Coming
Home
to
Mistletoe
Cottage

Celia Anderson lives with her husband as far away from the sea as you can possibly get in mainland UK. She dreams of buying a cottage on the coast, which explains the regular appearances in her books of seaside places with wide, sandy beaches. Celia loves walking, reading, having large, bubbly baths, eating, and drinking wine. Over the years, she has found that all of these activities bar the first may be done simultaneously, although this can be messy.

Previously a teacher and assistant head, Celia now writes full-time and is an enthusiastic member of the Romantic Novelists' Association, having graduated from their wonderful New Writers' Scheme. She is a doting grandma to Ida and Levi; loves flower arranging but tries to avoid gardening; plays the piano very badly; is a jigsaw addict; and has tried several times to learn to knit without much success (or joy). Some hobbies are best left alone . . .

🐦 @CeliaAnderson1
📘 CeliaJAndersonAuthor
📷 @CEJAnderson

Also by Celia Anderson
59 Memory Lane
The Cottage of Curiosities
The Secret Gift of Lucia Lemon

Coming Home to Mistletoe Cottage

CELIA ANDERSON

HarperCollins*Publishers*

HarperCollins*Publishers* Ltd
1 London Bridge Street,
London SE1 9GF
www.harpercollins.co.uk

HarperCollins*Publishers*
Macken House, 39/40 Mayor Street Upper,
Dublin 1, D01 C9W8, Ireland

First published by HarperCollins*Publishers* 2022

2

A catalogue record for this book is available from the British Library

ISBN: 978-0-00-846847-7

Set in Birka by Palimpsest Book Production Limited, Falkirk, Stirlingshire

Printed and bound in the UK using 100% Renewable Electricity by
CPI Group (UK) Ltd

I have always thought of Christmas-time ... as a good time; a kind, forgiving, charitable, pleasant time; ... when men and women seem by one consent to open their shut-up hearts freely.

CHARLES DICKENS, *A CHRISTMAS CAROL*

'Bah!' said Scrooge. 'Humbug!'

CHARLES DICKENS, *A CHRISTMAS CAROL*

Hope Conway's recipe book sits on the shelf by the kitchen window. Beyond the glass lies the garden, the wild sweep of sea marshes and in the distance, a golden stretch of sand and white-capped waves.

The book is showing signs of age now, but it still has so much to give. Sometimes it seems impossible that so much life experience can be held inside such a small space. Sights, sounds, smells, and an abundance of skills are between these tattered covers, all waiting for the daughter who will one day unlock them again. At the moment, Magda doesn't care enough, but soon her time will come. The magic of her mother's recipes is irresistible.

1

Monday, 4 December

Twenty-one Days Until Christmas

'We'll never get offered a break as amazing as this again. We absolutely have to go to New York next week,' Jared says. His knuckles are white as he grips the back of the kitchen chair. 'You've got to help us, Mum. I don't see what your problem is. It's only for a little while.'

Magda takes a deep breath and regards her son across the table. Jared and his wife can't be serious about this. She's always known how passionate they are about their careers and she's tried her best to be supportive, but this latest request goes way beyond a bit of babysitting now and again. Her hands are tightly clasped in her lap, almost hidden by the heavy oilcloth. She considers standing up to face his fury, but the effort seems too much on top of the shock she's just been dealt.

'Let me get this quite clear,' she says, trying to keep her voice steady. 'You and Annika have been offered a month's temporary contract with a New York theatre company, and you want to leave a week today. *A week today?*' she repeats incredulously. 'And you want *me* to look after the kids for *the whole time* you're gone?' This last point nearly sends her through the roof and Jared at least has the grace to look sheepish.

'Yeah. I know it's a bit last minute . . .'

'You're not kidding.' Magda feels her heart beginning to pound. A headache is starting behind her eyes. 'And why does it have to be New York, for goodness' sake?'

'Well, because that's where the job is . . . What's wrong with New York?' Jared responds, seeming to not entirely understand this part of the questioning. Magda doesn't answer, because she can't. It's much too difficult to explain her feeling of dread, especially in the middle of an argument. Jared presses on. 'It's a musical called *The Little Drummer Boy* and there are two parts for British actors. They've been doing really well in the provinces and they've just moved to Broadway, but some of the cast have had flu and the two lined up to replace them are already committed to other things over Christmas. Work, family stuff—'

'I guess most sensible people would be, Jared,' Magda interrupts bluntly.

There's an uncomfortable silence as Magda tries to crush the rising sense of panic that her son's request has set in motion. New York. It's the very last place she'd want him to go. Just the name of the city brings back shadowy memories that still haunt her.

'But why you? And why Annika?' she says eventually.

'You don't need to sound so surprised.' Jared is clearly affronted by this question, his own voice rising. 'We've been getting a good reputation in the business since we toured with the last musical and this new agent of ours is really earning her money. They wanted people who could sing as well as act and who could go over there immediately.'

'Immediately being the operative word.' Magda can hear her

4

voice getting shriller, but she can't seem to control it. 'So, in a nutshell, I get to look after the twins for *an entire month*, single-handed. And not only are you giving me a full-time job when I'm just getting into the swing of being retired, you'll be away for Christmas Day, too? For the whole of the run-up to Christmas, and New Year's Day, come to that.'

'After all the babies you've brought into the world, looking after our two will be a doddle, surely?'

'Helping women to give birth isn't quite the same thing as this, Jared. I was a midwife, not a nanny. *Are you actually for real?*'

'Stop shouting. You'll wake the kids.'

'I'm not shouting!' Magda bellows.

'Yes, you so are.' Jared's eyes are blazing now. 'And anyway, when did being in your own house on Christmas Day become so important to you, Mum?'

His words render Magda speechless and seem to bring her son up short too. She's still formulating a cutting reply when Jared squares his shoulders and goes on with what now feels a lot like an attack.

'Being around for me at Christmas wasn't exactly your top priority back in the day, was it, Mum? Think back for a minute. How often were you called away at the last moment to deliver a baby? How many times was I shipped off to a neighbour while you did your duty, or handed over to Fliss when she bailed us out yet again?'

'That's not fair. I tried my best for you. It wasn't easy being a single parent.' Magda's voice is husky now and she curses this heavy load of guilt. It's something she's carried with her for years and she's had to learn to live with it. There was no choice, after all. Somebody had to bring in the money, even if, in Magda's case, she had loved her job so much she'd have happily done it for nothing. Tears sting her eyelids and she blinks hard. He's not going to make her cry. No, he isn't. But Jared hasn't finished.

'Well, if you'd made any sort of effort to look for the man who apparently fathered me, we wouldn't have been on our own after he left us, would we?'

Jared's words lie between them like a thick fog. His father's permanent absence is a subject that very rarely gets mentioned and this is a very bad moment for Magda to think about the yawning gap in their lives. Her mind, as always, flinches from the gauntlet Jared's thrown down.

'I think we've gone slightly off topic here,' she manages. 'What about the children? What are Will and Desi going to think if you two desert them just before Christmas? Are you happy to leave me to pick up the pieces?'

Jared attempts to interrupt, but Magda holds up a hand. Sitting in this cosy room in the home where her mother had always been such a source of guidance and security for Magda, the realization that she'll never see that dear face again is suddenly overwhelming. Hope Conway's death is too recent for Magda to be able to think about her without stomach-clenching pain.

'No, let me finish,' she says. 'There's something else. Have you forgotten that it'll be our first Christmas since your grandma died? It's going to be hard enough to cope as it is, and now you're not going to be here either? It's only been six months since we lost her.'

'I . . . I haven't forgotten. Of course I haven't. I miss Gran too, you know that.'

'You can't possibly miss her any more than I do,' Magda

says quietly. She still battles with waves of pointless anger when she thinks about Hope leaving the family so suddenly. As each month passes without her mother's comforting presence in the house to support them all, the regrets snowball. Magda knows that she never listened properly to her mum's endless stories, tips for living a happy life and recipe ideas. What a waste of all that knowledge and wisdom. As her mind turns yet again to the wonderful food her mum used to produce so effortlessly, an awful thought occurs. Magda stares at her son.

'Jared . . . who's going to cook the Christmas dinner if you go away?'

'Is that really all you can think about, Mum? Who's going to make your dinner?' Jared turns away, not even trying to hide the sneer on his face.

'Don't be so scathing, it's important. Christmas is going to have to be all about chicken nuggets and chips if it's left to me. I wonder if you can get turkey nuggets?' she muses, glancing over to the large freezer in the corner and back to Jared, eyes wide with alarm.

'Yeah . . . I can see why you might be worried about that one the most. I'd have thought by your time of life you'd have worked out how to cook a turkey without me or Gran to supervise.'

The sarcasm of Jared's words cuts Magda to the quick. 'You're making me sound ancient. *By your time of life?* I've only just turned sixty and I bet I'm just as fit and active as you are.'

'Oh yeah?' Jared glances down at his own perfectly toned body.

'I am! I walk at least five miles a day, I swim, I sing in the chapel choir, I even sometimes go to Zumba for goodness' sake.' Magda can hear her voice getting alarmingly loud again.

She takes a couple of good, deep breaths and focuses on the subject in hand. 'Look, I didn't take early retirement to swap long shifts for full-time childcare and I've never pretended to be a great cook. That was your gran's forte. It's always been impossible to live up to her standards.'

'I know, Mum, but there's great and then there's adequate, isn't there? Ever since we moved to Mistletoe Cottage when I was fifteen she's been nagging you to at least have a go at using the oven. Did you ever really try? And if Gran hadn't taken the time to teach me the basics, I'd be exactly the same.'

'But you *like* cooking, especially baking. I . . . just don't.'

Jared sighs. 'I didn't take to it at first, Mum. There were a few times when whole batches of cakes went straight in the bin or out for the birds. Gran just helped me to start again from scratch.'

'Really? It always just seemed as though it came naturally to you both.' Magda feels again the lump in her throat that any mention of Hope triggers, this time doubly painful when it dawns on her how much of this period in Jared's life she doesn't recall. She'd noticed his growing bond with his grandmother and delighted in it, of course she had, but dealing with his teenage angst at being uprooted on top of settling back into her old life and relaunching her career had absorbed all her spare energy. She swallows hard.

Her son smiles sadly. 'No, you wouldn't have noticed. I expect the smell of burning had gone by the time you finally got home from work.'

The words cut deep, but Jared's voice is gentler now. He makes a move to come around the table towards Magda, and she stiffens automatically. She hopes he isn't going to try and hug her. They don't usually go in for that sort of thing, and today isn't the time

8

to start. 'I know some parts of looking after the twins will probably be difficult and strenuous, and I'm really sorry to put this on you,' he says. 'But Mum . . .'

Magda puts a hand up as Jared comes closer, unable to bear any more for the moment. He stops speaking abruptly as the kitchen door opens and his wife comes in. As ever, Magda is struck by Annika's beauty. Will and Desi have both inherited her blonde curls, but their eyes are as dark brown as Jared's. At just five years old, they still look like twin cherubs. Magda's heart sinks. Cherubic, her grandchildren most definitely are not, even if they both look angelic.

Annika frowns at them. 'Have you two been arguing again?' she says. Light dawns. 'Ah. You've gone ahead and told your mum about the plan, haven't you? I was hoping you'd wait for me.'

Jared glances at his mother and then down at the floor. She's reminded sharply of her son as a toddler and then all through his growing years. He could never meet her eyes when he knew he was in the wrong.

'To soften the blow?' Magda asks. The sadness has gone from her voice now, and she's back to pure incredulity. 'I don't think that would have helped in this case. I can't believe you're even considering such a mad idea, especially at Christmas. The kids will be heartbroken. How can you think of doing this to them? You've both completely lost the plot.'

Jared runs a hand through his hair, making it stand on end in short, liquorice-black spikes. Magda feels a pang of nostalgia for the handsome little boy who used to do this every time he was ruffled in any way. His sudden rage has more or less abated, just as it always does, Magda reflects with a pang. Similar in the way they react to confrontation, their arguments through the years have often been like this. Brutal, but soon over. She has a horrible feeling that this one won't be so easy to resolve. Her son takes a deep breath, looking up at his wife for reassurance as he defends them both from Magda's accusation.

'We haven't lost the plot. We're actors and musicians. We have to take the work when it's offered and we want to pay our way.'

'Well, that's great,' Magda says, 'but I'm sure we can manage without this sort of desperate measure.'

'No, we really can't, Mum. It's time we faced up to it.'

'That's my problem, surely?' Magda can't see why Jared is suddenly getting so stressed about their finances. Her mum's family have lived at the top of the cobbled street in Periwinkle Bay for generations. Okay, so there's always work that needs doing on it, but nobody's ever needed to dump their children and go to America to fund it before.

Annika comes over to sit at the table on the other side of Magda.

'We really, really want to give it a try. It's not such a massive ask, surely? Only a month out of your life, and you love the kids. You know you do. It'll be fun,' she says.

'But they're so excited about Christmas,' Magda falters. She can tell she's losing the battle now. 'What about the tree? You always love decorating the tree, Annika, that's always been your job!' She's desperate now, trying to find anything to convince Annika to stay.

Annika's face falls. Although Desi and Will have their own little silver tree for the kitchen – one of the few things Magda brought with her when she and Jared finally came home to Mistletoe Cottage all those years ago – the family's main

Christmas tree is always a real one, huge and magnificent. Every year, without fail, it's bought from the town market and dressed with almost fanatical attention to detail by Annika. It stands in the hallway, proud and sparkly, right up until Twelfth Night, scenting the whole house with the smell of pine forests.

Annika pushes her hair back from her face, irritation seeming to take over from any last-minute doubts. 'Oh, you'll manage,' she says. 'And the twins will help.'

It's these words that really bring home to Magda how desperately her daughter-in-law wants this opportunity. If the thought of handing over her favourite job of the year doesn't change Annika's mind, nothing will. Nobody else has ever been allowed to touch the main tree since Annika married Jared. Actually, even before that, come to think of it. Magda remembers newly engaged Annika quietly but firmly taking over this important task. Magda herself had relinquished it gratefully, happy to be able to escape back to work, always rushing, always busy. Magda doesn't respond. They both know the twins certainly won't help.

'I can get all the decorations out before we go, and write you instructions about how it needs to be done,' Annika says, rallying quickly and giving Magda her biggest, brightest smile. She breaks off and looks around the room. 'Where are those little demons, actually? I came in here to look for them. Haven't seen them for ages.'

There's a silence as all three ponder on this question. Finally it's broken by the muffled sound of sobs from under the table. Horrified, Magda lifts a corner of the oilcloth.

'We're here,' says Will, his voice gruff. 'Are you really going to go away and leave us behind at Christmas?'

2

Friday, 8 December

Seventeen Days Until Christmas

Magda slams the front door behind her and steps out into the lane, turning at the last moment to admire her daughter-in-law's latest handiwork. Even in the midst of her frantic packing and organizing for the trip, Annika has filled two hanging baskets with a collection of giant silver and gold baubles and added ivy and mistletoe from the back garden. How she managed to find the time Magda can't imagine. It's galling, but she has to admit that the woman is unstoppable.

Around the ancient wooden porch Annika has woven strings of white fairy lights, which twist amongst the branches of wisteria that cover Mistletoe Cottage in purple glory and delicate fragrance every summer. A hook on the door holds a Christmas wreath of Magda's own creation, of more ivy, holly with its cheerful splashes of crimson berries, and a liberal sprinkling of fir cones, and over the door hangs a large bunch of the garden's trademark mistletoe.

Magda sighs. She's never felt as confident as Annika when it comes to crafting, but this is her first attempt at a wreath and she's proud of the way it's turned out. Her own artistic talents have previously always been in home-making, with the occasional foray into junk modelling with her small son. Magda has an instinctive knack for making a place look cosy with bright cushions and rugs scattered around and well-chosen pictures and mirrors on the walls, mainly gleaned from charity shops and car boot sales. Even in the tiny flat she shared with Jared in Leicester she'd made the most of the space. Settling in a strange area with no spare cash for luxuries was a small price to pay for following her dream of completing her nursing training so that she could eventually become a midwife, but it hadn't been easy to give up the home comforts of Mistletoe Cottage.

Magda takes a last look at her wreath and wonders how she's ever going to find the time or inclination to try some new skills. She'd been hoping to get more adventurous and start a few new arty hobbies at the local primary school back at the start of autumn. Every summer since she and Jared had returned, she'd read the brochure for the September classes and promised herself that when retirement came, she'd plunge in. But this year, the shock of her mum's death drained away what little creative urges she had, and now being a full-time granny is going to put paid to her plan of signing up for the Christmas craft week they're running. Resentment towards her son and daughter-in-law burns again and she tries her best to crush it. This bitterness is very tiring.

Wrapping her scarf more snugly around her neck, Magda resolutely pushes such grumpy thoughts out of her mind and makes her way down the steep hill towards the market. She tells herself as sternly as possible that it'll do no good carrying on feeling hard-done-to, and it's certainly not Desi and Will's fault that she's feeling as if her newly retired status is being kiboshed. She needs to make sure she doesn't take this out on them. Thankfully, the salt marshes and fields around Periwinkle Bay are criss-crossed with well-worn paths, and striding down the track to the sea always lifts Magda's spirits. Born and bred in the small town, she knows every highway and byway for miles around, not to mention plenty of the places that casual visitors never discover. Her years in the Midlands forging a career and bringing up her son have only served to intensify her love of the wide-open spaces and sea breezes, even though at times the place had felt stifling to a somewhat wayward teenager.

Magda's glad she's put on her walking boots to negotiate the slippery cobblestones this morning because there's a lot of Christmas shopping to be done before Jared and Annika leave, and the weather seems to have taken a turn for the worse. An icy wind is making her normally tidy hair stand on end, so she pulls a red woolly hat out of her pocket, ramming it down over her ears.

For years, Magda's hair has been a delicate silvery white, turning from ash blonde when she was only in her thirties. She came to terms with the transformation quickly, knowing her mother's had done exactly the same, and now has it trimmed into a shortish bob that frames her heart-shaped face. Even so, this morning she feels her age, and in seconds, the underlying gloom is back. *I look a wreck*, Magda thinks, catching sight of herself in a shop window as she reaches the edge of the little town. *I expect my nose has gone red with the cold and I haven't even got any lipstick on. It's not so long since I felt full of energy and happy in my own skin, but finishing work and losing Mum has changed me. What's more, lovely as they both are, I'm going to be up to my ears in children soon. I'm not a woman with the power to turn heads, not a midwife who people respect. Nothing, really.*

This unaccustomed burst of self-pity is so pathetic that she even makes herself smile. Red hat or no red hat, she's never been ashamed of her looks up to now. She dresses well in colours that flatter her warm skin tone, and her favourite, most faded Levi's still fit perfectly. To her secret delight, she was voted Rear of the Year in a tongue-in-cheek competition at the Periwinkle Bay fair last summer, earning her the biggest round of applause of the day. At the time, she'd wondered if the prize had only come her way because she was by far the oldest contestant at almost sixty and the townsfolk felt sorry for her, but she's long since let that thought go. It doesn't matter a jot what the reason was. The resounding cheer when she collected her trophy and champagne was heart-warming, and almost made her cry. Magda's standing in the close-knit community of Periwinkle Bay doesn't seem to have suffered since she hung up her uniform for the last time. People instinctively like her, and she likes them right back. Mostly.

Giving herself another silent pep talk about the dangers of all this introspection, Magda heads into the market. The red and white striped awnings block out much of the wind chill and the pungent scent of pine drifting over from the Christmas tree stall takes her right back to Mistletoe Cottage Christmases in the past.

'Are you okay, ducky?' the lady on the candle stall shouts as she passes. 'Our Victoria said to send her love when I saw you next. She's expecting. I can't wait.'

'Fancy that. Have I been back in town so long that the babies I delivered are having babies of their own?' Magda turns with a smile in the direction of the voice.

The woman cackles. 'I know, it's hard to believe, isn't it? You haven't changed much since those days, mind. The sea air must suit you.'

Magda congratulates her on the coming grandchild, and walks on. Victoria was one of the first babies she'd helped bring into the world after arriving back at Mistletoe Cottage, fresh from her years in a hospital in the heart of the city. Becoming a community midwife in a small town was a challenge, very different to what Magda had been used to, and Victoria's birth had been far from easy. It's hard to believe that tiny, determined scrap of humanity is now going to be a mother herself. The last twenty years have gone by in a flash.

Magda continues to work her way through the market, lost in thought, before pausing to chat by the Christmas trees. She and the stallholder, Clive, go back a long way. She remembers him at primary school, when he still had hair. Neither Clive nor Fliss ever made any secret of the fact that they thought she was mad to desert Periwinkle Bay for the bright lights of the city, but they were good-humoured about it on the whole and, to give them their due, they both welcomed her back with open arms when she eventually returned with Jared in tow.

'You'll be coming back to choose one soon, I hope? Like you always do, with your glamorous daughter-in-law?' Clive says wistfully. '. . . And Fliss, of course, and the kiddies . . .' he adds, seeing Magda's disapproving frown. Clive has always made what she considers a ridiculous fuss of Annika.

'Well, yes and no,' Magda says. The gloom descends again. 'I'll be bringing Desi and Will, but Annika and Jared are off to America in three days.'

'Really? So close to Christmas?'

'They've been offered a month's contract in New York. There's a new play being launched. It's a musical. They've toured in some popular shows before and they've both got great voices. Classically trained, you know . . .' Magda cringes inwardly as she hears herself going over the top with her defence of the two of them, but the thought of anyone but herself criticizing her family isn't to be borne.

'A month? But that means—'

'Yes, I *do* know what it means, actually,' Magda interrupts, in a voice that's sharper than she intended. She can feel her frown lines getting deeper and Clive takes an involuntary step backwards, knocking over a nearby stack of tree stands.

'Oh well, at least you'll have Fliss!' he says, his attention caught by something over Magda's shoulder. 'And talk of the devil, there she is, over by the candles. Actually, I haven't seen her around much lately. Is she okay?'

Magda turns to look where he's pointing, and sure enough, there's her oldest friend, bending over the huge range of scented candles, no doubt about to buy another to add to her extensive collection. She hasn't seen Magda yet.

'Yes, I think she's all right,' Magda says, losing interest in Clive, her eyes instead on her best friend. 'Why wouldn't she be? Anyway, I'd better be going. See you when we come for our tree.'

Clive starts to speak again but Magda suddenly can't wait to catch up with Fliss, and leaves him mid-sentence. Weaving her way through the shoppers, Magda makes her way over to where the familiar figure is still standing. As she walks towards her, it begins to dawn on her just how long it's been since she's seen Fliss for a proper chat. Lately, there seem to have been so many other things to think about.

'Hi, love,' she calls as she approaches the stall, suddenly feeling brighter, knowing if anyone can lift her gloom, it will be Fliss. 'I was hoping I'd bump into you today.'

This isn't strictly true, as keeping in touch with people, even Fliss, has been far from Magda's thoughts lately, but seeing Fliss, neat and elfin with her dark hair and trademark black jeans tucked into ridiculously high-heeled boots, she realizes how much she's missed her.

Fliss still seems absorbed in choosing a candle. Perhaps she hasn't heard Magda calling her name. She tries again, louder this time.

'Oh, it's you,' Fliss finally turns round. 'Hello.' Her voice is surprisingly cold.

This isn't right. They've always greeted each other with a huge hug, and now Magda can barely recognize Fliss's tone as she speaks. Also, something else isn't as it should be. Magda peers more closely. Fliss's roots are showing. That's odd. Up to now Fliss has never given in to the silver streaks. Not only that, her light dusting of freckles is standing out more clearly than usual due to the pallor of her cheeks, and there are violet shadows under her eyes.

'Fliss?' Magda says nervously. 'What's up?' She takes Fliss by the arm and draws her out of earshot of the small group around the candles. 'Are you okay? You don't seem like yourself today.'

'Well, maybe *myself* wasn't who I wanted to be like today, eh?' Fliss pauses, rubbing a hand over her eyes. 'It's been a while since we spoke, hasn't it? I expect you've been busy with the family and suchlike.' Her tone is languid, almost bored. Magda starts to reply but Fliss hasn't finished. She yawns widely and carries on. 'Yeah, all those cosy dinners around the kitchen table and roaring log fires in the evenings. It's a tough old life you've got at Mistletoe Cottage. How are the twins doing?'

Magda pushes away the niggling thought that Fliss doesn't seem at all pleased to see her, and instead blurts out all her pent-up worries about the next month.

'. . . and they'll be away for the whole of Christmas. The kids are really sad. Will's being naughtier than ever. This morning he squeezed all my toothpaste into his mum's slippers and then took Jared's playscript and drew hideous faces all over it. Desi laughed so much she wet herself and she hasn't done that for ages.' Everything comes out in a rush, but Fliss hardly seems to be listening. She answers with a sort of non-committal sound, but Magda presses on anyway.

'And not only that, I'm going to have to do all the cooking as well as the childcare. I haven't even thought about making Christmas puddings and cake. I'll have to buy them this year. My mum would be horrified. Oh Fliss, how am I going to cope?'

Fliss regards Magda dispassionately. The awkward silence lengthens until Magda can't stand it any longer. Nothing like this has ever happened before. She and Fliss have barely had a cross word since they met on their first day at school and there's certainly never been an atmosphere like this between them. 'So anyway, sorry I haven't been in touch,' Magda says now, her voice suddenly quiet and unsure. 'I've been a bit preoccupied. It's so odd without Mum around the house and the twins haven't settled very well in their new class this term, for some reason.'

'I'm not surprised, are you? They miss Hope. We all do. She was such a big part of our lives. I thought you might have messaged to see how I was doing, actually. Hope was more of a mum to me than my own mother had time to be, before . . . you know . . .'

The guilt pangs strike Magda hard, but she rallies quickly. 'Well, what about *you*?' she replies defensively. 'It works both ways, you know. You haven't rung me either.'

The two women stare at each other for a second, then, before Magda can say more, Fliss turns on her heel and makes a beeline for the edge of the market. Magda is too surprised to try and stop her at first, but as she rouses herself to follow, Fliss picks up speed. She bumps into a couple of people on her way out but doesn't pause in her flight.

Magda fights back another wave of guilt. This isn't fair at all. Doesn't Fliss realize how hard it's been for them all since Hope died so suddenly at the end of June? It's been difficult enough to keep herself and the family going without worrying about everyone else whose lives Hope touched. A voice inside her head whispers, *But Fliss isn't just anyone, is she? Who else has kept you going like she has, all through the tough times? Who else knows you inside and out?* She makes her way out of the market and emerges by the giant Christmas tree in the square. There's no sign of Fliss. The right thing to do would be to go and see if she's headed for home, and try and get to the bottom of why she seems so out of sorts.

Magda takes a few steps in the direction of Fliss's house but a wave of sadness and exhaustion makes her shudder. It's all too much effort. She stops for a moment by her favourite café, admiring the beautiful window display of sparkly white lights and angels dancing on top of huge Christmas cakes. Someone opens the door to leave, and a delicious waft of coffee-scented air hits her. A few minutes getting warm and making a proper shopping list won't hurt, will it? Fliss will have to wait. The ache that lives constantly in Magda's heart these days is quite enough to deal with for one day.

Christmas Day, Thirty-five Years Ago

To begin with, Magda can't think where the shrill noise is coming from. It's late afternoon and she's fallen asleep on the sofa with the TV blaring and Jared snoozing fitfully on her lap. When she realizes it's her phone that's ringing and sees Fliss's name on the caller display she almost doesn't answer it, but curiosity overcomes her dragging inertia.

'Hello?' Magda croaks.

'Hello Mags, are you ill? You sound dreadful.' Fliss's breezy voice comes down the line loud and clear. 'Get off your backside and let me in. The doorbell isn't working and I've been knocking for ages.'

'You're here? In Leicester?'

'It certainly looks like it from where I'm standing. Come on, hurry up. I'm freezing.'

Shaking her head to get rid of the dizziness brought on by lack of sleep, Magda puts Jared over her shoulder and stumbles to the door, flinging it open to see her friend standing on the doorstep wearing an enormous red duffle coat and carrying two bulging shopping bags.

'About time too, my fingers are dropping off,' Fliss says, dumping the bags on the hall floor and wrapping her arms around Magda and Jared. 'My life, you look even worse than I expected. How long is it since you washed your hair? Give that baby to me and go and have a shower right now. No offence, but you don't smell too good.'

Still baffled as to why this miracle has happened, Magda doesn't argue. She heads for the bathroom and in seconds is standing under a stream of blissfully hot water, soaping herself all over with the last of the shower gel. She can hear Jared's habitual hungry wail begin to gain momentum and her breasts automatically start leaking milk, but Fliss is shushing him, and soon her friend is singing softly to Jared. It's not a nursery rhyme. Magda sticks her head out of the shower to listen. It sounds more like an Abba medley. But it seems to be working because the crying gradually stops.

Fifteen minutes later, dressed in warm and vaguely clean clothes, and sitting at her narrow breakfast bar now Jared is for once peacefully asleep in his Moses basket, Magda watches in amazement as Fliss unpacks her shopping bags. Packet after plastic box after foil-wrapped parcel come out one after the other until the small kitchen seems full to the brim of festive food. Magda also spots a separate bag of toiletries including baby bath, expensive shower gel and a whole lot of other luxuries that she hasn't been able to afford, or even bother to buy for a while.

'How did you . . . I mean why . . .' Magda can barely get her words out, although she's not sure if that's from the shock or simply her exhaustion.

'Hope was worried about you. You know how much she wanted you to come home with Jared this year, but until this morning when she rang to wish you Happy Christmas she assumed that you were going to be with friends and someone would feed you.'

'I'm quite capable of feeding myself, thank you,' says Magda, as sniffily as she can manage, but the sight and delicious smells of all these home-cooked goodies is completely putting paid to her efforts to look self-sufficient. She doesn't push it.

'So how did you end up on your own on Christmas Day?' Fliss asks instead, changing the subject. 'No, don't tell me, I can probably guess. He let you down at the last minute again, didn't he?'

Magda sighs. There's not much point in making up excuses for Jared's absent father. Fliss knows her too well. Even so, she has to try. She loves Giovanni. He can't help being torn in two at this time of year.

'If you must know, he's gone back to New York to spend Christmas with his family,' she says, trying to make it sound as if it's the most natural thing in the world for a new dad to abandon his partner and baby over the festive season.

'Right. And you're perfectly okay with that, are you?'

'Yes, it's fine. He says they have traditions that go back years and his mother would be heartbroken if he rocked the boat. A big, jolly Italian Christmas. He described it to me and it *did* sound wonderful. You can't blame him for wanting to be there.'

'Hmm. And he'll be back straight afterwards, will he?' Fliss has her arms folded now and her expression is on the chillier side of grim.

'I . . . I expect so.'

Fliss regards her friend dubiously. 'But you only got together a few months before you fell pregnant with Jared, didn't you? And in that time he's been home for mini-breaks at least three times. They must pay junior doctors more than I thought.'

'His mum always treats him to his flights.' The words are

out before Magda's tired brain has time to filter them and she sees her friend's mouth twist in derision.

'Of course she does,' Fliss says.

'He'll be back here soon, I'm sure he will.' Magda's voice doesn't sound so certain, even to herself. There's an uncomfortable silence. Fliss seems to be deciding on her next tack. Magda holds her breath. She's way too tired for this.

'Never mind, I'm here now,' Fliss says eventually, keeping things light to Magda's intense relief. 'When your mum realized you were going to be on your own, she decided to send the whole Christmas dinner to you anyway. I've got turkey, stuffing, cooked veg, gravy in a jar, Christmas pudding and brandy butter. You name it, it's here.'

Jared is awake now and he waves his fists and begins to make the noise that says he's going to need feeding very soon. Magda glances across at him, willing him to stop, even if just for another couple of minutes. Her eyes are gritty from lack of sleep and she's very close to tears, but Fliss is unperturbed.

'Right, I'll get your dinner together while you feed the little milk monster, and then he can doze on my knee while we eat chocolates and your mum's mince pies and watch a nice peaceful Christmas film, okay?'

'He won't sleep,' says Magda resignedly, scooping her son up and heading for the sofa.

'Oh yes he will. They call me the baby whisperer of Periwinkle Bay these days, didn't you know? I'm in big demand for babysitting around the town. It pays for my cookshop habit. I can't stop buying kitchen utensils at the moment. It's ever since I got my own place. I've got to say, your small person is my absolute favourite of them all, though.'

Magda gazes down at her beautiful dark-haired baby,

listening to Fliss rattle on. Right on cue he opens his big brown eyes and looks straight at her, giving her his first real smile. Her heart melts. Who cares if Christmas Day has so far been the worst of her life? Her best friend in the world has come to rescue her, and she's sitting here with her perfect, healthy boy on her lap. Bursting with love and gratitude, Magda holds Jared close and feels the initial pangs of pain and then the pure relief of his contented suckling. This is where she should be. Everything is going to be fine now.

3

Monday, 11 December

Fourteen Days Until Christmas

The day of Jared and Annika's departure comes around way too quickly for Magda's liking. It only seems like five minutes since she was facing her son across the kitchen table, and now she's preparing to say goodbye. The taxi driver is already outside revving his engine when Annika tiptoes downstairs soon after dawn. Jared is busy loading their cases into the boot, avoiding all but the most necessary contact with his mother, but when the two women meet in the hallway, Annika sweeps Magda into a huge hug.

'Please take good care of them for us,' she whispers, as Magda tries not to choke on the waves of musky scent. 'I know you will. We really do appreciate this, and it'll seem like no time at all until we're back.'

'Yeah, right,' Magda mutters under her breath, but she musters a smile and stands in the open doorway waving until the cab has trundled its way down the street and out of sight.

The twins are still fast asleep, having said their tearful goodbyes the night before. In the brief moments of peace before they wake, Magda goes into the kitchen and sinks down on to the saggy sofa that Jared's been threatening to take to the tip for years, clutching a mug of tea in both hands. Like many of the pieces of furniture in this house, the kitchen sofa has seen better days, but today she needs the comfort of this old friend. She burrows into the heap of soft cushions that her mother made and embroidered, tucking her feet underneath her. In her hurry to see Jared and Annika off she's forgotten to put her slippers on, and the uneven flagstones of the hall and kitchen floor strike cold.

Despair washes over Magda as she contemplates the weeks ahead, stretching away endlessly. She's daunted by the prospect of having to keep her beloved grandchildren happy, safe and well fed. Magda can hardly remember Jared at this age. She'd still been living in the poky flat in Leicester at that point, working long hours and random shifts, and trying to make herself believe that Jared would one day understand that following her dream of being a midwife was necessary for both their sakes.

Often, when Fliss had breezed in to visit and been such a hit with Jared, Magda had seriously doubted her own capabilities as a mother. Her friend made the whole thing look so much fun, but juggling day-to-day work and childcare responsibilities proved to be very hard. Her son became more and more vocal in his demands as he got older, and the spectre of being a failure was always lurking. Magda doesn't see how looking after young children full-time will be any easier for her now than it was back in the day. She has a feeling she only just escaped Jared's childhood with her sanity intact.

Now, Magda stretches her shoulders and sips her tea. Perhaps she and Annika are more similar than she's previously realized, when it comes to the crunch. Annie loves her work, and she's openly admitted she wants success for both herself and her husband while she and Jared are still young. Opportunities are out there and she is determined to grab them with both hands, just as Magda herself has done over the years. Even so, this desertion at Christmas feels way too much.

Without warning, Magda suddenly hears the thump, thump, thump of two sets of feet running down the stairs. Will bursts into the kitchen first.

'Where are they?' he yells. 'I wanted to give them another hug.'

He looks around wildly, while Desi, coming in more sedately, begins to cry quietly, tears dripping off her chin. Her nose is running, and Magda automatically reaches for the tissues, still on the table from last night's goodbye scene.

'They've already gone to the airport, my loves,' Magda says, holding her arms out to them both. 'They told you it was going to be an early start and they wouldn't wake you up, didn't they? You gave them lots of cuddles last night.'

Both children ignore her, moving together in a huddle, their curls becoming one big tangle. Magda can see Desi's lips moving, and although no sound is coming out, William is nodding and patting her back. The twins have been able to communicate in their own way ever since they were toddlers, maybe even before that, and now they're five years old they're better at it than ever. The largely unspoken conversations are a bit unnerving, but at least Desdemona has stopped crying.

'Let's all have breakfast,' Magda says, trying to seem bright, then hesitating for a moment. 'Shall I make pancakes?'

Admittedly, this is a massive risk. The last time she attempted pancakes, Magda ruined Hope's best frying pan and set off two smoke alarms in the process. Luckily, both children shake their heads.

'Cornflakes,' says Will. 'With sugar on.'

He regards Magda defiantly. His parents don't allow sugar on cereals. She sighs.

'Just this once. But after today, it's back to the rules, okay?'

The children come to the table and climb on to their usual chairs, leaning close to each other. They eat in silence, and Magda takes the opportunity to nip upstairs to check that their school clothes are still laid out in their room. Distracted by the search for two matching pairs of shoes, it's a few seconds before she registers there's an uproar coming from below. She takes the stairs two at a time, entering the kitchen just in time to see Will dancing in the middle of a heap of cornflakes. He's clearly delighted with the crunching sounds he's making, and Desi is clapping her hands and jumping on the spot. She sees Magda just before her brother notices their granny and both hands fly to her face.

'What on earth do you think you're doing, William?' shouts Magda above Will's shrieks of glee. 'For goodness' sake, I only turned my back for one minute. Stop that immediately or . . . or . . . no TV for a week!'

'Knickers! I hate you,' Will replies. 'You're not our mummy.'

'Absolutely,' Magda responds, before she's had time to think. 'If I was, I'd be wondering why you were acting like a two-year-old when I know for sure you're five.'

This causes a mutiny. Will starts kicking the shattered remains of the cornflakes around the room and Desi crawls under the table to escape Magda's wrath. Eventually, order is returned to the kitchen and Magda, teeth clenched to avoid further battles, shepherds Will and Desi upstairs to get ready for school. *Excellent work, Magda,* she tells herself with heavy sarcasm. *Morning One has got off to a great start.*

Twenty minutes later, holding a subdued twin firmly in each hand, Magda marches them into the school playground. They make it just in time for the bell, but instead of careering over to join their class, who are lining up by the door, Will and Desi fling themselves on Magda, attaching themselves to her legs and breaking into wild sobs.

Magda looks around helplessly. They've never done this, even in the early days of school, when they looked so tiny in their brand-new uniforms and held hands tightly as they walked into their classroom. Luckily, Periwinkle Primary's head teacher, Denis Archer, is still in his usual place by the gate, greeting everyone as they arrive as he likes to do. He spots Magda's agonized expression and comes straight over.

Long-legged and wiry, with dark hair that's showing rather fetching silver streaks at the sides, Den somehow seems much more dynamic than most of the other residents of Periwinkle Bay. He's generous and kind to a fault and favours those he particularly likes with a wide, sardonic grin. Others tend to get a more formal, professional smile. He's a well-known figure around the town, striding about in either his baggy tweed work suits and brogues, or his off-duty battered old jeans, an even tattier leather flying jacket, and big clumpy boots.

Magda bumps into Den regularly both as organist of the choir she sings with and as the leader of Periwinkle Bay's fund-raising committee. Although she doesn't know him well, she's very much aware he's no soft touch, and that this is a man who gets things done. She feels her tense muscles relax slightly, relieved that it's Den coming to the rescue and not the twins' rather starchy class teacher.

'Now then, Will and Desi, what's all this about?' Den says. Magda looks up into his warm, sea-green eyes and feels the tension in her shoulders instantly relax. She can tell he knows the score. Jared and Annika have been in touch with the school to explain the situation, and Magda has the distinct feeling that Den doesn't approve of what's happening. She's torn between an unexpected mother-tiger instinct to defend her son's actions, and a feeling of relief that someone understands her plight.

'I think Will and Desi are having a bit of an off day, Mr Archer,' Magda says, trying without success to detach the children from her thighs while also maintaining a light tone, trying not to reveal her own despair. She can feel their tears soaking right through the thick denim, and the hiccupping sobs don't seem to be getting any less.

'You could be right,' he says. 'Let's see what I can do to help. Will, Desi . . . let's all get out of the cold. My toes are frozen solid and I think we need to have a chat.' When the children still make no move to detach themselves from Magda's legs, the headteacher resorts to what is clearly a tried and tested last resort. 'If you come into my office, you can meet Blondie.'

Mr Archer is now in sole charge of a gorgeous, honey-coloured cockerpoo. His wife left him rather suddenly a few months ago, apparently with the aim of leading a simpler life on a remote farm on the Welsh borders.

'Blondie's the dog?' she asks, just to be absolutely sure. 'Definitely not the pop star?'

He grins. 'She is. Not as talented as her namesake, but still very cute. I've had an arrangement with the local grooming parlour to look after her in the daytime for a while, but they closed last week, so for now Blondie's taken over as the school mascot. Are you coming inside, guys?' Here, he turns back to Will and Desi. 'It's the start of Christmas Crafts week today, and your class has bagged the cracker-making workshop. You're a lucky pair. I wish I was doing that instead of boring computer stuff. Are you joining in with the grown-ups' version later on, Magda?'

She shakes her head. 'No babysitter,' she says.

'Ah. That's a pity. We were planning on having a crèche but it'll be a bit late for most of the kids to be out anyway.' He shrugs. 'Let's go inside, kids, or it'll be morning break before we get you to the classroom,' Den says, holding out a hand to each twin.

Will and Desi look up at Magda and then at each other. Some sort of wordless conversation is taking place again. At least they've stopped crying, thinks Magda. She realizes she's been holding her breath, but as Den smiles down at them, she feels them move away from her slightly and begin to edge towards him.

'Off you go,' says Den, raising his eyebrows at Magda over the two blonde heads. 'They'll be fine now. *We can ring if we need you,*' he adds in a whisper out of the corner of his mouth. He jerks his head towards the gate when he sees that Magda is still lingering, and she takes the hint, making her escape while the going's good.

Heading for the centre of town, Magda can feel the now-familiar headache building up behind her eyes and her shoulders are once again stiff with tension. She feels as if she's been run over by a truck. It's only the first morning and already she's dealt with carnage in the kitchen, a full-scale battle over the wrong pants from Will, and now this. At least she's remembering to hide her toothpaste now. On impulse, Magda reaches for her phone. In times of trouble, she always turns to Fliss. She might have been cold the other day, but Fliss knows her better than anyone, and Magda is sure she's bound to want to help.

At the first attempt, there's no answer from her friend's phone, so Magda instead leaves a voicemail, asking Fliss to call her back as soon as possible. But when she's killed some time admiring the automated Nativity display in the window of the delicatessen and bought some chocolates to give to the twins' job-sharing teachers on the last day of term, her patience runs out. Standing under the giant Christmas tree in the centre of the square, Magda tries again, and on the last ring is rewarded by the sound of Fliss's voice. The 'hello' from the other end of the line doesn't sound very enthusiastic.

'Hi love, are you busy?' Magda asks, ignoring the lack of enthusiasm and instead already planning to get the drinks in at the café. The craft shop where Fliss works is always closed on Mondays, so there's no reason why she shouldn't be free.

The silence that greets her question is unexpected, but Magda presses on. 'Fliss? Can you hear me? Are you up for a hot chocolate with whipped cream and marshmallows? I'm outside the café. I need to talk to you, it's been a hell of a morning.'

There's still no response. 'Jared and Annika have only just left and the kids have been a nightmare so far. They're so upset . . .'

There's a harsh sound from Fliss that could be a cough or a laugh. '*They're* upset? And so are you, I suppose?'

Magda frowns. She continues tentatively, confused by Fliss's words. 'Well, yes, I am. I feel as if I've been abandoned.'

'Oh, really? Well, join the club.'

'What did you say?' Magda can hardly take in the hostility that's coming down the line. Fliss never gets cross with her.

They've been friends since they started school together, in the same building where she's just left her traumatized grandchildren. Remembering their small, tear-stained faces, Magda swallows the lump in her throat – and her pride – and tries again to tell her friend about her day. 'It was awful dropping them off at school today. Look, how long will you be? I'll go in and order. Do you want a cake? The mince pies look good.'

'I'm not coming.'

There's a silence as Magda digests this. Maybe she misheard the brusque words, but somehow Fliss's tone implies that's unlikely.

'Not coming? But . . . but why not?'

There's another pause, in which Magda hears Norris, the one-man-band who likes to stand by the Christmas tree, start to tune up. He launches into a spirited reggae version of 'Mary's Boy Child' just as her friend finally replies. A cold breeze blows Magda's hair across her face and the sudden drop in temperature is echoed in Fliss's voice.

'I'll tell you why not, Magda. Over the years I've supported you through thick and thin. I came to stay with you in Leicester loads of times to help with Jared, I got you through his stroppy teen years when you came back here to live, I did all sorts of things to make life easier for your mum, and after all that I propped you and Jared and Annie up during Hope's funeral. Isn't that true?'

'Yes . . . yes, of course it's true, but why—'

'You're going to ask why I'm saying all this now. It's because, Magda, not once have you picked up the phone to see why I haven't been in touch lately.'

'Oh. But I've been—'

'Busy. Preoccupied. Upset. Yes, I get all that. But so have I,

Magda, and you haven't even noticed. So, no – I'm not coming to the café to listen to you bang on about how tough your life is, and no – I don't particularly want to see you right now. If you've got any sense you'll have a good long think about all this. For the moment though . . . just leave me alone, okay?'

The line goes dead, leaving Magda standing with her mouth open as the opening bars of the calypso carol fill the square. She puts her phone in her pocket and turns to face the Christmas tree. The blue and green lights are twinkling and the music is warm and festive, but a frosty feeling of impending doom is settling somewhere deep in Magda's stomach. There must be some way of fixing this disastrous misunderstanding, but try as she might, Magda has no idea where to begin.

4

Tuesday, 12 December

Thirteen Days Until Christmas

Will and Desi wake very early the next day. Magda can hear Will's voice through the wall, rising and falling in what sounds like the start of what she always thinks of as one of his chuntering days. He doesn't get these very often, but when they happen, distraction is the only way to cope. Desi is usually pretty good at turning the situation around when her brother's in one of his moods because she hates arguments, but this morning there is no answering murmur as Will gets louder and louder.

Groaning, Magda gets up and puts on her thickest dressing gown. It's still dark outside and the heating hasn't yet kicked in. She stomps to the bathroom to clean her teeth and splash her face with water. There's no way she can face the twins unless she's woken herself up properly.

'What's all this then?' Magda says through gritted teeth, pushing the twins' bedroom door fully open. 'You two are up before the seagulls today.'

Two pairs of eyes regard her balefully. Will and Desi are both in the bottom bunk with the duvet drawn up to their chins. Their fair curls are rumpled.

'Did one of you have a bad dream?' Magda says, yawning so widely that her jaw cracks. She imagines Jared and Annika safely tucked up in some giant hotel bed with its smooth Egyptian cotton linen and room service only an arm's length away. Or maybe, with the time difference, they haven't even made it to their room yet. They could be at extra rehearsals or an after-show party or even hanging out with the stars. It's hard not to seethe with envy, but the two troubled faces catch at her heart.

'We were just saying that Mummy and Daddy are prob'ly missing us,' says Will. 'I bet they wish they could come home right now, but they can't because YOU won't let them.'

He points a finger at Magda as he says this, and Desi nods furiously. Magda is thrown. She wonders what on earth can have brought this on. Going over to sit on the edge of the bed, she crouches to fit her head under the top bunk.

'I don't understand what you mean, Will.' She tries to keep her voice calm and level, refusing to let her panic bubble to the surface. 'Your mum and dad wanted to go to America so they can do their work. They'll be missing you lots, that's for sure, but *I* haven't said they can't come back. Where did you get that idea?'

'We heard them. They said they have to make money so they can pay you to let them live here.' Will prods Magda in the chest, and she winces. 'If *you* said they could come home, they would. Before Santa even starts delivering the presents.'

Both the children have tears in their eyes now. Magda feels unutterably weary. It's still only six o'clock. That's three more hours before they're in school and someone else's care. More specifically, before they're in Den Archer's care. She thinks back to the calm patience with which the headteacher dealt with the children yesterday, praying to find even a tiny amount of that patience within herself. Magda's vaguely aware Den has grown-up twins of his own. Ben and Ted are living up north at university now, but Magda feels sure Den never would have got in a flap with his boys when they were Will and Desi's age. Her thoughts of the headteacher steady her somehow. A few deep breaths are all that's needed, she tells herself. Breathe in . . . hold for five seconds. Out . . . nice and slowly.

'I think you've got the wrong end of the stick, Will,' she says finally and firmly.

'What stick? I haven't got a stick. Desi hasn't got one either, have you?'

His sister shakes her head but doesn't speak. Come to think of it, Magda's hardly heard her say a word since they were both found under the kitchen table. Desi's not nearly such a chatterbox as Will anyway, but this can't be right. Perhaps she just needs a bit of encouragement.

'Desi, I'm a bit worried about all this. Why are you and Will so cross with me?' she asks, reaching out as if to stroke her granddaughter's hair.

The little girl pulls the covers over her head and Will steps in again. 'Desi doesn't want to talk just now,' he says. 'So, what stick?'

'It's just a saying,' Magda tries to explain, sighing in frustration and thinking all this would be so much easier if she had a mug of coffee in her hand. 'And I think when you overhear people talking, you don't always get exactly what they mean. Your mum and dad like to earn money so they can help me out with the expenses.'

'What's expenses?' Will asks, frowning even more.

Magda doesn't answer. The thought has just struck her that

she hasn't been online this week to settle the gas and electricity bills, but Will isn't ready to let the subject drop.

'You've got loads of money. Why can't you just pay for everything? Chelsea says you must be the richest person in town because Mistletoe Cottage is the nicest house on the hill. She says you're being really mean, not letting us live here for nothing. The others in our gang said it must be true.'

It takes a moment for this statement to sink in. Chelsea is Magda's least favourite of Will and Desi's friends. She has the most elaborate birthday parties, the swankiest holidays and the most expensive designer clothes of any of their class, and her mother makes sure everyone knows it. And now, the thought that the other children are discussing the Conway family's affairs is mortifying. Some of their parents must be generating these ideas. Up to now, Magda has always felt comfortable with the locals of Periwinkle Bay. As a popular community midwife, who worked hard to always try and create trouble-free, relaxed home births whenever it was possible, she's always held a respected position in the town. Or rather, she thought she had.

'I'm not rich, Will,' she says, trying to think how to explain the situation in child-friendly terms. 'Mistletoe Cottage belonged to your great-grandpa and grandma and their own parents before that. It takes a lot of money to keep it going because it's rambling and very old. I don't know why whoever built it called it a cottage really. It's much too big to have that name.'

Both twins are looking puzzled now. 'What do you mean? If it's ours, why do we have to pay for it?' Will asks. Magda can't help but think they've gone slightly off track now.

'Oh, you know the sort of thing . . . there's food and electricity and logs for the fires . . . and all the other stuff we need,' Magda says. Warming to her theme, she continues '. . . and the roof leaks quite often and the house costs a lot to run and it's not very easy keeping it warm. I love us all living here together but we have to share the bills.'

'Hmmm.' Will's clearly unconvinced. 'You should definitely tell them to come home now though, cos you're just being nasty to our mum and dad.'

'And then there's the garden,' says Magda, rather desperately, ignoring this last comment. 'I have to get all the trees pruned so they don't get too big. The holly's going crazy and the old oak tree where all the mistletoe grows is enormous now.'

'But we like big trees, don't we, Desi?' says Will, folding his arms across his chest. His sister pokes her head out from under the covers but still doesn't speak. 'The oak tree is where our swing lives, and Dad says he's going to build us a house in it next summer. You shouldn't chop bits off it. Desi's really looking forward to the treehouse.'

'Desi? Aren't you going to say anything about this?' Magda says hopefully.

'She won't talk to you. Don't bother trying,' says Will matter-of-factly.

'But . . . why not?' Once again, she feels her panic levels start to rise.

'Desi says she's not happy and she won't speak until she is. Okay? And it's ALL YOUR FAULT.'

This last line is delivered at top volume. Magda starts to remonstrate but Will slides down the bed to be closer to his sister, covering them both with the duvet. Sighing, Magda gives up and goes downstairs to put the kettle on.

* * *

By half past nine, Magda's back in the kitchen, feeling as if she's already done a day's work after an even worse drop-off at school than yesterday. It took all Den's persuasive powers plus yet another promise of a cuddle with Blondie to get the twins into their classroom. Will is permanently surly today and her granddaughter still hasn't uttered a word.

When she's made a pot of strong coffee and found the emergency chocolate biscuits, Magda sinks into her mother's rocking chair next to the Aga and tries to keep her eyes open. To give in and have a nap so early in the day seems defeatist. It's important to get through until lunchtime, when she'll feel justified in lighting a huge crackling log fire in the living room and putting her feet up in front of some mindless daytime TV. She has an alarming flashback to her rare weekends off from work when Jared was small. He always woke ridiculously early too, full of boundless energy. Magda's exhaustion was often overwhelming and the early evening hours seemed to drag. There must be a way to make the time from school pick-up to bedtime more bearable.

The soft cushions seem to mould themselves into the shape of her back and the slow tick of the grandfather clock in the corner is soothing as Magda rocks back and forth gently, listening to the familiar creak of the ancient chair. She glances around the room, taking in the collection of blue and white china on the dresser and the six copper-bottomed pans hanging from a high shelf. It's a comforting feeling, knowing that her mother sat here often and enjoyed the same peaceful scene. But even so, the kitchen still seems very empty without Hope's reassuring presence.

Above the gleam of the pans and right next to the window is a shelf holding the tightly packed row of recipe books that carried Hope through her married life, her safety net to pull her through all the catering and entertaining she loved and did so well. Some of the books are older than Magda herself, but the glossier ones are more recent gifts from friends and family. On a whim, Magda reaches for the book on the end. It's a collection inspired by a TV show that her mum enjoyed; regional specialities from around the country. Rejecting that one as tediously wordy with too many photographs of the smugly beaming host of the programme, Magda pulls out another, which turns out to be mostly about curries, and then an older book, with a towering gateau on the cover.

This one is better. It has bigger print, simple instructions and tempting pictures of high-rise sponge cakes and plates of melt-in-the-mouth cookies. Magda flicks through it, and a sudden inspiration brings her to her feet, clutching the book to her chest. *That's it!* When she was a small child and still thought baking was fun, Hope always used cake-making as a way of making a bad day better. Maybe she can find a recipe to prepare for the twins. Or . . . better still . . . she could let them help her to get a cake ready for their tea. If they can be motivated to do something positive like baking with her after school, surely Desi and Will should begin to feel better.

The thought of this potential challenge is alarming, but it can't be that difficult. If Magda can hold down a demanding career, lead a home-birth team, deliver numerous healthy babies, *and* single-handedly raise a son, a simple cake shouldn't be beyond her. For a moment, Magda's heart sinks when she visualizes all the mess that baking involves. Even worse, if everything she tries to make goes wrong the children will think she's a complete failure as a granny. But one of Hope's favourite phrases had been *nothing ventured, nothing gained*. Magda can almost hear her mum saying it in the quiet of the kitchen that she'd loved so much.

Magda's mind is whirling now. The book in her hands has page after page of tempting pictures showing delicious cakes and biscuits tastefully displayed on classy crockery and surrounded by jars of jam, glowing like jewels and styled to look perfectly symmetrical. She knows she can't produce anything so professional, but something simple must be worth a try. There are plenty more recipe books on the shelf and in a burst of feverish enthusiasm, Magda tugs out another three. They're more complicated and are soon discarded, but the baking book is still providing a glimmer of optimism and telling her that she might have a chance of success if she just keeps it simple.

She casts her mind back to her early baking sessions with her mum, when Magda was still just a small child and when Hope still thought she'd make a confectioner of her daughter. The weighing and mixing had been the best bits. The results . . . not so great. But Will and Desi should at least have the chance to experiment.

Magda flicks through the book in her hand for something easy, eventually settling on jam tarts. The cupboards are well stocked with flour, sugar and the like, and Magda already has butter and margarine in the fridge, although she hasn't bought lard since Hope died. How hard can it be? There's even a nursery rhyme about tarts. If the Queen of Hearts can do it, so can she. A jar of her mother's home-made strawberry jam is soon unearthed from the back of the pantry and Magda sets everything out on the table, keen to get going as soon as the children are home.

As she strolls down to the school to pick them up that

afternoon, it is with a much lighter heart than when she started the day so blearily, and she hugs the twins warmly as they come running out to greet her.

'I've got a surprise for you at home,' she says, as she takes them both by the hand and sets off back up the hill.

Will stops in his tracks. 'Is it Mummy and Daddy?' he asks, letting go of Magda and beaming. 'Have they come back?'

Magda bites her lip. That was a bad choice of words. 'No, love,' she says gently. 'They won't be here for a while yet, you know that. The surprise is that we're going to do some very special baking.'

Her words aren't quite met with the response she might have wanted. Desi is still holding Magda's hand, but at this she lets it drop, instead covering her face with her school bag. There's a high keening noise coming from her that's so unlike a child's normal cry that Magda's heart feels as if it's being trampled on.

'Oh Desi, don't do that, darling,' she says, bending to cuddle the little girl. But Desdemona is having none of it. She wriggles out of Magda's grasp and begins to run towards home, stumbling slightly as she negotiates the cobbles.

'Wait for me,' Will yells, galloping after his sister. Magda's walking boots aren't designed for speed, but the fear that Desi will decide to take off in another direction gives her feet wings and she also takes off, reaching the front door only seconds after her grandchildren.

'Don't do that again,' she yells. 'You scared me.'

'You're shouting, Granny. Mum doesn't shout at us.' Will looks near to tears but Magda hardens her heart.

'Your mum and dad have left me in charge of you, and that means keeping you safe,' she says, trying to keep her voice even.

Shouting at them won't help, but her heart's still pounding at the thought of how easily they could give her the slip if they really tried. '*Do not* run away like that again. It's very worrying and what's more, it's dangerous. You could get run over. Or . . . or lost . . . or something. Okay?'

Desdemona's reproachful face says she doesn't care tuppence if Magda was worried. She follows Will into the house and immediately locks herself in the downstairs cloakroom.

'Now you've done it,' says Will in his now all-too-regular I-told-you-so voice.

The buzz of enthusiasm for the cooking session that Magda felt on the walk to school quickly fades away as she contemplates the closed door.

'Now what do we do?' she asks Will.

He shrugs. 'Last time she did that, she was in there ages. Mum tried everything to get her to come out.'

'So how did she manage in the end?' Magda tries to keep the desperation out of her voice. Will already looks far too much in control of the situation for her liking.

'Chocolate,' says her grandson calmly. 'She'll do anything for chocolate buttons.' He kicks off his shoes. 'So what's for tea?'

'Well, that was actually part of my surprise,' Magda says wearily. Then, louder and clearer, so that her voice will carry through the toilet door, she adds, 'We're going to make the best jam tarts ever created.'

Will immediately looks sceptical. 'Are we? But you hate baking. And you aren't very good at it ether. GG told us,' he adds, in answer to Magda's questioning look. 'When she was showing us how to make Rice Krispie cakes.'

'There's no need to be rude, Will. We can't all be brilliant at baking.' Magda bites her lip, trying to keep her irritation inside. This day is going downhill fast.

'I wish GG was here instead of you. She'd definitely make us some good tarts.' Will's bottom lip is sticking out now, and not for the first time Magda is reminded of Jared as a truculent five-year-old.

'Me too, my love. I really do.' Will and Desi had always called Hope GG, 'Great Gran' being too hard to say when they were just learning to talk. Will's use of it now tugs at Magda's heart. She ruffles Will's hair but he pulls away.

'I don't really want to bake stuff,' he says. 'I want to watch TV.'

'Oh, but you can do that anytime,' Magda says, suddenly desperate to try out her plan now the chances of it happening seem to be dwindling. 'Let's give it a go, Will. You can be in charge of putting the jam in, if you like.' She raises her voice. 'And Desi can put the pastry in the tins.'

There's a scuffling noise from inside the cloakroom. Will looks at Magda sideways and then makes his decision, leaning forward to bang on the toilet door.

'You'd better come out now. Jam tarts time, Desi,' he shouts. 'And I know where they hide the chocolate buttons.'

The door opens very slowly and Desi emerges. Wisely, Magda says nothing, but leads the way to the kitchen and supervises hand-washing. She props the recipe book on the table and they set to, working together in the kind of harmony that makes all the previous hassle worthwhile.

The results, however, are a disaster. Both children are covered in flour – something made even worse by the fact that Magda hasn't remembered to tell them to change out of their school uniforms or even to put on their aprons – and the pastry has a definite grey tinge to it after the twins have finished pummelling and rolling it, stretching it out in strange, lacy folds over the work surface.

'You forgot to put flour under it. And you didn't even use the big wooden board,' says Will, and Magda can't help but think she's hearing his I-know-better-than-you tone all too often today.

Desi nods, and points to the flour tin and then at the thin pastry sticking to the oilcloth.

Belatedly, Magda remembers this useful fact. 'You could have told me,' she says wearily, forgetting for a brief moment that she's supposed to be the adult here.

'But we're only five and you're . . . old,' Will points out. 'Why don't you know that stuff?'

'I . . .' Magda can't finish the sentence. She *should* know this stuff. Memories of the times when her mum has tried to teach her these basic skills come flooding back. Of course she knew they should have floured the big board, and the rolling pin too come to think of it, which now also has lumps of pastry sticking to it.

'Well, I think they'll taste fine anyway, and that's what matters,' Magda continues, trying to claw back some authority. 'Desi, you need to cut out the circles and then Will can pop some jam in.'

Half an hour later, she's not so sure. Desi even puts a hand over her mouth as Magda lifts the tray of cremated tarts out of the oven.

'Are they supposed to be like that?' Will asks, peering over as Magda chips them out of their tray. 'They look a bit . . . burnt. I think GG used to do something with the tins so they didn't stick.'

'Yes,' says Magda grimly, holding on to her patience with

48

difficulty. 'You're meant to grease them. I forgot that too. And I didn't set the kitchen timer so they were in the oven a bit too long. I don't think baking is really my thing.'

She flops down on the sofa and closes her eyes, close to tears. She can never, ever live up to Hope's genius in the kitchen. But even as Magda makes the conscious decision never to try anything like this again, she hears footsteps getting closer and feels a small hand in each of hers.

'We're making a Granny sandwich,' says Will, as the twins sit down either side and both put their other arms around her. 'It doesn't matter about the tarts. We don't like them much anyway, do we, Desi?'

His sister shakes her head, burrowing into the warmth of the hug. Magda breathes in the comforting scent of their shampoo mingled with a lingering smell of school dinners and a hint of chocolate from the buttons Will has unearthed.

'Are you very sad about the black tarts, Granny?' Will asks, snuggling closer.

Magda holds them both tighter, finding it hard to speak. This lovely closeness is a novelty, and she longs to make it last. Will leans to one side to look up at her.

'We can try again tomorrow, if you like?' he says.

Desi starts to giggle, and Magda hugs her closer. Will grins too.

'Really? Do you think we should after today?'

'We might do,' he says. 'But we could use a different book next time? You prob'ly just picked the wrong one. We should get the other.'

'The other what?'

'You know, the special one. Come on, Desi, let's go and play zoos under the stairs.'

He gallops out of the room followed closely by his sister, and Magda frowns, totally confused.

She stands up and stretches her tired body, glancing along the row of recipe books. It's as if they're all sitting up there mocking her. *What would Hope have done in this situation, with the children on the verge of being feral at times and the days until Christmas scrolling endlessly ahead?* Magda thinks bitterly. *What would Fliss do? She'd no doubt have all the answers.* Overwhelmed with loss at the thought of her mum and the growing conviction that she's alienated the only person who can help her at this point, Magda fights the urge to let pessimism win. She mustn't give up just because she's lonely and struggling.

For some reason, unknown even to her, Magda feels certain that the key to all this lies in the books on the shelf. Hope Conway's skills are going to come to her rescue at long last, she's sure of it.

Christmas Day, Thirty-four Years Ago

Sitting at the kitchen table early on Christmas morning, nursing a steaming cup of tea with her mother and Fliss, Magda can already see that this is going to be a very difficult day for them all. Hope has already sobbed her heart out twice, once because the turkey hasn't completely thawed and then again on hearing 'In the Bleak Midwinter' playing softly on the radio in the corner. It's only a month since Magda's grandmother fell ill with a bad dose of influenza, which along with an undiagnosed heart condition carried her off within a week. The loss of Granny Partridge has left a huge gap in Mistletoe Cottage and Hope still seems numb with grief a lot of the time. Both widows, Hope and her mother have brought Magda up together, and been a constant source of good food, undemonstrative affection and an infectious delight in their cosy home and rambling garden.

'I'm sorry that I haven't been better organized this year,' says Hope. 'I feel as if I've let you all down. If you hadn't taken over the Christmas food preparation, Fliss, we'd have been in a much worse mess. I don't know what I'd have done without you.'

'It's no trouble,' says Fliss stoutly. 'We all know Magda wouldn't have been able to do it!'

She laughs and Hope tries to join in, but Magda doesn't feel in the least bit amused. She's helped as much as she can with all the other arrangements, and organizing a funeral for

51

someone as popular in the town as her grandmother has been a steep learning curve. Fliss carries on, apparently not noticing Magda's sour expression.

'You say you weren't organized but you'd already got all the recipes, Hope, and most of the ingredients in the pantry or the freezer too. It was just a case of pulling everything together . . . and for that I just needed your special book.' Her eyes flick gleefully over to a well-thumbed, handwritten recipe book lying on the kitchen table. 'And,' she continues, drawing out her word in suspense, 'I've also got a bit of a surprise for us. I know how awful these last few weeks have been for you, but it was too late to make Granny Partridge's usual Christmas cake this close to Christmas. So instead, I made the one you invented yourself, Hope, with a tin of crushed pineapple in it.

'It tastes just as good and it won't need to be left for weeks to mature either. Which is lucky because I only made it last week. I snuck in and borrowed your recipe book while I was tidying some bits in the kitchen!'

Hope and Fliss smile at each other, and not for the first time Magda feels completely left out. She supposes it's her own fault for having no interest in baking, while Fliss, on the other hand, loves to cook, but she sometimes wishes she shared this connection with her own mother. It's the one time she doesn't feel totally like her mother's daughter. The three women freeze as a loud wail breaks the comfortable silence.

'It feels as if I only just got Jared to drop off,' says Magda, her shoulders sagging with weariness. Much as she adores her one-year-old son, he has never really taken to sleeping. He still wakes several times in the night and only naps in the daytime when exhaustion overtakes him.

'Stop worrying, Mags,' Hope chides her daughter. 'Fliss here can keep helping me in the kitchen and you can fetch Jared and then come back down and have another nice cup of tea. Jared can sit in his highchair and watch us. He might even learn something. Handy for the future.'

The barb doesn't go unnoticed. Magda goes up to fetch her son without a word. It's not worth an argument, and she's too tired for one anyway. The past year has been even harder than she expected, which is saying something, considering moving far from home, working shifts as a midwife, and raising a child on her own had never seemed like an easy task to begin with. Finding reliable childcare while she worked shifts had been especially tough, and the temptation to throw in the towel and move back home to her mum and gran has been strong. But she'd been determined to stick it out in Leicester, even after Jared's father made it clear he wanted no part in his son's life. And so stick it out she had.

Now, when Magda comes back downstairs with her newly changed, and much refreshed, baby boy, her mother is at the table showing Fliss her own recipe for custard, ready for the Boxing Day trifle. Fliss wants to try her hand at making it. Of course she does.

'How are you going to stop it curdling?' asks Magda. 'It does sometimes, doesn't it? I remember you telling me that, Mum.'

Even to herself, Magda sounds as if she's trying too hard to appear interested. She yawns. Who cares anyway? This team of two super cooks doesn't need her input.

'I'm definitely going to have a go at doing it the old-fashioned way,' says Fliss. 'But I bet Hope's got a tin of the powdered stuff hidden away in the cupboard for emergencies. If it goes wrong, we'll just slosh some cream and a bit of sherry into it. Nobody will mind, I'm sure!'

Magda passes Jared to his grandmother and sits back with relief as she then slots him into his highchair and gives him a wooden spoon and a saucepan to play with. The kitchen is large, with a sofa and rocking chair in one corner, and Magda closes her eyes for a moment. If only Jared would get the hang of sleeping. And if only his father ... but there's no point in thinking about what might have been. Giovanni's brief return from New York had only served to show her that he wasn't in the least bit committed to Magda and his son. The chance of a shiny new job back home was all the lure he needed to return to the bosom of his family, and incidentally to the girlfriend he probably should have married long before now. The desertion has hurt Magda very badly and made it even harder to be patient with her energetic baby who seems to think sleep is for losers.

Magda gives herself a little shake and tries to be positive. Her mother managed perfectly well as a solo parent and so will she. The women in this family have always been strong and she's determined not to be the first to go under. 'Oh, it's so good to have you two here with me,' she hears Hope say. 'Together we can face anything, can't we, girls?'

Magda smiles at her mum and then, with a bit more of an effort, at Fliss, both of them so happy bustling around. Realization dawns that for some time now she hasn't even been trying to face her own problems. She's just been ducking them and hoping they'll go away.

'Doesn't anything ever faze you, Mum?' she says admiringly. Her mum's life has been full of pitfalls and yet she never seems to be tempted to give in to gloomy thoughts.

'Not really. There's no point in getting stressed about things you can't avoid. Best just to look your problems straight in the eye and then tackle them.'

Magda takes in these wise words, telling herself that she'll make more of an effort to put them into practice when she goes back to Leicester. Perhaps this Christmas won't be so sad after all. She must just try not to resent Fliss for liking cooking, because actually it's very lucky that she does. If the food's good and the house is warm, they can't really go wrong. The warmth of the Aga and the sound of the chatter of the other two is soothing. As she settles further into her chair, she watches the long-winded preparation of the custard with barely disguised horror. Why would anyone go to all this trouble when they could just open a carton? She sighs. There are some things about her mother and Fliss that she will just never, ever understand.

5

Wednesday, 13 December

Twelve Days Until Christmas

The new day brings yet more chaos into Magda's previously tranquil world. She's woken by the full force of Will's weight landing on her chest.

'I can't sleep,' he mumbles into her ear.

Magda wriggles out from underneath the chunky little body, desperately trying to wake herself up. She'd been in the middle of a lovely dream, where she was on the deck of a fabulous ocean liner. The shock of seeing Will's furious face is not pleasant.

'What time is it?' she murmurs, blinking at the bedside clock.

'I dunno. But I think Desi's wet the bed,' he answers. 'She smells funny.'

Dragging herself out of bed, Magda heads for the twins' room to find Desi in a huddle under Will's duvet. Her pyjamas are on the floor and sure enough, the top bunk is a tangle of sodden sheets. Magda's head throbs. Every bone in her body is telling her she needs more sleep. With an effort, she holds on to her patience.

'It's okay, darling, don't look so worried,' she says, hoping her tone is calming rather than obviously aggravated. Wearily, she starts to strip the bed. 'Are you feeling poorly?'

Desi purses her lips and doesn't respond. Will is standing in the doorway with his arms folded. 'She's sad,' he says. 'I told you she won't talk. It's your fault!' At this, his voice rises again, all signs of the tranquil little boy who comforted her last night completely erased. 'Why don't you just ring up Mummy and Daddy like I told you? We want them to come home!'

'Will, I can't do that,' Magda responds, feeling once again that she is scrambling to get a hold of a situation that is fast running away from her. 'They're working, remember? It's what they want to do. It's important to them.'

'Ha! That's what *you* say.' Will turns away.

A couple of difficult hours later, just as Magda is rejoicing to finally be able to hand the twins over to someone else, she is surprised to notice a text from the school ping on to her phone as she hurries the twins down the hill. She reads it with growing alarm, while simultaneously trying to stop Will from tripping his sister up and Desi from pinching him in retaliation.

Good morning Magda. Could you pop into the office for a chat this morning when you've done the drop-off? The kettle will be on. See you soon, Den

Magda runs through the possible reasons for this summons in her mind, starting with the least worrying. Maybe Den wants to discuss the carol performance with her? The choir have been practising for ages and, as resident organist, Den likes to have charge of the programme as much as possible. They're taking the lead at the Methodist service on Christmas Eve this year. But no, they planned all that last week, so it seems unlikely.

Just as soon as she's got that worry out of her head, thoughts of the choir prompt the realization that Fliss hasn't turned up for practices for at least a month. This definitely should have rung alarm bells before now, but she'd always assumed that Fliss was just busy. The craft shop she shares with her ex-partner Laurence always takes up a lot of her time in the run-up to Christmas, when all the creative types in the area decide they want to make their own cards and decorations. Looking with hindsight now, though, it's clear that Magda had just been giving herself a lazy excuse to not check in with the one person she should always check in with. Fliss, an energetic do-er at all times, was never 'just busy'.

Magda's stomach flips uncomfortably. She really must bite the bullet and ring her friend later. By the time they've reached the playground and she's had another battle to get Will and Desi inside their classroom, Magda has run through every reason possible why Den would call her into his office and has finally accepted the fact that Den probably wants to complain about the twins' behaviour. Den's concerned expression as he opens his office door in response to her tentative knock convinces her that she's right.

'Come in and have a seat,' he says, his voice kind. 'I've been here since seven o'clock this morning and I'm gasping for a coffee. You must be ready for one too. And take your coat off,' he says, gesturing at a hook by the door where she should hang it, 'or you won't feel the benefit when you go out again, as my granny used to say.'

Magda is unable to speak. The warmth of the little room, the peace after the hubbub of the yard outside and the friendliness of the man now spooning coffee into huge mugs brings home to her how bereft she's been feeling since Jared and Annika went away. She suddenly realizes that her only proper human contact with someone her own age was with Fliss, and that ended so badly it was worse than none at all.

She looks around, as Den starts to hunt for biscuits. She's only been in here once before, when Annika asked her to drop off the registration forms for the twins. As she was on that occasion, she's struck by the fact that the room doesn't look anything like her idea of a head's office. There are no forbidding metal filing cabinets, just fitted wooden cupboards all along one wall painted in a mellow shade of moss green. The one large window looks out on to the wood that backs on to the building, where the children do the forest schoolwork that Will and Desi love so much. There are leafy ferns and other plants on a side table, alongside several photographs of Den's sons, framed in bamboo. The whole effect is of an extension of the outdoor area, softly lit by an elderly standard lamp in the corner whose charm is only slightly marred by a large white 'PAT tested' sticker on the base.

'So, how do you think it's all going?' Den asks, sitting down in the easy chair next to Magda instead of behind his desk. He puts the two drinks down on the coffee table and pushes a tin of biscuits in her direction.

Inhaling the fragrant steam with her hands clasped around the mug, Magda feels a bit stronger but there's still no point in mincing words. 'It's a disaster so far,' she says. 'Desi wet the bed this morning and Will's getting naughtier every day. This morning he poured bubble bath into the toilet cistern then watched from behind the door when I flooded the bathroom with foam. I was still mopping up two minutes before we had to leave the house. My slippers, the bath mat and the landing carpet are all sopping wet.'

Den's eyes are twinkling and he seems to be stifling a grin. Magda glares at him. 'It's not funny. It was the last straw. And Desi won't talk to me. At all.' Her voice wobbles and she pauses to pull herself together.

'Desi won't talk to anyone,' says Den quietly. He's definitely not smiling now. 'Her teacher mentioned it in the staff meeting last night. And then there's Will's . . . erm . . . spirited behaviour.'

'Oh, goodness. It must be bad if they've all noticed too. What's Will been doing?'

'This and that. He seems very angry a lot of the time, which isn't like him. Will's usually one of the most civilized children in the reception class, but lately he's been pushing and shoving his best friends around outside and getting into quite a bit of trouble in the classroom.' Magda can't think of a response.

Den leans forward and pats Magda's arm. 'Don't look so tragic. It's not the end of the world. They're only small, and they're both upset. We can help them to get through this. We just need to think of the best way to tackle it.'

They drink their coffee in silence, both lost in their own thoughts. It strikes Magda, apropos of nothing, that this is the first time she's ever been alone with Den. They've previously only bumped into each other at choir practice or in parish meetings. She's grateful that at least this conversation is happening with somebody she knows, even if not very well. It would be so much worse if Den was some crusty head teacher straight from the pages of a 1950s children's story. Even so, this is serious. Her frustration with Jared and Annika is turning to full-force fury now, bubbling away inside her.

'I told them not to go,' she bursts out. 'I knew this would happen, especially with Christmas coming. It's unbelievably selfish. I *told* them. And this is probably the only time Desi will ever be chosen to play Mary in the Nativity. I reminded them about that and Annika just said that she'd asked one of her friends to video it, as if that's a substitute for being there.'

'Were there arguments? Before they left, I mean. Might the twins have overheard?'

Magda nods solemnly. She and Jared hadn't held back. They'd waited until the children were in bed, but sound still carries, and neither Will nor Desi had been settling very well at night.

'Right, well at least we know what the problem is. They're feeling lost without their parents and it all happened quite quickly, so you had no time to prepare them.'

Magda leans back in her chair, beginning to relax slightly. Den is making all this sound perfectly normal and understand-able in the circumstances. His voice is particularly soothing, and the rising panic at the escalating situation with the twins is ebbing away.

'Try not to worry so much and let me deal with this. It's not your fault if they're unsettled,' he continues.

'They seem to think it is.'

'Well, it isn't. Everyone likes someone to blame when things go pear-shaped, don't they? Looks as though the twins are no different.' Here, Den gets out a notebook and pen and makes a few unintelligible squiggles. 'Now all we need to do is make a plan to help the two of them to get through this and still enjoy Christmas. And you too.'

'Me?' Magda's heart sinks. What she knows, deep down, is that she didn't do the childcare stuff very well the first time round. Memories of her own small son are flooding back. She'd been called in unexpectedly for an interview with the head teacher of Jared's school when he was only a little older than Will and Desi and had decided to tell his entire class and teacher that he was going to run away from home because his mummy was always taking him round to the next-door neighbour's house so she could go out. That had been a very sticky interview. Magda had explained that she was a single mum working full-time. Not only that, but the lady in question was a registered childminder and one of the kindest people she'd ever met, but the constant feeling that she was failing her son had intensified that day.

'I'm not sure we should be thinking about Christmas being fun for me,' she says. 'It's all about Will and Desi, isn't it? Especially this year, with their parents so far away.'

Den smiles at her. 'Don't be so hard on yourself. Christmas isn't just for the children. Let's think about you for a change. You're the one holding all this together, after all.'

6

'Look, I don't know anything about the ins and outs of your family life, Magda,' says Den, starting to do that irritating thing where people click their pen on and off. He sees her looking at him and puts the pen down. 'Sorry, I've been told before that's one of my most annoying habits.'

'Could be a lot worse,' Magda lies. 'Go on with what you were saying.'

'Okay. I'm not trying to stick my nose in, but I'm worried about all this. Anything that affects the pupils here is my business, so it stands to reason I'm allowed to interfere. It's clear that this year you've put the family first but it doesn't mean your own Christmas should be a damp squib, you know.'

Magda frowns. This is a new thought. For a brief moment, she allows herself to wonder whether in fact she's been shouldering too much guilt, unnecessarily. Well, if she has, it's mainly because some of the accusations Jared was throwing around before he left managed to hit home in a big way. Magda would be the first to admit that she hadn't quite noticed the extent to which the early years in the flat in Leicester, when it was just the two of them, have left their mark on her son.

'For goodness' sake stop beating yourself up,' Den is squinting at her, as though trying to read her thoughts. 'Whatever you say, I'm certain you've done a great job so far. You've raised a well-mannered, talented son. He seems to be

Celia Anderson

happily married, which as I know is no mean feat. The younger Conways have produced two children who are usually full of beans, in a good way, and you've had a great career yourself.'

'It's nice of you to say so.'

'Not just me, the whole town sings your praises. You've always been everyone's midwife of choice, apparently.'

Magda can't help smiling at this. 'Delivering babies for so many years was a privilege, but to be brutally honest, I was just really looking forward to early retirement. And now . . .'

'And now you're suddenly back to full-time mothering.' The ease with which Den understands Magda's predicament shocks her.

She thinks about his words for a moment and then responds, 'Well, I suppose. But it's not really a case of *back to* mothering with me, Den. I was never a stay-at-home mum. Jared still holds that against me. I can't help but think this must be some kind of payback.'

Den drains his coffee mug and looks as if he's searching for the right words to say next. 'I doubt that very much. I guess I'm something of a solo parent myself, these days. I know my lads are much older than your two, but Virginia, my wife, has sort of . . . left me, I suppose. Maybe you've heard . . .' His voice trails off. The truth of it is that the whole *town* seems to know about Virginia's departure, so of course Magda is aware. She doesn't want to tell Den this, though; he seems uncomfortable and sad enough as it is. Instead, she keeps quiet, and Den ploughs on.

'The boys weren't impressed to begin with, big as they are, but they're getting used to the idea. Anyway, that's enough about my life,' he says briskly. 'Let's get on with the plan. So, what are your Christmas priorities, Mags?'

64

She's glad he's gone back to the name all her friends call her. *Magda* sounded so formal in his text and none of the choir or her other friends ever use it. 'How do you mean?'

'Think about it. If you had to design the perfect Christmas for you and Will and Desi, what would it look like?'

The sound of the reception class's loud rendition of 'Jingle Bells' can be heard from the nearby hall as Magda struggles with her answer. This question, or rather, this whole *conversation*, is on a much more personal level than the usual exchange of mildly sarcastic jibes and one-liners that the choir bat back and forth with their organist.

'Come on,' Den prompts, as the reception class moves on to 'Away in a Manger', the one that Magda expects will leave no dry eye in the house at their Nativity service next week. 'Give me something to go on. We're talking about you, Magda Conway, pillar of the community, retired midwife, with more fans in Periwinkle Bay than you can shake a stick at. What would make your Christmas great, assuming we can't magic the wanderers home?'

Magda clears her throat. 'Okay, here goes,' she says. 'It all comes down to fun, I guess. More than anything, I would like to be able to make the twins happy, hear them giggling and being silly with me.'

'Go on,' Den encourages, pushing Magda into her stride.

'We would wrap up warmly and go for long walks through the woods and down to the sea. We would go and visit Santa in the Town Hall Grotto. I want to get them to help me buy the family tree and decorate their own little silver one for the kitchen.'

She pauses, remembering Jared decorating that same tree, when there were just the two of them in the flat, and wondering whether she had ever allowed herself to actually *enjoy* doing those things with him, or whether she'd been too busy trying to juggle work and childcare without losing her marbles to even care properly.

'And most of all, I'd like them to feel as if they can tell me when they're feeling sad and angry instead of getting into trouble or going silent. And we need to have the delicious smell of home cooking in the background, to make us all feel cosy and loved.'

'That's a great list. So what's stopping you? Your Christmas and mine haven't gone on hold just because three of the main players have gone AWOL.'

'Four, if you count my mum,' says Magda, in a small voice.

'Ah. And there we have it. The elephant in the room. I can't believe I didn't think of it before. Look, Mags, even if the others hadn't upped sticks and left you in the lurch, this Christmas would have been difficult and painful, wouldn't it?'

'I suppose so.'

'Of course it would. You're only human. And I think I've got the answer, or the start of one anyway.'

Magda waits, already grateful that here is someone who's prepared to make the effort to help her tackle everything going on. Den picks up his pen, starts to click it, and then pulls a face and puts it down again quickly.

'Sorry. It helps me to think, somehow.'

He stands up and takes the tweed jacket off, flinging it over another chair, as though preparing for something big.

'So, I reckon you need to make some subtle changes in your routine from now until the big day, and also some bigger ones,' he says. 'Trust me, I know what I'm talking about here.'

'I don't get it.' Magda feels as if she's wading through thick fog. Exhaustion and the warmth of the room are making her long to stagger home and sleep until pick-up time. 'What are you saying?'

'My dad died very suddenly a couple of years ago, in mid-December. Mum insisted we did everything the way we'd always done it, just as he would have wanted. She went through the motions of putting up decorations, we all went to our usual Christmas market and the carol service and so on together and we finished it all off with Christmas dinner at her house with an empty chair at the table. She even laid him a place. It was a nightmare.'

'That sounds so very sad.'

'Yes, it was. It just brought home how nothing was ever going to be the same again. The next year we all went on holiday to Spain – me, Virginia, the boys, Mum, and a couple of her single friends. We still missed Dad like crazy but it was much better than trying to pretend everything was normal.'

Magda's definitely interested now. 'I think I see what you're getting at.'

'I'm saying that Christmas can still be just as good, but in a different way. And I reckon the first thing you need to do is to conjure up that kitchen full of gorgeous cooking smells again, like it was when your mum was around. Set the scene, like you would for a play. Let the kids help you.'

'But that's not a change, is it? We've always had lovely food.'

He grins. 'It's a change for you to be in charge of it, I'm guessing.'

Magda sighs. 'I think everyone who knows me in the town must have heard about my reputation for avoiding anything to do with baking,' she says. 'You're right though. I did try last night. I made some jam tarts with them. It wasn't a success.'

She pulls the sleeves of her oversized sweater down to cover her hands, suddenly chilly even though Den's office is so cosy. 'I wish . . . I so, so wish I'd let Mum show me some of her tricks for making perfect cakes and pastries. I haven't even cleaned the kitchen to her standards lately.'

'So there you have your starting point. Call it Plan A. Go home, do a quick online shop to stock up with all the essential store cupboard ingredients and then put some festive music on and give the kitchen a good scrub. You'll feel loads better and you'll have set the scene for the next part.'

'Right. If you say so. But then what?'

'We'll work on that later. As you know, I'm alone and not got much else to do – I'll help as much as I can.'

The relief of not shouldering all this alone floods through Magda. She stands up, suddenly feeling rejuvenated. 'Right, I'm off to start Plan A,' she declares, slipping her arms into her coat and heading for the door, wrapping her scarf around her neck as she goes. Den is ahead of her and opening it before she can reach for the handle.

'I'll call you later. And Mags . . .'

She turns and looks up at him. 'Yes?'

'Like I said before, try not to worry, eh?'

Striding back up the hill, with Den's words echoing around her head, Magda has a feeling that will be a lot easier said than done.

7

The Herculean task of kitchen blitzing takes longer than Magda expected, and she's still mopping the floor at half past two, having done a big online shop and missed lunch. It's nearly time to fetch Desi and Will but not before she's had a much-needed breather. Magda's stomach rumbles as she sinks into her mum's rocking chair to give the tiles time to dry, glad she's thought to have a pot of tea and some biscuits within reach.

Leaning back, Magda relaxes for the first time that day. Following Annika's example, she's attached long strings of white fairy lights along the beams and across the dresser shelves, and they sparkle cheerfully in the afternoon gloom of the chilly December day. There are tall church candles ranged along the windowsill and dresser, all ready to be lit later on. The hum of the washing machine in the pantry, the gentle sound of Christmas music on Classic FM and the fresh, zingy scent of a variety of cleaning fluids is soothing. Now all she needs to do is decide what to try and cook with the twins when they get home. If she can make a better attempt at baking tonight, all might not be lost.

Glancing around the sparkling kitchen with the satisfied feeling of having for once done what her mother managed to achieve all the time, Magda's eyes come to rest on the shelf of cookery books. She stands up, carefully avoiding treading on the dampest part of the floor, and reaches to run her fingers along the row. Hope always enjoyed dipping into all these old favourites. Their spines reveal an eclectic mix. There are books on Thai cooking, gateaux, chocolate indulgences, an ancient Be-Ro book, a tattered pre-war collection and a whole set of Delia Smith's finest.

It strikes Magda that Will mentioned that they were using the wrong book yesterday. It's most likely to have been just one of his random comments though – there probably wouldn't be a right cookery book for her, even if she had a whole library of them at her disposal. She looks at the shelf more closely. One of the books is sticking out further than the others. Magda frowns. She's sure she lined them all up neatly when she dusted the shelf earlier. Her hand stops when she reaches the one that's out of kilter. There's a strange tension in the air, as if the kitchen is waiting for something. Even the music on the radio stutters for a moment. Magda touches the slimmer volume lightly. It's wedged between a thick vegetarian tome and a hefty book on how to make the most of cheese. Memories stir inside her, some good, some less so. She pulls it out, holding her breath. It's a long time since she's had this one in her hands, but it's still the book she remembers the most. *Of course,* Magda says to herself. This must be what Will was getting at. Her mum's collection of handwritten recipes, added to over and over again through many years of happy cooking.

Back in her chair, Magda looks down at the treasure in her lap. The much-thumbed pages are bound in a hessian cover, mottled with all sorts of food splashes. As Magda opens it, a mysterious scent of cinnamon wafts into the kitchen, seemingly from nowhere. She peers down at the first pages but there are no specks of spice to be seen. Odd. The familiar fragrance brings back memories of her mother, poignant but reassuring. Revelling in the image of her mother making one of her mouth-watering fruit cakes, Magda reads the inscription, precious words that Hope had loved.

> *To our Hope,*
> *For The Future, on her tenth birthday – may your baking always be as scrumptious as your smile.*
> *With all our love, Mum and Grandma.*

Feeling part of a long line of strong, loving women is something to celebrate, Magda tells herself, even if she's letting the side down at the moment. Tears prickle behind her eyelids. She blinks them away and turns to the index. Hope had had an unusual way of categorizing her personal recipes, and underneath the inscription, she's written an extra note, seemingly added a lot later than its predecessor. In the quiet of the slumbering afternoon kitchen, Magda reads the words out loud.

> *All my recipes should be made with love: to help you to love yourself, for those you love, or with those you love. Togetherness in the kitchen is one of life's great joys.*
> *PS But never lend anyone your knives!*

Magda shivers. She can almost hear her mum's voice as she says the words. The ink is fading slightly now but the message is clear. It's almost as though, for a moment, Hope is reaching out to Magda from beyond the grave. Magda shivers again, shaking off the thought. But the note reminds her she should persevere with Will and Desi, and maybe they'll inherit Hope's skills, even if she can't.

She turns her attention to the recipes themselves. Tags stick out from the pages all along the edge, handwritten in neat black lettering. Some sections are much longer than others. Magda reads the titles of each aloud, as if it's an incantation.

Extra Easy Ideas, Picnics and Holidays, The Squishiest Cakes Ever, Comfort Food For Bad Days, Quick Dinners, Perfect Pastry, Posh Parties To Impress, Christmas Countdown Made Simple, and The Ones That Look A Mess.

The words have an enchanting feel to them, almost as if Hope is back in her kitchen, her warm, reassuring presence telling Magda that everything's going to be fine. Magda recites the list of categories twice more, and each time she feels stronger. She closes the book and holds it close to her chest. A very slight tingling that seems to come from right inside the pages makes her spine prickle. She closes her eyes and as if bound by some unwritten rule, lets the sensation develop. Her whole body feels as if it's being . . . what? The only word that comes anywhere close is *loved*.

The grandfather clock in the corner creaks as it prepares to strike three and Magda sits up with a jolt. Only fifteen minutes to get to school. She places the book carefully back between its friends and leaves the kitchen at a trot, grabbing her coat and keys and remembering at the very last minute to swap her old trainers for boots.

It's very cold outside now, but Magda hardly notices. All the way down the street, her mind whirls and the book's section titles sing themselves in her head, to the tune of 'The Holly and the Ivy'.

She tries singing the words aloud as there aren't many people on the street at this time of day. The more she repeats them, the closer her mum seems, almost as if Hope is reaching out through the years to get her secrets across. As she reaches the town centre and the streets grow busier, Magda stops singing, but the message is still there, warming her. She can smell coffee and the scent of freshly baked fruit cake as she hurries past the café, but it lingers longer than that too, as if following her towards the school. This is how her kitchen should be, full of the promise of delicious home-made Christmas goodies.

8

The twins are in a better mood this afternoon when they emerge from their classroom. Will puts his arms around Magda's waist and hugs her hard and Desi smiles up at her, showing the endearing gap in her front teeth.

'Has today gone well?' Magda asks and they walk back up the hill hand in hand.

'Yes. Jarvis has got chicken pox so now I'm going to get to be Joseph in the play,' Will says gleefully.

'Oh my goodness, poor Jarvis,' says Magda automatically.

'We don't like Jarvis, do we, Desi?' Will says.

'What's he done now?' Magda is getting a sinking feeling in the pit of her stomach. This boy's name is depressingly familiar to most of the parents in the twins' class.

Will shrugs. 'He's just naughty,' he says virtuously. 'He hits people.'

'That's bad. I'm glad you two aren't nasty to your friends,' Magda says. Will looks down at his shoes and doesn't answer.

'Anyway, it's good news that you're going to be Joseph,' she adds, deciding not to press this point just now. 'Desi will like that.'

Desi's eyes are shining. She beams up at Magda.

'Were you worried about Jarvis being Joseph, darling?' Magda says, wondering what else the small tyrant has done to upset her granddaughter.

74

Desi nods, and Magda feels a fierce protective wave wash over her. 'Well, thank goodness it will all go smoothly now your brother's stepping in,' she says.

'Not if they keep trying to make Desi speak,' says Will. He's let go of Magda's hand and is kicking a stone along. He still doesn't look at her.

'I didn't think it was a speaking part. What's Mary supposed to say?'

Desi, unsurprisingly, doesn't answer. Will gives his stone one last kick and turns to face them. 'She's meant to say "I'm going to call him Jesus", and she won't do it. But it's a waste of time anyway because we all know that's his name. And anyway, it's not even a real baby. It's a doll. *And* it's a girl doll,' he adds, pulling a hideous face. 'It should have a willy if it's Jesus,' he adds. 'I coulda told 'em that.'

Magda turns to Desi, ignoring most of what Will says. 'Do you still want to be Mary?' she asks the little girl.

Desi nods again much more vigorously.

'She wants to be Mary so she can wear the blue dress and the white thing on her head.' Of course it's Will who responds for his sister.

'I was talking to Desi. Let her answer for herself, Will,' Magda says, trying her best to be patient.

'But she doesn't want to. She told me last night she's not going to talk to anyone except me until Mummy and Daddy come home.'

Magda bites back the urge to say *But maybe she would if you didn't keep jumping in,* and smiles down at them both.

'And I'm not going to be good until they're back either,' Will says, as though he doesn't want to be left out.

He stops in his tracks and glares at Magda. Desi pauses

too and goes over to stand shoulder to shoulder with her brother.

'Unless . . .' He breaks off and looks thoughtful. Desi nudges him and he leans closer to her. Magda can't hear the muffled words properly, but Will doesn't seem to be having a problem understanding.

'. . . unless we can do Christmassy baking with you every single night until they come back,' he says. Desi nudges him for a second time.

'And she says you mustn't burn anything else either.'

For a moment, Magda is stunned. Baking something different every day sounds terrifying. It was only yesterday that Will seemed so unsure about cooking with her.

'Are you sure? Every single evening?' she says.

They both nod vigorously. Magda looks down at the two upturned faces, both so hopeful, and her heart melts. This has got to be doable. She remembers her mother's words in the book. Baking should be done *with* those you love.

'I think you've got yourself a deal, kids,' she says. 'I promise we'll have a very good go at getting it right. You'll have to help me as much as you can though, okay?' Will and Desi nod again in unison and start to run back towards the cottage.

The twins start to look a little less sure as Magda unlocks the front door when they get home and ushers them into the kitchen. Nevertheless, they put their slippers on and wash their hands dutifully when instructed. It might be the first time they've willingly followed orders since Jared and Annika left.

'Go and get changed into your old clothes, this might be messy,' she says next, and sure enough, the twins disappear upstairs and are soon back, dressed in jeans and hoodies.

Magda herself is already struggling in the kitchen. She's staring up at the cookbooks when they re-enter the kitchen, frozen with trepidation at the idea of choosing what to make that she won't completely fail at. 'Maybe we should do some painting instead?' Will asks, noticing her distress. 'We can cook tomorrow night.' Desi is already on her way to the crafting cupboard when Magda puts a hand on her arm.

'No, we can't give up so soon,' Magda says firmly, reaching for her phone. 'We just need a nice easy recipe.'

'Hmmm. P'raps the other book was too hard for you,' Will says kindly.

'Possibly . . .' Magda grins at him. 'What do you suggest then?'

This time, it's her granddaughter who responds, albeit without speaking. Desi claps her hands and then points to the shelf. Magda follows the direction of her granddaughter's finger and sees that even though she was sure she'd put it back neatly, the slim volume of her mum's recipes is once again out of line with the others, as if just waiting to be pulled from the shelf. She must have been in more of a rush earlier than she'd thought. Magda reaches for it and feels a gentle warmth flowing through her left hand and down her arm. She glances down at the nearest radiator that sits underneath the window, stretching her other hand out to touch it. The heating doesn't usually come on until later because the heat from the Aga is enough to keep the kitchen cosy, and she chastises herself for accidentally leaving it on, when bills are already tight. But sure enough, the radiator is still cold. Odd.

'Come on, Granny, let's look at GG's book!' Will interrupts her thought process and she is forced to push it from her mind. 'We like that one! She'll know what we should do next.' Desi claps her hands and the two of them sit down on the sofa, leaving a space for Magda between them.

She settles herself in the gap and lets the covers fall open. They give off a slight rustle as they move apart. This time, an evocative scent of freshly ground nutmeg flows from the pages, and Magda is instantly transported back to Hope's epic rice puddings.

'Can you smell anything?' she asks the children.

They shake their heads dismissively and lean in for a better look. The book has opened at a recipe within the Extra Easy Ideas section. 'Chocolate Weetabix or Rice Krispie Cakes,' Magda reads aloud. 'You can make them with cornflakes too, but I seem to remember someone crushed all of those.' She turns to look at Will.

To his credit, he at least blushes, while Desi giggles. She turns to grin at her grandmother as if the two of them are sharing a joke and Magda's heart swells. At least one person is having a better time tonight.

'But we want to make Christmas food. How can we make them all Christmassy?' Will asks.

Magda wracks her brains and then remembers that her mum kept a stock of different paper cases. They're in a rainbow of colours, some shiny and glittery, and if she remembers rightly, there were even some gold ones decorated with tiny Santa Clauses and reindeer.

'We'll sit them in special cases to make them feel festive,' she says now with false authority, 'and we can put some sprinkles on top. Right, let's read the instructions. I know we've got the ingredients because there are only two. Cooking chocolate and Weetabix. Simple.'

Will stands up and beckons to Desi. 'We don't need instructions, we know about this already. We did Rice Krispie cakes with GG.' Then he looks witheringly at Magda as she also stands, and reaches for a trusty saucepan hanging from above the Aga. 'That's not the right one,' he says, almost bored, and clearly much more aware of his way around the kitchen.

'Really?' Magda frowns. 'We probably don't need a pan anyway. Can't we just use the microwave?' She turns back to the recipe book. *'Take a double saucepan and bring some water in the bottom half to a gentle boil,'* she reads aloud. Her mother's handwriting is achingly familiar. *'Break the chocolate into chunks and place in the top half. Let it melt slowly, stirring occasionally until smooth.'* Then she sighs, defeated. *'Don't be tempted to melt chocolate in the microwave because it's very easy to burn it that way.'*

Will laughs. 'It's like she knew you were going to try and cheat.'

'Hmmm. What's a double saucepan anyway? Have we got one? You did this with GG, didn't you?'

There's a short silence as Will and Desi ponder this question. Finally, Will goes over to the dresser and lies on his stomach, rummaging right at the back until he pulls out a pair of battered aluminium saucepans that fit together, one on top of the other. 'There you go. There's two of 'em. Double trouble, like me and Desi. That's what GG used to call us.'

Desi gets up and potters over to the dresser where Hope kept her baking ingredients and digs around until she finds what she's looking for. She holds out a large bar of cooking chocolate.

Magda is torn between delight that Desi is joining in, and chagrin that her grandchildren know Hope's kitchen better than she does herself. She reaches up to the highest cupboard where she remembers seeing the cake cases. Sure enough, there they are, all wrapped in brown paper bags and neatly labelled.

'Now what?' Will says.

Magda's stomach is in knots. For goodness' sake, it's the simplest recipe in the book, there's no possible way she can ruin this one. As she approaches the table with the air of a bullfighter edging into the ring, the sound of the doorbell makes her jump.

'Who can that be at nearly teatime?' she asks pointlessly. The twins shrug, and Magda goes along the hall to investigate. The looming shape behind the stained-glass panels looks ominous, and Magda wonders if she should be opening the door when it's already getting dark and she's in sole charge of the twins, so she puts the chain on. The door creaks open a crack and she peers into the gloom.

Den's voice emerges from the shadows. 'Hello, Mags,' he says uncertainly. 'I . . . erm . . . just wondered if you were all okay? After our chat today and . . . Well, the twins were still unsettled today and I thought . . .' His voice tails off when Magda doesn't answer. Blondie is sitting at his feet, her tongue lolling out of her mouth as if she's smiling.

'Can I come in?' Den says eventually, shivering in a sudden gust of wind which makes his coat flap. 'Or is it bad timing? I was just passing on my way back from walking the dog and I saw the kitchen light was on.'

'Yes, of course you can. You're *both* very welcome. I was just surprised to see you. We're baking . . . sort of . . .'

'That sounds fun.' Den lowers his voice as they get nearer to the open kitchen door. 'I actually came this way on purpose, if I'm honest. It was a bit of a soul-searching chat we had this morning, wasn't it?'

Magda is so touched she can't think of anything to say. Will and Desi look totally amazed to see their head teacher on their own turf which renders them speechless too, but Blondie breaks the ice by bouncing up at them ecstatically and they're soon kept busy finding her an old blanket and settling her near the Aga.

'What are you baking, kids?' he asks. 'My boys always liked to cook. We always used to make a chocolate yule log at Christmas time.'

'It's Weetabix cakes,' says Will shyly. 'Granny can't burn those.'

Den grins. 'Can I help to bash the Weetabix? That's my favourite bit. I need to take my jacket off though. Didn't have time to change.'

'You'd better borrow something to protect your school clothes,' Magda says. 'Chocolate and white shirts don't go well together.'

He grins, and takes the pinafore she's holding out. It's one of Jared's, a navy and white striped butcher's apron. Rolling his sleeves up further, he ties the strings and goes over to the sink to wash his hands.

'Right, bring on the challenge,' he says. 'I always wanted to be on *Bake Off*.'

Magda concentrates on making sure the chocolate melts properly while Den, Desi and Will arm themselves with wooden spoons and a big mixing bowl. They're soon mashing the cereal bars to smithereens, ready for Magda to pour the molten river of chocolate over it.

'We can put more Weetabix in, Mr Archer,' Will says. 'Then there'll be more cakes.'

'Nope, doesn't work like that. If you put too much of the dry stuff in, you can't make it stick together when the chocolate goes hard again. Trust me, I've tried,' says Den.

'Mum's written that in the book! There are lots of tips.' Magda's flipping through the Extra Easy recipes. 'Thank goodness,' she adds quietly to herself.

Soon there's a tray on the table covered in rows of rough clusters of crunchy chocolate in brightly coloured paper cases.

Magda gives Will and Desi some sprinkles each to add a festive touch. 'Can we eat them now, Mr Archer?' Will asks hopefully, scattering brightly coloured sugary sparkles around.

'No, they've got to set first. Anyway, I need to get Blondie home now. She needs her supper. Look at the poor girl.'

They all look round at the dog, still on the rug but sitting up hopefully, nose twitching. She sniffs the air and dribbles slightly.

'Can she lick the bowl out? GG used to let me and Desi do that if we were good. We weren't always,' Will says, with disarming honesty.

'No, dogs aren't allowed chocolate. It makes them very poorly. I'll take her back and give her what she likes,' Den explains, taking his pinny off and heading towards the kitchen door. 'See you tomorrow, folks.'

'We could bring you a cake in the morning, if you like, Mr Archer?' Will's voice is hopeful, more excited than Magda's heard it in a while.

'That'd be great. I'll have it with my coffee. Sleep tight, all of you.'

The atmosphere in the kitchen suddenly seems very flat without the bouncy dog and her owner, who is just as full of vitality. Magda looks down at the twins, who are now sitting cross-legged on the floor, shoulders slumped.

'Let's have some blackcurrant squash,' she says brightly, and the twins glance up at her and blink as if they've forgotten she's there. 'I need to organize something quick to eat before it's bedtime. Why don't you two pop up and get your pyjamas on and we'll have tea in front of the fire?'

'Cheese on toast? With the telly on?' Will squeaks.

'Go on then, just this once.'

Desi smiles at Magda, sadness forgotten. Thank goodness

children are fairly easy to distract. As soon as they're on their way upstairs, Magda slips out of the back door. In the garden, the cool air is calming and she feels her equilibrium returning. Perhaps she's been starved of single male friends these last few years. The Weetabix cakes are a success and it was good to have Den around tonight, he's great company. But she mustn't get used to it. This evening was lovely, but she can't see someone who works with children all day long wanting to spend his time off doing something similar.

I was right to stay single all these years. I don't need a man to make me happy, Magda tells herself firmly. *This Christmas is going to be all about fun. I can do that on my own. I'll show Jared that I can get this mothering lark right this time. We're going to have Fun with a capital F. Just watch us!*

9

Thursday, 14 December

Eleven Days Until Christmas

The next morning, Will and Desi are a little more amenable than usual, even when Magda realizes she's overslept and they are going to have to rush, although Desi's idea of seeing how many raisins she can push up her nose almost results in a trip to A&E. Luckily, Magda catches sight of the second one disappearing and is able to put a brake on this particular experiment. Desi is still brushing toast crumbs off her school jumper as Magda tries to zip up her coat and Will spends the mad dash to school telling Magda how it's about time they got themselves a puppy.

'I liked it when Mr Archer came round, didn't you, Granny? Will he come again and bring his dog?' Will says, galloping along beside her as Magda takes the hill at a trot.

'Hey,' she says, an idea occurring to her as they reach the marketplace and level ground. 'How about we ask Mr Archer if we can collect Blondie after school and take her for a walk? We could go to the park or along the river a little way?'

Desi immediately starts to spin as she walks and Will hops

from foot to foot in his excitement. 'Can we really?' he asks, hurrying along after his sister.

Magda bites her lip. Uh oh, rookie error. She should have remembered not to suggest something that might not be possible before she'd checked with Den. In the twins' minds they are already Blondie's chief dog walkers.

They're outside the school gates now, and Magda decants them into the playground and goes to search for Den, who luckily is delighted at her idea.

'Can you pick Blondie up from my neighbour on the way to fetch the twins later? That'd be brilliant. And then I'll come and get her when I finish here. Are you cooking again with them tonight?' he asks. Magda wonders if he's angling for an invitation to join them, but then chastises herself. Being surrounded by children all day is probably enough to make any teacher want to lie in a darkened room with a large glass of wine when they finally get home.

'I don't know. I feel as if it's a great way to keep them amused, but I'm just not the sort of person that baking comes naturally to. My mum tried. Oh boy, did she try, but it's not my thing at all.'

'You must have cooked with Jared when he was little though? The usual fairy cakes and biscuits?'

Magda shrugs, not keen to share her experiences of parenting with a man who must find it all so easy.

'Anyway, I'll collect Blondie and get out of your hair quickly tonight, so you can get on with the job. And then it's choir practice later, but I guess you won't be able to come, now you're in charge of Will and Desi?' continues Den.

Disappointment washes over Magda. Choir practice and the

hour she and her friends spend in the pub afterwards is usually a highlight of her week.

'Ah. I hadn't even thought of that,' she says. 'No, I'll have to give it a miss. What a shame. I could do with being there because of the carol service. Never mind, the kids come first. And I haven't got anyone I could ask to babysit. We've always looked after the twins between us . . .' Magda's voice trails off as she remembers the other thing she'd been psyching herself up to do.

'Why are you pulling that face?' Den asks, and Magda realizes that she's been frowning.

'Oh, I was . . . erm . . . planning to go and find Fliss to see how she is,' Magda says. She doesn't want Den to think she resents her grandchildren and it's true, she really should go and sort things out with her friend. The friction between them was awful when they met in the market. She says goodbye and heads towards the main street, making a snap decision to call in at the deli for something to take as a peace offering, to make right whatever it is that's gone so badly wrong between them. The olives with oily cloves of garlic tucked inside are Fliss's favourite and she can get some Camembert and a loaf of the crusty artisan bread. Maybe they could even have lunch together. Preoccupied with this plan as she arrives at the shop, Magda flings the door open and barrels slap bang into Fliss herself, who is on her way out at speed.

'Oof! Watch where you're going,' Fliss snaps, teetering on her spiky-heeled ankle boots before crashing to the floor. She lies still for a moment in a pool of smashed eggs. 'You total idiot, Magda. Look what you've done. I've banged my elbow. Ouch!'

Immediately, three people rush over and bend down to try

and help Fliss up, and the shop owner, Belinda, goes to fetch a cloth for the mess. Magda can see that her friend is close to tears, which never happens. Fliss has always maintained that crying gets you nowhere.

Magda herself is in total shock at the coldness of Fliss's words, and the anger with which they were delivered. 'I'm *so* sorry,' she snaps. 'I was actually coming in here because I planned to get you something nice. I thought maybe . . .'

'Well, whatever you thought, you were wrong. Just back off and leave me alone, can't you?' Fliss is finding her balance now as her rescuers lift her to her feet. 'Knew I should have ditched these boots before now. Wellies for me from now on,' she mutters. 'Oh, sod it all.' Fliss is out of the door and away up the street before Magda can say another word.

'Well, you've certainly rattled her cage this morning,' says Belinda. 'What was all that about? Although to be fair, I'd be hopping mad too if you knocked me over in a pool of egg. I was only just asking her if you two had got the preparations for your usual bake sale under way and she slapped some money on the counter and rushed off,' she continued. 'So if you think about it, it wasn't really your fault you collided. Have you done something to upset her?'

The bake sale. Those three words send a chill right through Magda's body. Usually, Hope would have begun baking for the annual Periwinkle Bay Christmas Fair weeks ago, with Fliss as her willing assistant. There's never a shortage of people wanting stalls every year, but Hope's booking was a regular one, so she both expected and got a prime spot in the Town Hall, amongst the tables of crafts, plants and sundry other goods. Magda's role in the past had been to drum up contributions of baking ingredients from the local shopkeepers and to publicize the event. In fact, it had been her idea to have the bake sale in the first place. Their stall had always been one of the most popular at the late-December fundraiser.

'I . . . I can't . . .'

'Oh, I know what you're saying, pet. I should have known better than to mention it, with hindsight. Without your mum it can't possibly happen this year. It's a shame though – a lot of people rely on your stall for their Christmas treats. I'll miss the mince pies the most. The ones we sell in here are lovely, but your mum's were melt-in-the-mouth.'

For a brief moment, Magda wonders if she was wrong to completely discount doing the stall this year without even talking to Fliss about it. She pushes the idea away. She's far too busy for anything but keeping the twins entertained at the moment, and even if they both wanted to make it happen now, she's left it way too late to plan anything. Thinking back to previous years, it was usually Fliss who got the ball rolling, pulling Magda into it with her contagious energy. With them not having spoken recently, Magda had barely even noticed she hadn't heard anything about it from her friend. Funny that Fliss hasn't been in touch about it already, now Magda comes to think of it. Maybe she's realized that, without Hope's help and guidance, the whole thing would just be too sad. That must be it.

More customers have piled into the little shop while Magda's been thinking everything through, so she gets in line to be served while Belinda goes behind the counter to clear the backlog. When she reaches the front of the queue, Magda remembers that the only reason she was in here was to buy something for Fliss, and that plan's gone out of the window. Her shoulders slump, but she feels as if she needs some sort of consolation now, so decides to press on anyway. She chooses some robust-looking Stilton, an enormous slice of pizza and adds a tub of salad to make her feel as if she's being healthy.

'Will I see you tonight at choir practice?' says Belinda, as Magda pays. 'Oh, but I suppose you're tied to the house now, aren't you, with the twins? Do you need a sitter?'

A glimmer of light pierces the gloom that's settled over Magda. 'Why? Do you know someone I could ask?'

'Well, there's always our Fiona. She's saving up for her gap year. She knows Desi and Will from helping out at Sunday School, doesn't she? She loves kids.'

'Oh wow, that'd be brilliant. Would she come at such short notice, do you think? Will and Desi absolutely love her.'

'I'll text her when I get my break and let you know, okay? But I can't see why it would be a problem.'

With a much lighter heart, Magda picks up her provisions, leaves the shop and walks back up the hill. There's a dog walk to look forward to, and now perhaps even a chance to sing all her favourite carols later. The only immediate cloud on the horizon is Fliss. Something will have to be done about that situation, and soon.

Christmas Day, Twenty-nine Years Ago

Jared sits at the breakfast bar swinging his legs and kicking the high stool every now and again. Magda glances at him, wondering how he can look so bright and breezy when he's been awake and demanding attention since way before five a.m. She's desperately trying to make sense of the instructions on all the various packets and cartons that contain their ready-made Christmas dinner.

'Stop making that noise, love,' she says, trying to keep her voice cheery. 'We'll never have this ready if you don't let me concentrate.'

'Gran never gets her dinner in boxes,' Jared says, pulling a face and carrying on kicking. 'Why couldn't we go to her house again?'

Magda sighs. 'You know why, I explained. I was working until late last night. That was why you had a babysitter. There wasn't time to take the train to Periwinkle Bay this year, and I've got a morning shift again tomorrow.'

'Why couldn't you tell them you were busy?' Jared's dark eyes are full of tears and he blinks them away angrily. At seven years old, he already thinks big boys shouldn't cry. Magda wishes he'd let her hug him more often, but her son is prickly about demonstrations of affection, although she's noticed that her mother and Fliss always get a cuddle when they see him. She grits her teeth and slams a few trays of food into the oven.

'You're always cross,' says Jared. 'Can't we do some fun stuff today? I want to make those little pancakes that Gran does. She let me help her last year and we did them in the frying pan in all sorts of Christmas shapes with those metal things.'

Magda turns to look at her son. He stares back at her. She leans back on the worktop and folds her arms. There's so little room in the poky flat that she can see right the way through the living room to the bedroom where Jared sleeps. It's very tidy. He always puts his toys away, and he's already taken his newly opened presents in there and found places for them. A sudden longing for her old home makes her swallow a lump in her throat. Jared's right, she could have been more forceful and booked the time off to give them a chance to get to Mistletoe Cottage for a few days. Why didn't she? The painful realization that she prefers being frantically busy delivering babies at the hospital to entertaining her own child makes her wince.

'We haven't got any of the metal pastry cutters that Gran uses,' Magda says, dodging the rest of Jared's enquiry. 'You could open your new Lego?'

'Will you play with me if I do?' Jared says hopefully. 'And then afterwards we could cook something. It doesn't have to be pancakes.'

'Actually, there isn't any flour either.' Magda stifles a feeling of relief that she has a good excuse for not cooking. 'I know, let's make another decoration for your tree.'

They both turn to admire the little silver Christmas tree that Magda bought last week to make up for not giving Jared the chance to have all the traditional Periwinkle Bay fun. Last year he'd especially loved the lantern parade, visiting Father Christmas in the Town Hall and the walk down to the beach after their enormous lunch. He'd even sat quietly through the carol service, eyes wide with wonder at the magnificence of the Methodist church in its full festive glory.

'Okay, we could do that, I s'pose,' Jared says. 'Who's looking after me tomorrow? I hope it isn't Mrs Fishy-Smells again.'

'No, it isn't, and please don't call her that, She's a very kind lady. She just really likes to eat kippers for breakfast.' Magda lives in fear that their lovely child-minding neighbour, Janet, will for some reason decide not to help her out any more, especially in emergencies. Childcare is a constant juggling act when you work shifts without a partner to help.

'Who is it then? Maybe they'll do some baking with me if you get some flour from the corner shop.' Jared's baking line of enquiry is clearly not going to end any time soon.

Squashing the never-ending feelings of guilt, Magda smiles. 'I think you're going to be lucky with that one, love,' she says. 'Aunty Fliss is setting off really early in the morning so she can be here for when I go to work.'

At this, Jared's face lights up with joy. 'Hooray! I love Aunty Fliss. She's definitely going to want to bake with me! Thanks, Mum.'

Relief that Jared is happy with her arrangements mixes with sadness that she doesn't seem to be enough for him on her own.

'We'll go home to Mistletoe Cottage for Easter instead, I promise,' she says. 'And I bet Gran has metal cutters in the shape of Easter eggs and bunnies too.'

Smiling, Jared goes to fetch his junk box, full of scraps of card, empty egg boxes, glitter, coloured paper and glue. Magda grins back. At least junk modelling is something she can do right.

10

The after-school walk with Blondie goes off without a hitch, although the twins are both horrified at the thought of what goes on with the poo bags.

'That's yucky,' says Will, as Magda stoops to clear up after the dog, and Desi wafts a hand in front of her face.

By the time Den arrives to collect his dog, Blondie is asleep on her blanket and the twins are practising their spellings while Magda sits in Hope's chair and alternately tests them and flicks through the recipe book. This strange way of being in contact with her mum is already becoming addictive. The feeling of luxurious warmth is there again and today she thinks she can smell orange rind as she flicks through the pages and reads Hope's instructions and side notes. The evocative scent is relaxing but also energizing, making her want to spring into action and bake. It's certainly not a feeling she's experienced before. Magda still can't tell exactly where the smell is coming from; there are no obvious splashes of ingredients on the pages she's read so far. It's unnerving, but comforting at the same time.

'Have you found something else to try? I asked Will and Desi earlier if they were baking tonight and they didn't seem too sure,' Den says, as he strolls into the kitchen, already looking at home.

'I was only saying Desi doesn't want us to burn anything

again, that's all. She gets worried,' says Will, looking up from his spelling book. 'Do you know how to spell pie, Mr Archer? I keep forgetting it has an e on the end.'

'Funny you should say that,' Magda says. 'I thought we'd have a go at a cheese and potato pie first. It's in the comfort food bit. I remember Mum making it on cold, wet days to cheer me up if I'd had a bad day at school. I don't think I can possibly ruin something this simple,' she adds, with more confidence than she feels. 'It's basically a big ovenproof dish of very buttery potato that's been cooked with a chopped onion, mashed quite roughly, with lots of grated cheese in it and some crispy bacon pieces. Then you put more cheese on top and grill it till it's all nice and brown.'

'That's not proper baking,' says Will. Desi shakes her head and pouts.

'Well then, we'll make Scotch pancakes while it's cooking, if you give me a hand.' She's thinking back to how much Jared used to love his own grandmother's pancakes. Magda registers that Den looks interested and wonders if she should ask him to stay and help, but decides it's probably a cop-out. If she's going to do this cooking thing properly, she needs to stand on her own two feet, something her mother always told her to do.

Den calls Blondie and sets off for home as the others start to work, clearing away the school books and settling around the huge kitchen table as if they've been doing this sort of thing together for years. Desi and Will beat the pancake batter while Magda peels potatoes and an onion and gets them boiling.

While they're cooking, Magda explains that Fiona is going to look after them while she heads off to choir practice.

Will and Desi put their heads together for a moment to

confer, before Will says, 'We've decided that's okay. So long as she reads extra stories. Fiona does all the voices.'

Relieved, Magda gets on with her pie, reading the instructions carefully and making herself take her time instead of rushing the vital parts or substituting random ingredients instead of hunting for the right ones. This recipe really is easy as well as comforting, and as she grates the cheese, she glances down at Hope's book.

Watch out for your fingers on the grater, she reads. *Nobody wants extra protein in their dinner.*

Pulling a face, Magda mashes the now-cooked potatoes and onion, adding way more butter than she thinks is necessary, because, of course, Hope's side note says she should.

Never stint on the butter. The comfort of this dish depends on it. Add some sea salt at this point. And make sure you grill the bacon until it's properly crispy. Stand next to it while it cooks. Don't go off and watch TV/read a book/ phone a friend. Blackened bacon is almost worse than grated finger-ends.

Magda smiles to herself, taking the liberty of firing off a quick apologetic message to Fliss while the bacon cooks, but there's still no response. By this point, she didn't really expect one.

The Scotch pancakes are mostly successful, although the first few are very dark brown. Magda's managed to find the battered metal pastry cutters and they've chosen a Christmas tree, a holly leaf and a solidly built angel to trim them to shape when they're cooked. The scent of vanilla is everywhere and Magda can't tell any more whether it's coming from the pancakes or Hope's recipe book. As Magda inexpertly flips them over, Will and Desi give her marks out of ten for each one and applaud madly. They're all hysterical with laughter by the time Fiona arrives, and despite the fact that the twins are clearly in desperate need of some calm time, for the very first time since Jared was born, Magda feels as if she's on the way at last to learning what it is to be a proper mum and granny. It's a start.

'I remember your mum making Scotch pancakes with us at Sunday School a couple of times,' says Fiona, when the twins go upstairs to get ready for their bath. 'She sometimes called them *drop scones.*'

'That would have been more accurate tonight,' says Magda. 'I dropped at least three of them. The birds are going to have a good breakfast tomorrow, especially with all the trimmings we've ditched.'

'I loved your mum.' Fiona's looking sad now. 'We all miss her at Sunday School, especially her puddings. At least you must be glad you can bake lovely things just like she did though.'

Magda stifles a giggle and leads the way upstairs. *If only you knew,* she thinks.

11

The way to the chapel is always lined with the best displays of Christmas lights, winter foliage and decorations in town, Magda thinks, as she makes her way between the lighted windows, admiring the gaudy ones just as much as the elegantly tasteful. The neighbours down the hill and along the main street vie with each other for the finest results, but as their ideas of excellence vary so much, there can never be a clear winner in Magda's eyes. All of them are wonderful, and all of them make her slightly bruised spirits soar.

This is a very familiar route. Magda's parents were both staunch Methodists, largely due to their love of belting out the old hymns, or so Hope told her. Archie Conway died when Magda was a baby so she has no memories of her father, but the old photograph albums show an upright, kindly-looking man with very bushy eyebrows that remind Magda of two caterpillars squaring up to each other for a fight.

Christmas is still Magda's favourite time of year in the chapel. The Methodist building isn't anywhere near as attractive as the town's ancient church. It has no arched stone doorway, bell tower or picturesque graveyard, so it's never been popular for weddings. But despite its lack of potential for romantic photo shoots, the chapel comes into its own at Christmas. The more active and enthusiastic church members always put up a large stable at the front, complete with manger and wooden animals, and there's a tall Christmas tree with random, and often home-made, decorations and brightly coloured lights.

As she approaches the building for choir practice, Magda views the place with her usual mixture of affection and criticism. Although even its most ardent supporters couldn't call it pretty, with the front door open and the light streaming down the foot-path, it feels welcoming and cheery. There's a new addition to the stable, and Magda stifles a giggle as she recognizes the large stuffed horse that usually belongs at the school in the reception class farmyard. It's now wearing a pair of large furry ears.

'Isn't that Shergar?' she whispers to Den when she meets him in the aisle as he heads for his usual seat at the organ. 'Has he been promoted?'

'Of course it's not,' he replies. 'Don't you know a donkey when you see one?'

He grins at her and goes to take his place, which is on a raised plinth behind the pulpit, right at the front of the church. Soon, the room is filled with the resounding music of Christmas. Den warms the singers up with his own arrangement of 'The Holly and the Ivy', and Magda's mind automatically flips back to her mother's recipe sections and the way they perfectly fit this tune. She feels the now-familiar fizz in her stomach as she thinks of the book, waiting at home for her to be brave enough to make further inroads into its depths, but her mood is damp-ened when she suddenly realizes that Fliss, once again, hasn't turned up for practice.

'Have either of you seen Fliss lately?' she murmurs to the two people next to her. They shake their heads and shrug. Magda reaches for her phone to send her best friend another message and then switches it to silent as the conversations around her stop. It's time to sing.

The choir practice goes by in a flash. They move from a spirited rendition of 'Hark the Herald Angels' to a beautiful, melancholy version of 'In the Bleak Midwinter' with barely a pause, and before long they've covered all the traditional carols they'll be singing on Christmas Eve. Belinda from the deli has recently taken over as conductor, and she and Den make a great team, working together with only the odd glance at each other to move things along or tweak the choir's performance.

As the last strains of the final song, 'Silent Night', fade away, Magda notices she isn't the only one blinking away tears. Christmas brings a whole host of memories along with the festive spirit, she reflects, shrugging her arms back into her coat as the pub regulars get ready to scuttle through the brightly lit street to the comfort of the blazing log fires at the Pig and Whistle in the marketplace.

'Are you coming to the pub, Den?' she hears Belinda call. 'They've got their special eggnog on tonight, and pork scratchings. I know you've got to rush back, Magda. Although I expect you could tempt our Fiona with a few quid more if you fancy a drink?'

'I really want to get home for Blondie,' says Den. 'She's been on her own too much lately.'

'And I want to make sure Fiona's okay,' adds Magda.

'Why don't you fetch the dog and both join us in a little while?' says Belinda. 'Although . . . yeah . . . you're probably right to check on the kids, Mags. They're bound to be a bit unsettled at the moment.'

'No, it's okay. I'm ready for home if Magda is,' Den says, raising his eyebrows at her. She nods gratefully. The time after practice in the pub is always fun, but dealing with the twins is leaving her ready for her own bed as soon as they're safely tucked up in theirs most nights.

'That was tricky,' Den says. 'Belinda's great but she does like to organize everyone, and last time I took Blondie to the Pig and Whistle she was so excited she knocked over someone's pint and tried to steal someone else's pie. Come on, I'll walk you home.'

'There's no need, honestly,' Magda responds, admittedly without much conviction.

Den seems hellbent on getting away from the church as fast as possible, and they find themselves naturally walking towards Mistletoe Cottage together.

They wind their way up the street, the cobbles now dangerously slippery, and Den offers Magda his arm as she slithers around.

'There's frost in the air,' says Den. 'It's going to be a beautiful starry night.'

Magda looks up at the clearing sky, wispy clouds making way for the spectacle later. She's glad Den took no notice of her saying she didn't need an escort. This feels strangely like some kind of luxury. She isn't used to being looked after.

They reach the porch of Mistletoe Cottage, and Magda reluctantly lets go of Den's arm, immediately missing his warmth. Den makes admiring noises as he looks at the doorway.

'It looks so festive with all those white lights around the door frame and the coloured lantern,' he says. 'I'm glad you haven't had the ivy cut back.'

Magda looks up at her home. Its ivy-clad frontage has always struck her as welcoming too. The wisteria with its garland of lights shares its space with the ivy, and at the back of the house on the sunniest wall there's more of both, with the second ancient wisteria that drips gorgeous lavender flowers in the summer, and on the side wall, a rampant creeper turns deepest russet red in autumn. The house is almost covered with foliage, which looks wonderful but probably isn't so good for the elderly brickwork. Magda sighs as she remembers all the small repairs that are her responsibility now Hope isn't there to organize the work.

'You've done even more than your mother used to do at this time of year, is that right?' says Den.

Magda's heart swells with pride. It's not been easy getting into the Christmas spirit this year and the wreath wasn't easy to construct, but it looks pretty good considering it's her first try at anything so ambitious. Her mother always favoured a market-bought one, but she wanted to make use of some of the mistletoe that gives the house its name. There have always been oak trees in the garden, and mistletoe grows there in abundance.

'I didn't know you liked doing all this stuff,' says Den. 'You could have come into school and done some flower sessions with the Year Sixes. You've never mentioned it.'

Magda laughs. 'That's because I've never dared to have a go before,' she says. 'Mum always insisted on everything being done the same way every year and Annika's a complete control freak with the big tree. So I always used to just leave them to it.'

'Isn't the wreath a problem though?'

'In what way?'

'Well, all that mistletoe just hanging there. It's asking for trouble. Don't you find everyone who comes to the door wants to kiss you? Must be a bit trying with the postman and the milkman. And if you get a lot of Amazon deliveries . . .'

Magda looks up at him, suddenly nervous, but he just smiles at her, eyes wide with innocence.

'Anyway, I'd better be off. Blondie will be by the door with her legs crossed. See you in the morning.'

Magda has a sudden urge to have company for just a little while longer. She almost asks Den if he wants to come in for a portion of cheese and potato pie, but can't find the courage. Instead, she stands on the porch and waves him off.

'See you in the morning,' she responds, a hint of sadness creeping into her voice.

12

Friday, 15 December

Ten Days Until Christmas

Once the children are safely at school on Friday morning, Magda decides to try a different approach to contacting Fliss. It might be easier to talk to her when she's at work in the craft shop. Perhaps the situation will seem less fraught if Laurence, her ex-partner but current business partner, is there too. Magda has always felt sad that Laurence and Fliss didn't stay together. Their working relationship is cordial, but Fliss has moved back to Periwinkle Bay now, while Laurence still lives over the shop, which is in the next village over.

The roads are icy today and she's glad she hasn't bothered with running a car since she finished work, but it does mean she has to find a public transport alternative instead. The bus to the neighbouring village leaves the marketplace every half-hour and she catches one by the skin of her teeth, climbing up to the top deck to avoid having to chat to the gaggle of townspeople already in place, all on their way to the monthly farmers' market.

From the upper level, Magda has an excellent view of the surrounding countryside, right across the salt marshes to the sea. The sky is a misty grey. It definitely feels cold enough for snow today. She shivers as an icy blast from the ill-fitting window finds a crack between her scarf and her coat. It's not a good day for an outing.

When the bus drops everyone off at the centre of the next village, Magda pulls on her red woolly hat and heads for the shelter of the market hall. She considers having a good browse amongst the cheese and vegetables but knows that's just putting off the moment when she'll have to face her friend. She makes her way down the twisty streets with a feeling of dread growing in the pit of her stomach. The dark green awning outside the shop is classy, and the enormous arrangement of silver branches in the window is artistic, twined with tiny white lights. It's breathtakingly beautiful, but to Magda's experienced eye it looks suspiciously as though it's not her friend's handiwork. Fliss is more of a fan of sumptuous reds, golds and greens at Christmas.

'Hi, Laurence,' Magda says, as she enters the warmth of the shop. The evocative scent of pine greets her before the proprietor does, but she soon sees the tall man emerging from behind the counter. Laurence is almost as familiar to her as Fliss is.

'Magdalena. I wasn't expecting you,' Laurance replies, looking her up and down. She can't help noticing the slight chill in his welcome, and he doesn't reach forward for a hug as he normally might. Tall and elegant, he's dressed in a crisp striped shirt and a very smart three-piece suit in a discreet shade of grey. In a concession to the festive season, he's added a crimson brocade waistcoat. Laurence is the only person who calls her by her full name, and he's always said it in an affectionate way, but today she realizes it doesn't sound friendly at all.

'Is Fliss here?' she says, biting the bullet, and realizing Laurence might not be up for small talk today. 'I really need to see her.'

'Well that's unfortunate, because you've come to the wrong place,' Laurence says. 'Fliss hasn't been here for over a month. She's off sick,' he continues, registering Magda's shocked expression. 'But I'm in regular contact with her still and I gather that you two haven't been in touch lately.'

'Off sick? What's wrong with her? Is it something serious? Why didn't she tell me?' Magda is beginning to panic now.

The shop bell jangles as a customer comes in. Laurence turns away from Magda with what looks like relief. 'You'd better ask her those questions yourself, especially that last one. Anyway, have a good Christmas. I need to be getting on.'

Magda leaves the shop again, mere moments after having arrived, with a leaden feeling in the pit of her stomach. Fliss is ill and Laurence is angry. *What is going on?* Fliss has never been one for having time off work, unless it's for a very good reason. Magda knows there's really only one thing for it now.

Back on the bus, she stares unseeingly across the wintry landscape towards the distant sea. A cool breeze has sprung up and anyone out walking along the way is wrapped up tightly in scarves, hats and gloves. How could she have let the situation with Fliss get out of hand like this? They've never lost contact for so long before, even when they lived hundreds of miles away from each other.

By the time the bus pulls back into Periwinkle Bay at the stop nearest to the mews cottage where Fliss has lived alone since her break-up with Laurence, Magda's stomach is churning. In all the years the two of them have been friends, she can count the times she's dropped in unannounced on the fingers of one hand. Fliss hates surprises. She's a great hostess if she knows you're coming, incredibly hospitable and madly generous with her food and wine, but she does love to plan ahead for these occasions.

The doorbell rings its mournful peal as Magda stands on the step, already regretting her snap decision, but when there's no answer the first time she can't give up without a struggle. On the third ring she hears footsteps and the door opens a crack.

'You again? What the hell do you want?' says Fliss. 'Didn't you get the message when I ignored the bell?'

Magda's natural instinct is to say 'Sod you then,' and beat a hasty retreat, but she's got this far, so she grits her teeth and waits.

'Well?' Fliss almost shouts. 'Go on then. What's so urgent you need to disturb me when I'm sleeping?'

'Laurence told me you were off sick. I couldn't not see you. What's up, Fliss? Please can I come in? I guess you've been thinking I'm a lousy friend, and that's true, but at least give me the chance to say sorry.'

Everything hangs in the balance for the next moments, and then Fliss opens the door just wide enough for Magda to slide in. As she follows Fliss down the hall, the first thing she notices is the overpowering stuffiness. Her friend has never before been keen on turning the heating up unless there's a blizzard, but the atmosphere is as warm and steamy as a tropical night. Even more alarmingly, Fliss is wearing fleecy pyjamas, a thick dressing gown and slippers so furry that she has the appearance of a pint-sized yeti.

They reach the open-plan living area and Magda can see that there is a mountain of dirty crockery piled up in the sink.

Alarm bells are really ringing now. A messy kitchen is one of Fliss's pet hates.

Fliss gestures for Magda to sit on the sofa and goes over to the kitchen area. 'I suppose you'll be wanting a cup of tea?' she asks, in the tone of someone offering hemlock.

Magda nods and settles herself on the elegant if rather uncomfortable chaise longue while Fliss clears enough space to make their drinks. When she's handed a brimming mug with a teabag floating in it, it's the final straw. This is a woman who's always been a stickler for the proper rituals of teatime. She normally offers a wide choice of drinks, likes to select from a variety of teapots and cosies of different sizes, has trays with freshly laundered tray cloths to fit and only uses the very best china cups and saucers.

'Thanks,' Magda says, wondering what she's meant to do with the soggy teabag but deciding to ignore it as much as possible. 'So, what's going on? You've made your point. I've got the message that you're furious with me for being a rubbish friend loud and clear, and I'm more sorry than I can say, but now's not the time for sulking. Come on, love, spill the beans.'

The familiar endearment seems to be the catalyst that pushes Fliss over the edge. She bangs her own mug down on the coffee table and starts to howl, startling Magda so much that at first she can't move. But a mere second later, and Magda has snapped into gear. Fliss's anguished wails bring Magda to her knees in front of Fliss's chair and her arms are around her friend before the other woman has the chance to resist.

'It's all bad . . . so bad . . .' sobs Fliss, pulling away slightly. 'How could this happen to me? I'm healthy. I go to the gym and everything. I eat proper meals and I've never smoked. Well, only that time behind the bike sheds with . . . whatever his name was . . . Colin, wasn't it? So why me? What have I done to deserve this?'

'Deserve what?'

Magda doesn't realize she's holding her breath in the long pause until Fliss says, 'It's MS. I've got Multiple Sclerosis. There's no cure.'

In the silence that follows, Magda has plenty of time to wrack her brains for anything she might know about MS. It turns out to be very little.

'What . . . what are your symptoms?' she asks.

'I'd been getting clumsier and clumsier. Laurence thought I was just being careless to begin with, but he knows that's not my style. I've been putting off doing anything about it for weeks and it was him who persuaded me to go to the doctor's. They referred me for tests and asked me lots of questions. I've been exhausted a lot of the time, but I had just put it down to turning sixty and trying to expand the business even more. And then I realized my fingers have been tingling. So it all started to add up.'

Magda tightens her grip for a moment and then makes a decision and gets straight to her feet.

'Right, it's time you got yourself dressed and came home to Mistletoe Cottage with me for a little while. I'll load the dish-washer and tidy the kitchen here quickly, then I'll come up and pack a bag for you. The bed's all made up in our guest room. It's yours for as long as you need it, okay?'

'Can't you just go away and leave me alone? I . . . I don't want to be with you just now.' Fliss's words are defiant, but Magda can tell from her tone that she's faltering.

'Yes, that's pretty clear, but this place is a mess and you're not coping. Being at Mistletoe Cottage for a little while might be the best of a bad job at the moment. Shall we try it for a day or two? You don't have to like me. Obviously I'd rather you did, but I can take it if you're determined to be like this.'

The two women look at each other for a long moment, then Fliss gets to her feet with a slight wobble. She steadies herself.

'I'm really grumpy just now,' she warns.

'So what's new?' Magda says, risking a smile.

Fliss ignores her comment, but Magda thinks she sees a dimple appear in her cheek. 'I do need some help, I know that, but if I come home with you, it doesn't mean everything's okay between us again. I don't want to seem ungrateful but I'm . . . I'm just so angry with you, Magda.'

Being called Magda instead of the usual Mags is a bad moment, but Magda squares her shoulders and tells herself this is the only way of getting to the bottom of what's wrong. The shock of Fliss's news has left her reeling.

'I know that,' she acknowledges. 'There's clearly a lot for us to talk about. But come on, we can do that later.' She sees the look on Fliss's face and adds, 'If you want to, that is. If not, at least you can let me look after you for a few days.'

13

Half an hour later, they're walking into the comforting warmth of what Magda still thinks of as Hope's kitchen.

'I still half expect to see your mum in here, cooking up a storm,' says Fliss, sinking into the old sofa with a sigh. 'She was the inspiration for our bake sale when you first came home to Mistletoe Cottage, did you know that?'

Magda cringes slightly at the reference. The sale has been on her mind ever since Belinda mentioned it. She puts the kettle on and joins her friend. 'No, I didn't. I always thought it was my idea?'

'That's what you were meant to think. She was a clever woman, was Hope Conway. And she was like a mum to me. She tried so hard to compensate for what I was missing at home. My mum's illness meant she wasn't up to much in the way of mothering for her last few years, and after my dad left us, I think she pretty much gave up on me. But you know all that.'

'Yes, I . . . I'll never forget how sad it was for you. I think Mum really wanted you to move in with us at that point. You were only just eighteen when she finally died, weren't you? But then you decided to keep the house and be independent.'

Fliss smiles. 'I did, but Hope still kept a close eye on me, just in case I went off the rails.'

Magda tries not to mind being reminded of the closeness between Fliss and Hope. Over the years, the thought of it has

110

been a thorn in her side. Why couldn't she have that relationship with her mother? But of course, the answer's always been clear. Fliss was still in Periwinkle Bay when Magda herself left and, even more importantly, she shared Hope's joy in everything baking related.

When they both have their hands round mugs of tea, Magda turns to Fliss, alarmed by the pallor of her cheeks and the dark shadows under her eyes. 'Do you want to talk about your diagnosis now, or are you too tired?'

Fliss sighs. 'Now is fine, I guess. Although you know we can't just flip back into how it was with us?'

'Fliss, I've said I'm sorry but I really don't get what I've done to make you feel so furious.'

'No, I don't suppose you do.'

'Go on then . . . tell me, for goodness' sake.' Magda can hear the sharpness increasing in her voice. The thought of Fliss feeling bitter and full of fury is making her shrivel up inside. Fliss puts her mug down, rubs her eyes and leans back in the chair.

'Okay, here goes. I feel as if all these years you haven't really seen me as a person. You were desperate to get away from here and start your training in Leicester. I think you'd have gone anywhere to escape at that point, to be honest. And we kept in touch, of course, but it was always me who made the effort to travel to you.'

'I thought you liked our mad weekends? You always said it was a brilliant change to go out in the city and see a bit of life.'

'I did. I loved it. But you were so busy with your own plans that you hardly ever asked about mine. Then, of course, there was *the lovely doctor*. He always had first dibs on your time.'

111

Fliss has always been one to speak her mind but in all the years they've known each other, Magda has never before heard her friend speak with such withering sarcasm. 'It wasn't like that, Fliss . . .' she begins.

'Oh, but it was. And then Jared came along and everything got more complicated. If you're honest, you knew that Giovanni was no good for you, didn't you? You must have done. How many times did we discuss it? I tried so hard to understand how you felt about him and to steer you away from him tactfully. But you still went ahead and had his baby.'

'I loved him, Fliss. I didn't mean to get pregnant, you know that, and . . . I couldn't have . . .'

'Oh, I know you couldn't have done anything else, but it made your life so much more difficult being a parent. He didn't ever want you to live with him, did he, even afterwards? Then he just upped and left the country to go home and marry someone else without so much as a goodbye, even though Jared was still tiny. And did you ever hear from him afterwards?'

Magda doesn't reply because Fliss assumes she knows the answer to this one, but her friend hasn't finished yet.

'You must have twigged how much your mum wanted you to come home then, but you still waited until he was fifteen and as stroppy as hell.' Fliss's voice is rising now, as though she's regaining some of her old self. Magda just wishes this wasn't the moment for her to feel more spirited.

Magda thinks back to all those difficult years before she came back to Periwinkle Bay. Some of the memories are precious. Jared's first tooth, his first faltering steps. A lot are painful. It was often a tough kind of life bringing him up as a solo parent and still trying to make her way up the career ladder with the shift work involved, but she was determined to go it alone and prove that she didn't need a man, and certainly not the one who'd let her down so badly.

'When you finished your nursing training and managed to get on to the midwifery course, just like you'd planned, Hope was so very proud,' continues Fliss.

'Was she? I always got the impression she thought it was a daft move and I should be content with part-time bank nursing.' Magda knows she's being defensive, but it irks her that Fliss thinks she knows her own mother better than Magda does. This was exactly what had given *her*, Magda, grief for decades.

'Not at all. She wanted you to follow your heart. It's just that she would have liked to help more with her grandson. By the time you came back to Periwinkle Bay, he was past the point of needing her.'

This is too much and Magda has to intervene in the tirade. 'That's not true, actually. It might have looked that way on the surface, but Jared and my mum had a lot of time for each other once he'd got over being furious that I'd dragged him away from his friends and the bright lights of the city. He needed his grandma in a different way . . . just like I've needed you, Fliss, all the time. All down the years.'

Fliss closes her eyes, utter weariness making her voice fainter than usual. 'That's enough for now. I can't do this today. Couldn't I just go to bed for an hour or two?'

Magda wants to tell Fliss that *no*, she can't go to bed until all this is solved, but she knows she has to give Fliss what she needs. Her relationship with her best friend has always been one of the joyful constants in her life, there through thick and thin, strong and true. She has never even considered that Fliss felt it was one-sided. There must be a way to right the balance before it's broken beyond repair, but for the life of her, Magda can't think what it is.

14

Saturday, 16 December

Nine Days Until Christmas

After a quiet Friday evening sitting curled up in Hope's chair by the Aga at Mistletoe Cottage, Fliss looks much less stressed when she emerges from her room the next morning, although she's still very pale and her expression is aloof bordering on angry. Her cheekbones have a sharp look that emphasizes her recent weight loss. Magda guesses this is probably less about Fliss's illness and more that she's lost interest in cooking for herself.

'I'm still not sure this is the right thing for me right now, but if I'm going to stay with you for a while, I need to know I'm not getting in the way of what you want to do,' Fliss says, when Magda gets back from dropping the twins off at a birthday party.

Magda wonders how to tackle this subject. It's painfully clear that although Fliss went along with her impulsive plan yesterday, she's not comfortable with it. Their friendship has existed for so long, Magda's never had to consider what might happen if it wasn't there. The thought of living alongside this frosty, switched-off version of her usually warm and energetic friend is alarming. She can only hope that Fliss will thaw as the days go by. It's unthinkable that Magda might never break through this icy barrier.

'You'd never be in the way here,' she says eventually, resisting the temptation to try and hug Fliss, who's leaning on the sink with her arms folded. 'This has always been your second home. Actually, if anything, it's been your first home. My mum would be horrified if she thought you felt that way.'

The mention of Hope seems to create a fragile link between the two of them as their eyes meet. Just at that moment a gust of wind comes through the open kitchen window and Hope's recipe book, which is lying on the kitchen table, blows open.

Magda shivers as she closes the window. 'I burnt the toast again,' she explains. 'I was trying to get rid of the smell before you came downstairs.'

'That's your mum's special book, isn't it?' Fliss says, going over to the table to look.

Magda battles a sudden protective urge to scoop the book up and put it safely back on the shelf. The connection she's been feeling with Hope through those pages is so personal that she can hardly bear for Fliss to touch it. She pushes her hands firmly into the pockets of her jeans.

'Your mum used to let me look at these recipes sometimes,' Fliss muses, as she flicks through the pages.

'I know that.' Magda can't keep a touch of bitterness out of her voice. The bond between Fliss and Hope had been so strong that she'd often felt like an outsider. Luckily Fliss doesn't notice, absorbed in the book.

'I learned so much from her in this kitchen,' she says. 'Oh!' Fliss bends to look more closely at the page now revealed and Magda comes to join her, keeping a wary gap between them.

'What's up?' she asks.

'It's just . . .' Fliss points to the elegant writing in the margin of the page. The recipe is for Hope's mother's Christmas puddings, an old family favourite.

Magda's shoulders slump. There won't be any of those this year. They should really have been made on Stir Up Sunday and that's long gone. 'I guess we'll have to have bought puddings this year,' she says.

Fliss shakes her head. 'Not necessarily. Look what she's written here.'

The date jotted down above Hope's extra note is one in December six years previously. 'Read it out,' Fliss says, sitting down at the table as if her legs have refused to hold her up any longer.

Magda clears her throat. The familiar writing never fails to bring on a wave of loss.

Don't panic if you haven't made your puddings on the right day. When I was playing the piano for the ladies' group today, I found out from my friend Freda that there's a way round this. You can microwave them instead of all that steaming and then it doesn't matter if it's all last minute!

Fliss smiles. 'She hated the microwave, didn't she? She can't be being serious?'

Magda carries on.

If you use exactly the same recipe you can microwave them on that day and then again on Christmas morning. Freda says they taste just as good. The important thing is the love you put into them, like everything else. I might give it a whirl sometime.

'There you go,' says Fliss. 'It's not too late. You can still make some.'

'But you know all about me and cooking. They'll be disgusting if I do them. I've been trying to get the twins interested in baking this week, but this recipe is way too complicated for us. Look at all the ingredients, Fliss. Spices, apples, lemons, breadcrumbs, even grated potato and carrot. I can't do it.'

There's a silence as Fliss regards Magda dispassionately. She looks as if she doesn't care either way, but after a moment she shrugs. 'I suppose I could supervise you and the kids if you get the stuff in later. I'm not doing them for you though. I'm not in the mood.'

Just at that moment Magda's mobile rings. It's an unknown caller. She answers the call, expecting it to be some sort of hard seller or scam that will need a stern rebuff, but the voice is familiar. It's Natasha, who's often to be seen helping out in the reception classroom these days. She's only been living in Periwinkle Bay for six months and is bending over backwards to fit in by offering her services for anything and everything. Today she's volunteered for the job of party supervisor at the church.

'Hi Magda. I'm sorry to bother you but I thought you ought to know that Desi's very upset,' Natasha says. 'She won't say why, but I think you should come.'

Magda's muttering an explanation to Fliss and grabbing a coat almost before the woman has finished speaking. Desi *had* seemed even quieter than usual this morning, but Magda had put it down to excitement about the birthday party. Glad she hasn't changed out of her old trainers, she jogs the short distance through the streets to the Methodist Church Hall where the party's taking place. There's no sign of Desi, but one of the other mothers sees Magda and points to the open door leading through to the main church. Magda strides across and goes in, only to find Desi in a corner on Natasha's knee, sobbing into a wad of tissues.

'Look, here's your granny,' says Natasha brightly. 'I told you she was coming.'

Desi looks up, and the relief on her face tugs at Magda's already thumping heart.

'Do you want to come home now, love?' Magda asks. 'Have you had enough of the party?'

Desi nods, and turns to beckon to Will, who Magda now sees has been standing close by in the shadow of a vast Christmas tree.

'I'm ready,' he says quietly, going to fetch their coats without even being asked.

Ten minutes later, after a silent walk home during which neither child will speak, Magda flings open the front door with relief, longing for a mug of tea and five minutes to tell Fliss what's happened. She opens her mouth to suggest the children go upstairs to change into their comfy clothes, but before she can speak, Fliss comes into the hallway and Will and Desi hurtle towards her.

Fliss drops to her knees and opens her arms to them and both twins wrap themselves around her as if they haven't seen her for weeks. Desi's sobbing again and Will's face is pale with distress.

'I'm guessing that wasn't the best party ever, kids?' Fliss says, holding them close.

Magda decides to leave them to it for a moment, and fighting back her envy at the calm, loving way Fliss copes with her grandchildren, she heads to the living room to make sure the fire is ready to light for later.

When she returns, the other three are in the kitchen and Fliss is on the sofa with a twin either side of her. They're snuggling into her comforting warmth like baby birds who are afraid they might fall out of their nest. Fliss herself has never had children. At times such as this, when Fliss is displaying such natural abilities to be maternal, Magda has found herself wanting to ask Fliss why this is. Occasionally, she'll get a non-committal response about how you should never have babies with the wrong man, but Fliss never expands further than that. There have definitely been a couple of relationships with men who could fall into this category, for both of them, so Magda can't help feeling her friend has had a lucky escape.

'Leave them with me,' Fliss says. 'We'll have a little chat about what's happened, okay? Why don't you go to the shops and get stocked up ready for later? I can cope. Reminds me of the Leicester years, this does.'

The barb hits home. When Jared was small and Fliss came on her regular visits, she had often been the one to save the day when he was distraught about various small worries or was just overtired and fractious. Their eyes meet over the twins' heads and Magda tries hard to swallow the sharp pang of sorrow that she isn't the one sorting out the problem. Fliss makes it look so bloody easy. She makes *everything* look easy. Magda should be the one doing this. But after a moment, common sense prevails, and she grabs the recipe book, stows it away in her biggest shopping bag, and heads for the town.

When Magda returns, Fliss and the twins are sitting at the kitchen table with glasses of milk and a plate of freshly baked cookies between them.

'We made biscuits with Fliss and now we're helping to write a list of some nice Christmassy things you're going to do with us,' says Will. 'Fliss is letting us use her best felt-tip pens.'

Desi says nothing, but beams up at Magda and holds out her arms for a hug. Feeling the confiding warmth of her grand-daughter's sturdy little body and smelling the delicious scent of the shampoo Annika buys for her children, Magda is filled with love. There's so much that can go wrong in the life of a five-year-old, but also so much happiness waiting to be discovered every day. Somehow, Desi has gone from one extreme to another in the space of a very short time, and that must be largely thanks to Fliss's tranquil approach to sorting out worries.

Magda bites back the urge to say that supervising the list should be for her to do. Clearly Fliss is doing a good job. Her mind flips back to that first Christmas when she'd been at the point of despair, and Fliss had arrived to save the day. Some people are born comforters and organizers. Maybe it's time Magda accepted that fact and just appreciated her friend's talents instead of constantly comparing herself unfavourably with Fliss.

Fliss takes the paper from Will and holds it up. 'Look, bullet points and everything,' she says, smiling at the twins. 'Desi did those. And the first thing on the list is to buy the big tree.'

'That was what made Desi upset at the party,' says Will. 'She wanted us to have that tree from the chapel. We usually get one before now and Mummy decorates it and then we do our little pretend one that lives in here.' He waves an arm around the kitchen as if trying to conjure up the silver tree that Magda had originally bought for Jared, all those years ago.

'So that's easy to sort,' says Fliss. 'When we've had our milk we can go and choose one from Clive on the market. There's still time before he packs up for the day. He can get it delivered by the time we're back.'

'Do you feel up to it?' Magda asks. Fliss is still looking rather wan but her eyes have got a definite gleam now.

'Look, if I'm going to stay here, you need to promise not to fuss,' says Fliss. 'My doctor says I have to listen to my body. When I'm tired, I rest. When I really want to do something, I pace myself. I come with you and Annika and these guys every year to get the tree, don't I? It's traditional. And then we always go to the café for hot chocolate with marshmallows.'

Will and Desi both cheer, as Magda says, 'I suppose that must have been why I've been putting off getting it. Without you and Annika, it seemed like an ordeal.'

'It won't be the same without Mum,' says Will, his bottom lip wobbling.

Fliss ruffles his hair. 'The thing about doing the same thing every year is that although it's kind of cosy, it makes you panic if it can't happen. I think that we should all tweak our routines every now and again. It's like spring cleaning,' she finishes.

'It's funny, that's very much what D— I mean Mr Archer was saying the other day,' Magda says wistfully. At Fliss's inquisitive expression, she adds, 'I'll explain when we've got more time, Fliss.'

'Yes, you do that. But for now, let's get moving! We've got a big tree to order and a little one to get out of the loft, I expect. Is that where you keep it?'

'Yes! And the decorations. Don't forget the decorations. They're in a giant suitcase!' With this, Will jumps down from his chair and start to run in circles around the table, followed by Desi, who's shrieking like a steam train.

'I'm really glad you're here, Fliss, but can we take turns with having the rests?' Magda says, catching Desi and inserting her arms into her coat.

'As long I get first refusal on the naps,' says Fliss, grabbing Will and giving him his own coat to put on. 'There have got to be some advantages to being a crock.'

'Do you really feel like a crock?' The twins are in the hall now looking for their shoes and in the sudden calm the two women face each other.

'Only some of the time.'

Magda is standing very close to Fliss now and the urge to wrap her arms around her is almost irresistible, but the underlying fear that it's too soon and Fliss isn't quite ready to thaw completely stops her in her tracks. The familiar scent of her friend, a mixture of Fliss's favourite fabric softener, rosewater and the wool of the soft hand-knitted sweaters she loves, almost makes Magda cry. But now is not the time for tears, and it's still definitely too soon for hugs, by the look on Fliss's face.

'It's nearly Christmas,' Magda says. 'Let's get this show on the road.'

Christmas Day, Twenty-eight Years Ago

Looking down at her son making some sort of balsa wood model on the floor by her feet, Magda's heart swells with pride. She's made it home to Mistletoe Cottage and Jared is loving every minute. If only she felt well enough to appreciate being here herself. A bad dose of flu has laid her low for a fortnight and she only decided last week that she could make it. Fliss offered to fetch her in the car, which was the only way it could have worked. The thought of lugging everything on the train was just too much.

Now Magda's actually here, the contrast between the tiny flat and her old home seems even more obvious. It's not the lack of space she minds. She's made it cosy and colourful, and anyway, a bigger place would be impossible for her to clean regularly with her long working hours, or to afford to heat properly. So it isn't Mistletoe Cottage itself, exactly, that she's missing, but the feeling of being cared for and being part of a family. The responsibility for trying to keep Jared clothed, fed and happy yet to still make progress at work is gradually grinding her down.

Magda's flu has left her bone-weary and it'll be a long time before she can climb into bed. Hope and Fliss are busy cooking up a storm ready for the huge Christmas dinner that they're aiming to eat at around four o'clock, and they've said they don't want her to help but that she needs to go and set the table soon. Five more minutes and she'll go.

Magda looks up as the doorbell rings. 'Can you get that, love?' her mum asks. 'It'll be Vera and Ruby. They're early.'

Hauling herself out of the rocking chair, Magda heads for the front door, yawning. On the doorstep as predicted, she finds her mother's twin cousins. Both auburn-haired and well-rounded, they exude comfort and well-being. They're carrying a cardboard box each, and are smiling broadly.

'We thought you might like a few extras as we're descending on you for dinner,' Ruby says. 'You look shattered, you poor pet. Your mum said you'd been poorly.'

'We've brought lots of goodies,' Vera adds. 'My apple jam won joint first prize in the WI competition last month with Ruby's lemon curd. It's my own recipe. There's a hamper here with three jars of each and a whole lot of mince pies and cakes in it. We hope you don't mind?' She pulls a face. 'They won't be as good as your mum's, obviously.'

Magda can't help smiling, tired as she is. Rivalry between the cousins has always been fierce when it comes to cooking. Thank goodness the WI judges had the sense to call a tie.

'You're absolute darlings to think of us. Have you come on the train or did you drive? Oh, of course you wouldn't have been able to bring all this on the train. I'm sorry, my brain's on a go-slow today. I'm blaming the flu. And lack of sleep,' she adds. Jared still wakes up ridiculously early, full of energy and raring to go.

'We came in our *new* car. Ruby did very well. She didn't get lost once.'

'That's because I had such a good navigator,' Ruby replies, beaming at her sister.

Magda is relieved to find the twins are having a benevolent day. Sometimes the atmosphere between them is spiky to say the least, but they were a constant in her childhood even though they live so many miles away, and still they make her feel secure just by looking at them. The journey from Scarborough to Periwinkle Bay isn't straightforward, and Magda knows Hope is deeply touched that they've made such an effort, especially on this day of the year.

That Christmas Day is one of the happiest that Magda's had for years, even though she's exhausted by the end of it. Having Ruby and Vera there takes the pressure off in the kitchen so that even Fliss isn't really needed. The two of them watch a film with Jared while the cousins cook and drink Hope's favourite brand of dark, sweet sherry, bringing each other up to date on the gossip. The dinner is a triumph and Jared is allowed to stay up way past his usual bedtime.

'I wish it could always be like this. I wish I could just stay,' Magda whispers to Fliss as her friend says goodnight, having elected to go back to her own house rather than stay over. Magda has a feeling Fliss isn't too happy that the twins have dropped into their roles in the kitchen so easily. She's probably feeling displaced.

'Well, why don't you come back? What's stopping you?' Fliss's tone is icy now, the earlier warmth between them lost in this sudden, resentful question.

Magda blinks. Fliss has never tried to change her mind about going away and has certainly not interfered in her life in Leicester except to help. She opens her mouth to speak but her friend gets in first.

'You had your long-term plan all in place before you even told me about it, didn't you? First the nursing training, then moving on to being a midwife as soon as you could. Then you went and got yourself pregnant but you still didn't want to come home. What is it about this place that's so bad? Or is it us? Is it your mum and your friends?'

'I . . . no, of course it's not you, Fliss, and it's not Periwinkle Bay either. Okay, I was keen to spread my wings to begin with and have a different kind of life, but I don't feel that way now.'

'So why not move back?' Fliss's voice is wobbly and she swallows hard. She reaches for her coat and slips it on. 'Your mum would love it. And so would I,' she adds quietly.

'I just can't, that's all. Oh Fliss, you know it's not always like it's been today, don't you?'

'How do you mean?'

'With Mum not minding that I don't like cooking. She's been too busy competing for best chef award today to bother with me.'

Fliss frowns. 'I don't know why you don't just bite the bullet and let her teach you,' she says. 'You know that's what she wants. All those lovely recipes going to waste.'

'But they're not wasted, are they? You're learning to make them instead of me. Taking one for the team.' Magda laughs but even to herself she doesn't sound convincing.

'If you say so.' There's no hug as Fliss turns away, and the atmosphere is still chilly.

Magda closes the door after Fliss and leans on the wall for a few moments, almost too tired to go to bed. Tonight, her heart aches with longing to be a better daughter. She could do it if she tried. She should probably move back home, get a job here, learn all the skills that her mother wants to teach her. It's all about independence, though, and standing on her own two feet. No, Magda's way is better. Maybe one day, but not yet.

Because what if Giovanni comes back? Returns to Leicester and tries to search her out, to reconnect with his son? If she leaves now, he might never find her again.

15

By the time Magda, Fliss and the twins reach the marketplace, afternoon is drawing in quickly and the town is
lighting up. Periwinkle Bay's Christmas lights are famous for
miles around, and by now the market square is humming with
visitors. The roasted chestnut stalls are doing a roaring trade,
and the café owner has set up a trestle and several bistro tables
outside his shop to accommodate the constant demand for
hot drinks and mince pies.

Desi nudges Magda and points upwards at the giant fir tree
that dominates the market, with its blue and green lights and
shining gold baubles.

'Wow, what do you think of that?' Magda asks automatically,
and then bites her lip as Desi turns away.

Magda exchanges glances with Fliss. 'Desi's not spoken to
anyone except Will since her mum and dad left,' she whispers,
under cover of the nearby Salvation Army band bursting into
a loud rendition of 'Good King Wenceslas'. 'I've been so worried.
It's not natural.'

'Give her time. It's been a shock to her system. Nasty
surprises can get you like that. I didn't say a word to anyone
except Laurence for a week after my diagnosis.'

'Oh Fliss, I'm so sorry I wasn't there when you needed me.'
Magda swallows a lump in her throat. 'I wish you'd phoned.'

'Well, I didn't, so there's no point in banging on about it

any more,' Fliss responds briskly, not interested in the conversation. 'We need to give the twins some fun today, so this is no place to discuss that. Come on, folks. Let's get this tree chosen and then we can have . . .'

'Hot chocolate!' Will shouts, and even Desi lets out a squeak.

Clive gives them a look that says, *Where have you been until now? I was about to pack up,* but plasters on a smile for the children and lets them spend a happy half-hour discussing in intricate detail and then rejecting the vast majority of his trees.

Eventually, he loses patience. 'So, what you're saying, kids, is that none of these fine beauties is quite right for your hallway?'

Will nods. 'You see, it's tall.'

'What is?'

'The gap.'

Magda tries to explain more clearly. 'The stairs go up at right angles and the tree always stands in the square part of the entrance hall.'

'Is it my fault if you live in a bl— in a stately home that calls itself a cottage?' Clive mutters.

Fliss pokes him in the ribs. 'Don't be such a misery. You've been in Magda's house, you know exactly what they need. Haven't you got any more back at the yard? We want one that's absolutely perfect for the space. It's very important.'

With all four of them gazing at him hopefully, Clive seems to know when he's met his match. 'Well, there are a couple more, I suppose. But I was keeping them in reserve in case Lady Foxton wanted a spare.'

'Tough. She's left it too late.'

Clive thinks for a moment and then nods. 'Fair enough, I'll get it sent round shortly. You'd better buy one of my new stands too. A whopper like this one needs a firm base and Annika always insisted on putting it in a pot. It'll cost you though, Magda. This tree's a stunner.'

Magda pays up without a murmur and they head for the café, with Will and Desi high-fiving each other as they go.

Back at home, getting the decorations out is going to take some time. Just as Magda's wondering how she's going to get them down to the landing with Fliss busy supervising the twins in the kitchen, she hears voices in the hallway and Fliss calls up that Den is here.

'Is this a bad time?' he asks, as Magda comes downstairs, wiping dusty hands on her jeans. 'I just called by to see if you wanted an extra pair of hands for the daily bake tonight? I don't want to get in the way, though. Good to see you, by the way, Fliss. You probably don't need me, Magda, if the expert here is around.'

'It's a brilliant time, as long as you don't mind getting a bit dirty,' she tells him. 'I've just been up to the loft for the first time in months to get down the Christmas decorations and it's a complete shambles up there. So many heaps. Someone with long arms to wind the lights around the tree would be a real help when I've sorted out what we need.'

'Count me in,' says Den, following her upstairs. Magda scrambles back up the ladder and takes a closer look, finding that actually everything has been labelled by her mum and it's just a case of passing box after box down to Den. Downstairs, Magda can hear Will singing 'We Wish You a Merry Christmas' to Blondie, who's totally overexcited and capering around the hallway.

'Better get a mop and bucket at the ready,' says Den, as they join the others in the kitchen. 'Blondie's bladder's a bit unreliable.'

'Join the club, mate,' mutters Fliss. The other two stop to look at her, but she just shrugs. 'Don't ask,' she says.

The twins are kept busy for a good half-hour putting the trinkets and tinsel on their own little silver tree that will live in the kitchen, and by this time a ring at the doorbell tells them that Clive has lived up to his promise.

The tall, graceful spruce that is fed through the front door in its net takes Magda's breath away. The overwhelming scent of pine takes her back through the years to her own childhood, and also to all the times since when she made the effort to come home for Christmas with Jared. Now they've been back for good for twenty years, it's the ones that got away that tug at her heart strings. All those times when work was so intense that she decided there weren't enough hours in the day to travel home and back over Christmas.

'It's magnificent,' says Fliss. 'We were right to stick out for the biggest and best.'

Den fetches scissors and comes forward to cut the net away. He helps with the tricky job of manoeuvring the tree into its shiny new stand and after a lot of crashing and banging, the three of them stand back in admiration, craning their necks to see the top branches that reach right up the stairwell and brush the ceiling.

'I'll get the lights on it first and then we can decorate it,' says Den. He sounds even more excited than Magda feels.

Hearing the commotion, Will and Desi come careering down the passageway from the kitchen followed by a madly barking Blondie. After a moment, Den, unsurprisingly, quietly takes himself off to look for the mop and bucket and the twins follow him.

'I can't wait to see this with the decorations and lights on it,' says Fliss. 'Annika would never let us touch the big one but Jared always loved decorating his little silver tree, didn't he, Mags? Do you remember that Christmas when I brought all the tiny woodland creatures to perch in the branches and the only one he'd let us put on it was the squirrel because it reminded him of the ones in the garden here?'

Magda nods. She does remember, and the memories of that year aren't all good.

Christmas Day, Twenty-seven Years Ago

Jared's delight on that particular Christmas morning when he opens his best presents seems to be shadowed with anxiety.

'What's the matter, love?' Magda asks, yawning and stretching. Her son's usual waking time of five o'clock has moved forward an hour in honour of Christmas Day and even though she's halfway down her first mug of strong black coffee, it's hard to stay alert. She leans back on the sofa and watches him as he rootles through the small pile of gifts. At last, he smiles.

'This one's squishy,' he says. 'I think Santa's remembered.'

Tearing off the paper, Jared reveals a magnificent fluffy grey squirrel. Magda has searched for weeks to get exactly the right one. The red variety were much prettier in her opinion, but she knows that her son will want an animal just like the ones that leap through the trees in the back garden of Mistletoe Cottage.

'Wow,' he breathes, lifting the toy up to his face and pressing his nose into the fur. 'This is brilliant, Mum. Santa's really clever, isn't he?'

'He definitely knows his stuff, does Father Christmas,' says Magda. 'Right, what's your Christmas morning breakfast going to be? We need to get organized because Aunty Fliss will be here in a couple of hours. She's already texted to say she's on the way.'

Jared whoops with joy, and not for the first time, Magda feels a wave of gratitude for the generosity of her best friend, who has been up even earlier than Jared, and never minds the long drive.

Their first breakfast is over, and Magda is thinking about a second, when she hears the sound of Fliss's car pulling on to her allocated parking space under the window. As she's about to go and open the door, Magda's mobile rings. The number is familiar and unwelcome.

She answers the call as Fliss staggers in, laden with bags, mouthing an apology as she tries her very best to get out of the emergency call-out.

'But I've promised my son and my friend faithfully that I'd be here today,' she says. 'Well, there must be somebody else. Oh . . . well, why didn't you say so? I'll get my bag.'

She turns to see Jared's reproachful eyes on her, and Fliss with a similar expression.

'I'm so, so sorry, guys,' she says. 'It's Mrs Glenfield.'

They both look puzzled and Magda hears herself start to gabble.

'It's just that she's asking for me personally. She's forty-five and it's her fifth baby. There have been problems all along. I'll need to dash. Fliss . . . can you . . .'

Fliss doesn't meet Magda's eyes but she smiles brightly. 'Of course you'll have to go. We'll be fine, won't we, Jared? I don't expect you'll be too long.'

The last sentence is clearly meant to reassure Jared, and Magda nods gratefully, grabbing her work bag and coat and pulling on her boots.

'She only lives up the road. I'll let you know how it's going and be home as soon as I can,' she says as she hurries from the room. Glancing back at the window when she reaches the street, she sees Jared gazing after her. Fliss is standing behind him, her hands on his shoulders. Magda waves, but they've already turned away.

It's a long, frightening day involving an emergency journey to the hospital and several crisis points. Magda has never yet been so close to losing a baby, and the mother refuses to let Magda out of her sight, clinging on to her like a life raft. The newly born baby boy survives but it's touch and go. Arriving back at the flat many hours later, exhausted and blood-stained, she finds Jared and Fliss in their pyjamas, asleep under a blanket on the lumpy old sofa. Jared is still cuddling his squirrel.

Her friend sits up, startled, and then relaxes when she sees Magda.

'He was determined to wait up for you,' Fliss puts a finger to her lips and whispers, but Jared is awake already, blinking up at Magda in the glow from the white tree lights.

'Is it still Christmas, Mum?' he asks eagerly, as Magda scoops him into a hug and gets ready to take him to bed. Fliss follows, yawning.

'No, darling, it's past one o'clock now,' she says, tucking him in and bending for a kiss, but he pushes her away, his face contorted with rage.

'You promised you'd come back in time to play a game with us before bedtime,' he says. 'You've been gone for ages and ages. We've had dinner and tea and even supper while you were out.'

Guilt washes over Magda as she registers Fliss's exhaustion. 'I'm really sorry. Both of you must have been really fed up with me for not coming home sooner but the baby didn't arrive when he was supposed to . . . and then he couldn't breathe properly . . .' she tries to explain, but Jared is having none of it, and turns his back on her before falling instantly back to sleep.

'Don't say another word,' says Fliss. 'Let's go to bed too. You're even more tired than we are. It was fine. We had a good day. Next year will be better.'

'It will, I promise,' Magda says, but in her heart she's not so sure. Her promises don't seem to be good for much these days. There must be a better way of finding a balance between work and Jared. She vows to herself to try her best to find it.

16

Back in the kitchen, with Blondie now snoozing by the Aga and the twins getting ready for action, Magda glances across at the grandfather clock and tries to calculate how long it will be before she's tucked up in bed. At least she's not having to entertain the twins single-handed, though. Den has fixed the tree lights and is now supervising hand-washing, and Fliss is sorting the pinnies for them all.

Hugely relieved to have this help in managing her grand-children, Magda reaches up for her mum's recipe book, now in its usual place on the shelf. As she touches it, a wave of joy seems to spread all the way down her arms and around her body, almost like one of Hope's hugs. She stands very still for a moment, luxuriating in the sudden feeling of well-being.

'What's up?' says Fliss, turning to see why Magda's gone quiet. The pinched look seems to be gradually disappearing from her face and Magda thinks the anger might be fading too. Even so, she hesitates to say what's on her mind.

'Oh, nothing . . .'

'Yes, there is.' Fliss points a finger at her friend. 'Spill!'

That single word has always been the ultimate command between them to stop messing around and spill the beans, right from when they were at primary school. Magda checks that Den and the twins are still out of earshot and tries to think how to say what's on her mind without sounding cheesy or weird.

'It's this book,' she says eventually. 'I can't help feeling as if Mum's trying to tell me something every time I open it. You know how I've been . . . how I *still am* about baking and so on. It's never been my thing. But there are all these notes in between the recipes, and such a lot of memories in the pages and so . . . oh, this is so hard to explain because I don't really understand it myself, but it's as if my mum is helping me along. Each time we try and bake something, it seems less stressful. It must be because Mum was so good at putting in the extra details and descriptions in her recipes. Her notes make it seem as if she's giving me a nudge. All the little things she'd say if she was here, the tips and short-cuts and so on.'

'I know what you mean. But you had a funny look on your face. It seems like there might be something more?'

Magda pauses, choosing her words carefully. This feels almost too fragile to analyse. 'Fliss, I can't get my head around the fact that every time I open it, I get the warmest, most comforting sensation ever, and I'm sure I can smell herbs and spices and even sometimes lemons and . . . all kinds of things. It's a different scent every time, almost as if the book has a memory of its own. Do you think I'm going crazy? Missing Mum so much I'm imagining things?'

Fliss looks at Magda a little oddly but doesn't seem too fazed by this.

'Well, I've always believed in the echo of past atmospheres, and your mum was such a strong, loving woman that it wouldn't be beyond belief that she's still here, in a way,' she says. 'Especially in her kitchen, where she was happiest, wrapped in her old apron and looking over her glasses at us when we tried to eat the biscuits straight out of the oven. If there's still something of Hope in that book, I wish she'd share it with me too.'

Fliss's words warm Magda's heart but even so, she half-wishes she hadn't said anything. The book is hers, and hers alone. But she grits her teeth and tries to be magnanimous. 'Mum loved you, Fliss. I expect you've got nearly as many memories of her as I have.'

'More, probably,' says Fliss. The smile that her reminiscences triggered is fading now. Magda feels as if the sun is going in.

'Well, I wouldn't say that, necessarily,' Magda says, holding on to her patience with difficulty.

'It's true,' says Fliss. 'I was here a lot of the time you were away, remember? Somebody had to do all the stuff you were too busy for.' They had had a brief moment's respite and now here they are, straight back to the coldness.

Before Magda can react again, the rest of the party burst back into the room, a sure sign they're ready to start another bake. Today they've settled on making mince pies, and as the children clamber up on the kitchen table next to her, Magda opens Hope's recipe book at the festive section. The mingled hit of brandy-laced mincemeat and spices rising from the pages is so strong that it takes her breath away. Magda glances at Den and Fliss. They don't seem to have noticed anything. She rubs her eyes. It must be her imagination, but she misses Hope so much in that moment that she can't speak. Den leans over and looks at the recipe for mince pies as she's struggling to find words.

'Oh, that's a surprise,' he says. 'Your mum used a food processor for her pastry. I always had her down for a back-to-basics cook, doing everything by hand.'

'No, Hope was always finding new ways to cut corners,' Fliss says. 'She said life was too short to stick to the old-fashioned ways.'

Magda bristles at the way Fliss is making it sound as if she knew Hope best, but takes a deep breath and tells herself not to be petty. Soon, the food processor is unveiled from its dusty plastic cover, the scales are out and the table is laden with ingredients.

'I don't know what it all says but the writing in GG's book says OZ next to everything.' Will is looking puzzled.

'Great reading, Will. It means ounces,' says Magda. 'Changing all her recipes to grams was a step too far, even if she *did* like labour-saving devices. Look, there's a button on the scales that lets you weigh in ounces.'

She clicks the button and helps Desi to measure out eight ounces of flour. They add two ounces of soft margarine and two of lard.

'How much is a pinch of salt?' asks Will. Desi pinches him on the arm, which starts a fight.

'Hey, pack that in,' says Den calmly, and the two gaze at him, immediately silent.

'How do you do that?' Magda wonders aloud.

'Years of experience,' he says, grinning. 'It's my superpower. That and mince pies, obviously,' he adds.

Magda looks at him quizzically. 'You're a mince pie expert and here we are making mince pies?'

'I'm always the one to make them in our house,' Den explains, before adding, quietly, 'well, I used to.' Louder again, though, he says, 'I used to have to do them the vegan way, of course. Virginia didn't eat anything from an animal, so I became an expert at pastry without butter or lard.'

'Well, we'll see about that,' Fliss interrupts, clearly wanting to focus on the task in hand. 'Will, this is what the recipe means.' She pours salt on to a saucer and pinches some between her thumb and first finger. 'Not too much. There, it's in. Look Magda, your mum's written some extra notes here.'

Magda peers at the book. The letters are very small and crammed into the margin.

'*Your margarine and lard should be softened beforehand because that makes the mixing process quicker,*' she reads. 'Well, we can give them a few seconds in the microwave to sort that one.'

She grins at them and carries on reading.

Only ever make one batch of eight ounces of flour at a time. Trying to double up just gives you tough pastry. This will make twelve mince pies if you roll out carefully and don't waste the scraps. When the mixture in the machine looks like breadcrumbs, add the water a teaspoon at a time. You need one teaspoon of water for every ounce of flour. NO MORE THAN THAT. Then tip the mixture on to a large floured board or worktop and squeeze it together gently until it sticks and makes a ball. NO MORE WATER!

'Why does she keep going on about the water?' Will says. 'She sounds a bit scary. I don't remember GG being bossy.'

'She just wanted it done properly, that's not being bossy. I'll always remember Hope telling me that the more water you put in and the more you handle the pastry the harder it will be,' says Fliss. 'But she always said the most important thing to remember is that you should never make pastry if you're in a bad mood because it'll end up as heavy as your heart.'

Magda takes in these wise words. Her heart has definitely felt much too heavy from time to time although the weight seems to be gradually lifting with every moment she spends sharing this newly discovered baking fun. Better to be on the safe side, though. She makes a conscious effort to put her shoulders back and smile.

'Away we go then,' she trills, in an unnaturally bright voice. Den and Fliss look at her rather oddly but don't comment, and soon the baking is underway.

They finish the process between them as quickly as possible, helping Will and Desi to roll the pastry out thinly without making holes. Soon, a baking tray is greased and lined with twelve pastry cases. Magda supervises spooning just enough mincemeat into them and they all help to put the tops on.

'Mum used to make lemon curd tarts too in case anyone didn't like mincemeat. She used Aunty Ruby's lemon curd recipe. I did think about having a go,' says Magda, glancing at the recipe book.

Fliss rolls her eyes. 'Steady on, let's see how we go with the basics first, shall we? Right, fifteen minutes in a hot oven,' she says, directing Den to do the dangerous part even though Will and Desi would like to have a chance to get the oven door open.

'I want to eat them now!' Will calls, as soon as the pies are in the oven.

Magda leaps in to prevent a meltdown. 'Why don't we go up and do your baths and then come back and see if they're ready? They'll take fifteen minutes and then we still need to wait for them to cool so you don't burn your tongues,' she says, although as soon as the words leave her lips, she realizes how weary she is at the thought of two excited children and a lot of soapy water. They head up the stairs, both twins reaching out to touch the tree as they pass by. The fresh scent of pine when the branches are disturbed is intoxicating, and a wild ripple of child-like excitement takes Magda's breath away. She can really do this.

Following the children as they clamber upstairs, Will muttering away happily about all the mince pies he's going to eat as soon as he's out of the bath, it dawns on Magda that she's had a whole evening without her all-too-familiar feeling of panic about the children. Somehow – and she strongly suspects it's due to the help of both Fliss and Den – she's managed to tick off some Christmas activities, without her sadness over Hope or her frustration with the children getting in the way. She *can* make Christmas fun, she tells herself now, allowing herself a small smile.

17

Half an hour later, bedraggled and soaked to the skin from Desi's sudden urge to slide down the bath and make tidal waves 'like the Little Mermaid', Magda sends the squeaky-clean children downstairs to Fliss and Den for a mince pie tasting session before bedtime while she gets changed.

In the quiet of her bedroom, she glances at the photo by her bed. In it, an angelic small boy with very dark eyes and short black hair is holding a fluffy toy squirrel in his arms. The little silver Christmas tree, now in pride of place in the kitchen, stands in the background. The fairy lights are shining because it's still dark outside. Sinking down on to the bed and leaning back on her pillows, Magda allows herself a blissful five minutes' peace. She thinks about her son and the long-ago Christmas Day when that photograph was taken and remembers again his joy when he'd opened the parcel containing the squirrel, the only thing he'd been sure he wanted that year.

If only making him happy had been as easy every day since, she reflects. Still, looking back there had been plenty of moments when everything would suddenly fall into place, even if only briefly. Granted, everything had gone pear-shaped later, but that first hour had been magical. *Hold on to those memories*, she tells herself. *You got it right sometimes. You can definitely do it again now. But first you need to tidy yourself up a bit.*

Magda quickly changes her shirt for a clean, even baggier

one in blue and white stripes, looks at herself in the mirror and drags a comb through her hair, tucking it behind her ears. For once it stays in place, although it could definitely do with a good cut. Her eyes look huge in the dim light from the bedside lamp, and when she's added a spritz of perfume and a slick of lipstick, she feels almost human again. Her favourite gold hoop earrings complete the picture. A fleeting thought that Den might think she looks okay tonight flashes through her mind, and when she enters the kitchen again she can see by his look in her direction that he's registered the slight difference.

She reaches for Hope's book once again, keen to hang on to the warm glow that's been growing inside her all afternoon, and the jolt of happiness when she opens it is stronger than any of the previous tingles she's felt when she's held it in her hands.

I think I'm getting somewhere with this baking lark at last, Mum. It feels as if you're cheering me on.

Fliss has been busy decanting the mince pies from their tin and sifting a light dusting of icing sugar over their tops. She gestures to the plate. 'Let's try these and see how we're doing so far. They're still a bit warm, so go steady.'

The twins need no second bidding and neither does Den. The mumbles of approval from all sides show that this first attempt has been a huge success, and soon, soft crumbs of pastry are all that's left.

'I'll take these two up to bed while you two handle the washing-up,' Fliss offers, fixing Will and Desi with a firm stare. To Magda's amazement, they follow Fliss without a murmur.

Magda and Den start to load the dishwasher. The silence between them lengthens, and seems to crackle with suspense. The sound of 'The Little Drummer Boy' playing in the background makes Magda think of her son, now acting in a musical of the very same name. She is also reminded of the time Jared was chosen to bang the drum at his school Nativity, and she'd moved heaven and earth to be there. So there *were* times I got it right, she tells herself. And now my small drummer is making his music all the way across the pond.

'It was nice all baking together tonight,' she says, keeping her back turned so Den can't see that her eyes are wet.

'It's been great,' says Den. 'I hadn't realized how empty my house has been since Virginia left, until I came round here and joined you lot.'

'Do you wish she was coming back for Christmas?' The words are out before Magda can stop them. She closes her eyes and wishes she was somewhere else. It's no business of hers how Den feels about his wife being away.

'Do you want the honest answer or the one I probably should give you?' he says, folding his arms and leaning on the sink as he regards her. He doesn't look offended by her nosiness, and Magda begins to relax again.

'Oh . . . well . . . let's have both and I'll pick the one I like best,' she says, grinning up at him.

'Okay. So . . . Option A. Yes, I'll miss Virginia so much that I won't be able to enjoy a single moment. The Christmas dinner's going to taste like sawdust without her to share it and I'll probably cry myself to sleep.'

'Right. And Option B?'

'We've got two great sons and it's been good in a lot of ways, but we've been drifting apart for a long time. We've got such different ideas about how life should be lived, I guess. I think we both know it's time to move on.'

The last sentence is said in a very low voice and Magda isn't

147

sure if she's heard correctly, but the way Den is looking at her across the kitchen tells her she did.

'So which is your favourite option?' Den asks, breaking the silence that has stretched between them.

Footsteps on the stairs make them both jump, and Den finds himself suddenly very keen to take Blondie out to the garden. He leaves the kitchen just as Fliss comes in. She looks at Magda suspiciously.

'What's going on?'

'Nothing. Why?'

'You look proper shifty, that's why.'

'Do I?' Magda widens her eyes and Fliss snorts.

'Don't give me that innocent look. You're blushing. I've had my suspicions you've been flirting with Den before now . . .'

'I *so* have not!' Magda hears the outrage in her voice, an echo of her teenage self whenever Fliss had teased her about liking one of the boys from the town. She can't help grinning. 'You know I wouldn't mess around with someone who's not long come out of a big relationship.'

'Come on, Mags, this is me you're talking to. There's some sort of chemistry between you two. It's obvious. How do you really feel about him? Cut to the chase, quick, before he comes back inside. Is something going on?'

Magda shakes her head vigorously. 'No! No, there isn't.'

'But would you like there to be something? That's the real question.'

'I . . . well . . . it's not like that . . . but anyway, I wouldn't want to rock the boat. He's probably still getting himself back on track.'

Fliss laughs. 'I wouldn't worry about that. He's a grown man and Virginia's been gone ages. Denis Archer can look after himself.'

'I certainly can,' says Den, coming in and catching the tail end of Fliss's words. He smiles at them both. 'But why is that fact up for discussion?'

Magda and Fliss gaze at him, both feeling their faces burning and wondering how to wriggle out of this one, but he just laughs and bends to make a fuss of the dog. 'I think these two have been doing a bit of character analysis,' he tells Blondie. 'We'd better head for home before they start on you.'

Christmas Day, Twenty Years Ago

Jared comes into the kitchen and goes over to the fridge. He takes out a large bottle of apple juice and drinks from it noisily, banging it down on the worktop and going through to the hallway without a backward glance at his mother.

Magda sighs. This wasn't how she'd imagined life with a growing son to be. Visions of long walks along the beach skimming stones and collecting shells like they used to do on their visits when he was younger have been replaced with arguments, sulks and high decibel banging of doors. Jared is not one bit impressed that Magda has uprooted him from the bright lights of the city and his large group of friends.

Ah, those 'friends'. Magda's prepared to put up with a good deal more teenage tantrums to see the back of that lot. She forces herself not to think about them.

She wonders if life would have been different if she and Jared's father had been together. Being Mum to a large, happy brood had been her aim once upon a time but really, how realistic was that? She's struggled enough with one. Only Fliss seems to understand her son these days. She expects that's where he'd really like to be now, if it wasn't Christmas morning. Fliss and her partner Laurence have bought a derelict retail space in the next village and are busy doing it up. They're going to open a craft store, and Jared loves nothing better than helping to strip old wallpaper, slap on emulsion and get absolutely filthy in the process.

'You're looking melancholy again, love,' says Hope, coming into the room and going straight over to the oven. She takes out the turkey, sizzling in its deep baking tray, and pokes a skewer deep into its side. 'Don't be sad about Jared. He'll come round, you mark my words. The dinner I'm cooking would cheer up a much gloomier face than that. He loves his gran's roasties. Do you . . . do you want to have a go at the stuffing? I forgot that Jared only likes the basic kind. He won't eat my apricot and chestnut creation. You could do some sage and onion?'

The hesitation in her mum's voice cuts straight to Magda's heart. Hope must think she's not even able to add boiling water to a ready-made mix. But even as she nods and goes into the pantry to look for the packet, she knows she's only got herself to blame for this show of no-confidence.

The fridge door is still swinging open and the apple juice has been left without its top. Magda sighs. The sound of thumping music comes down the stairs and the phone in the hall is ringing again. It won't be for her, so there's no point in going to answer it. Hope's circle of buddies always like to wish each other a Merry Christmas before they get too involved in their respective culinary extravaganzas. A wave of loneliness washes over Magda and she pushes it away. She's living the life she's chosen in her small home town now, and she's even managed to land her dream job as a community midwife. And at least her son's here with her, safe and sound. She shouldn't even think about wanting more.

They've got each other, she, Jared and her mum. A tight little unit of three, with Fliss there whenever they need her. Odd times, in the small hours when she can't sleep, Magda lets herself imagine how it might be to meet someone wonderful, who would have her welfare at heart, who would love Jared like a father and understand how much she adores her work. But such a man doesn't exist, she always tells herself. If he did, she'd have found him by now. This way is best. You know where you stand with your family.

18

Sunday, 17 December

Eight Days Until Christmas

Sunday morning dawns with low clouds and a hint of snow in the air. Magda looks out of the window at the frosty cobblestones and wonders how Fliss will manage the steep hill if they decide to go to church. They've both always loved the time of Advent in the Methodist Chapel, when the world seems to be holding its breath waiting for something very special to happen, and the candles in the Advent ring are lit one by one as the weeks leading up to Christmas go by.

By the time Will and Desi are up and dressed, Magda can see that her friend is having a bad day energy-wise, although she's starting to look a little less ferocious at last.

'I think I did a bit too much yesterday,' Fliss admits when Magda asks about going to chapel. 'Do you mind if I don't come to the service? I want to be able to help decorate the tree and make puddings later. It seems to be all about pacing myself now. Boring, but it can't be helped. I'm due back at the hospital soon for more tests and a proper treatment and management plan. It's early days.'

'I'll stay here with you, shall I? Fiona's said she'll pick the twins up for Sunday School anytime, so I don't have to go.'

'But you want to, don't you?'

Magda considers this. 'It's partly the book,' she says slowly, trying to make sense of the elusive instincts that are guiding her. 'I've been reading my mum's comments and thinking back to all the happy times we spent. I know I disappointed her when I didn't want to learn to bake, but that wasn't all we had. One thing I especially liked was that she used to take me to chapel and try and explain what the minister had said.'

'Did you get it?'

Magda laughs. 'I didn't really listen very well. I just liked hearing her voice and having her all to myself for a little while. After that she was busy getting the lunch organized.'

'You haven't answered my question. Do you want to go to church today? And I don't mean just to ogle the gorgeous organist.'

Magda ignores this remark, and the unexpected pang of uneasiness the thought generates. 'Yes, I do want to go, actually. I'll take the kids with me and you can have a rest. But obviously it's nothing to do with Den!' she adds, laughing and rolling her eyes. Fliss doesn't smile back, just raises her eyebrows.

'Anyway,' Magda continues hastily, 'Den and Blondie can come round afterwards if he wants to. Jared and Annika are FaceTiming this afternoon. We've barely spoken to them since they've been gone. It's not been a great success so far for them, trying to communicate with each other from so far away. The kids will need the distraction of decorating the big tree and we can have Sunday dinner together later on. I'll need you *and* the book to help me if I'm going to attempt Yorkshire puddings with the beef, though.'

Fliss looks quite gratified at this, and Magda begins to hope that the thaw really is underway between them. They've managed another full conversation without any snide remarks, which feels like it hasn't happened for a while. Being at odds with each other is so unlike them that it makes her feel constantly anxious. Fliss has been her security blanket for so long that she can't imagine life without her. *But who wants to be thought of just as a comfort blanket?* a small voice inside her says. *Maybe Fliss is right to be so angry with me. How often have I shown any appreciation?*

Magda and the twins make their way to church, slipping and sliding their way down the hill. Magda has shelved her disturbing train of thought for the time being, concentrating instead on the food they're going to prepare later. It hits her how far she must have come already if she's even contemplating making a full roast dinner. It's true that having Fliss as back-up and guide makes everything a lot less daunting, but even so, she knows there's more to it than that. The recipe book is affecting her somehow. The baking secrets inside and the pithy comments from her mum are making her think about the past more than she's done for years.

It's difficult to face up to some of the memories that are emerging, but it feels as if the process, even when it's painful, is necessary. And finally she's beginning to get past the panic of looking after the twins, and instead get to know them better, even in their worst moods. The delight of it is starting to take hold of her. Even the prospect of a possibly confusing conversation for the twins with their parents isn't enough to burst the bubble.

Inside the chapel, the first thing Magda hears is the stirring sound of the organ playing. She cranes her neck to look at

Den but she can only see the back of his head. She's texted him to see if he wants to come round after church and had a thumbs up emoji as a reply but nothing else. Hopefully he doesn't think she's flirting. Magda's face feels hot when she thinks about the things Fliss said.

Den's now playing an old Christina Rossetti carol. It had been Hope's favourite, and as Magda settles the twins, one either side of her, ready to be called for Sunday School, the words sing themselves in her head.

> *Love came down at Christmas, love all lovely, love divine.*
> *Love came down at Christmas, star and angel gave the sign.*

Quiet and peaceful for once, Will and Desi lean on her and gaze wide-eyed at the church all decked out in its festive finery. The tree is majestic, lit with twinkling white lights and decorated with small gilt angels and stars, but the biggest, brightest star is reserved for the topmost branch. It sits in all its glory, tilting slightly as usual. She remembers her mother's friend Freda grumbling one year about the way the star always leant to the left and after the service fetching a step ladder to fix it. The next week it was back at its usual crazy angle. Hope had smiled at Freda's chuntering.

'When will you learn, pet? Things don't have to be perfect to be beautiful,' Hope had said, and Freda had gazed back, baffled at this idea. Magda had thought it an odd concept at the time but over the years she came to understand that this was Hope's attitude to everything. If you always do your very best, that's quite enough.

'I like it here, don't you?' Will whispers.

'I do too. What do you like best?' Magda responds, pleased that Will is enjoying the morning, just as she had always done with Hope.

'The candles in that circle at the front. Will they light them in a minute?'

Magda looks to where he's pointing and sees the Advent ring. It looks as if the minister, Jean, is doing her usual frantic search for matches.

'Yes, Jean will do that soon, but only three of them because the last of the four red ones is for next Sunday and then the one in the very middle is for Christmas Day. They light an extra one every week.'

'And after they light the middle one, Mum and Dad'll be coming home?'

'Not right after it, but soon. Desi, what do you like best?' Desperate to change the subject, Magda forgets for a minute that her granddaughter is very unlikely to answer.

Desi unexpectedly reaches up to give Magda a kiss, pointing at the tree and then making both her chubby hands into a heart shape.

Too moved to speak, Magda wraps an arm around each child even more firmly and watches as the matches are at last located and the candles are lit. '*Love came down at Christmas*,' the voice in her head sings. She's glad her conscience is giving her a rest and as the congregation stand to begin 'Hark the Herald Angels Sing', Magda can't help thinking that the words could be meant for her.

When they return home, they realize Fliss has been far from idle, even though she still looks tired and there are deep violet shadows under her eyes. She's put the beef in the oven to slow roast and is just about to start on the vegetable preparation.

'That smells amazing,' Magda says, breathing in the delicious aroma and hearing her stomach rumble loudly. 'It felt as if my mum was here waiting for us when we came in, just like the old days.'

'I'm sorry if I'm a disappointment,' Fliss snaps back. 'I can never replace Hope.'

'Oh, stop being so touchy. You know I didn't mean that. It was meant to be a compliment.'

Magda's words hang in the air and she holds her breath, wondering if she's gone too far, but eventually, Fliss shrugs.

'Sorry, Mags, I'm just tired and it makes me grumpy when I have to accept I can't do as much as I used to,' she says. 'Let's have coffee and you can tell me all about the service.'

Magda breathes a sigh of relief and goes to put the kettle on. It clearly doesn't always pay to pussyfoot around her friend. She's going to have to play it by ear and somehow be a bit less worried about offending Fliss.

The time for the FaceTime call is imminent, and Magda gets the twins as peaceful as possible, sitting on the kitchen sofa with milk and cookies. Unfortunately, Den arrives just as the call starts and Blondie escapes from his clutches and dive-bombs the children, sending the milk flying and ambushing a biscuit. Magda can see that Jared and Annika aren't amused. It's very early in New York and Annika has never been good at mornings.

'Can everyone just calm down, please?' Jared has to raise his voice to be heard above the hubbub, and Den hustles Blondie outside with an apologetic look at Magda.

'Sorry,' he mouths.

Magda turns to give the screen her full attention. She would have liked to show Jared and Annika that things are under control, that she's better prepared than she'd been when Jared was younger, but this is a more realistic depiction of life in Mistletoe Cottage, she reflects, giving herself a break. She expects her son has forgotten how chaotic family life is here, in his charmed world of hotels and chauffeur-driven cars to the theatre, so actually it's a good thing for him and Annika to be reminded about what she's coping with on a day-to-day basis. Desi's holding her favourite teddy in both arms and has buried her face in its soft fur but she doesn't seem to have any intention of speaking. Magda had hoped that seeing her parents would trigger some sort of verbal response, but it's not happening.

'So, are you having a good time with Granny, guys?' Jared asks.

He's met with a wall of silence. Magda leans forward.

'Tell Daddy what you've been up to,' she says. 'They've both been really busy, haven't you?'

There's still no response from either twin and the atmosphere is becoming more and more uncomfortable. Magda is mystified. Will and Desi seemed very excited about speaking to their parents when they were on the walk home from church, but their mutinous expressions make it very clear they don't want to chat. She's assumed their anger at being left behind was only directed at herself, but it looks very much as if they're just as cross with their mum and dad.

Annika makes a sterling attempt at conversation next, telling the children about the show they're performing in and how there hasn't been a dry eye in the house when she sings her main song. They're obviously unimpressed, and Magda starts to feel desperate. She doesn't want Jared and Annika to think she's somehow turned their children against them by blaming them for this situation.

'Well, I think these two are just tired out,' she says brightly. 'It's a hectic time for them in school, all the play practices and so on . . .'

She sees the look on Annika's face and feels like kicking herself. Her daughter-in-law probably thinks she's making another dig at them for not being here for such an important event in the school calendar. Oh, hell.

'I need a wee,' says Will loudly. 'Can we go now?'

'Aren't you going to blow Mummy and Daddy a kiss before we go for our breakfast?' Annika says, shooting an agonized look at Jared as Will tries to stand on his head on the sofa.

'See yah. Wouldn't wanna be yah,' shouts Will rudely and gallops from the room. Desi follows without a backward glance, the teddy under her arm.

'Oh, I'm sorry. I don't know where he got that from,' says Magda, trying not to giggle. 'They've been so well behaved all morning at Sunday School too.'

'Well, that explains it. Brainwashing again, Mum,' Jared retorts.

Magda takes a deep breath. The last thing she wants is a huge fall-out with Jared, but it had slipped her mind that his religious views are, to put it kindly, flexible. Sometimes he's happy for family traditions to be upheld, but on other occasions he's been positively anti-Church. Clearly being woken up early, having no breakfast yet and then seeing both his children disappear without a goodbye, is making him veer towards the second opinion.

'It's nearly Christmas, Jared,' she says mildly. 'They love the carols and the decorations . . . and . . . and everything,' she ends feebly, inwardly berating herself for not standing up more strongly for her own views. As a defence of the Christian religion this leaves a lot to be desired, and Hope would be disappointed in her, but there's an ocean between them and the peace needs to be kept.

'I know all that,' Jared says. 'Sorry to be tetchy, Mum. I guess it's just that we miss them even more than we thought we would. Roll on mid-January.'

Thankfully, they manage to end on fairly amicable terms, and Magda heaves a sigh of relief as she clicks off the call. She goes over to the cupboard on the wall as Den and Blondie come back in. 'In this house, we always have a glass of port when we start to decorate the tree,' she says. 'And we eat crisps and olives and cheese straws and stuff while we're doing it. Let the fun commence!'

19

The roast beef dinner is a huge success, although even with Hope's fail-safe recipe, the Yorkshire puddings are somewhat flatter than Magda would have liked. Fliss had resisted her offers of help to begin with but soon gave in when Den said he'd like to join in too. She'd winked in a most embarrassing way at Magda and made herself scarce, taking the twins off to watch TV in front of the fire.

'I told you before we went in the other room that the oven wasn't hot enough, but you wouldn't wait,' says Fliss. 'You've always been impatient, Mags.'

Magda doesn't say anything. There's no point in ruining what's been a mainly peaceful day.

Will takes the last Yorkshire pudding to mop up his gravy. 'These ones aren't zackly like GG used to make but they still taste nice, Granny. Can we finish decorating the tree next?' he asks.

'That'll have to wait until later, we've got other work to do,' says Magda, thinking longingly of the days before Jared and Annika went away, when she would make her excuses and slope off for a nap at this point on a Sunday.

'Is it time to make the Christmas puddings then?' Den asked. 'I'm ready for the master class.'

Fliss looks shattered now. She groans at Den's words but

doesn't object when Magda gives in and starts lining up the basins and Will and Desi rummage in the spice rack.

'Which ones do we need?' Will asks, turning the jars over in his hands. Desi opens the white pepper and sneezes three times. They collapse into giggles as Magda says, 'Just bring them all.'

She can see Hope's recipe book on the shelf out of the corner of her eye. Surely it's moved again. It's definitely sticking out further than it did when she last put it away.

'Have you been looking at Mum's book?' she asks Fliss.

'No, why would I? I know most of her recipes off by heart,' Fliss responds, in a somewhat cold tone.

Once again, Magda bites back an acid reply. There's a time for standing up to Fliss but this isn't it, when they're all flagging. It's not easy, this peace-making lark, especially when any mention of her mum and Fliss's closeness brings on nasty jabs of envy. She reaches for the book and thankfully is immediately soothed by the feeling of cosiness and the delicious scent of cinnamon that greet her as she opens it.

The Christmas pudding ingredients are soon assembled on the kitchen table and Magda dons her mum's favourite apron in honour of the occasion. The feel of the soft, oft-washed cotton under her fingers as she smooths it down is like a hug.

As Magda shows Will and Desi how to weigh out the suet and cut the glacé cherries into halves, Den's mobile on the edge of the table near to Fliss begins to ring and vibrate.

'I hope that's not a work crisis,' he mutters, going over to pick up the phone. He sees the name on the caller display and falters. 'I'd better take this in the other room,' he says.

'I really wanted Mr Archer to do our stories tonight when

we've finished the puddings,' says Will. 'He said he'd borrowed some books from the school library to read to us. Is he going to be a long time?'

Magda and Fliss exchange glances. They've both seen the name of the caller. 'I hope not,' says Magda. 'Let's carry on with our baking, and maybe he'll be back by the time we've finished.'

She puts on some Christmas music, partly to motivate the twins, but also to drown out the sound of a very loud conversation coming from the other side of the hall. Magda's never heard Den raise his voice before. He's not quite shouting, but it's clear he's not at all happy.

'What's that noise? Is it Mr Archer? He sounds cross,' says Will, seeing Magda's furtive attempt to slide nearer to the door. 'He doesn't yell at school.'

'He isn't yelling,' Magda says absently, leaning closer.

Fliss claps her hands. 'Come on, you lot. It's none of our business what's going on in someone's private conversation, is it?'

Just as Will opens his mouth to argue, Den comes back into the room, his expression thunderous.

'I'm really sorry, chaps, but I'm going to have to go,' he says.

'What? Before stories?' Will's face crumples, and Desi goes over to Den and takes him by the hand. She's holding an armful of story books and she offers them to him hopefully.

Den smiles down at her but then his face falls.

'I'd love to read those to you another time, Desi,' he says. 'But right now I need to go home.'

'Well, can Blondie stay here for a sleepover then?' Will's not giving up without a fight.

'Not tonight. I'm sorry,' Den says. The dog comes over to him when he calls her, tail between her legs.

'See, even Blondie's sad,' says Will.

Magda follows Den into the hall, sending the children back to Fliss. 'What on earth's happened?'

He turns to face her and the desolation on his face takes her breath away. 'It's Virginia. She's back,' he says.

'Back? As in . . .?'

'I don't know. It sounds as if she's home for good. She said something about giving us another try.'

'But . . .'

'I know. There's no need to say any more. I'm going to have to talk to her and find out what's going on. Look, I'll be in touch as soon as possible, okay? Thanks for . . . for . . . well, making me so welcome over the past few days.'

Den seems to be about to bend and kiss Magda's cheek but changes his mind at the last minute. Instead, he pats her shoulder and strides off down the hill, Blondie bouncing around his heels. After a few paces, he stops and bends to put her lead on. As he straightens up, he looks back up the street to where Magda is standing in the light of the porch.

'I'll miss you . . . all,' he calls. 'This has been really great.' He turns and heads for the town.

Magda watches him go, her emotions all over the place, swinging between sadness and rage. His words seem oddly final. He surely can't think it's okay to drop everything like that, just because Virginia clicks her fingers. His wife left him without a backward glance, or so it appears, and now here she is again, making demands. It doesn't seem right or fair. If the word in the town is correct, Virginia has long since begun a new, back-to-nature life in the Welsh mountains. It's unreasonable to expect just to waltz straight back into her old world.

What about the twins? What about helping with the

cooking? Fliss is too exhausted to do much. Magda would never have started a task like Christmas pudding-making with Will and Desi so late in the day if she'd known they weren't going to have an extra pair of hands. She goes back into the kitchen to where the others are sitting in a row at the table, looking despondent. Taking a deep breath, Magda calls on her mother's stoicism and energy to get through the next hour without tears or arguments. She plasters a big smile on her face and claps her hands.

'Come on, let's do this!' she cries. 'Turn up the Christmas music, and we'll get chopping and stirring. Did you know that when you're mixing up this sort of pudding, everyone has to make a wish? It has to be a secret though. Start thinking of what you're going to go for. Christmas wishes always come true.'

Too late, she realizes what an extravagant promise this could turn out to be. It's going to be a disaster if the twins wish for their parents to appear or for a helicopter to land in the garden ready to whisk them off to see Father Christmas in Lapland. She hopes fervently that they'll pick something manageable and that Fliss won't wish for a spell to make Magda even sorrier than she already is for neglecting her friend.

As for herself, Magda needs to consider what she'll ask for as she stirs the spicy mixture. Perhaps to make sparkly Christmas fun possible for the children. Or, more selfishly, for the return of Virginia to her haven in the hills. *Purely because we need Den here, to help Fliss and me get the festive spirit going*, she tells herself. *That's absolutely the only reason.*

20

Monday, 18 December

Seven Days Until Christmas

As Mondays go, Magda thinks this one is starting off very badly. Fliss has a hospital appointment, so she'll be out of the loop for most of the day, and there's been no word from Den since his hasty exit.

'Did you really think he'd be able to call us last night?' Fliss asks, hunting around the kitchen for her handbag, when Magda mentions that she hasn't heard from him. 'He's bound to have been a bit . . . well . . . preoccupied.'

'Just a quick text would have been good though,' says Magda, listening with growing dismay to the pounding of small feet upstairs.

'A text such as what? "I'm sorry my wife has come back all of a sudden but I'll still come round as often as I can to do Christmas baking with you and the kids"? As if.'

Magda doesn't deign to answer this. She realizes, too late – again – that her focus should be on her best friend's health and hospital appointments, not on some trivial problem in her own life. Fliss looks nervous, Magda notices now, and is tight-lipped and even paler than usual. Magda knows this appointment could be gruelling. More test results should be handed over today and she'll have a clearer idea of what the future might hold for her, energy and mobility-wise. Unable to think of anything encouraging to say that doesn't sound trite, Magda braves rejection and gives her friend a quick hug, which is reasonably well received, all things considered, then goes to the bottom of the stairs to shout for the twins. 'Could you two please speed up? We're going to be very late.'

'I can only find one shoe. I'll have to go in my trainers,' calls Will. 'And Desi's got a tummy ache.'

'Nice try, but look again. They won't let you in if you're wearing trainers and Desi was perfectly okay when she ate two bowls of cereal. Now *hurry up!*'

Eventually they're on their way to school, having waved Fliss off in a taxi. She's going home to pick up more clothes and then, as the craft shop never opens on Mondays, Laurence is taking her to her appointment. As she hustles the bickering children down the hill, Magda reflects that Fliss and Laurence get on much better now, as friends and business partners, than they did for most of their closer relationship.

As they walk the now-familiar route down the hill, away from Mistletoe Cottage and towards the school, and the twins entertain themselves by having a hopping competition, Magda finds herself wondering whether Fliss will ever settle into a permanent partnership, or even marriage. The idea brings her thoughts uncomfortably back to her own carefully preserved single status. Unexpectedly, an overwhelming feeling of loneliness takes her breath away. She's never had a Laurence-type person in her life, and has always convinced herself that she didn't need one. Maybe she was wrong to push anyone away who showed signs of wanting to get closer.

Magda realizes she's let her mind wander too far. Looking down at her watch she shouts, 'Come on, kids, let's jog the last bit, we can still make it on time if we run,' pulling herself together and grabbing each twin by the hand. They hurtle into the playground just as the bell goes, but as Magda waves Will and Desi off, she sees Den disappearing into the school round the side. He doesn't look back, but he must know she's there. So that's how it's going to be, is it?

Cursing both the unpredictable Virginia and her jelly of a husband for taking her back so readily, Magda stomps back up the hill, wondering how to fill her day. Earlier that morning, Fliss, unable to sleep and hearing Magda moving about before five o'clock with similar problems, decided they needed a distraction, and insisted on showing Magda how to make one of Hope's Christmas cakes. Fliss had directed operations from Hope's rocking chair with the recipe book on her knee, and in the comforting warmth from the Aga with carols playing in the background, the atmosphere seemed almost back to normal as Magda obeyed her mum's orders to the letter. It's a shame the calm of the evening hadn't lasted until this morning, but Magda can't blame Fliss for being stressed about facing the hospital appointment.

The cake is now sitting on the wire rack in the kitchen, and as she enters, Magda can smell the mingled aromas of the dates, sultanas, cherries and spices. Her mouth waters. This one is only half the size of Hope's traditional creations, but they're planning on making a bigger cake with the twins tonight if Fliss feels up to adjudicating. Magda tells herself it's probably her duty to eat a piece for quality control purposes.

Switching the kettle and the radio on, Magda is once again

grateful for the constant cosy temperature of her favourite place in the house. She feels chilled to the bone, both inside and out. This morning's apparent cold shoulder from Den has upset her more than she wants to admit, and the thought of a long day alone is deeply depressing.

What's wrong with me? she asks herself, making coffee and settling in Hope's rocking chair with a substantial slab of fruit cake and a chunk of Cheddar to go with it. *I never used to mind my own company. Mostly, I welcomed it. Am I turning into some kind of pathetic creature who needs a man's approval to function?*

The local radio station is playing its usual morning selection of upbeat Christmas hits from the past, and gradually, as the opening strains of 'Step into Christmas' flood the kitchen, Magda begins to thaw in more ways than one.

Jumping to her feet, she starts to sway to the music, remembering Hope's fondness for this song. It was always a kick-starter for all the festive fun.

As Magda ramps up her dance to take in the whole of the kitchen space, she thinks of her mum and of the recipes she'd loved to swap with her two cousins. They'd all vied with each other for the best food-based Christmas present ideas every year. Ruby's speciality had always been lemon curd. As the song ends and Magda feels her heart pumping energetically, she has a sudden urge to cook. She flicks the radio to Classic FM and stretches up once more to the shelf for her mum's recipe book, flopping into the rocking chair to get her breath back.

Gradually, the combined effects of the more tranquil music and the book work their way into Magda's system, and she feels content for the first time that morning. She drinks her coffee and takes a huge bite of cake. It's not quite up to Hope's standard yet. They left it in the oven for ten minutes too long, Fliss says, having been distracted by the children stirring upstairs. Even so, the combined flavours seem perfectly balanced, so tonight they'll get it spot on.

A rather scary thought creeps into her mind. For now, as she hasn't got Fliss as a safety net, what a great surprise it would be to make something easier to impress her friend with when she returns. She imagines the look on her friend's face if she was to produce something edible all on her own. Holding the book in both hands, she opens it. The zingy scent of lemon rind is the first thing she notices. That's odd. She was just thinking about lemon curd. Flicking through the book, she wonders which section that particular recipe would fit into. It's not in the 'Extra Easy Ideas' part, nor 'Christmas Countdown Made Simple'. Then she remembers that not only was lemon curd produced as gifts, it was the essential filling for one of her mum's 'Squishiest Cakes Ever'.

Magda drains her coffee mug and finds the relevant section and, as expected, there it is. *Aunty Ruby's Lemon Curd*. She reads through the ingredients and instructions with a sinking heart. It sounds much too tricky for someone going solo for the first time. There's a part where it might curdle. Despondent, she's about to close the book and give up when another elusive fragrance catches at her senses. What is it? Cider? Pear drops? Surely not. The smell gradually becomes more potent and at last Magda recognizes the familiar smell of cooking apples, like the ones that flourish every year on the tree in the back garden.

Closing her eyes, Magda pushes away the troubles of the moment and lets her thoughts flow freely. She's sure it can't really be anything to do with the book, it's just her mind playing tricks again, but she has the strongest feeling that her mum still wants to be in touch with her. Perhaps Hope never really went away. As Fliss said, when somebody has a personality so powerful that many of their family and friends remember them often, with smiles and with love, surely some of the pure essence of them is bound to stay around.

As Magda's mind drifts through the years, Christmas memories are at the forefront. She pictures herself as a small child sitting at the long table, waiting for her mum to carve the golden-brown turkey. All around are dishes of roast potatoes, buttered parsnips, sprouts and countless other treats, but the background scent of this memory is coming from a little china dish right in front of Magda. One of her very favourite parts of the meal, golden and deliciously sticky. Apple jam.

Magda opens her eyes, blinks, and turns back to the book. The scent of apples is even more noticeable now, and as she turns the pages it intensifies when she gets to the Extra Easy section. And there is the recipe in her mum's handwriting, with notes to go with it.

Aunty Vera's Apple Jam
(We often have this instead of regular apple sauce – it's a great way of using up some of the fruit from the garden, keeps for ages and it goes well with chicken, turkey, pork, sausage . . . anything, really! It's the easiest thing ever to make.)

Hope has also written an extra line underneath in red. *I made this with Jared after he came home for good, although we did it in a saucepan like Vera showed me. Excellent results. But now I've gone all modern and I use the microwave.* And next to it, she's drawn two linked hearts.

Magda can almost hear her mother's voice now. Not reproachful this time, just reassuring. Jared could do it. If he could do it when he was younger, so can she. She traces the lines of the two hearts with her finger, reminding her that she did the right thing all those years ago in bringing her son home to his granny at last, even if it took a while to get there – and even longer for him to understand the decision. There's no room for regrets that she didn't make the move sooner; this is all about celebrating the now, as her mum had done. *You can do it too,* Magda tells herself again.

She skims through the ingredients. Yes, she's got everything she needs to make the apple jam, and it really does look super-easy. There's still a stash of Hope's empty jam jars in the pantry that Magda's been meaning to recycle but keeps forgetting to deal with. She's got lemons, plenty of sugar, and the last of the cooking apples are stored in the outhouse, wrapped and layered in newspaper.

Suddenly full of energy, Magda fetches her mum's apron from the back of the kitchen door, washes her hands and gets down to work. Thank heavens for the microwave, and for the fact that every step of the way is explained, so she shouldn't be able to fail. Although Hope herself had always been adventurous in her cooking, flinging in extra ingredients or experimenting with flavours, and refusing to weigh anything unless she was making pastry, both of Hope's cousins had been accurate and meticulous in their detailing of their recipes.

As Magda works, sterilizing the jars in the oven and peeling, coring and chopping what seems like far too many apples, she thinks about the three beloved women, Hope, Ruby and Vera.

The bond between them had been unbreakable even though distance meant they didn't see each other as often as they'd have liked. Their boundless strength and positivity links them together in Magda's mind. All of them moved with the times when it came to their kitchens, competing with each other for who had the best gadgets. Neither Ruby nor Vera had ever married, and they'd lived together contentedly in a bungalow in Scarborough until their later years.

When circumstances persuaded them it was time to go into a residential home, the only real regret they'd had was who would inherit their kitchen equipment when their house was cleared. Much of it was still, even now, neatly packed away in boxes at the back of the pantry in Mistletoe Cottage. Until now, she's never had the slightest interest in the contents of the crates, but she imagines the delight of the two old ladies if she was to ring them with the news that she's beginning to discover the fun of baking and using some of their treasures to help her.

Magda presses on with the job in hand. She pictures Fliss's face when she returns to find a row of jars of apple jam all ready for the store cupboard. While the mixture bubbles away in the microwave, Magda gets out her phone and quickly browses classy-looking labels, ordering some that make her think of Hope, with their colourful borders of leaves and fruit.

Decanting the finished product into the jars is the hardest part, but Magda gets away with only one small burn from a splash of boiling jam. The notes in the side margin tell her she should have waited a while before filling the jars. She sighs. Fliss is right, patience has never been one of her strong points. Next time. Other than that, so far, so good, and it's heart-warming to feel as if her mum's still watching out for her, knowing her foibles and guiding her along.

Magda briefly wonders what Hope would think of her efforts as she clears up the incredible amount of mess she's made. It was worth it though. The euphoric feeling of producing something that's edible on her own for the very first time goes a long way to dispelling the gloom of the morning. She places the shining jars in a row on the kitchen windowsill and a shaft of afternoon sunshine makes them glow as if they were filled with nuggets of amber. Getting out her phone, Magda takes a photograph to preserve the triumphant moment of her first independent cooking project, and with no disasters either. She thinks about messaging the photo to Fliss but decides to surprise her later instead. Maybe they'll open some fizz and drink a toast to Magda's new kitchen skills!

Checking her watch, Magda sees it's almost time to head for school. More worryingly, though, she realizes Fliss should have been back by now. As she picks up her phone to send a text, Fliss's name lights up on the screen, calling her.

'Hi,' Magda picks up, still on a high from her baking success and her voice bright. 'I was just thinking about you. Will you be home soon?'

There's a pause and Magda thinks she hears a sob.

'Fliss? Are you okay?' she asks, suddenly afraid.

'No. I had a sort of funny turn. They think I was probably just tired. It's been a bit of a day. Anyway, the doctor's insisting on keeping me in, at least overnight, to run a few more tests. Oh, Mags, I'm so fed up. I thought I was getting my head around the whole MS thing but it's as if I'm taking one step forward and three back. And not only that, I really wanted to crack on with the cakes later.'

Magda swallows hard. On top of her worry about Fliss is

the thought of being alone with the twins again, and there's no Den around to help this time.

'Try not to fret, love. We'll be fine here. You need to rest and get your strength back. Have you got everything you need for tonight?'

'Yes, Laurence has been a star. He went over to mine and fetched some night things and a couple of my old romantic novels because they're so comforting. I'm fine really, I just feel so frustrated. I thought I was moving forward, getting to grips with the thought of dealing with all this in the future.'

'You'll be home very soon,' Magda says, with more confidence than she feels. Having made the mistake of googling Multiple Sclerosis one night when she couldn't sleep, she's now in posses- sion of way too much information. But Fliss is only sixty and otherwise fit and healthy, she tells herself firmly. This is a blip, that's all. And, Magda realizes with a pang, this is the first time in her illness that her best friend has actually come to Magda for comfort and help. It gives her a small thrill deep in her stomach, even despite the circumstances. Perhaps the worst of their own hiccup is over at last. With a friendship this long and strong, nothing should be allowed to get in its way.

Magda says a hasty goodbye, mindful that she has to collect the twins, rings off and sets off at a trot down the hill. Luckily, the sunshine has melted the earlier frost. The gulls are wheeling overhead and the air is fresh and clean. She's just thinking about texting Den and asking if there's any chance she and the twins could take Blondie for a walk, when she remembers with a jolt that Virginia is back. As if her afternoon needed to get worse. And as she knows, the dog is said to be very attached to her wandering mistress, and Virginia will quite likely now be in sole charge of walks.

A deluge of misery almost swamps Magda as she reaches the school gates. She can see Den over at the other side of the playground but he still doesn't look her way, and now Fliss isn't going to be there to talk to tonight. She feels nostalgic already for the past week the three of them have shared. It's been so lovely to have Den and Fliss to chat and laugh with, and already she misses them. She knows it's foolish to miss something that was so brief, but it had felt so special, she can't help it. It feels as if nothing will ever be the same again.

Christmas Day, Fifteen Years Ago

The book on the kitchen worktop is open at the page for lemon curd. Magda knows her mum is planning to make Ruby's recipe and fill a few jars for last-minute Happy New Year gifts for her friends, saving some to make tarts for Jared because he isn't a big fan of mince pies.

'Do you want to give me a hand with this?' she asks Magda, who's sitting on the sofa leafing through a glossy brochure. 'It's a bit fiddly. There's quite a lot of stirring involved and if the phone rings or someone comes to the door, I can't leave it without it spoiling.'

Magda drags her eyes from the magazine, exhaustion making her grumpy. 'What did you say?' she asks, as her mum's words register. Whoever is going to come to the door or even phone? This is the evening of Christmas Day, for goodness' sake, and even at this late hour her mother is still thinking about cooking. Magda's only had two days off so far. She spent yesterday dashing around the town picking up all the last-minute shopping and even now it seems she's not to be allowed to do anything in peace.

'Magda, you were miles away. What are you reading?'

'It's a booklet from Birmingham university. Jared sent off for it. He says it's time to get his act together and do something with his life. He's looking at drama courses.'

'But I thought he was happy with his apprenticeship? Why

178

in heaven's name does he want to go dashing off to the Midlands again? You've hardly been home five minutes.'

'Mum, we've been back here for five years and you know all Jared's ever wanted is to be an actor. You were really proud of him when he took the lead in *The King and I* in the summer.'

'Yes, but that was Am Dram, love. It's not something you'd want to make a career of, is it?'

'It's what he needs to do. I'm not going to stop him. He can sing, he can act . . . somebody has to make it. Why not Jared?'

'Oh Mags, think of the disappointments in store for him. He's going to have to deal with being knocked back time and time again, surely? Why can't he just settle down here, meet a nice girl and have a family? He wouldn't even need to move out – this house is plenty big enough for us all.'

Jared comes into the kitchen at this moment and Magda fixes her mother with a glare, shaking her head slightly. Hope opens her mouth but then closes it again.

'Oh Gran, you're not still at the cooker, are you?' Jared exclaims. 'It's Christmas. There's a great film on in ten minutes. I wanted us all to watch it in front of the fire and have coffee and some of that weird cherry liqueur Fliss bought you.'

'I've just got to finish up here, love. I can't leave the lemon curd half made. If I had some help I'd be done in time for the film.'

Magda and Jared exchange glances. He goes to wash his hands and she heads for the kettle to make coffee. They know their roles well by now.

'I'm so glad you came home,' Magda hears her mum say to Jared as he lines up the jars. You love it here at Mistletoe Cottage, don't you? I couldn't manage without your help in the kitchen.'

Jared gives his gran a brief hug but doesn't answer the pointed questions, instead getting on with the job in hand. Magda has no doubt he'll follow his own path and nothing will get in his way. He's single-minded. Just like his father.

21

The twins are disgruntled when they come home to find that not only is Fliss missing, but Blondie and Den won't be making an appearance either.

'But what will we have for our tea?' says Will piteously.

'We didn't starve before we had company, did we?' says Magda, who has been wondering that same thing herself. 'What would you like?'

Will and Desi put their heads close together and Magda can hear a low murmuring, but no words are clear. They've been able to do this even before they could talk properly. After a few moments, Will says, 'Jacket potatoes and baked beans with cheese on top, please. And can we finish the tree now?'

Magda thanks her lucky stars they didn't say something more complicated. They put the potatoes in the Aga to cook and go into the hall. She opens the suitcase that contains the last of the decorations and the three of them make short work of adding the final touches. Magda tries to make sure she's hanging the most fragile of the old ornaments high enough for safety, while Will and Desi seem happy to place the little wooden angels and stars further down.

'How was your day?' asks Magda as they work, feeling as if she's interviewing her two youngest relations for a job.

Desi pulls a face and Will shrugs.

'That good, eh? What went wrong?'

'Everyone was grumpy,' says Will. 'We got kept in at snack time because it rained a bit and as soon as our break was finished, the sun came out. Then Lucy told the teacher I'd pushed Stanley into the sandpit.'

'And did you?'

'Yes.'

'Erm . . . why?' Magda already feels out of her depth in this conversation. She wishes she'd offered to go and fetch fish and chips.

'He said I'd only been picked to be Joseph because Desi's going to be Mary. It's not true. They chose me because I can sing really loudly. Like Mum and Dad,' he says proudly.

'So that's when you pushed him?'

'No . . . it was a little while after that.'

Magda reaches up to hang a particularly delicate glass bauble on one of the top branches, wondering how to proceed with this. Her own equilibrium feels as fragile as the iridescent bauble. Jared and Annika have always dealt with school issues without telling her up until now. This situation is getting worse by the minute.

'And what made you do it, then?' she says. 'Push him, I mean.'

Will and Desi send each other a meaningful look, in which a lot seems to be being said without words. After a few seconds, she nods and he carries on.

'Stanley said our mum and dad don't love us any more. If they did, they wouldn't go away for Christmas.'

Before Magda can think of an answer, Desi clears her throat and utters one word. 'Santa.'

'Oh yes, and he said there's no Father Christmas, and it's

your mum and dad that get the presents, so this year, we . . . we won't . . .'

At that, both twins sit down on the floor and burst into tears, seemingly simultaneously. Magda is kneeling between them in an instant, an arm around each. They sob into her shoulders while she fights the rage that's making her want to go straight round to Stanley's house and give him and his parents a very large piece of her mind.

'It's okay, my pigeons,' she murmurs. 'What does Stanley know? He's younger than you and he's probably just jealous because your mummy and daddy are going to be super-famous.'

'Are they? Will they be in the movies one day?' Will says, between sniffs.

'Quite probably,' Magda says, hoping this is true or she's going to lose all her street cred. 'They're very talented, and sometimes that makes people say nasty things. I bet it happens to all the stars. Did you get into trouble?'

'Only a bit, because he punched me in the tummy after that, so he was told off more,' says Will, cheering up.

'I wonder why they haven't rung from school to tell me about this,' says Magda, half to herself.

'Oh, that's because Mr Archer came along when the teacher was telling us why we should be kind to each other all the time and he said he was going to phone you, so she was to leave it with him.'

As Will finishes speaking, Magda's mobile in the pocket of her cardigan starts to ring with that exact incoming call. She gives the children a final hug, asks them to put the remaining few decorations on the tree and goes into the kitchen to answer it.

'Den? I hear there have been problems today?' she says, trying to make her voice sound even more stern than she feels.

'I'm so sorry not to have rung before, Magda,' his voice is formal, almost cold, and Magda notices sadly that he's deliberately chosen to call her by her full name. 'I was called into a meeting just after sandpit-gate happened and then there were parents waiting to see me after school. But I guess the kids have filled you in. Well, Will probably has, anyway.'

The sound of his voice produces so many mixed feelings in Magda that she can hardly breathe. It's a heady mixture of anger at being cold-shouldered in the playground, disappointment that he seems to have let Virginia saunter back as if nothing's happened and sadness that she's not going to have the warmth and humour of him to help her any more.

'So, is it all sorted now?' Den continues, before Magda has a chance to respond, and sounding as if he's about to ring off. His attitude is way too flippant, in Magda's opinion. Through the open doorway she can see that the twins are busy with the decorations but still hiccupping, their crying only just abating properly.

'I was quite surprised I didn't hear anything from the school sooner,' she says. *Two can play at this game of formality*, she thinks. 'It sounds serious to me.'

'Well, anything that upsets one of our children is serious,' Den says. 'But I don't think a bit of a scuffle is too much cause for alarm, do you?'

'Yes, I do, actually. Did you hear what Stanley said to Will?'

'Erm . . .' Den sounds on the back foot now. 'I was just told that they'd had a scrap and made friends afterwards.'

Magda recounts the conversation, as told by Will. 'I've never had any cause to doubt his truthfulness,' she says stiffly. 'I know he's been . . . livelier than usual since his parents went away, but surely this isn't acceptable. He was provoked.'

There's a sharp intake of breath from Den. His tone has softened again when he next speaks. 'Ah. Right. I can see I only got part of the story. I'm so sorry. I'll get on to this first thing tomorrow. You're right, that's bang out of order. I'll talk to them both and clear the air, then speak to Stanley's mum and dad. Leave it with me, I promise I'll follow it up as soon as I can.'

Magda feels her fury dwindling in the face of his apology. 'It's not like you to leave something half investigated,' she says quietly. 'I know that.'

Den doesn't answer for a second or two, and Magda takes the opportunity to peep into the hall, where the twins are still quite happily adding the final touches to the lower branches of the tree. At last Den says, so quietly that she has to strain to hear, 'I've been bogged down with all this stuff with Virginia. Look, can we talk?'

'Not at the moment. I've got tea for the kids to organize, a fruit cake to make and Fliss has been kept in hospital so I'm on my own tonight.'

'No, I didn't mean right now. Oh, is Fliss ill? She mentioned an appointment. I hope she's okay.'

'It's a bit complicated. I expect she'll explain when she sees you. Whenever that is.'

Magda hears barking in the background and a high voice in the distance shrieking, 'Not upstairs, my sweetie. Blondie! Come back here.'

'I'm going to have to go anyway, it seems,' Den says. 'Apparently I've let the dog run wild while she's been away and the house is a tip.'

'And is that true?'

'No, and no, but that's my problem. Let's see if we can grab half an hour in the morning after I've spoken to Will and Stanley. How does that sound?'

If she's honest, that sounds as if it might be the high point of her day tomorrow, but she doesn't want to give him the satisfaction of knowing that, not when he's been so distant. Instead, she agrees unenthusiastically and disconnects. At least the jacket potatoes smell good, and grating cheese and heating up beans is well within her culinary scope.

'Come on, kids, lets organize some yummy food,' she calls. 'And afterwards, maybe you can both help me make a fruit cake.'

They make short work of the potatoes and soon have the table loaded with cake ingredients.

'Is it okay to do this without Aunty Fliss to watch us?' Will says.

'Of course it is. We'll be fine.' Magda's voice is giving off more confidence than she feels, but when Desi hands her the recipe book and she once again opens it at the festive section, a wonderful sense of calm comes over her.

'GG's book always makes you smile,' says Will, surreptitiously eating three glacé cherries. Desi nudges him and he passes her the same number. Magda is touched that he's noticed.

'Hey, stop that,' she says, but without much conviction. 'There won't be enough for the cake if you aren't careful,' she adds, leaning closer to read her mum's detailed instructions. She starts to laugh as she does so. 'Look at this. You must both take after your daddy. There's an extra note at the side here. *When making this cake with children in the room, beware of cherry thieves.*'

The twins giggle. 'Maybe she meant you, not Dad,' says Will. 'You were her little girl, weren't you?'

Magda thinks back. It's true that she *had* still joined in the baking when she was their age. It was only later that she'd rebelled. Either way, the book seems as if it's been waiting in the wings, ready to ease her through this process of getting back on track. It always seems to know the right thing to say at the right time.

The baking session with the twins, as ever, is noisy, messy and completely wonderful. They weigh and measure, stir and taste until Hope's best non-stick tin is filled with the rich, fruity cake mixture.

The baking goes well, and this time Magda puts the kitchen timer on so there's no danger of over-cooking.

She picks up her mum's recipe book to slip it back on the shelf and as she does so, she notices an extra note scribbled at the bottom of the list of cake ingredients.

When life's getting you down, tell yourself you're doing a fine job and have some cake. Nothing will ever seem so bad after that.

Magda nods to herself, puts the book away and fetches out the cake tin with the remains of the smaller cake in it.

'It's time for a pit stop, kids,' she says. 'We deserve a reward, because, you know what? We three are absolutely great.'

22

'Did you used to do this with our daddy? Baking, I mean,' Will asks, as they munch fruit cake and wait for the new one to be ready.

Magda frowns. She'd tried, she really had, but Jared had always seemed to sense her reluctance to reduce their tiny kitchen to chaos. It was partly her lack of skills, although Magda knows Hope had worked hard to get her interested as a child, making fairy cakes, gingerbread men and all sorts of other treats with her. The other problem with her son had been that there never seemed quite enough time for messy activities, so they'd tended to stick to Lego modelling and making things out of junk, that required a bit less clearing up afterwards.

'Not so much,' she admits, and the children frown at her.

'Why not?' Will asks.

'We did other things instead. Your dad liked to go to the park. He was mad on the slide. He used to scare me with the way he came down so fast and then shot off the end. We didn't have a garden like you two have here, so I had to find ways for him to burn off his energy. Anyway, let's tidy ourselves up a bit while the cake cooks. It's nearly time for you to speak to your mum and dad.'

Jared and Annika FaceTime the children tonight bang on cue, and to Magda's relief, this time both of the children are full of smiles. Desi still won't speak but Will is bursting with questions about Jared's daredevil days. Afterwards, Magda manages a quick call to Fliss, who seems in good spirits, although still looking shattered, even through the phone's low-resolution camera.

'Might be in here another day,' she says. 'They're giving me steroids. Are you coping?'

'We made more cake!' Will shouts. 'It smells great.'

The look on Fliss's face when Magda turns the phone screen so Fliss can see the successful golden-brown cake sitting proudly on the kitchen table makes all the effort worthwhile. If even Fliss is impressed, she must have done a good job. The twins are also triumphant.

Later, when Will and Desi are safely bathed and in bed and the kitchen has been restored to its usual state of almost-tidy, Magda lights the fire in the living room and stretches out on the squishy sofa with a glass of chilled white wine. She thinks she's deserved it today.

Taking a hefty sip, she reaches for her laptop. It's been a couple of days since she checked her emails and there are quite a few waiting to be read, but one catches her eye immediately. It's from Jared, sent only a few minutes ago. Why does he need to message her when they've only just got off the phone? The subject is *Unexpected Development*. She clicks to open it, suddenly alarmed.

Hello Mum.

    It was great to see the offspring looking so cheerful tonight. You're obviously doing a fantastic job.

Hmmm, thinks Magda. *Buttering me up. Why?*

> *This is a difficult email to write and I've been struggling
> with how to put it. I hardly know where to start. This is the
> third time I've drafted it out tonight but it's got to be done,
> Mum. Here goes. Try not to be angry with me.*
>
> *Here's the thing. I didn't tell you that I've been under-
> studying the lead actor/singer, Joshua McIntyre, in the
> show this week. Well, three days ago, I had to step into
> Josh's shoes at the last minute when he went down with a
> stomach bug. This meant that my name went out in the
> publicity material on the radio, there was a TV promo about
> the cast having to be so versatile and know several
> different parts, and I was given top billing on the boards
> outside the theatre.*

Magda's mind is reeling. Her son, headlining on Broadway!
How she wishes she'd known sooner; she wants to shout it from
the rooftops. Fliss will be so proud too, and the twins will no
doubt be bursting with excitement when she explains how important this is. For now, she reads on.

> *That's not my interesting development, by the way,
> although it is pretty cool, eh?*
>
> *No, the big news is that after the show last night, we
> were in our dressing room and there was a visitor. We get
> people dropping in all the time to say hello, they're a very
> hospitable lot here, so I wasn't surprised. But when I found
> out who the man was, I was absolutely gobsmacked. He
> introduced himself as Doctor Giovanni Brocato.*

To say this is a shock would be a huge understatement. Magda feels as if her blood has turned to ice and all her breath has been stolen. She gasps and puts both hands over her face, almost letting the laptop crash to the floor. Dizzy with the blow, it's a while before she can steady herself enough to carry on reading. A fortifying gulp of wine helps, and the crackle of a log shifting further into the fire calms her a little. Giovanni Brocato, in touch with Jared. It's her worst fear come to life. She'd known all along it was a mistake for Jared to go to New York.

You'll know where this is heading, of course.

Magda is almost too scared to read on, dreading the words that might appear in the next line.

He told me he's my father.

Magda is trembling now. As soon as Jared had mentioned going to New York, the old fear had reared its head. When Giovanni, soon after that first abandonment at Christmas, had left her for good to go home to the big city, Magda had hoped desperately for a letter or a phone call to say he'd made a mistake and wanted to change his mind and come back. Of course, that was never going to happen. In one last rushed conversation, Magda had learned that Giovanni had been unofficially engaged to the daughter of friends of his parents for years. He'd never intended to stay in England for longer than his two-year sabbatical and now he was cutting even that time short. Magda and Jared were complications he hadn't planned for. There wasn't even a proper goodbye. Giovanni had left Leicester at dawn the very next day without another word.

Fliss's words come back to Magda, repeated every now and

again in different ways. 'What has that apology for a human being ever done for you? He's a rubbish father, he was unfaithful when you were with him, he's the biggest flirt ever, he doesn't care about you or Jared,' and so on and so forth. Magda had listened and largely ignored her, even defending Giovanni when she couldn't stand it any longer. Fliss meant well. Her protective instinct often went into overdrive. But even so, it was hard for Magda to accept that she'd, albeit unintentionally, made such a phenomenally bad choice of father for her child.

She rubs her eyes and tries to think what this is going to mean. It had been difficult not to worry that it might happen, but with the size of New York and the fact that she didn't even know if Giovanni was still there, she'd finally been able to push the dread away. It's back now, of course. She forces herself to read to the end of Jared's email.

I was so stunned I couldn't take it in to begin with. It feels as though there's too much to say for one email, so I'll go now and let you have a think about this. I hope you don't mind, but I gave him your email address. He seems to have things to get off his chest, which I guess is not surprising.

Let me know how it goes if he does get in touch, Mum. I'm so sorry if all this has made you sad or angry (or both) but I can't help feeling glad it's all out in the open at last.

Love, Jared x

Reading and re-reading the email doesn't help: Magda is in a turmoil, her head pounding. She finishes her wine and goes into the kitchen on shaking legs to get a refill. As she returns to the fireside, the impact of the last part of Jared's email hits her. Giovanni has her contact details. What was her son thinking? Hardly daring to look, she picks up the laptop and goes back into her emails. And there it is, just below Jared's.

Subject: Long Time No See

Magda's heart is in her mouth. She opens it with a sense of foreboding, but she knows she has to read it.

My dear Magda,

   Where to begin? I saw our wonderful son perform on Broadway today. What a line to be able to write! I had no idea he was in New York, of course, but when I heard his name on the radio and looked him up online, I rushed straight to buy tickets. I couldn't help myself. It's clear what a success he's about to become. He and his beautiful wife were stunning in the musical, and it's a shame you couldn't get out here to see him yourself. I know he'd have loved you to witness his triumph, but at least one of us was there to represent his parents and to be proud of our boy.

   He tells me I'm now a grandfather of two theatrically named children. William for Mr Shakespeare and Desdemona after one of my favourite heroines of the bard. Perfect.

Our son? Our boy? Really? He's sorry I couldn't be there to see him? Giovanni had left them without a backward glance when Jared was much too small to even remember him. When he'd returned after that first Christmas away from her, Magda had forgiven him everything, so happy was she to have him home. But of course, Leicester never was Giovanni's home. It hadn't taken long for his mother and the girl who turned out to be his fiancée to pull the strings that would drag him back to New York for good. Those brief few weeks before he left again had been wonderful, which made the pain of his final departure so much worse. Magda can't bear to think about the depths of her misery when reality stepped in. Giovanni had really left her, and this time he wasn't coming back.

How dare he say all this now? He was always full of his own importance, but this feels like a step too far, even for him. Nevertheless, she takes a deep breath and carries on reading.

I guess this will have come as a shock to you. It did to me too. But Magda, isn't this a sign that I should get to know Jared? I have never stopped feeling guilty at having left you both.

Huh. *Not so guilty that you tried to keep in touch or help us out when we were stony broke,* thinks Magda. Or only that once anyway, and very late in the day. She bats away the thought that she did have one chance to let him back in, and worse, sometimes she wonders whether she should have done so, whether her life would have been easier as a result.

Now, though, an exhilarating rage is taking over from the initial numbness of this awful surprise. He can't be allowed to get away with emailing in this chatty, all-mates-together way about *our son*, as if the thirty-five years since he left have never happened. Giovanni was nowhere to be seen when Jared was teething, and waking every hour on the hour night after night. He was absent when the rent was in arrears, and all through the time when finding reliable childcare while Magda worked became harder and harder. Jared's father knows nothing of the little boy who grew into this talented, dynamic man. He has no right to step back into their lives now. No right at all.

I've suggested to Jared that when he's home, I could come over to England and spend some time with you all. I think it would be good for us. Apparently you're still single? My wife, Chantelle, sadly passed away earlier this year. I have three daughters aged thirty-two, thirty and twenty-five, but they all have their own lives now, and none of them as yet have given me any grandchildren. I would so love to meet William and Desdemona and to catch up with you again. We always got on so well, didn't we, Magda? Britain in the spring will be magical and perhaps it's time for us to get to know each other all over again. How does that sound?

Yours, waiting for a reply with great anticipation,

Dr Gio x

How does that sound? To be frank, Giovanni, it's my worst nightmare come true, thinks Magda, knocking back the remains of her second glass of wine. The fury that's built up as she's been reading threatens to swamp her, and she lies down on the sofa to try and control it. How dare he? And to use the old nickname too, as if they were still together.

'Yes, we got on well, Giovanni,' she says out loud. 'That is until the lovely Chantelle reeled you back in.' *Just like Virginia has done with Den,* a small voice in her head taunts.

'And you can think again if you're planning some sort of step-back-in-time move,' she continues, punching a handy cushion so hard that a dust cloud rises and makes her sneeze. 'I'll tell you the moment you can come back into my life. When hell freezes over, that's when.'

She heads to the fridge for more wine. This is definitely not a stopping-at-two-glasses kind of night.

23

Tuesday, 19 December

Six Days Until Christmas

Magda wakes with the sort of crushing headache that would send you right back to bed if you had the luxury of being a free agent. Instead, she shuffles to the bathroom, cleans her teeth, splashes her face with water in the hope of some sort of recovery, and totters downstairs.

There's only one thing for it, she tells herself sternly. Bacon sandwiches. Ignoring the churning of her stomach, she makes tea, swallows two painkillers, and sets a frying pan on the hotplate. The clang of metal on cast iron makes her head pound even more but she perseveres, thanking the god of hangovers for the joy of a Calor Gas-fired Aga and not something along the lines of the ancient range Hope grew up with. If she'd had to stoke and cajole the beast to make it function, Magda thinks she'd have definitely given up the ghost before hot drinks were possible.

Gradually, as warmth seeps into her tired body and the bacon begins to sizzle, Magda comes back to life. She sips her tea and listens to the clattering of footsteps above. The twins will be down here soon demanding her attention, food, clean shirts, last-minute spelling practice and the million and one other things that are now part of her mornings. She'd thought she had actually been starting to get the hang of the full-time granny lark, but then this bolt from the blue had to come and derail her completely.

There's an ominous trickling noise coming from above now. Remembering the toilet incident with horror, Magda stumbles upstairs, an unfamiliar sickly scent going a step further to let her know that something's badly wrong, and she shouldn't really be able to smell roses at this point.

'What on earth are you doing?' she croaks, going into the bathroom. The sink is full to overflowing and the water slopping over the top is a garish shade of purple.

'Desi wanted to make perfume for Mum ready when she comes home. And I'm helping,' says Will cheerfully, not meeting Magda's eye.

'But . . . what are you using?'

'Just some stuff we found in your cupboard.'

Magda sees the discarded packets of bath crystals and eau de toilette. She reaches down. 'Will, Desi, these were very expensive presents from your mum and dad. I was saving them for a special occasion.'

'But they stink,' says Will. Desi holds her nose and giggles wildly.

'They're not supposed to be all mixed together.' Magda feels much too fragile to lose her temper, and anyway, the damage is done. She pulls out the plug to ferocious screams from the twins. 'Now, if you two don't hurry up and get yourselves downstairs there'll be no . . .'

Magda wracks her befuddled brain for a suitable punishment, but Will helps her out.

'Don't say it!' he yells, starting to cry. Desi is in tears too. They fling their damp arms around her waist.

'Don't say what?' Mystified, she pats their heads automatically.

'We want to bake again tonight. We want to do it every night. You mustn't stop us, it's not fair.'

This last word comes out as a wail. Magda is somewhat shocked to hear this. She knew the twins were enjoying their baking evenings, but she hadn't realized they were so attached to them. Now, she finds herself too touched to be angry any more. They *want* to cook with her, she realizes, with a pang. She's done it! She's somehow managed to make it fun!

'Of course I won't stop. I love baking with you,' she says affectionately. The years of feeling as if she was getting it wrong with Jared at last begin to fade into insignificance as she looks down at the two earnest, tear-stained faces. 'Come on, get a move on. We need to find today's recipe. Probably something to cheer up poor Fliss when she gets home, what do you think?'

'That's a nice smell,' shouts Will, bursting into the kitchen ten minutes later, now fully dressed and de-perfumed and ready for school. 'Are we having a fry-up? Is it Saturday? Dad always makes one on Saturdays.' Magda nearly left the bacon to burn as she'd dashed upstairs, but thankfully she'd made it back down just in time.

'Shhhh,' she says desperately. 'Less noise, please. I'm just making bacon butties. Sit at the table and you can have one.'

'Can you do that?' He sounds incredulous, and Magda, not for the first time, wishes she hadn't given herself this sad reputation of Non-Cooking-Granny.

'Yes, I can just about manage it, I think,' she snaps, patience running thin. 'And *please* could you be a little bit quieter, Will?'

'With red sauce?' he says, at a slightly lower volume.

'Naturally. Where's your sister?'

Desi comes into the room, dressed in the full costume of Mary, mother of Jesus.

'Why . . . what . . .?' Magda stutters, then remembers that the children had both brought their play outfits home to be ironed ready for the big performance on the last day of term. 'But you can't wear that for breakfast, darling,' she says. 'You'll get ketchup on it.'

Her granddaughter's eyes fill with tears again. It's incredible how one small child can contain so much water, Magda thinks as she passes Desi a tissue. She's running low on sympathy this morning.

Will unexpectedly reaches out to pat Magda's arm. She looks over at him and, for the first time, actually sees him as an ally. They exchange glances and he nudges Desi.

'It's gonna ruin everything if you get ketchup on Mary's dress or her white head thing,' he says. 'They hadn't invented tomato sauce when Baby Jesus was born.'

Desi looks doubtful and Magda can understand why. A world without red sauce for your bacon butty seems unimaginable for her, too. After a moment, her granddaughter nods and climbs down from the table and potters out of the kitchen. Will grins at Magda and they high-five. When Desi comes back, her sandwich is waiting and she's wearing a tutu over her pyjama top, and wellies.

It's a small victory, but it cheers Magda up considerably. Her headache begins to subside as they eat, and she shelves all thoughts of absent fathers crawling out of the woodwork to be dealt with later.

* * *

At the school gates, Den waves to her as soon as he spots them arrive and leads her to his office, a big improvement on the shifty avoidance of the past two days. He puts his Do Not Disturb notice on the door and closes it firmly, blotting out the hustle and bustle of the morning. Magda sits down and watches as Den makes drinks.

'You can't already have talked to Stanley, and Will's only just arrived. I thought we were going to discuss their fight?' she says.

'We need to do that later, but there's something much more important. This definitely isn't the place for the sort of conversation I want to have with you, but if we don't talk now, who knows when else we'll have the chance?' He hands her a mug of coffee. 'First, I need to apologize.'

'Yes, you do,' Magda answers confidently, although she's somewhat shocked to hear him say this straight away. 'That'd be a good start, for sure. I thought we were friends. Sliding off every time you see me isn't the way friends act, is it?'

'No. But that's just it.'

'Just what?' The headache's looming again, and Magda starts to feel the need to shake him. 'Get on with it, Den,' she says wearily. 'I'm not feeling so great today.'

He looks taken aback at her abrupt tone, but perseveres. 'Right. I'm sorry. Truth be told, I was avoiding you.' *Yes, I'd noticed*, Magda thinks. 'I really wanted to talk to you, but Virginia coming back has complicated everything.'

'Has it? Why?' Magda feels the need to make him work at this. The cold-shouldering hurt, and she's not ready to forgive him without a fight.

'Because . . . oh, I know she hadn't been gone long and you and I, we were only just . . . baking . . . but . . .' He pauses, as though unsure where to go next.

Magda waits and drinks her coffee. Let him sweat and burble.

'Okay, I'm going to be honest with you.'

'Excellent.'

He pulls a face. 'Oh Mags, stop being such an ice queen. I'm trying to tell you how things are with Virginia and me. Although, to be fair, I don't really know that myself.'

'But why do you need to explain your marriage to me?'

Den scratches his head. 'Well . . . um . . . because I've never had a female friend like you. I was starting to feel as if I could tell you anything.'

Magda's shoulders slump. For once, she feels the full weight of her sixty years. Den's ten years younger than her. *Of course* he just sees her as a mate, that's all. She can't believe she had really begun to let herself imagine anything else.

'Go on. Always here to listen,' she says, beaming at him rather too brightly, desperately trying to pretend there's nothing wrong with what he's just said.

He blinks, but carries on. 'Well, to be honest with you, when Virginia left, I was so relieved I could have danced. I thought everything was starting to make sense at last. The long silences between us. Her extended trips to see these mysterious friends in Wales. The way she gradually moved into the guest bedroom because she said her habit of grinding her teeth in her sleep must be disturbing me. It was, of course, but I hadn't said anything. And then she bought herself a fancy new mattress and some muslin drapes for the spare room window and set herself up with a new radio in there. She even put a bolt on the door.'

Magda nods enthusiastically, encouraging him to continue. 'I just thought that maybe this was how marriages get if you're in it for the long haul. We've had a good life, two great sons. So when she left, really left, it was a shock, but I definitely wasn't heartbroken. We'd been friends but not . . . not *lovers*, for a long time.'

Magda feels her cheeks burning. 'Why are you saying all this to me, Den? I've got a horrible feeling it comes under the heading of "way too much information".'

'It's just that . . . you seemed to like me. I started to feel human again. We did the cooking together, we made each other laugh. It was all so different to how things had been with Virginia. I'd almost forgotten it was possible to have fun like that.'

Magda looks at Den properly at last. His soulful green eyes are full of passion and she has a sudden longing to reach out and smooth his ruffled hair, to put her arms around him and feel his warmth, his strength.

Stop this, she tells herself. *The last thing you need is a man in your life. And Virginia's still here. Den sees you as a friend. This isn't ever going to be more than friendship. It can't be.*

'But she's home again now, so all this is pointless,' Magda says briskly. 'And anyway, even if she hadn't reappeared, my life's about to get way more complicated.'

Magda pauses. She doesn't want to say the next words because when they're out there, the whole nightmare will become even more real, but it's got to be said. She takes a deep breath. 'Jared's father has been in touch.'

She hadn't meant to be quite so blunt, and the effect on Den is electric. 'He's . . . what?'

'I think you heard me perfectly well. The man who fathered my son and left us when he was a baby has crawled out of the woodwork and made contact with Jared at the theatre. It seems as though he finally wants to get involved. It's a long story.'

'Oh Mags, what a horrible shock for you. It must have been the last thing you expected, not only for Jared to meet his father at last, but for the man to be somebody who might actually want to be in his son's life.'

'That's exactly it.' The relief of telling someone and having her fears understood so quickly is beginning to overshadow her bitterness at Den's sudden disappearance from her life. But this still is no time to weaken. 'But almost worse than that is that he . . . Jared's father . . . wants to reconnect with *me* too. Look, Den, you and me being friends . . . it's been great.'

'But that sounds as if it's in the past.' Den finishes her sentence before she has a chance to.

'It is. You need to sort things out with your wife once and for all, decide what's best for both of you and not just for Virginia. Let's face it, she's not going to want you coming round to do baking with me and the kids, is she? And I've got to face up to the fact that Giovanni coming back into my life was always a possibility, and now it's happened, it needs dealing with. So we'll be friends, always that, I hope. Give me a ring when you've had the chat with Will and Stanley.'

Before Den can stop her, Magda's out of the room and heading down the corridor. She nods to the receptionist at the front desk, who gives her a quizzical look but doesn't comment on her flushed cheeks, and is soon on her way home, glad of the winter chill and a few flakes of snow to cool her whirling thoughts.

The house welcomes her home and she sinks into her mother's rocking chair, hardly realizing until she's sitting down that she's instinctively reached for Hope's recipe book. With it in her hands, she leans back in the chair and feels the familiar wave of comfort that the book always gives her. Amazement at the scene that's just unfolded in Den's office mingles with sudden grief that the one person she wants to pour out her troubles to will never be here again. 'Oh, Mum,' Magda whispers. 'What am I going to do now?'

The book sits in her lap and then there's a faint rustling as the pages open. Magda looks down at the section revealed. It's the festive one again. Christmas shortbread. She remembers how Hope had loved to make up numerous tins of her short-bread at this time of year. She frosted the biscuits with a swirl of snowy icing and added tiny sprigs of fake holly and, of course, the trademark mistletoe. Her mum has written in the margin of this recipe.

Christmas is for sharing. My family love food, and food is on a par with love in this house. When someone eats the buttery, melting shortbread I've made for them, they know they're in my thoughts. At that moment, we're connecting. Whoever's reading this, and I can't help hoping it's my darling Magda, take note . . . there are many different ways of sharing and connecting. Sometimes you have to just go with your instincts and wait until the time is right.

Magda frowns. Her mum always seems to be able to get straight to the point. It's as if she has some secret link to Magda's troubled thoughts and insecurities. Magda shakes her head at her own silly thoughts, putting them down to tiredness and a general feeling of anxiety about where her life is going. She doesn't want to have any sort of connection with Giovanni

Coming Home to Mistletoe Cottage

and she won't let it happen if she can avoid it. What she *is* prepared to admit to herself is that she *does* want to stay connected with Den, in whatever form that takes. His marriage has been long and she assumes it's largely been good. He and Virginia need to be left alone to sort themselves out, so if Magda's only going to be friends with Den on a strictly impersonal basis, with no visits to the house and no private conversations, that's fine. It'll have to be.

Christmas Day, Ten Years Ago

Magda can hear the doorbell ringing through a fog of sleep. It's late on Christmas afternoon, the time when all sensible people are settling themselves in front of the fire for a nap. Who can that be? The ringing comes again, for longer this time, and Magda remembers that Jared and Annika have gone for a walk by the sea and Hope will probably still be fast asleep under her ancient feather eiderdown, earplugs firmly in place. She gets to her feet, yawning, and stumbles to the door, cursing the idiot who dares to disturb one of her rare days of rest.

Outside on the step is an unexpected sight. Den Archer, newly appointed head of the primary school and much-needed church organist, is wringing his hands and looking distraught. Magda stares. So people actually *do* wring their hands. She's only read about it in books up to now. She blinks away the last of the sleep and tries to focus.

'I know we haven't met properly yet, if you ignore that awful first choir practice when the organ refused to work, but I've been told you're the best person to contact. I need a midwife urgently.'

Magda views the tall, slim-hipped figure with the five o'clock shadow. She's sure she'd have heard if the Archers were about to have a baby, so the emergency can't be his.

'I'm really sorry but I'm not on call today,' she says. 'I don't know what the problem is, but whoever needs the midwife will need to ring the emergency number.'

'We've tried that, but the number keeps going to answer phone and the ambulance is going to take at least an hour to get here. It's our neighbour. She's gone into early labour and she's in agony. None of us can drive her to the hospital because we've all had a drink. It *is* Christmas Day,' he says apologetically.

Magda pauses for a moment, but realistically she knows what the answer has to be. 'Okay, I'm coming. Just give me a minute to get my bag and put my boots on.'

They both look down at her new slippers, a joke present from Jared. Two pink rabbit faces peer up at them.

'Good idea,' Den says, grinning for the first time as he comes into the hall, a dimple appearing in his left cheek. In seconds, Magda is striding alongside him down the hill, getting as much information about the situation as she can. The midwife on call is still not picking up. Magda grits her teeth. Heads will roll for this, she tells herself.

When they reach Den's Victorian semi a few streets away, Magda can see that all the lights are blazing in both houses and Den's wife, who she's only glimpsed in passing at the health food store up to now, is in the open doorway of the right-hand house, also wringing her hands. It must be a family trait, Magda thinks, as she greets the other woman and follows her upstairs.

'She's in here. I'm Virginia, by the way,' Den's wife says. She has long red hair and her clothes mostly seem to be layered cheesecloth in shades of green and brown. She reminds Magda of a very pretty autumn leaf.

On the bed lies a younger woman, curled in a ball and moaning loudly.

'This is Gemma,' Virginia says. 'She's been like this for half an hour. I don't know what to do. I've got twins but they're ten now and anyway I had them by C-section so I was out of it. Is she going to have the baby right here and now? I've sent her husband to see if he can find a doctor. He was making her worse, to be honest.'

'The only doctor who lives in town has gone away for the holidays,' says Magda, putting her bag down. 'Where can I wash my hands?'

Soon, she's examined Gemma, calmed her down and established that the baby is in no danger of appearing before the ambulance arrives. Once the latest contraction has ebbed, she gets Gemma up and walking around the room, leaning on the back of a chair when the waves build up again.

'First babies often take ages and this one's in no hurry,' she tells the girl, rubbing her back.

'Thank you so much for coming, you're an angel,' gasps Gemma, as the pains die down again. 'Have you got children of your own?'

'One son. He's twenty-five now and married.'

'Did it hurt like this? Was your husband any use? Mine isn't much good in a crisis, I'm finding out today. Oh, here he is back again,' she says, as they both register the sound of the man in question bursting back into the house and bemoaning the fact that no doctor can be found.

Magda thinks back to her own labour. Giovanni had been nowhere to be seen, unsurprisingly. It had been Fliss with her doing the back rubbing, murmuring soothing words and wiping her face with a blissfully cold flannel.

'I'm sure he'll redeem himself when the baby's here,' she says. 'Give him lots of chances to be part of it all. It's all too easy to leave the dads out of the first few days if you're not careful.'

How have I even got the nerve to give advice like this? Magda asks herself, hearing the approaching wail of the ambulance's siren with relief. *I have no idea what dads do with their children.*

After the excitement is over, and Gemma and her frantic husband are on their way to the hospital, Magda goes next door for a much-needed cup of tea. The scene of domestic calm almost brings tears to her eyes. Twin red-headed boys are making a gigantic Meccano model in the middle of the carpet, Virginia is knitting and Den can be seen through another door loading a tray with mugs and cake. Magda feels a sharp pang of sorrow that she's never going to have this sort of life and that, even if she did, Jared's missed out on it already. How wonderful to be a tight little unit like this.

Den comes into the living room and deposits the tray on a side table, just as Magda finishes texting the family to say why she's disappeared so suddenly. She looks up into his warm green eyes and they smile at each other.

'You did well there,' he says. 'I don't know what we would have done if you hadn't come.'

'You'd have coped,' says Magda. 'And the ambulance didn't take long, as it happened.'

'But it might have been ages. You made Gemma feel safe. It's a massive gift you have there. We were really struggling.'

Magda glances across at Virginia and senses a slight cooling of the atmosphere. Maybe her husband's effusive praise is making her feel inadequate, but it's warming Magda through and through, getting rid of that nasty, niggling feeling of having missed out on something beautiful. Yes, she does have a talent for making the pains of labour seem natural and not so stressful. It *is* a gift. It's time she celebrated it and stopped looking back over her shoulder. The past is over and done with.

24

It's just after lunch by the time Fliss arrives back from the hospital in a taxi, looking frail and exhausted. Magda holds her breath, hoping against hope that the coolness between them will have lessened now that they've both had some time apart to think. It's been so hard to accept that all these years of friendship could come to a sticky end. She opens the door wide and goes forward to help with her bag.

'Welcome home, we've all missed you,' she says, and means it.

They make their way through into the kitchen and turn to look each other in the eye. 'The thought of going back to an empty house and having to think about getting it warm and what to have for dinner would have been too much to bear today,' says Fliss, seeming, for the first time, to be truly grateful to be back on speaking terms with Magda. 'I've got to start getting used to the fact that I'm not some sort of invalid now, but it's obvious that sometimes I might need to take things more slowly. I'm not going to sponge off you forever though, I promise.'

Magda bites her lip, desperately not wanting to say the wrong thing when Fliss finally seems less prickly. 'I think all the times you've bailed me out mean that you will never have to feel guilty about being here,' she says.

'You make it sound as if this is payback time. I promise it's

210

not like that at all. I've always loved helping you, Mags, you know I have.'

'Well, you're here now and we've really missed you these past couple of days,' says Magda. 'This place felt really lonely without you in it. I still can't quite believe we managed to make a fruit cake without you.'

She displays the fruit cake still sitting on the kitchen table with all the pride of a first-time mum, and Fliss applauds.

'But even better, look on the dresser.'

Magda waves an arm proudly towards the rows of gleaming jars of apple jam and Fliss gasps.

'You didn't?' She laughs. 'Well, you obviously did. That's amazing. It'll be great with our Christmas dinner. Your mum would be doing a happy dance if she could see these.'

'Perhaps she can . . . somehow . . .'

They smile at each other, and Magda at last has the sense of everything beginning to fall back into place between them.

'So what's today's recipe going to be?' Fliss says, flopping into her usual chair at the table.

Magda is making a large pot of tea, even setting a tray out, just how Fliss likes it, with milk jug, tea strainer and shortbread on a china plate.

'No tray cloth?' asks Fliss, grinning, as Magda works, before she even has a chance to respond. 'No, honestly,' she says, as Magda pulls a hideous face at her. 'This looks amazing. Hospital tea just doesn't hack it somehow. You didn't make the shortbread too, did you?'

'Well, it's nice to be able to offer you some home comforts now,' Magda responds. 'And no, I didn't. I was thinking of having a go at shortbread next, when the kids come home, so

I put these out as a benchmark to see if I can do better with Mum's recipe.'

While Fliss drinks her tea, Magda picks up the cookbook once again. It's still lying on the kitchen table from where she left it earlier. As she picks it up, the gentlest waft of air seems to stroke her cheek. She checks that the window is properly shut. It is.

'Did you feel a draught then, Fliss?' she asks.

'Hmm? No, did you?' Fliss seems more interested in munching the shop-bought shortbread.

Magda doesn't answer. She sits down in the rocking chair with her mum's book in her hands. She's getting a properly Christmassy feeling today, even despite the shocks of the past twenty-four hours. Now Fliss is home, coping with the turmoil of thoughts generated by Giovanni's email and Den's declaration suddenly seems a lot more manageable.

The white lights on the dresser twinkle and she's also switched on the coloured ones wrapped around the twins' little silver tree. She opens the recipe book and breathes in the delicate scent of vanilla, overlaid with the usual touch of cinnamon. Her mum wasn't a messy cook, so it's odd how the book keeps giving her this delicious hint of baking. Maybe the kitchen is still full of nice smells from earlier – the aroma of baking is still in the air from the fruit cakes. She sniffs the page again. No, the lovely new scents are definitely coming from the book.

'Have you found a recipe for shortbread?' Fliss is looking brighter already, now on her second piece. 'These are nice but we can do better, I'm sure.'

'It's in the Easy section again,' Magda tells Fliss, drinking in the feeling of warmth and reassurance as she reads the words her mother has scribbled next to the ingredients.

Only the very best butter will do here. I get it from the farm shop. Magda keeps on buying that horrible low-fat stuff, but I won't have it anywhere near my baking.

That's told me, Magda thinks, but she's grinning. She'd been about to substitute her own spread, but this is going to mean a diversion to the farm shop on the way back from getting the twins. No point in cutting corners. She closes the book for now and begins to pour out the story of Jared's email.

'Giovanni's back on the scene?' Fliss's voice completely echoes the horror in Magda's. 'But why? What can he possibly want? It's been so long . . .'

'I emailed Jared back in the end, because I needed to show him that I wasn't sulking just because he wants to see his father and find out more about him. It's understandable, if you think about it.'

'Sulking? You? As if.' Fliss laughs, and Magda gets a glimpse of her friend's usual, backchatting personality at last.

'Yeah, okay. No need to say more. Anyway, apparently Giovanni's widowed, and his three daughters haven't produced any grandchildren for him, so I suppose that's part of the reason he's keen to get in touch with Jared – and meet the kids, of course.'

'But he dumped you from a great height,' Fliss says. 'He can't just swan back in and act as if he's only been away for five minutes. You've made your life here. Surely you're not . . . oh, Mags – you're not going to meet him or anything, are you?'

Magda bites her lip. This is the question that's been spinning around in her mind ever since she read the emails. Her first reaction had been to dismiss any such suggestion out of hand. The pain of Giovanni's rejection is still somewhere inside her, even if buried deep. After he left the country, shedding her like a snake ditches its old skin and abandoning his small son, Magda had grieved for the man, even though he was still very much alive, and it's hard to forget sometimes that she did once have deep feelings for him.

She reminds herself that getting through each day with a young, demanding baby and a job that asked for long hours was an almost unbearable challenge to begin with, but she'd done it, and looking back now, she's proud of herself for managing to survive those dark times.

As if she's been following Magda's thoughts, Fliss groans aloud. 'You can't let him do this,' she burst out. 'I remember those days, Mags. You very nearly went under with the sadness and stress of it all. He almost finished you off.'

'We did it without him, though, me and Jared. And you, of course,' she adds hastily, when she sees Fliss's expression. 'And later on my mum was brilliant too. Who needs a fancy playboy doctor? I'm okay now, aren't I?'

'But *are* you okay?' Fliss digs. 'You've never had another long-term relationship, and I know you've had plenty of chances to get married and have more babies. Don't tell me you haven't been tempted.' Here, she pauses, as though wondering if she's overstepping the mark. But she ploughs on. 'And we never finished that conversation about Den the other day, but don't think I haven't noticed you eyeing him up lately, don't try and deny it. I bet you think it's all right to have a crush on Den because he's safely married again, now Virginia's back.'

'I absolutely *do not* have a crush on Den,' Magda snaps. 'Whatever makes you say that? I've never even thought about him in that way. Definitely not.'

'Well, it's nothing to be ashamed of! And if that *is* true then you must be the only woman of a certain age in the town who hasn't been admiring his manly charms,' Fliss says, starting to snigger. 'And you're protesting rather too much.'

'Manly charms? What sort of magazines have you been reading in hospital?'

Fliss is really giggling now. 'You should try them. I did a quiz to find out who my dream man would be. I brought it home for you in my bag. We'll try it out later.'

'We most certainly will not. I don't need a dream man. I'm fine on my own, thank you,' Magda says defiantly, before pausing to think. 'So, who did yours turn out to be? It's been a while for you too, if we're talking barren patches.'

Fliss stops laughing abruptly. 'Well, that's the weird thing,' she says. 'I answered all the questions and all it could come up with was that I'd probably already met him.'

'Oh. So . . . which one of your blasts from the past ticks all the boxes?'

'It's all rubbish. If I'd met my Mr Right, I'd have grabbed him and settled down, surely?'

'Well, so would I, in that case.'

'But would you, Mags? You're not exactly without emotional baggage, are you? Look, I've been meaning to say this but didn't know how to do it without offending you, so I'm just going to have to try.' Fliss pauses. 'The thing is, and I know you've not been freed from going to work for long and you're still grieving for Hope, but you're really stuck in a rut. You must see that?'

Magda lets what Fliss has said sink in, trying not to jump on the defensive. For years she's thought she was winning at life, at least in the area of her career. Being a midwife had been everything she'd hoped for, and being Jared's mother has been a challenge at times but a huge joy too. Perhaps, though, the time is right for a change. Magda's aware that over the years she's built an imaginary but very strong protective shield around her heart. Giovanni was the love of her life, or so she'd thought. The possibility of ever being hurt like that again is unthinkable.

'I suppose I always carried around a shed-load of guilt about not being enough of a mum to Jared,' she admits, unable to bear Fliss's steely gaze any longer.

'You *were* always plenty good enough, and more. You just didn't want to admit you needed help.'

'I've always let *you* help me, Fliss.'

Her friend regards her, head on one side. 'Yeah, right. You haven't always appreciated me very much though, have you? I supported you all along when you decided to leave home, even at first when your mum was so set against it. I used to come and stay with you at the drop of a hat when Jared was little, babysat while you worked, batch-cooked for your freezer. I was more like a mum than a friend a lot of the time.'

Magda still can't meet her friend's eyes. 'I know you were,' she says, so quietly that Fliss has to lean forward to hear. 'You've been a godsend. Literally.'

'Well, we're agreed on that, at least. An angel straight from heaven, that's me.' Fliss grins and Magda relaxes again.

'You might have a point though. I'll give it some thought. And even if I had been thinking about Den in that way – which I hadn't – he's still very much married and with a boomerang wife who can't be relied on to stay away.'

'Does Den want Virginia to stick around, do you think?'

'He doesn't seem to. So why doesn't he just end it, once and for all? I don't want to be messed around by Giovanni again after all these years and whatever you say, I'm never going to be interested in a man who lets himself be pushed around.'

'Good for you. Now, you'd better get down to the school or the magnificent Mr Archer will have you down as someone who doesn't care enough about the kids to be on time. And you don't want to get in his bad books whether you fancy him or not, do you?'

25

The children burst out of school and run to hug Magda, and her heart swells with pride as she looks down at the two curly blonde heads. This is much better. They really seem happy to see her today, and on the way home they can't stop talking about what they'll bake next. Magda tells them about how good Hope's shortbread used to be and how the bought version isn't anywhere near as nice.

'If we try that one, ours might be as yummy as GG's,' says Will.

'Oh, for sure. We're super-bakers now,' says Magda, high-fiving them both.

As planned, they stop in the farm shop on their way home from school, and when they reach Mistletoe Cottage, Magda can't help but notice that Fliss looks tired again. She attempts to send her friend to bed, but this idea is met with resistance from all sides.

'She can't go yet, she hasn't helped us to do the shortbread,' says Will. 'You promised, Granny.'

'Anyway, I'm not tired. I had a nap while you were fetching these guys,' Fliss says. 'We need to crack on, because I think we could pull in making some gingerbread Santa Clauses too if we hurry up.'

'Hooray,' shouts Will, and Desi capers around the kitchen table humming one of her own made-up songs.

'Lovely singing, Desi, but you know what we need for making Christmas gingerbread men and shortbread, don't you? Proper Christmas music,' says Fliss.

Soon, Elton John is singing about watching the snow fall for ever and ever and Will is at the window, telling them that, actually, it really is snowing now.

Magda feels the tension leaving her shoulders as they all take a moment to look out at the whirling flakes, lit by the streetlights. This Christmas is already shaping up to be much, much better than she expected.

Will tugs at her sleeve and she smiles down at him. 'Hey, I forgot to tell you,' he says, 'Mr Archer made Stanley say sorry to me in front of the whole class today.' He opens the little glass jar of ground ginger and sniffs rapturously. 'This smells nice,' he says. 'Can you smell biscuits already, Desi? GG made good gingerbread.'

His sister bends her head to sniff too, nodding her agreement, and then sneezes loudly. Magda tries not to think about germs. It's a good job they're only baking for themselves, and not . . . Her mind flinches away from thoughts of production lines in the past, in the weeks running up to their annual bake sale, and the familiar sight of her mum and Fliss wrapped in their pinafores, cooking up a storm.

'Let's get this show on the road,' she says. 'And maybe by the time we've finished, there'll be some snow on the fir trees in the garden and it'll look exactly like a Christmas card.'

The white lights on the dresser seem to be twinkling more strongly than ever. Fliss, joining in occasionally, but mostly sitting comfortably in the rocking chair, directs operations while the CD moves on to 'I Believe in Father Christmas'. Will is chattering about the merits of raisins for eyes as opposed to peanuts and Magda doesn't realize he's listening to the lyrics of the poignant song, until he says, 'Stanley said he made a mistake about Santa not being real, so we'll be okay on Christmas Day, won't we?'

His eyes are pleading, and Magda nods. 'Of course you will. He'll probably still deliver some presents for your mum and dad here though, so they can open them with you when they get back. We can have another Christmas then.'

When the shortbread is cooling and the gingerbread Santa Clauses are in the oven, Fliss claps her hands to get everyone's attention. 'While you were out, I was thinking,' she says.

Magda had been just about to round the twins up for a quick bath but they're already sitting at the table before she has time to intervene, looking at Fliss expectantly.

'I thought you were having a nap?' Magda says, looking at her watch. If they don't hurry up, it'll be time to take the other baking out.

'I had time for both. So anyway, it strikes me there's one thing we haven't discussed properly since I came to stay, and that's the bake sale.'

Magda's not sure where this is going. She's been asked several times in the town over the past week or so what's happening about the sale this year and she's put everyone off by saying it's not possible without Hope to help. She had thought, or at least *hoped*, that that would be the end of things.

Fliss is looking at her beseechingly now. Magda has a feeling of doom, suddenly dreading where this might be going.

'Right, I'm just going to come right out and say it. I think between us we can still get the sale together in time.'

'You're joking,' Magda says, but the twins are already cheering. 'We can't possibly.'

'Yes, we can!' bellows Will. 'We can do anything. You said we're super-bakers, Granny.'

'But . . . but . . .'

'I know you'll say it's too near to the sale date, but look how many biscuits we made tonight, and they're definitely good enough for the stall.'

Magda can't help but think that Fliss has a point, and that also, her suggestion to make gingerbread had been more planned than Magda had at first realized. Fliss goes over to the oven, checks the trays and fetches out the gingerbread people. Only one has a missing leg and the scent of ginger is mouth-watering.

'There you go. How yummy do they look?' she says. 'They just need icing, and the shortbread needs a frosting of icing to look like snow. So, here we go, my plan is that you three do the cooking and I mostly supervise. But I refuse to think of myself as ill any more. I just get a bit more tired now and I have to be careful not to stumble.'

She holds up a hand as Magda starts to make horrified noises. 'No, just listen. I first had this idea while I was hanging around in hospital, actually. I had hoped that Mr Archer would help but I guess he's not going to be so available now. But that doesn't even matter. We can definitely do this without him, Mags.'

Magda finds herself reaching for her mum's book, almost like a comfort blanket. She isn't convinced. 'But if Den . . . I mean Mr Archer is . . . busy . . . who's going to make all the mince pies? He was the one who said he was good at those and we can't have a Christmas bake sale without them. They're always one of the biggest sellers. And there'd be way too many other things to bake. We'd never be done in time.'

'You shouldn't be so negative,' says Fliss. 'Should she, kids? We'll all help.'

'We've been looking forward to doing the baking all day,' Will says, tugging on Magda's apron. 'I told Mr Archer me and Desi are making more things when I saw him at assembly and he said he was going to be having a go at some baking tonight as well. So he can't be too busy.'

'Oh.' Magda had imagined that she was reconciled to stepping away from her growing friendship with Den, but this new development complicates matters. If Fliss is going to try and involve him in some sort of marathon baking session for the sale, they'll be bound to meet again outside school and he might notice that she isn't immune to his charms. The thought is a mixture of alarming and exhilarating.

'Well, there you go,' says Fliss. 'You've got no excuse.'

'It's going to be great,' breathes Will.

'I haven't said *yes* yet,' Magda says, but her voice is drowned out by the noise of Will whooping, Desi clapping wildly and them both skipping around the room in opposite directions, narrowly missing colliding with each other.

'But it's going to mean lots more hours in the kitchen. We haven't got Santa's elves to help us here,' says Fliss, putting her hands over her ears.

Magda's phone rings just as the noise reaches an unbearable pitch.

'I'll go up with them and run the bath. I'm guessing that's himself?' Fliss whispers, as Magda goes into the living room.

'Hello, Den,' she says, wishing Fliss's earlier words didn't now make her feel like a guilty schoolgirl with her eye on the head boy.

'Magda, sorry for the delay again. I know I was supposed to get back to you about Will and Stanley, I've just been . . .'

'Busy. Yes, me too,' says Magda rather frostily, registering that she's become Magda again and not Mags. Maybe it was because Virginia was listening. 'It's fine, Will says everything's been sorted.'

'It has. Stan's parents were mortified and they've had a strong word with him. It won't happen again. I took the opportunity for speaking to the whole school when I did my assembly this morning. Just a pep talk about being kind to each other and some heavy hints aimed at the older ones about keeping the Christmas magic alive. I think most of them got the message.'

'Thanks. I appreciate that. Well, I'd better go. I've left Fliss in the mayhem of bath time and they're a bit hyper after the gingerbread session. Didn't burn anything,' she adds, not interested in hanging around and chatting to this overly formal version of her friend.

'Me neither. I've just taken two dozen mince pies out of the oven. Virginia's special request. That should get us in the Christmas spirit in good time. Vegan mincemeat, which smells delicious . . . as always,' he adds hastily.

Virginia's definitely listening, Magda thinks, saying goodbye as quickly as she decently can without being rude. She goes upstairs with mixed feelings about the day just gone. On the plus side, Fliss is safely back under her roof and she can carry on trying to repay the years when her friend has helped her through. Will and Desi have had a great baking session. The snow's still falling and making the garden and the street look just like the very best kind of Christmas card. Stanley's put things right with Will, and Den has done his best to make sure that particular bogeyman won't return.

But on the other hand, Virginia seems to have settled back at home with her husband, and if the mince pie session means they're spending Christmas under the same roof, there'll be no more cosy baking evenings with him at Mistletoe Cottage, and no extra help if she does agree to carrying out Fliss's mad idea of getting the bake sale together. Also, and much more worryingly, Jared seems keen to get to know his long-absent father and, most crucial of all, Magda needs to make sure she sends a forceful enough message to Giovanni to make sure he knows she never wants him back in her life.

Christmas Day, Nine Years Ago

The beach is almost deserted when Magda reaches the edge of the salt marshes. A brisk, solitary walk is just what she needs after all that delicious food at lunchtime, and the weather is perfect for a winter's day – crisp, bright and full of the scents of the sea. The tide is out and there's a huge expanse of firm sand just waiting for her footprints, but as she strides along, Magda notices that she's not quite alone. She can just make out distant figures and hear whoops of excitement as two adults and two boys take turns to throw a ball for a tiny, very excitable puppy.

For once, Magda's heart is full of joy on Christmas Day. Jared and his new fiancée Annika have made it to Periwinkle Bay for Christmas after flying back from a last-minute holiday in Italy, during which Jared apparently staged a very romantic proposal. It's not the first time Magda has met the glamorous Annika but she hasn't been to stay at Mistletoe Cottage for more than a couple of nights before and the two women are gradually getting to know each other.

Fliss's partner Laurence drove to the airport yesterday to fetch the visitors in his Range Rover, and the first thing on Jared's mind when he came into Mistletoe Cottage was to ask if Magda had got out his little silver Christmas tree because he wanted to decorate it with Annika for the first time. This moved Magda to tears and she had to make a quick excuse to leave the room. So her son *has* held on to some precious memories of the years when they spent Christmas in Leicester. The thought warmed her heart.

Her prospective daughter-in-law seemed underwhelmed with Magda and Fliss's other decorations, especially with those on the big tree in the hall, but she had the sense not to comment, and Magda pretended not to notice. It's early days after all.

Hope was so grateful to Laurence for his taxi service that she invited him for Christmas lunch, but he and Fliss have left now to visit his parents. He's a good man and her mother loves him. Magda hopes they stick together, but by the look on Fliss's face lately when Laurence has been mentioned, it seems as if he's always disappointing her in some way. They've got their business to consider though, so they need to make a go of it.

As she strides across the beach towards the other family, Magda recognizes Den Archer and his wife and sons. Virginia has picked up the puppy now and is kissing it on the nose, while it wriggles madly to be put down again. Den turns to wave to Magda as the boys hurtle towards the water's edge and start skimming stones.

'Hi,' Magda calls, waving back. 'Merry Christmas, or what's left of it anyway.' What an adorable family they make, she thinks, all so good-looking and healthy. Although Jared's obvious love of his little tree was encouraging, Magda can't help wishing that she and her son had been here more often for the holidays, and had been able to enjoy something so special as the sea air on Christmas Day, especially when he was at the age of Den's twins: not young enough to need constant care, but able to amuse himself with nothing but a wide sweep of sand and some satisfyingly flat stones.

She hears someone calling her name and looks back to see Jared and Annika in tracksuits jogging across the beach. They must have changed their minds about having some exercise. How they can run after the amount of food they put away earlier is beyond her, but she supposes they're young, energetic and they've probably both had a quick nap in front of the blazing log fire.

Virginia smiles at Magda. 'Are you taking a break from feeding the family?' she says. 'I'm trying to wean my carnivorous men away from traditional Christmas food but it's not working yet. I bet you've been cooking all week, haven't you?'

Jared's in earshot now and he laughs uproariously at this remark.

'Mum doesn't do cooking,' he says. 'We've all accepted that now. We've had to.'

'No, I don't, but *you've* excelled yourself this Christmas,' says Magda, looking at her son and wishing he wasn't quite so keen to make her seem like an inadequate mother, even at this age. 'Your gingerbread men are amazing. And the frosted shortbread is as good as your grandma's.'

She turns to Virginia, who's released the little dog at last. 'Jared got up extra early this morning to bake, even though he and Annie have been travelling round Italy all week. Baking isn't my scene. My mum and my friend Fliss have always done all that sort of thing in our house, and now the next generation's taking an interest so I'm really redundant.' This last comment is her attempt at a joke, but it falls flat. Perhaps everyone realizes that there's too much truth in it.

Den says he's sorry but he's just got to go and show the lads the right way to make a stone skip over the water. Magda's voice tails off, distracted by the sight of him running down the beach to join in the fun with his boys. She can hear their laughter and see the way they rough-and-tumble together. If only she'd had the back-up of a father figure like that for her own son.

She notices Jared's eyes following Den too and wonders if he's having the same kind of thoughts. Shaking off the sudden gloom, Magda pushes her hands deep into the pockets of her thick jacket and tells the others she's going to walk as far as the edge of the bay and then back to Mistletoe Cottage to make sure the fire hasn't gone out, and more importantly, to eat some of Jared's biscuits. She heads east, letting the sea breeze clear her mind. Today is for celebrating, not overthinking. Jared and Annika are home for Christmas, and all is well in Magda's world. Almost all, anyway.

26

Wednesday, 20 December

Five Days Until Christmas

The night has been chilly and there's still a light layer of snow everywhere when Magda sets out to take Will and Desi to school the next day.

'Is there enough for a snowman?' Will asks, as they slip and slide once again down the hill. Desi shakes her head sadly.

'The weather forecaster on the radio thinks there will be soon,' Magda says, grabbing a twin with each hand as they threaten to spiral off in different directions. 'They might send you home from school early if it gets too bad.'

'They can't do that. Mr Archer said we're having a go at the play this afternoon. I need to practise my singing,' Will says. 'I've got a solo now. Oh! It was supposed to be a secret,' he says, as Desi reaches round Magda to pinch him.

Magda swallows a lump in her throat. Jared and Annika would be so proud to hear this. When Will started at the school he was quite a shy little boy and now here he is, happy to take centre stage, even if it will probably be brief, and Desi's plucking up her courage to take a main part in the play too. She still can't reconcile herself to the fact that they're willingly missing such a moment in their children's lives.

'I'll pretend I didn't hear,' she promises. 'And they won't finish early unless they really have to. I bet everyone else will be in their wellies too, so you'll still be able to play outside at break. If you don't try and make slides,' she says, as an afterthought, remembering her own schooldays with a pang.

'Not allowed,' says Will sadly. Desi doesn't respond at all.

Magda looks down at her granddaughter as they reach the playground, trying not to mind that Desi doesn't feel comfortable enough to speak to her. She really hopes the little girl will feel able to talk again soon. Patience is hard when there must be so much that Desi wants to say, although actually, she was never particularly talkative even before Jared and Annika went away. Will has chattered from a very early age and now seldom pauses in his running commentary for long. But maybe Desi's quite content to speak only when it's absolutely necessary and to communicate with her brother in their private language the rest of the time.

'What do you think about small talk?' Magda asks Fliss when she's back at home and they're sitting at the table with coffee.

'Erm . . . how do you mean?'

'Well, Desi seems to have decided that any sort of chatting is pointless at the moment, but Will's more like you and me. We've always liked to talk non-stop, haven't we? Right from when we met on that first day at school?'

'I don't get what point you're making.'

'It just made me wonder. When I was with Giovanni, we only ever seemed to discuss the big, important things.'

'I guess that's because he wasn't around long enough for

mundane chit-chat,' says Fliss drily. 'He was either at the hospital being the super-impressive doctor with the most charm ever, or on the phone to his family in New York. The nurses and his folks probably got all his gossip and small talk. You got the leftovers.'

'That's harsh, Fliss.'

'But true. What are you saying? That you'd like to find a man who can talk about anything and everything? Anyone in mind? Anyone available, I mean.' She waggles her eyebrows and pulls a funny face.

Magda sighs. 'Nope,' she says firmly. 'Anyway, there's no point in thinking about it now. Let's get baking. What else can we do from Mum's book that'll be easy to bake? We've cracked the quick Christmas cake recipe, and shortbread, gingerbread men and the microwavable puddings. Oh, and I've got plenty more apples and jars for more jam.'

Magda takes the recipe book from Fliss and holds it in both hands, waiting for the comforting warmth to make its way through her body. It suddenly strikes her that it seems second nature now to communicate with Hope in this way. If only her mum could help with the rest of the chaos in her life. Magda suddenly longs to tell Hope about the dilemma with Giovanni. The identity of Jared's father has always been a closely guarded secret. Only Fliss knows what really went on in Leicester and how deeply Magda felt betrayed. She wonders what Hope's advice would be now. She would be quite likely to warn her daughter off from ever seeing Giovanni in the future. Then again, her mother had been well known for her positive outlook on life. She might not have condemned the man out of hand without even meeting him.

Magda had secretly longed to introduce the handsome

doctor to her mother. At the time, she was desperate to ask Hope's opinion of Giovanni but more than a little afraid that his glib patter would put her down-to-earth mum off. They hadn't been together, if you could call it that, for long, before Magda's pregnancy had forced Giovanni to take their relationship more seriously, so there hadn't really been an ideal opportunity to bring him home for a visit.

To give Giovanni small credit, he had tried for a short while to be everything she wanted him to be, but her morning sickness, constant backache and growing bulk had soon put paid to any romance in their lives. Giovanni liked his women to either be smart and crisp in their nurses' uniforms or primped and perfumed for a night on the town. Flowing maternity smocks and early nights weren't his style at all. In the time following his return from New York after the Christmas desertion, he'd shuddered at dirty nappies and Magda's painful cracked nipples and wondered aloud why she had insisted on having this baby when she clearly wasn't cut out for motherhood.

It's been a long time since Magda has let these harsh memories back into her mind, and at this moment, what she really needs is a hug from her mother to dispel the awful thoughts. She reaches for the next best thing to connect her to Hope, but before Magda has a chance to flick through the recipe book, there's a ring at the doorbell. She and Fliss frown at each other as Magda gets up to go and investigate.

'Could just be the postman,' she says as she leaves the room, but the figure she can see on the step through the stained glass of the window is much smaller than their regular man. She opens the door to see Sophie, Periwinkle Bay's best mobile hairdresser, beaming up at her. Sophie's sunshiny smile is always guaranteed to lift the spirits, and she's unfailingly friendly but also so discreet that she's the recipient of most of the big gossip in the town. A visit from Sophie is at least as good as seeing a therapist because you can pour out your deepest worries with no fear that they'll go any further. Nevertheless, Magda is puzzled. She can't remember arranging for her to call.

'Had you forgotten I was due here today?' Sophie says. 'This is the Conway family's regular Christmas slot. Your mum always booked it, so I've kept it for you, of course! I can go away again if you don't want me this time?' she says, doubt sounding in her voice when Magda continues to look shocked, rather than invite her in.

Suddenly, the thought of having her hair done is just the shot in the arm Magda needs. 'No, no, come on in,' she says enthusiastically, ushering Sophie into the kitchen. 'Let me carry one of your bags. I'm sorry I was being so gormless, it's just that I hadn't noticed your name on the wall calendar. Oh yes, there it is. *Lovely Sophie's Makeover Morning*,' she reads in her mother's handwriting, looking at it for the first time that day, potentially even that *week*.

'I knew Hope would have it written down somewhere!' Sophie says brightly. 'I do miss your mum, you know. She was such an important part of the community. Oh, hi Fliss. Are you going to have a trim too?' Sophie adds, on seeing Fliss sitting at the kitchen table.

'If you've got time, I can't think of anything better,' says Fliss. 'There's only us two here. The twins are at school and Jared and Annie are still in New York.'

'I thought I might just have Magda to do, but I've got all morning because the care home in town have cancelled me today. They've got a bug. Anyway, I can give you both a completely new look, if you like? How about a colour, Magda? Although the silvery look's very in now, so it seems a shame to spoil it.'

'I'd love something different, but just a cut. I bet Fliss'd be up for getting a new shade though,' says Magda. 'She could do with a bit of a lift too.'

Fliss looks doubtful for a moment, but then grins. 'Actually, why on earth not! Let's go the whole hog and dye it. My grey streaks have been depressing me. Not too dark though. I'd look like someone out of *The Addams Family* with these pale cheeks.'

Magda makes a big pot of tea and puts the radio on. Soon, the warmth of the kitchen and the sound of 'Fairy Tale of New York' turn what could have been a stressful start to the day into the sort of interlude that has its own recipe for happiness.

'I suppose Jared and Annie are having their own New York fairy tale at the moment,' says Sophie, as she gets down to business, settling Fliss in a dining chair with a plastic cape round her shoulders. 'I gave them a quick trim before they went and they told me all about it. What an opportunity, eh?'

'Yes, it is.'

Magda's brief answer doesn't stop Sophie in her tracks. 'Lucky them. They deserve it. I heard them both sing when they were doing that musical in Birmingham. They're amazing, and so good-looking too. I bet you're loving having the kids to yourself.'

Fliss snorts at this, but the band of anxiety that's been tightening around Magda's head ever since her son went away loosens slightly and she glows with pride. 'Yes, they do deserve a break,' she says. 'I'm happy for them.' And it's true. She *is* glad that their hard work's paying off. The twins seem to be slowly getting used to their mum and dad being away and now she thinks about it, her relationship with them has definitely got better. She hadn't thought it needed improving, but spending all this time with the twins and cooking together is finally making her understand what she missed when Jared was small.

'What are you going to have done to your hair, Fliss?' she asks, thinking a change of subject's needed. Too much soul-searching after the upheaval of the emails last night is more than she can stand today. All she wants is some light-hearted conversation to take her mind off everything. 'Have you got any ideas, Sophie?'

Sophie puts her head on one side and considers Fliss carefully. 'I'd suggest an even more cropped style, a little bit spiky on top.'

'That would suit her down to the ground. Short and spiky.' For a moment, Magda wonders if she's gone too far. But, luckily, Fliss lets out a loud laugh. It seems like old times are finally coming back.

'Sounds good to me!' she says. 'And the colour? Bright red?'

Sophie giggles. 'Like a post box? I know you're joking about the red, but we could do layers of chestnut and strawberry blonde? How does that sound?'

The rest of the morning passes peacefully, and by the time Magda looks in the mirror to check out her new style, she feels twenty years younger.

'I've kind of combined Judi Dench's look with that beautiful Naga Munchetty off the news programme,' says Sophie, looking at Magda to admire her hard work. 'You can see your lovely eyes properly now, they look huge! And the shape of your face is great for really short hair. You're looking great, Magda, but then you always do. And Fliss is going to be just as cool as soon as I dry her hair.'

Fliss rustles up omelettes for an early lunch, seeming energized by her makeover, and Sophie sits with them round the table and begins to ask about the bake sale. 'I look forward to it every year,' she says. 'I don't have much time for making cakes, so I always stock up on yours. The kids would be horrified if we didn't have Fliss's goodies at Christmas.'

Fliss and Magda look at each other with unease, and Fliss heaves a heavy sigh. 'The idea of the sale's still up in the air and if it does go ahead this year it'll only be because Magda's pandering to my whim that it can happen. It's not common knowledge around here yet, but I'm not firing on all cylinders at the moment,' she says. 'And that's not likely to change much.'

'How do you mean?' Sophie's face is a picture of concern, and Magda thinks, not for the first time, what a blessing she must be to the lonely people of the parish.

'I've got MS,' says Fliss. 'I'm trying out some new drugs at the moment but there's no cure. It's just a case of managing it as best I can.'

'Oh, I see now,' says Sophie. 'That must have been a horrible shock, but I'm glad you know what the problem is and it's being tackled. Anyway, you two stay there, I'll let myself out.' She gets to her feet and prepares to leave. As she approaches the door laden with her hairdressing kit, she turns. 'So are you saying it's on or off? The sale, I mean. If you're going to go ahead I can start telling my clients the good news. Get a bit of a buzz going.'

Magda takes a deep breath. She can almost feel her mum's warm presence cheering her on. It's now or never. She can do this.

'Okay, you've both convinced me. Let's go for it,' she says, grinning at the other two women, who both whoop with delight. Fliss looks as if she's blinking away tears.

'I don't know if you get what a big deal this is, Sophie,' she says. 'The baking for this year's sale is going to be mostly Magda's work. I'll just be supervising.'

'Really?'

There's an uncomfortable silence, and then all three women burst out laughing. Sophie's long history as the family's hairdresser means she's quite aware of Magda's lack of skills in that department.

'You're not serious about baking for the sale, are you?' Sophie says. 'Tell me you're joking.'

27

After Sophie leaves, on impulse Magda gets up and goes over to one of the highest cupboards. She stands on tiptoe and fetches out a long cardboard box. It's held closed by a faded red ribbon. 'I've been meaning to hand this over to you for a while now,' she says to Fliss, passing her the box.

Fliss opens her eyes wide as she takes it from Magda, carefully unties the ribbon and lifts the lid. 'It's your mum's favourite wooden spoon,' she whispers. They both look down at the spoon as Fliss lifts it from the box. It's bigger than most of the other kitchen ones because it was mainly used for preserves and pickles, which Hope always made in her big jam kettle. The wood is bleached from many washes and one side is slightly worn down from all the years of stirring boiling liquids. The handle is smooth, and as Fliss picks it up, it seems to fit her hand perfectly.

'You can't give me this,' says Fliss. 'It should be yours.'

'Yes, I can. You see, my mum was left-handed, like you, that's why it sits so well in your palm and the worn bit's in the right place,' Magda says. 'I could never use it properly.'

'But you might want to keep it for Jared or Annika.'

'You were as good as a daughter to my mum,' says Magda. 'You did lots of the things I should have been doing when I was living in Leicester, and when I came home you still propped us all up. She loved you very much, Fliss, and she was always

238

impressed with your baking. She wanted me to be the same. I let her down. I'm catching up now though, aren't I?'

'You sure are, and I'll treasure this. It means a lot.' Fliss stands up and takes a deep breath. 'Right, time to get moving. I guess *we* should really have spent the morning catching up on some baking,' she says. 'But Mags, Sophie's visit was so, so needed. I feel as good as if we'd had a day at a spa. She was right, we do look lovely!'

Fliss's new style is perfect for her petite figure, Magda thinks. The warm, layered colours give her cheeks a glow, showing her high cheekbones beautifully. And Magda's own even shorter cut makes her feel sassy and powerful. *Let Giovanni try and manipulate me*, she thinks. *I can deal with him. And Den can keep out of my way too. I'm an independent woman.*

At that moment, Magda's laptop pings with an incoming email, and as she sits down to read it, the positive thoughts go swirling right down the pan.

Dear Mum

Just a quick follow-up from our other messages. I've been doing a lot of pondering since I've been over here and we really do need to talk. It's definitely time to put the past behind us and part of that is going to be getting to know my father. That needn't affect you at all, unless you want to see him. I know he's keen. Have a serious think about it before you make the final decision.

I'll FaceTime soon, I love you very much.

Jared xx

Magda puts her hands over her face when she's finished reading, and Fliss comes to sit beside her at the table.

'What's up?' she says. 'Is the loathsome Giovanni demanding photos of the twins now?'

'If only it was that simple.' Magda pushes the laptop across so that Fliss can read the email for herself. Fliss scans the words quickly and then goes back to the beginning and reads it more slowly. Eventually, she stretches her arms above her head and smiles.

'Well, that seems to be that,' she says. 'Jared's a grown-up. You can't stop him wanting to find out more about the worm. And really, what harm can it do? Are you worried about the fact that Giovanni wants to see you? Remember that he's over there, and you're over here. He can't do anything from that far away. And he doesn't even know where you live.'

Magda turns to face Fliss. 'Ah, but that's where you're wrong. He does know where I live. After I came back home, Jared had a phase of really wanting to know about his father. He was very bitter that I didn't want to tell him any details and he went on and on about it, so I wrote to Giovanni several times, asking him to consider getting involved. I didn't tell Jared I'd done it and there was no reply, so I let it drop. I don't think Jared ever forgave me for not coming up with the goods. He was only fifteen and he was going through a very angry patch.'

'I remember.' Fliss pulls a face. 'It was around then when he went down to the beach and smashed a load of bottles by the windbreak. It was only because we found him in time to make him clear it all up that the police didn't get involved. I remember your mum was livid. Then there was the time . . .'

'Yes, I don't need reminding, thanks very much. He was wild for a while, I know. Let it go now, Fliss.'

Fliss looked apologetic and went back to the topic in hand. 'But when you wrote your letter to America, how did you know where that slimy toad lived? I thought he'd disappeared in a puff of smoke leaving you with no way to contact him?'

'I got his address from the hospital files. I had to sweet-talk the bursar, it was strictly against the rules, but it was still the one who'd been there in my time, and he'd always had a soft spot for me. He knew the situation. I was desperate. He could have lost his job for that – I should never have made him do it, it was bang out of order. I knew he felt sorry for me and he was so close to retiring he probably didn't worry so much about security any more. I played on his good nature until he gave in.'

'I'd probably have done the same, so don't beat yourself up. Even so, I can't see why you're worrying after all this time. Come on, Mags. Is he really going to go to all the bother of coming over here? It'll be way too much trouble, surely? Just how likely is it that he'll make such an effort when he hasn't been interested for nearly thirty-five years?'

Magda doesn't answer. The band of tension is back, tighter than ever.

Christmas Day, Eight Years Ago

Magda opens the pile of cards at the start of the day, while Hope is busy making porridge for them all.

'I can't believe you haven't done that before now,' says Annika, wandering into the kitchen dressed in a flowing, diaphanous robe. 'I have to rip mine open as soon as they arrive. Those have been mounting up all week.'

'I've been busy, if you hadn't noticed,' mutters Magda. 'That's what I do just before Christmas. Working, shopping for you all, you know the kind of thing.'

'Hey, don't snarl at me,' Annika says, grinning. 'Just saying . . .'

She floats off again and Magda concentrates on reading all the messages. Some are from people who live in the town who she sees often, but a few are from further afield. There are even one or two from friends from her early days in nursing, even though not many still live in Leicester nowadays. She gets to the last one in the heap and feels as if her heart stops beating for a second or two. The room spins and she clutches the table until her vision clears.

The envelope in front of her is from America, and the scrawling handwriting is all too familiar, even after so long. Doctor's writing. She reaches for a knife and slits the flap with shaking hands. Hope is singing along to a carol on the radio, happily stirring her pan as if nothing's wrong. Magda pulls the opulent-looking card from its envelope, wondering whether she

242

should have put it straight in the bin, but curiosity gets the better of her and she opens it.

A very Merry Christmas to you, Magda and Jared. It's been far too long and I've been thinking about you both. I've recently had a little scare with my heart. Nothing serious, and I'm fine now, but maybe this should be the year when we begin to make contact again. My address is here, along with my email and telephone number. The ball's in your court, Magda. All the very best, Gio xxx

Magda's initial reaction is one of pure anger. *Go stuff yourself, Giovanni,* she says inside her head, wishing she could say it to his face. *This is much too late. You can't send a fancy card and act as if all these years of ignoring us don't matter any more, just because you've had to face your own mortality for a moment or two.*

She stands up, ignoring the trembling in her legs, and goes through to the living room. A cheerful log fire is already blazing. Jared likes to get the room properly cosy before they open their presents. Without a second glance at the card, Magda flings it into the flames. She clasps her hands together to stop them shaking and then realizes it looks as if she's praying. Maybe she is.

28

Fliss suggests a cooking session to take their minds off the email, but Magda is finding it hard to shelve the crippling anxiety Jared's message has triggered. 'Let's give ourselves a couple of hours off and plan to do some more when the twins are back,' she says.

'There isn't time,' says Fliss. 'We really need to bake, Mags.'

'Well, we can't do anything until the next batch of shopping's delivered. I ordered a load more supplies as soon as we made the decision to definitely go ahead with the sale, and it's arriving at half past four, so we'll give the twins pizza and get going as soon as we're stocked up. Then if you pace yourself, like you said, we can carry on after they're in bed.'

'What about the mince pies?' Fliss asks. 'Are you going to ask Den to help with them but from home? We won't be able to do everything ourselves.'

'I'll go and see him just before pick-up time. I put mincemeat in the order in the hope that he'd be able to help. So if he agrees, we can give him all the stuff. I don't like asking, but I can't see any other way to have enough goods for a bake sale.'

'Good. Let's hope Virginia won't mind him using the regular sort of mincemeat in her kitchen.'

'*Their* kitchen surely? Right, I'm going to light the fire in the living room and we can watch *Love Actually* and eat chocolate, okay? That's always part of the Christmas run-up for me.'

'Wonderful,' says Fliss. 'It's snowing again though, so you might have to go down to school before the film ends.'

'That's fine, I know it off by heart. So long as I get to see the bit where the smouldering Brazilian man takes his shirt off. That's my favourite scene. Oh, and all the airport hugging. I wonder if we should go and meet Jared and Annika when they return? We could make them a placard?'

The rest of the afternoon passes peacefully. Magda makes a huge effort to take Fliss's wise words about Giovanni on board and put him out of her mind and, for a while, she's successful. By the time they hear the distant sound of the clock in the kitchen striking three, they're both in a state of happy relaxation.

'It seems as though a good haircut, a romantic film and a block of Dairy Milk is all you need to get your life back on track,' says Magda, hurrying into her coat and boots for the school run.

The town is sparkling like the best kind of Advent calendar as Magda makes her way down the hill. Most houses on her way to the school have lights either in the windows, on their trees outside, or trailing round smaller trees inside, and the switch-on is getting earlier every day. The low, snow-filled clouds make the day darker than usual and the giant tree in the marketplace is already resplendent with its blue and green twinkling bulbs. Magda's cheeks are pink with cold and she's wide-eyed at the beauty of the newly snowy landscape by the time she slithers to a halt at the school gates. She gets past the secretary's interrogation with difficulty, finally being met by Den at the door of his office.

'This is getting to be a habit,' he says. 'A nice one, that goes without saying,' he adds, seeing Magda's face fall.

'I need a favour,' she says, sitting down in what feels like her usual chair and forgoing small talk.

'Fire away.'

Magda tries not to look into those piercing green eyes but it's hard to resist, even though he has a wife who's now very much in situ. It's no good, her eyes are drawn to his, and for a moment she finds it hard to speak. Den seems to be having the same problem and for a while they gaze at each other. Magda is the first to pull herself together. She quickly explains about Fliss's bake sale suggestion and her own somewhat reluctant agreement, and then outlines the plans for the super-fast preparation.

'I know it can't be as elaborate as it was in my mum's day, but Fliss and the twins are so keen. I can't disappoint them, and people are still expecting it even though I've kept saying it can't happen. But Den . . .' she pauses, trying to find the words she wants to blurt out. 'This will probably sound crazy to you, but I've been getting a kind of weird, magical feeling every time I'm near my mum's old recipe book. It's as if she's here helping me. I feel warm and energized somehow . . . and loved. Anyway, it's making me feel as if I can do it. In fact, I *know* I can.'

Magda pauses and puts a hand over her mouth. She hadn't meant to say quite that much. He'll think she's flipped. Den leans forward. 'I reckon that's perfectly reasonable, when the book belonged to someone so important and precious to you,' he says. 'And if it gives you the confidence to do something as magnificent as the sale to raise money for the town . . . well, I think you're very generous for even considering it, under the circumstances.'

How is he being so reasonable about this? Magda thinks, in awe.

'You don't think I'm imagining it?'

He shrugs. 'Who knows? Does it matter? The result's great and it makes your eyes shine.' He blushes and seems about to say more, but changes tack. 'I've got no problem with making the mince pies anyway. I expect Virginia will help.'

He says this last bit rather doubtfully but Magda doesn't care, so long as they can rely on him to do his part.

'I'll bring the ingredients to you tomorrow morning,' she says. 'I really appreciate this, Den.'

'It's okay. Why don't I fetch it all later, sometime after five? Then I can make a start tonight. I'll do a couple of batches every evening between now and the sale, no problem.'

Magda hears the bell sound for the end of the school day and stands up. Den stands too. 'I'd better go. I'm so happy you're helping,' she says, feeling almost as if she should shake his hand to seal the deal, but that would be ridiculous.

'I'm glad I can. I just wish I could be with you . . . all . . . at Mistletoe Cottage to bake together, but you understand, don't you?'

'Of course. Your circumstances have changed.' Magda can feel the ice creeping back into her voice and forces a smile. 'See you later. I'll make sure everything's ready so you can get straight back.'

'Your hair looks great, by the way, Mags,' Den blurts out as she gets to her feet. He seems about to say something else but his secretary knocks on the door and opens it a crack. 'There's a parent to see you, Mr Archer,' she calls.

Magda makes her escape before she lets herself down by sounding sour. She gets into the playground just in time.

'Wow, look at you, glamorous granny. Loving the foxy hairdo,' says Natasha, who today is struggling with shepherding a line of excited five-year-olds into the playground. Their shouts of joy as they see the fluffy layer of settled snow echo across the concrete square, making Magda smile.

'Hey, your twins did a great job in the rehearsal this afternoon, Magda,' says Natasha. 'I've never seen a cuter Mary and Joseph. Den was very impressed.'

The casual dropping of his name into the conversation and the secretive smirk that follows it makes Magda grit her teeth. Maybe Natasha's hinting that Magda has a vested interest in impressing Den, even if it's through her grandchildren. She decides to weigh in with her own comment.

'I bet he's glad Virginia's back, just in time for Christmas,' she says, reminding them *both* that Den is a married man. 'Imagine how lonely he'd have been otherwise, with his mum and the boys away. At least they'll be able to cosy up together and have a great time now.'

'Oh, I'm sure *somebody* or other would have taken him in for the day,' Natasha says, smirking.

Magda's still trying to work out what the other woman means by this when the twins emerge and fling themselves at her legs.

'It's snowed, Granny,' shouts Will.

'I noticed,' says Magda, putting a hand on each head and feeling the usual rush of tenderness that always takes her breath away.

'Snowman time?' Will asks. Desi hops up and down on the spot, gazing up hopefully at Magda.

'We'll give it a go, if there's enough to work with. Now, let's get home and have some hot chocolate in front of the fire. We've got a whole lot of baking to do. Say goodbye to Natasha, and thank her for helping with your play today.'

'Thank you,' says Will, but already the twins are turning away to make snowballs with their friends.

Natasha's face softens. 'They're lovely kids, Magda,' she says. 'You're very lucky, you know. In lots of ways.'

The two women look at each other for a moment, and the unspoken words between them make Magda feel a pang of guilt for assuming Natasha had bad intentions. She knows Natasha's by herself a lot of the time. Her daughter is a high-powered businesswoman living in Germany, so Natasha only sees her own small grandchildren every few months.

'What are you doing for Christmas?' she asks.

'Oh, I'm off to the Black Forest on Christmas Eve,' Natasha says, brightening. 'It's going to be magical, just like being in Narnia. And I'll get to spend five whole days with the family. I can't wait.'

'Lovely,' Magda responds, from the heart. At least here's someone who is having the Christmas of her dreams. She'd almost been on the point of asking Natasha to join them at Mistletoe Cottage. Magda rounds up the twins and heads for home, thanking goodness Natasha's got other plans and won't be alone on Christmas Day.

Will and Desi are wild with delight when they see that the snow has drifted just enough in the back garden for them to make a small snowman. Fliss watches from the window, and when she considers they are all blue enough with cold, she opens the door and announces that hot chocolate, squirty cream and marshmallows are waiting for them in the kitchen, not to mention pizza. They've only just finished when the huge load of shopping arrives.

'Are we baking cakes tonight?' Will asks, when his moustache of cream has been dealt with.

'We've got to. There's a lot to be done,' says Magda, opening the recipe book. 'I think we'll make another batch of smaller fruit cakes and while they're cooking in the Aga we can get the old electric oven going and try some snowmen biscuits, to celebrate the one you made outside. I hope it still works. Mum only ever used it at this time of year, when the bake sale production line was in full swing.'

Will and Desi rush over to the window to check their creation is still standing and, satisfied he's safe, go off to wash their hands, ready for another baking session.

'The snowman one's in the Christmas Countdown section,' says Fliss. 'Your mum showed me how to make them for the stall and I did them every year. There are never any left.' The twins come rushing back, clad in their aprons, and Fliss continues. 'So, you make white chocolate chip cookies in two sizes, one for the body and one for the head. Then you stick them together with icing and put eyes, noses and mouths on them with more icing and cherries and stuff. It's a sticky job. Look, GG's even stuck in a photo I took of some of mine one year.'

'They're just like our snowman,' says Will. 'Cool.'

'Cooler than cool,' says Magda. 'Let's go.'

29

Den arrives that evening just as Magda is putting the last of the mince pie ingredients into two large shopping bags. She lets him in but he doesn't go straight through to the kitchen as usual.

'Hello, Mr Archer,' says Will, coming down the stairs two at a time with his sister close behind. 'Are you doing the baking with us again?'

'Erm . . . no, not tonight,' says Den. He hesitates, but Magda doesn't help him out with excuses. Eventually he says, 'I'm going to make my mince pies at home, it's easier in your own oven.'

'Oh.' Will goes to find Fliss without another word. Desi sighs heavily and turns her back to follow him.

Den pulls a face. 'I feel like such a killjoy,' he says, 'but I can't really spend all my time round here baking as soon as Virginia's back. It seems . . . I don't know, callous, somehow.'

'Of course you can't,' says Magda crisply. 'Off you go, we're fine here.' She turns to go after the twins, but Den grabs her arm. She can feel the warmth of his fingers through the soft cotton of her shirt.

'I wanted to say again that I really like your new haircut,' he says. 'And also . . . that I wish things were different.'

'What do you mean?' Magda wants to move away, but the urge to inch closer to Den is strong. Her whole body is tingling. *What's the matter with her?* The man's only holding her arm,

251

for goodness' sake. What would she be like if they actually . . . She tears her thoughts away from the danger zone and looks up at him.

'I'm getting the feeling that you're not enjoying this return to your old way of life as much as you probably should,' she says eventually, trying not to give away how fast her heart is pounding.

He shakes his head. 'It's not easy, that's for sure. I'd already got used to being on my own. Well, me and Blondie anyway. But Virginia's still my wife, I can't avoid that. If she wants us to still be together, I should make an effort. We've got history. The boys . . . the years of happy memories. It wasn't always like this, you know.'

Magda doesn't want to think about Virginia. She can hear Will calling her and the precious baking time is ticking away. She disengages her arm and opens the front door.

'Good luck with your marriage,' she makes herself say. 'See you at school, I expect. And thanks for all this.' She gestures towards the shopping bags and he picks them up.

'Bye, Mags,' he says sadly.

Magda heads for the kitchen. There's work to do.

It's a late bedtime tonight but the results – not to mention another evening spent with Fliss and the children – more than make up for it. The warmth of the kitchen, the tall candles flickering on the dresser and the windowsill and the little tree shining with its own multi-coloured flower lights make the perfect backdrop for the array of baking laid out on the table. Five fruit cakes sit in a line on their wire cooling racks and three large trays of snowmen biscuits are in rows, waiting for their icing to set.

The scent of nutmeg mingles with chocolate and cinnamon as Magda herds the twins upstairs, all three yawning. By the time she's got them into bed, sorted the next load of washing and tidied up after all the baking, she feels more than ready for sleep herself. She gets back downstairs to find that Fliss has finished the last of the drying.

'Goodness only knows what I'd do if you weren't here,' says Magda. 'I wish . . .'

She breaks off, and Fliss turns from the sink, dishcloth in hand, and raises her eyebrows. 'What do you wish?' she asks, smiling. 'For a handsome prince to gallop along on his charger and carry you off? I don't think so.'

'If I wanted one of those I'd have done something about it long before now,' Magda responds. 'No, I was just wondering . . . do you like living on your own, Fliss?'

The unexpected question seems to startle her friend. She frowns. 'Well, I haven't always been alone, but I've never minded when I am. Why?'

'Not minding isn't the same as liking it. I don't know how to say this without sounding pessimistic, but what's the long-term prognosis for your MS?'

'Do you mean am I going to get a lot worse and not be able to cope?'

Magda pauses, but then nods. 'Well yes, I suppose that is what I was getting at. I don't know much about the next stages apart from what Google's told me, and that was quite confusing.'

'I could probably sit an A-level on MS, I've read up so much on the subject, and adding that to what the doctors say, it boils down to the fact that there's no straight answer. Everyone's different. Again, why are you asking?'

Magda gestures for Fliss to come and sit with her on the

sofa and they lean together companionably as the saggy uphol-stery accepts their weight. The sounds of the house settling into the evening are all around them. The grandfather clock strikes nine, the old floorboards and water pipes creak as the heating goes off for the night and an owl hoots right outside the back window.

'I love it here,' says Fliss absent-mindedly, on hearing the owl. 'It's so peaceful.'

'Well, that's actually what I was coming around to, in a clumsy way. I don't think you should plan to stay on your own now.'

'You're not suggesting some sort of sheltered housing, are you? I know your aunties loved their bungalow but I'm fine at the moment, I promise. I'm not ready to give in.'

'Don't be daft. What I've been thinking is that Jared and I talked about converting our outhouses into a self-contained flat and putting it on Airbnb. We've already had plans drawn up and got all the permission we need, but we eventually decided we couldn't really afford to do it in style and we didn't want to skimp. But now, because of New York, Jared and Annika are going to get a mortgage to do the work if their income settles down to a more regular amount.' She realizes she's rambling and tries to get to the point. 'What I'm saying is, how about you sell your house and move in here? You could have a say in the alterations and live in the new apartment for as long as you'd like.'

'Rent it, you mean? But you said you wanted to do Airbnb.'

'I'd much rather you lived here than have strangers coming in and out. We could share the garden, eat together whenever we want to, and we'd only have to walk a few steps to do it . . .' Her voice trails off as she waits for Fliss.

Fliss doesn't answer. Her expression is unreadable.

'What do you think?' asks Magda, suddenly terrified that she's overstepped the mark. 'I don't expect you to give me an answer right now. You should think about it first.'

'It's . . . it's a lovely idea, but . . .'

'But what? Go on, tell me why I'm not a genius.'

Fliss flicks Magda's ear. 'Genius or big-head? Right, here's why. For a start, you haven't talked about this with Jared and Annika. No, let me finish,' she says, holding up a hand.

Magda tries to speak again but Fliss talks her down. 'And then there's us. What if we can't live that close to each other without falling out? We've never tried it, and as we both know, we've had our ups and downs recently. Part of me is scared of losing what we have again.' She seems as though she wants to say more, so Magda gives her time without interrupting her. 'And the worst scenario is that I get a lot worse and you feel honour-bound to look after me.' She rushes these last words out, as though she's been holding on to them for weeks.

At last the real reason is out. Magda bites her lip. She mustn't show any kind of pity.

'Look, we're back together again after a bad patch, which was horrible while it happened and was completely my fault.'

'Go on. I love it when you take all the blame,' says Fliss, grinning.

'Make the most of it, I shan't do it again. But as I was saying, *this* is how it should be: us being friends and looking after each other. Right?'

'Yes, I guess so.'

'And for the most part, you've done the looking after throughout this friendship so far. Well, you know what, it must be my turn. Wherever you're living, if you need me, I'll be there helping you. Think how much easier my life would be if we were under the same roof.'

Fliss laughs at this. 'So, once again it's all about you?' She puts her arms around Magda and hugs her so hard Magda yelps. 'The idea's definitely growing on me, even if only for the share in the garden. But Jared and Annika would have to be up for it too, without you twisting their arms.'

Magda thinks this is the best response she's going to get. It will do, for now.

30

Thursday, 21 December

Four Days Until Christmas

The level of excitement in Mistletoe Cottage the next morning is almost off the scale when Desi and Will look out of their bedroom window and find their snowman is still standing, although the snow around him is showing patches of green.

'It's all melting,' says Magda. 'I'm afraid he'll be gone by teatime. Don't cry though,' she adds quickly, as they both look up at her with stricken expressions. 'We want the snow to go because if it freezes or snows more, not many people will be able to get to your play or the carol service or the bake sale.'

She congratulates herself on her quick save. They're slightly mollified at this, and slither down through the remaining heaps of slush to school without much protest. Den is waiting by the gate, making sure the children go straight into class instead of soaking themselves in the last of the drifts.

'How's it going?' he asks Magda. 'Are you going to be able to get to choir practice tonight or is there too much baking to be done?'

She avoids looking straight at him, afraid her hard-won

peace of mind will crumble if his eyes have their usual effect. 'I was going to ask Fliss to babysit so I could be there,' she says, 'but then I realized that she really ought to be coming with me. She's missed a few recently, but I think she's in a better frame of mind now. I might stay at home and she can go instead. We'll be cooking all day so one of us can have a break at least.'

Natasha passes by at this point and overhears. 'I was talking to Belinda when I called into the deli for a coffee on my way to school. She mentioned choir practice and that you might have trouble getting there. She was going to call you later. She said Fiona's free tonight if you need her again. You don't need to worry about taking advantage, Fiona needs the cash. I'll go and finish the last bits of scenery for the play ready for the final rehearsal ahead of tomorrow, Den, but I'd better make you a coffee first. If this rehearsal is anything like last time, we'll need it.'

She smiles at Magda and carries on into school. Magda tries not to be annoyed. She doesn't like people talking about her situation behind her back, but at least it means she's got a willing sitter, she reminds herself.

Den tuts. 'Take no notice, Mags. The last rehearsal wasn't that awful. And anyway, your two were fine, so at least the key players aren't going to throw a wobbly or wet themselves on stage. I'll have to dash now. Don't want my coffee to get cold, do I?' He gives Magda an exaggerated comedy wink, and she can't help laughing. 'See you tonight, hopefully,' he says.

Magda watches Den weave his way across the playground, stopping every now and again to have a word with groups of children. She thinks about the reputation the school had before he took over. He'd been the deputy head at another school thirty miles away and she remembers hearing how much Den had hated the tedious drive along country lanes, especially in the winter. He'd often had to come straight to choir practice from work without even time for a cup of tea. Magda had been on the board of governors at the time and remembers the tussle some of them had to convince the others that it would be fine to have a head teacher who was based in Periwinkle Bay.

'He'll never have a moment's peace,' their Chair of Governors, Bill, had said. 'The kids will pester him when he's out and about in the town and parents will stop the poor chap in the street to bother him with silly questions about their little darlings.'

'Denis Archer doesn't strike me as a pushover, Bill,' one of the others had said. 'He won't stand for any nonsense. And look at the state of this place. If we don't get someone dynamic, we'll be closed down within the year. Numbers have dropped, discipline's not what it should be, and people are voting with their feet. They're taking the children out and sending them to Midcaster Primary, even though it means a five-mile car journey instead of a walk.'

The decision to choose Den for the job was the right one. The school has gone from strength to strength in his care, so much so that Jared and Annika had no doubts at all when they were applying for places for Will and Desi. Magda's thinking about all this as she walks back home, and doesn't notice Fliss's worried expression when she enters the warm kitchen.

'Your laptop's been beeping,' Fliss says, gesturing to the machine sitting on top of the dresser. 'You'd better have a look, hadn't you? It might be *that man* again.'

Biting her lip, Magda comes and sits at the table. She opens

259

her emails and stares down at the new message. Sure enough, it's from Giovani.

Subject: Are you out there?

My dear Magda,

I must admit to being a lot more impatient these days than I used to be back when we first knew each other. You haven't replied to my last message and I can't wait a moment longer to see how you feel about us getting back in touch.

Shall we have a Skype chat? I'd love to see your beautiful face on the screen. I hope you don't mind, but our son has showed me a photograph of you. I expect you miss all that long blonde hair that you used to put up in a bun in your nursing days. Do you remember how you used to let me take the pins out of it when we were alone, and how I loved seeing the curls flowing over your shoulders? Ah well, I guess we've all changed, but my daughters tell me I'm very well preserved for my age!

Ciao, beautiful Magda, I can't wait to hear from you.

Dr Gio xxxxx

Fliss, with Magda's permission, has been reading over her shoulder, and makes retching noises. 'What an arrogant piece of . . . well, there isn't a word bad enough for him, that's all I can say. Just tell him you've decided you don't want to revisit the past because it was hellish,' she says. 'Better still, ignore it.'

'I can't keep on ignoring him and pretend it's not happened, Fliss. I need to draw a line under this. It'll bother me like mad if I don't answer.' Magda clicks to reply, and types quickly.

> *Giovanni,*
>
> *I've read your emails with astonishment. Why you should want to reconnect with me after you abandoned us is beyond me. My life has moved on considerably and I have no desire to go backwards. Please don't try and get in touch again.*
>
> *Magda*

She presses *send* before she can change her mind and sits back with a sigh of relief.

Even Fliss seems to be impressed at this very un-Magda-like reaction. 'Well done! That's sure told him,' she says. 'He won't bother you a third time, I reckon. He was always full of his own importance and he won't want to risk being put in his place again. People like Giovanni don't take kindly to being slapped down. Now, let's get some baking done. We're nowhere near up to the amount we usually make.'

They work together until lunchtime, with Fliss directing operations from her seat at the table while Magda produces two trays of rock buns studded with cranberries and walnuts and the same quantity of the oddly named Freda's Eggless Nutties. But even holding Hope's recipe book doesn't help Magda to muster up much enthusiasm today so, disappointed, she hands it over to Fliss. Finally, Fliss closes the book and looks up with a gasp.

'Mags, I've just realized why everything feels so difficult for you today. It's your mum's birthday! Why didn't you say something? Here I am slave-driving and you're having to deal with all this Giovanni rubbish and feeling extra sad at the same time.'

Magda shrugs. 'Her birthday shouldn't make a difference, should it? It's just another day. I miss her all the time.'

'I know, but anniversaries and that sort of thing are always hard, and it's the first one without her. Look, you've got over two hours before you need to fetch the twins. Why don't you grab a bunch of flowers for your mum's grave and a sandwich or something for your lunch from the corner shop and take a walk over to the cemetery? Would that make you feel any better?'

Magda thinks about the idea and comes to the conclusion that, as ever, Fliss seems to know her better than she knows herself. This is just what she would love to do. Wasting no time, she hugs Fliss, wraps herself up warmly in a fleecy coat and woolly hat, and heads for the coast, only pausing briefly to buy a snack and some glorious yellow roses at the One-Stop.

The road to the sea is lined with stunted, windswept trees to begin with, and it's not until Magda turns a corner and comes out into the open that she notices what a beautiful day this has turned out to be. The winter sunshine has melted away the last vestiges of snow clouds and the sky is a brilliant blue. There's a hint of frost still around, and the air is crisp and fresh. Soon Magda can feel her face glowing as she heads out towards the distant graveyard.

When she reaches the cemetery gates, Magda thinks, not for the first time, that if you're unfortunate enough to need to be buried, this must be one of the best places around for it to happen. Hope loved this stretch of coastline, often packing up a picnic and a flask of hot chocolate to take a walk to the furthest point of the wide bay. Today, Magda enters under an archway of twisted clematis branches that in the summer will be a riot of colour with its purple blossoms, and makes her way along familiar paths to the family plot. Hope's family, the Montagues, have lived around these parts for centuries, latterly always in Mistletoe Cottage.

Magda sits down on the bench opposite Hope's headstone and reads the familiar words, proclaiming that here lie Hope and Archie Conway, beloved parents of Magdalena, resting in peace. Hope's name is a much more recent addition to the family stone but the lettering for Archie's is getting slightly worn now, because he had died in a motorbike accident when Magda was only a baby. Her mum had never been one for visiting his grave on anniversaries but had dropped by whenever she felt the need. Since her mum's death, Magda has decided she'll do the same and not be tied to specific dates, but today feels different. The urge to be here on the first birthday without Hope is too strong to resist. It's the right thing to do.

Looking down at the headstone, Magda thinks about how lonely Hope must have felt at times, after her only daughter had escaped to the city lights. Thank goodness Fliss had still been in Periwinkle Bay. She thinks of all that Fliss has done for their family through the years, and vows to herself that she'll make absolutely sure her best friend is never without love and care in the future, whatever direction her condition takes. Hopefully Jared and Annika will agree that converting the outhouses into a comfortable flat will be the best thing all round.

31

The yellow roses in the vase set into the earth are a bright splash of sunlight against the grey stone, and Magda stands back and bows her head, silently honouring the two who gave her life but especially her mother, who provided the confidence for Magda to go out and make her own way in the world.

'I know twins aren't unusual in your family, Mum,' she says aloud. 'Ruby and Vera weren't the only ones. But this latest pair are very, very special. I'll bring Desi and Will down here when the weather improves and let them arrange their own flowers for you. They'll like that.'

She pauses, wishing so much that her mum could answer. There are still many, many questions to be asked, and now it's too late.

'I wonder if your cousins had a secret language too when they were little?' she continues. 'Ruby and Vera can't hear very well on the phone now. I was going to visit them up north this week but it's too far to take Will and Desi on the train. As soon as Jared comes back I'll go up to Yorkshire, ask them more about what they were like when they were young, and tell them I'm baking, and that I'm going to start digging out all their utensils and other kit. They'll hardly believe it after all the years I resisted.' She's nattering away to her mother about nothing in particular, she knows, in the same way she would have done if they were

264

both sitting at the kitchen table in Mistletoe Cottage. Even just feeling as though there is someone to listen to her thoughts is enough to comfort Magda.

As she straightens up, she sees a lone figure coming towards her, long Burberry coat belted tightly against the wind. He's wearing a black fedora and carrying a holly wreath.

'Laurence?' Magda says, when he's close enough to hear, eventually recognizing the approaching man. 'I didn't know you had anyone buried here?'

He smiles at her and gives a little bow as he takes off his hat. 'Hello, Magda, I thought it was you. Yes, my parents are over in the far corner. I always make them a wreath at Christmas. It was my mum who taught me how to do it.'

Magda looks down at the magnificent creation. The red of the holly berries contrasts strongly with the shiny dark green leaves, and woven through the ring are fir cones, candied orange slices, bunches of dried cranberries and nuts, carefully but loosely attached.

'I like to make something beautiful but still let the birds have a snack when the ground's frozen,' he says, gesturing to the fruit and nuts. 'Erm . . . Magda . . . I'm glad to catch you if I'm honest. How is Fliss doing? I mean, how is she *really*? When I ask, I just get the usual "I'm fine, stop fussing," but she can't be fine, can she? That diagnosis rocked her world.'

Magda regards his kind face and sees the frown lines gathered between his eyes. Something she's completely missed before suddenly becomes blindingly obvious as she sees the distress written there. 'You still love her, don't you?' she asks. 'Not as a friend, I mean, or rather, not *just* as a friend anyway.'

Laurence runs a hand through his short grey hair. He looks as though he doesn't even have the energy to argue. 'Yes, of course I do. Who wouldn't? I've never stopped loving the woman, but she couldn't seem to believe how much I cared for her when we were together. I gave up trying to convince her in the end. I've had to accept she likes having me as a business partner but nothing else. But it's not easy.'

'I know.' Magda smiles at him and pats his arm.

She blows a kiss to her family's grave and walks alongside Laurence as he makes his way to a corner plot under a yew tree. From here, they can see the expanse of flat golden sands across the salt marshes, and hear seagulls wheeling and crying above.

'They loved that beach, and going out in their boat,' Laurence says, as he places his wreath on the very last grave in the row. 'Happy Christmas, folks. I wish you were still here, but sleep well wherever you are. I'll have a shot of rum to toast your memory tonight.'

Magda turns away, giving him a moment with his parents. Then, in an unspoken agreement, the pair head out of the graveyard and down the lane towards the gap in the dunes, where they can see the white caps of the waves moving back and forth. Magda hands Laurence a doughnut out of her bag and they munch contentedly as they walk.

'It was a bit of a grab and run snack stop today,' explains Magda. 'I've got a couple of apples and a sandwich too. Fliss said I needed to come to the cemetery for my mum's birthday to make me feel better, and she was right.'

'She's usually right. It can be annoying sometimes,' Laurence says, grinning down at her.

'We've been using Mum's old recipe book to do some baking. It's given us the boost we needed to get the bake sale back underway, but we're still not up to speed compared to other years. It's all very last minute and it's going to look a bit sparse however hard we try.'

'For goodness' sake, Magda, give yourself a break for once,' says Laurence. 'You've been looking after lively twins and Fliss has had plenty to think about herself. To be doing any sort of sale is a miracle this year, and you'll need all the help you can get. I tell you what, I'll make you some of my chocolate truffles tonight. I've got lots of little gift boxes at the craft shop. They'll probably sell well for last-minute presents.'

'That'd be great,' says Magda, feeling as if she's got to know Laurence better in this last half-hour than she has in all his time with Fliss. They walk to the end of the bay and then pause on some flat rocks to take in the view and breathe in the fresh sea air. Magda hands over half her sandwich and they tuck in before finishing off with an apple each.

Eventually Laurence turns to Magda. 'I know you and Fliss have been having a few problems lately.' He sees the expression on Magda's face and puts a hand on her arm. 'We haven't been gossiping about you, honestly, but she does talk to me about things that worry her. Can I say something without offending you?'

'Well, you can try,' Magda says, grinning at his serious tone. 'I'm not that scary, am I?'

He doesn't answer the question. 'Well, what I wanted to point out was that it's always looked on the surface that Fliss has kept you afloat over the years. She's rushed to help you out in Leicester when you've struggled, held the fort here with your mum, been a constant support . . .'

'I know all that,' Magda says, trying to keep the irritation out of her voice. 'You don't need to make me feel any more guilty than I do already.'

'And that's just it. I don't think you have any idea what a two-way process it's been. Fliss has never wanted children of her own. You and Hope have been the family she never had and your lovely son is very, very precious to her. Now there are the twins and Annie too, and she adores you all. Imagine what her life would be like without the Conway gang?'

The words take a moment to sink in, and then Magda feels relief and warmth flooding through her body. 'Really?' she says. 'You're not just being protective of her and trying to make sure we don't fall out again?'

He laughs. 'I wouldn't mess around with something this important. Your friendship is very special. But enough of this soul-searching for now – let me give you a lift back to town so you can pick up those two young rapscallions. I've got the rest of the Christmas wreaths to deliver to customers so I'm heading that way. Will you give my love to Fliss?'

'I will. But I think you need to have a better go at getting that message across yourself, don't you?'

'What message is that?'

'Don't be obtuse. That you want to give her your love?'

Laurence makes no reply, so Magda doesn't push it. He drives in silence when they're back in the car, lost in his own thoughts. When he pulls into a lay-by near to the school, Magda thanks him, and tells him how glad she is they bumped into each other.

'It was great to have a walk with you today. I think we both needed propping up,' she says.

He nods. 'I ought to have spoken to you about Fliss before and how I still feel about her, I suppose. I know we both want what's best for her in the long run. You can ring me any time, you know, if she seems worse . . . or . . . anything . . .'

'I will. Team Fliss, that's what we are. And maybe you two can sort things out between you when she's properly adjusted to the idea of a different kind of life. It's the unpredictability of it all that scares her, isn't it?'

'It terrifies me, too. Fliss has always been such a powerhouse of energy. But whatever happens, I won't stop loving her.'

Magda waves him off, her delight that Fliss has a man who adores her so wholeheartedly, even if she doesn't know it, tinged with only a small drop of envy. Perhaps it's not too late for Fliss and Laurence to try again. But Magda's no expert at relationships, she reflects, as she watches Laurence drive away. Far from it.

At the choir practice later that evening, everything that possibly could go wrong does go wrong. The heating hasn't come on, three singers have been struck down with sore throats, half the musical scores have mysteriously gone missing, and the organ has developed a strange groaning noise.

'This is a nightmare,' Natasha says as she and Belinda ransack the Methodist Church Hall for the lost copies of the songs, and Den wrestles with the organ stops to get a decent tune out of the old instrument.

Eventually the music turns up in a box of carol sheets left ready for the service and the organ decides to behave itself after much tinkering, but by this time half their allotted slot has been wasted and everyone is very cold and grumpy.

'Don't worry, it'll be all right on the night, as they say.' Den's optimism gets him a beam of approval from Natasha, but Magda and Fliss, huddled together for warmth in one of the back pews, are finding it hard to look on the bright side of all this.

'I shouldn't have persuaded you to come,' says Magda. 'The last thing you need at the moment is to get a chill because some dozy person messed with the timer.'

'I'm fine, don't fuss,' says Fliss, and Magda's reminded of Laurence's words. She hasn't mentioned their earlier meeting yet because Will and Desi were so excited when they got home from school that sensible conversation was out of the question, but now, under cover of all the flapping around, she fills Fliss in on the bare bones of the afternoon.

'Laurence is such a kind, talented man. He'd made a beautiful wreath for his parents,' Magda says. 'Afterwards we walked along the beach and shared my lunch. He's really concerned about you, love.'

'Oh, he's a sweetie, right enough, but he feels sorry for any underdog, he's that sort of bloke. I don't need his pity. The lifts to hospital are useful though,' Fliss says, grinning.

Magda's about to say there's a lot more to it than that, but at this point Belinda shushes them all and finally gets the rehearsal underway. As they swing into a lively rendition of 'Angels from the Realms of Glory', Magda casts a sideways glance at her friend. *There's more to life than relationships with men,* Magda tells herself, singing away lustily. *Fliss doesn't need Laurence, he should have spoken up long before this and won her over instead of letting her go. And Giovanni's old news. The main thing is that Fliss and I are back on track. Together, we can tackle anything.*

The two of them walk home arm in arm through the starlit night, still singing. Magda feels invincible. With hindsight, she should have waited awhile before having these thoughts, but then hindsight is a wonderful thing.

32

Friday, 22 December

Three Days Until Christmas

The sound of wild screeching brings Magda into the twins' room at a run the next morning, only to find them both whirling on the spot in the middle of the room. They're bright red in the face and gasping for breath.

'It's today!' whoops Will when he sees his granny. 'It's the play! Play today, today the play, hip hip hooray, it's the play today!' he intones over and over again as he spins.

'Stop that at once!'

Magda's yell brings them to a sudden standstill and Desi crashes into Will, knocking them both to the floor. She starts to wail, rubbing her face.

'Oh, terrific, you're going to be Mary, the mother of Jesus, with the added feature of a broken nose,' says Magda, scooping her up and sitting with her granddaughter on the bottom bunk bed. Will trails after them, his face a mask of concern now he's stopped careering around. Magda examines Desi for damage but finds to her relief that the button nose is just pink, rather than squashed completely.

'It was Desi's fault,' says Will. 'She's being going on and on all night about being Mary. I didn't get much sleep.'

Magda regards Will doubtfully. *Going on and on* isn't a phrase she associates with Desi these last few days. Will sees her expression.

'She has, honest,' he says. 'It's just that there's only me can understand her just now.'

'Ah, the secret language of twins,' says Magda, half to herself.

'It's not a secret. It's just, like . . . we're twinnish.' Will guffaws at his own witticism and Desi joins in. Magda holds a hand up.

'Ssshhh, you'll wake Fliss, if by some miracle she's managed to sleep through this racket already. So, what you're saying is, Desi can still speak good twinnish to you, even though she doesn't want to talk to the rest of us?'

Desi and Will nod. Magda's known this interesting fact for a while now, but it's different having it put into words. She gazes at her grandchildren with mingled respect and frustration.

'Do you think you'll want to talk to me in the usual sort of way anytime soon, Desi?' Magda asks hopefully.

Desi shrugs, and Will says, 'She's going to, when Mum and Dad get home. If *you* ever let them.' He points an accusing finger at Magda. She bites her lip and refrains from answering. *Not this again*, she thinks. She'd really hoped they'd have dropped this by now.

'Granny, we had a thought when we woke up,' says Will. 'We haven't got a Christmas present for Mum and Dad. Desi told me she wants us to make something.'

Magda sighs. This isn't going to be a quick conversation after all. 'Any ideas?' she asks wearily.

'No. It's got to be really, really good though. Did you make things for people's presents when you were little?' Will says. He's climbed back into the top bunk by now, and has positioned himself so he's hanging upside down over the edge, opposite Magda, all the better to fix her with a steely gaze.

Thinking back, Magda can remember them making all sorts of random things with egg boxes, cereal packets and the insides of kitchen rolls, but nothing stylish enough to give as a gift. Then, as she delves further back in her memory, something glimmers.

'Shell boxes,' she says, half to herself.

'What?' Will drops to the floor next to Magda and Desi comes over to sit the other side.

'I used to make things decorated with shells with GG,' Magda says. 'We used plaster of Paris. It's a white powder and you mix it with water to make a paste, then you spread it all over a little box and stick the shells on to it.'

'Why?'

'Oh, erm . . . well, it makes a useful box to put things in.'

Desi frowns and Will shakes his head. 'Shells are good,' he says. 'But our mum's got lots of boxes for stuff, hasn't she?'

Magda has to admit the truth of this; Annie is an avid buyer of small containers of different sizes. Another idea occurs to her. 'How about plant pots?' she says. 'We've got lots of those in the shed. They look great with shells all over them.'

'Do they?'

'Yes,' says Magda, warming to her theme. 'The plaster of Paris goes hard really quickly and then all you need to do is paint them with a coat of varnish so they look shiny. It brings out all the pretty colours too. You could do them one each and then we can call at the market and get them a plant to go inside. How about that?'

The twins' eyes are shining now.

'But we haven't got time to go down to the beach and collect shells because of all the baking, so you'll need to use some of my collection,' says Magda, before they can rush off looking for their wellies. 'I've got lots. They're in boxes in the loft. I used to go down to the bay most weekends and I could never bear to throw any away. I'll get everything ready while you're at school.'

'Promise?' says Will, putting his arms around her waist while Desi mirrors the action from the other side.

'Absolutely. And Laurence will probably have some plaster of Paris in his shop. It's like an Aladdin's cave in his stockroom. If Fliss asks him nicely I bet he'll bring us some.'

Magda leaves them to begin their daily job of hunting for their shoes and goes downstairs to put the kettle on. Fliss joins her seconds later, yawning widely. As she grinds beans and waits for some much-needed coffee to brew, Magda fills Fliss in on the conversation she's just had. She's aggravated that still, after all this time, anything Desi wants to say to her has to go through Will.

'I just wish Desi wanted to talk to me like she does to her brother,' she says. 'I feel as if I've failed everybody, especially lately.'

'What's that supposed to mean?' Fliss looks as if an intro-spective whine like this is the last thing she wants to hear right now, but she sits on the sofa, leans back and prepares to listen.

Magda pours the coffee and flops down next to Fliss. Laurence's comforting words are already fading from her mind and the guilt is firmly back in place. 'Well, I wasn't there enough for Jared when he was growing up, and it's clear he still resents me for it. I didn't let my mum teach me to cook, and now Desi's so traumatized she won't speak properly and I can't figure out a way to help her. And then I went and let you down when you needed me most.'

'Have you quite finished feeling sorry for yourself?' Fliss asks, digging Magda in the ribs. 'Is it my turn to have a say?'

Magda turns to face her, wrapping her arms around herself.

'That's better. Silence for a change,' Fliss says. 'Right, here goes. You were a working mum, you had to be.'

'But I wanted to be too. I loved my job.'

'Yes, and you did the best you could at the time for Jared, even after that loathsome piece of manhood did a runner and hurt you so badly. If you'd had a job you hated, you'd have been in an even worse state. It's good for kids to see grown-ups loving their work. Anyway, your boy's turned out brilliantly. You've probably got a few things to discuss when he's home, if not before, but that can be sorted.'

'If you say so. Go on.'

'Not everybody has the urge to produce wonderful cakes, and I benefitted from you not wanting to cook with Hope because of my own mum being poorly for so long. Your lovely ma filled a lot of the gaps for me. I didn't learn to be a baking whizz by accident, you know, and she taught me other things much more important, about life . . . and so on . . .'

Fliss pauses, lost in her memories, and Magda waits, unbelievably touched. Eventually her friend reaches for a tissue and carries on.

'The twins are fine, you're doing a great job and Desi will talk in her own good time, which I expect will be right after the wanderers return. And as for the last thing, you haven't let me down. You were a bit preoccupied with what life was throwing at you for a little while but you came to find me as soon as you twigged something was wrong. You've given me a purpose by letting me help you learn to bake and you've even offered me a roof over my head in case I need back-up later on. How ever is that failing?'

They look at each other and Magda opens her mouth to reply but Fliss stops her. 'No, I haven't quite finished. One of the reasons I was so devastated after I had my diagnosis was that I was terrified I wouldn't be able to help look after all of you any more if I got really sick. It wasn't that I was angry with you, really; it was the fear that my whole life was going to change. But now you're showing me that it's not that different, and whatever happens we can cope.'

'Together. It won't be so one-sided in the future,' Magda replies, finally getting a word in. She's about to say more but she hears the familiar thunder of the twins' feet on the stairs. She reaches out to hug Fliss and they cling together for a moment. 'Thank you,' she murmurs.

Fliss pulls away as Will and Desi burst into the room. 'So now all you need to do is make sure to never see that tosspot of a doctor again, and find a way to stay friends with Den,' she says quietly. 'Mags, for goodness' sake stop trying to pretend you're not into him. You'll just have to deal with the situation as best you can.'

Not for the first time, Magda wishes she didn't blush so easily whenever Den's name is mentioned. It's a dead giveaway and Fliss never misses a trick. 'But even if he was single and I was interested, Den's much too young for me,' she says. 'A ten-year age gap's way too much.'

'Don't be silly, ten years is nothing. If it was the other way round and *he* was that much older than *you*, I bet you wouldn't even think about the difference.'

Magda opens her mouth to remonstrate but Fliss gets in first. 'Anyway, as things stand, it's irrelevant. If friendship's what he wants, you can still have part of him, you know? As a mate. Just maybe not the parts you were thinking of,' she says, pulling an 'Ooh, Matron' kind of face. 'Don't try to deny it, I know you too well.'

Magda giggles, still red in the face, and gets to her feet to make breakfast. Her heart is so much lighter for the pep talk that she feels as if she can face anything.

'Pancakes?' she suggests rashly.

'Hang on, let's not run before we can walk,' says Fliss, getting up to take over the supervision of the microwave porridge.

The walk to school is easier today. All the snow has gone and there's a light frost that makes walking fun for the twins as they slip and slide over the cobbles. They make it to school with only one tumble for Will, which merely results in a damp bottom for his grey uniform trousers.

'It doesn't matter, Granny,' he says. 'I'll be putting my Joseph clothes on soon. We're having a last go at the play this morning. It's called a dress rehearsal. I think it's because all the costumes are like dresses.'

Natasha is already checking with various parents if they've booked tickets for the afternoon's performance when they reach the school.

'It's just that the school hall can only take so many,' she says officiously, ticking names off on a clipboard. 'Mr Archer's left me in sole charge of the lists, so woe betide me if any extra slip in. We've got fire regulations to think about.'

She sees Magda about to make her escape and calls her over. 'I've got you down for two,' she says. 'That would be you and Fliss, I'm assuming? No chance of your son and his wife turning up unexpectedly, is there? Because if they did, we'd never fit them in at this late stage. Mr Archer's left me in . . .'

'Sole charge. Yes, so I heard. And no, there's no chance. They've got two shows today and two more tomorrow. The musical's really taken off and every performance has sold out. Jared's still standing in for the lead,' Magda says, her pride brimming over, so she shares more than she probably needed to.

'Ah well, never mind. At least they've got Granny. Obviously, the safety procedures mean parents can't film the play, and . . .'

'Not film the Nativity? But I know Annika particularly asked one of her friends to video it for her. Surely it's not a problem if everyone agrees?'

'Rules and regulations, Magda. Since I've been working here, I've learned an awful lot about safeguarding issues. You'd be surprised.'

Back at Mistletoe Cottage after the drop-off there's baking to do, but first, Magda must reply to her son's email.

Dear Jared, she writes, trying to get the words down without overthinking them.

I can't deny it was a shock to hear you'd met your father, and even more of a surprise to get a couple of messages from him myself. I've thought about it and I definitely don't want to take that side of things further, but I will never stand in your way as you get to know him better.

The history between Giovanni and me is just that – old news.

I love you very much. Let's FaceTime again very soon,
Mum xx

Writing this is cathartic, and Magda knows she could never have got here without her pep talk from Fliss this morning. There shouldn't be secrets between them after all these years of friendship, and knowing that Fliss is aware of her feelings for Den somehow seems to make everything seem more normal and manageable. Also, for the first time, Magda can feel herself really beginning to break free of the corrosive link she's reluctantly had with the memory of the time with Giovanni. All she needs to do now is to get properly back on track with her son, and get enough baking done to fill their stall. She has a feeling that the second of these tasks will be easier than the first, and that's really saying something.

33

Before long, the kitchen is humming to the sound of Elton John again, and Magda and Fliss are stepping into Christmas in a big way. A couple of hours later, there's a row of small fruit cakes waiting for their marzipan topping, and Fliss is filling some of Hope's airtight containers with more frosted shortbread.

'It seems a waste that not many people know Hope's recipes,' muses Fliss as she works. 'Oh, I know she shared them with some of the townsfolk from time to time, but wouldn't it be brilliant to get them properly published? They'd make a fabulous recipe book, much better than anything similar out there.'

Magda's stomach clenches. *Fliss wants to let everyone into Mum's life*, she thinks to herself, panicking slightly. Even worse, Magda's worried she might lose the special link she's been feeling with Hope every time she opens the book.

'And who's going to find the time to do that, may I ask?' she says.

'Erm . . . you?'

Fliss is still busy putting biscuits away and doesn't seem to pick up the panic in Magda's voice. After a moment she turns and sees the expression on her friend's face.

'It was just a thought,' she says apologetically. 'I know how protective you feel about the book. Forget I mentioned anything.'

After a lot of strong black coffee and a hasty lunch of mainly chocolate-based snacks, Magda and Fliss feel fortified enough to head for the school, ready for the play. Laurence has been round to drop off a bag of plaster of Paris and seeing him, even so briefly, seems to have perked Fliss up no end.

'That's one of the good guys,' Magda tells her, as Laurence drives away. 'He reminds me of Brian Ferry, and you know you had a poster of Roxy Music on your wall for years. Don't try and tell me you don't still fancy the pants off Laurence, my girl.'

'Don't be ridiculous,' says Fliss. 'You're just trying to take the spotlight away from you having this enormous crush on Den. Your mind is in the gutter, as usual.'

'Ha! Pot calling the kettle black there?'

'Not at all.'

Even so, Fliss is smiling broadly all the way down the hill to the school.

Although they both have places booked for the Nativity play, Magda knows that competition for the best seats will be fierce and, sure enough, by the time they reach the gates, the queue of excited parents and grandparents is winding its way all around the edge of the playground. Natasha is standing at the main door with her clipboard and red pen at the ready.

'Only five minutes to the big moment when we open the doors,' she calls. 'Can we avoid pushing please, ladies and gentlemen? There's plenty of room for you all inside.'

'Always the optimist,' mutters Magda. 'We'll be crammed in like sardines. I heard on the grapevine it was so hot in there last year that one of the older grannies fainted and nobody noticed for ten minutes because she was propped up so closely either side.'

'That's awful. Did she not see the rest of the play?' Fliss asks, focusing, as ever, on the important bit.

'Oh yes, she was fine. Her daughter poured cold water over her face and she came round immediately and joined in with the singing in the finale. Nobody leaves until they absolutely have to.'

The people in front of Magda and Fliss are beginning to shuffle forwards now, but Natasha is making sure not a soul gets through the door unless they're on her list. This holds up the proceedings considerably as several families have tried to sneak in an extra person or two. When a full-scale war seems about to break out, everyone is mightily relieved to see Den in the doorway.

'It's okay, folks,' says the elderly man in front of Fliss. 'The boss is here. Nobody messes with him.'

Magda watches as Den sorts out the problem quickly and tactfully and then turns to the queue.

'Sorry for the delay, everyone. You'll be pleased to know that due to a quick reorganization of the PE equipment by my wonderful staff, we've managed to create an extra row of seats, so you'll all get in.'

'But ... Mr Archer ... the booking list ...' Natasha's pointing to her clipboard, her face thunderous.

'Don't worry, Mrs Trotter,' Den says. 'It's all under control. You can let everyone in now without ticking them off. It's much too cold to leave everyone waiting outside. We'll have people dropping with hypothermia if we're not careful.'

He gives a cheery wave to the crowd and goes back inside to the sound of cheering.

'What a bloke,' says the lady behind Magda. 'He's really turned this school round, and he's a lovely man to boot.'

'Nice chap,' her friend agrees. 'Shame about his wife though. Listen to this. I heard it from Freda Dawson. She lives across the street from the Archers. Virginia's gone off again.'

'Ooh!' The first lady is clearly delighted to be hearing this piece of gossip. 'Are you sure?'

'Yes!' her friend confirms. 'Freda says a taxi turned up before six o'clock this morning, pipping like mad. Freda wasn't best pleased, it woke her up.'

Fliss and Magda can't help overhearing this fascinating conversation, and are both wide-eyed. They file into the hall in silence and squeeze into seats near the back. The sound of Wizzard wishing it could be Christmas every day is thumping away in the background and the muggy warmth hits them as they try to unwind themselves from their layers of scarves, coats and woolly hats.

'So Virginia's done a flit again,' whispers Fliss. 'Has she gone for good this time, do you think? And what's that going to mean for you?'

'Who knows if she's finally left? She's probably just gone off on one of her jollies. And it won't mean anything for me.' Magda is defiant, determined not to get involved in this mess yet again.

'But he could be free now.' Fliss is nothing if not persistent, her whispers getting dangerously louder. 'And don't give me all that rubbish again about him being too young for you. When two people click like you have, age doesn't matter a jot.'

'Look, Fliss, just drop it, okay? Even if she doesn't want him, and let's face it, she's not likely to have gone away perman-ently this near to Christmas, I don't need Virginia's rejects.'

Slade have now taken over from Wizzard and the decibel level in the room is ear-splitting. Preoccupied as she is with

Magda's love-life, Fliss doesn't notice that Den's walked out on to the small stage at the front of the hall and held up a hand. In the sudden silence as the music is turned off, she bellows, 'But don't you ever want to have sex again, Magda?'

There's an outbreak of tittering around them and Magda feels her cheeks burning. She nudges Fliss so hard her friend cannons into the woman next to her. Luckily, she thinks Den's too far away to hear. He smiles around at everyone.

'Welcome to our Nativity play,' he says. 'It's one of the most popular events of the school year and it couldn't happen without all the hard work of my amazing staff, not to mention Mrs Trotter's skilful organization. Let's give them a round of applause before we start.'

As her face cools down, Magda sees Natasha beaming around at the audience. 'I bet she's thrilled with that mention,' Fliss whispers to her. Magda doesn't answer. She's still too cross.

'We must also thank you lovely parents for your help in getting costumes together,' Den adds, when the clapping dies down. 'It never ceases to amaze me how you manage to produce the goods so efficiently.'

'*He's* obviously never had to magic up an angel costume from a pillowcase and some tinsel,' says the lady next to Fliss.

'They get them off Amazon these days,' says her friend. 'Times have changed. Shepherds in tea towels are a thing of the past.'

'And now for the main event,' Den says. His eyes meet Magda's across the sea of parents and grandparents. 'A huge amount of practising has gone into this performance and although we always pride ourselves that Periwinkle Primary is one big family, this year, for the first time ever, we have a set of twins as Mary and Joseph, and a gang of cousins and second cousins as the three Wise Men. Well, five Wise Men, if we're being accurate,' there are small titters of laughter from the crowd at this. 'I'd like to introduce you to . . . our children. The reception class present *A Christmas Birth.*'

As he finishes speaking, there's a commotion near the door next to the stage and a voice calls, 'Is my mummy here yet? I need to tell her I've done a wee in my donkey suit.'

This holds up the start of the play, but not for long. Soon, the age-old story is being acted out by the angelic host of chubby-faced infants. Magda is sure that their two teachers must be on the verge of exhausted collapse, and in dire need of the bottles of wine and gin that a handful of the more generous parents have sent in for them today, but they don't let it show. By the time Will and Desi are in position by the manger and Desi is reaching forward to pick up her baby son, both Magda and Fliss are close to tears. Fliss reaches for Magda's hand and they cling to each other, all thoughts of the past few weeks of anger between them far from Magda's mind now.

'Thank goodness Desi doesn't have to speak after all,' whispers Fliss. 'Oh!'

The gasp is brought on by Desi stepping forward, holding out the swaddled doll to show the audience. She clears her throat. 'I'm going to call him . . .' she says clearly.

There's an agonizingly long pause. Magda hears the nearest teacher hissing, 'Jesus. You're going to call him Jesus.' Desi turns and glares at her witheringly. She starts again.

'I'm going to call him . . . William,' she says proudly. 'Because that's my brother's name.'

Will is red to the tips of his ears and Magda expects he'd like the ground to swallow him up as the hall erupts with delighted laughter. The teacher looks mortified, but Magda is so happy that Desi's finally managed to say a whole sentence that she doesn't care.

'She can call him Rumpelstiltskin if it means she's going to talk to us again,' Fliss says, echoing Magda's thoughts, as the two of them wipe away happy tears and clap along with the rest of the crowd.

The final rendition of 'Away in a Manger', as Magda predicted, has everyone fumbling for tissues, and Will's solo in the second verse is pure and clear. He's so pleased with himself that he bows to the audience before the whole carol is finished, meaning a pause for extra applause is needed before the last verse and the children finish singing a while after the music stops, but nobody minds. They all join in a rousing chorus of 'We Wish You a Merry Christmas' and the Periwinkle Bay Nativity Play is over for another year.

'Those poor teachers deserve far more pay than they're ever going to get,' says the lady next to Fliss. 'I bet they're knackered. Hey,' she nudges Fliss and leans forward to peer round her. 'We all want to know the answer to that burning question. *Does* your friend ever want to have sex again?'

Magda pretends not to hear.

Magda and Fliss wait in line in the playground to collect the twins, who come running to them, arms outstretched.

'Were we good?' shouts Will.

'You were both amazing, my loves,' Magda says, hugging them both and kissing their curly heads.

'Desi said the wrong words though,' Will says sadly, as they walk home.

'I didn't. I said the right words. William's a much nicer name,' says Desi.

Magda and Fliss exchange glances. Apart from being a little husky, Desi's voice is as sweet and precise as it always used to be. Magda wonders if it's best to mention the fact that she's speaking properly again or just pretend it's normal, but Will gets in first.

'Desi said she's fed up with being quiet and she likes being with you two and me a lot,' he says. 'So she's going to talk again now.'

'Going to talk a lot,' says Desi, beaming up at Magda and swinging their hands together as they walk along.

'That's absolutely brilliant news, poppet,' Magda replies, grinning and deciding to question it no further. All that matters is that Desi is back to her normal self. 'And now all we need is to work hard tonight to get ready for the bake sale tomorrow morning! Are you two ready to help? We need you to be as grown up as possible to get everything sorted. We still haven't got enough cakes to fill the tables.'

'And we've still got to do the shell presents for Mum and Dad,' Will adds. 'We'd better not forget that. Do you think we could ask Mr Archer to help? And Blondie? I bet they'd like to come round.' Magda groans internally. She'd almost forgotten about the plant pots.

'I don't think that's likely,' she says in response. 'He'll be very tired. The last day of term must be extra hard work.'

'But why? The teachers don't do the work.'

'It's us that does it all,' agrees Desi. 'They just watch us. So why?'

Magda decides this is a conversation for another day. They're back at the front door now and the warmth of the house welcomes them in. She switches on the fairy lights to distract Will and Desi. The tree in the hall glitters, the white lights shining on its many baubles and strings of tiny gold bells.

'Let's get your little tree lit up in the kitchen too,' she says. 'Then we can get to work.'

While the twins run upstairs to get changed into comfy clothes and Fliss goes to hunt for her slippers, Magda flicks the kettle on and gives herself five minutes to sit down in Hope's chair with the recipe book.

'Oh Mum, I miss you so much,' she whispers, clutching the book tightly to her chest and feeling the comfort spreading through her tired body. 'You'd have loved seeing the twins in their play today. I'm still gutted that Jared and Annie missed it. How am I going to get through the next days? Christmas and New Year without them and without you are going to be so hard. But I can't let myself be gloomy, it's not fair on the others.'

She puts the book on her lap and lets it fall open. Unsurprisingly, the page where it settles is part of the festive section. Looking down, she notices a comment in the margin that she hasn't read before. It's next to Hope's special recipe for mulled wine.

Please note that my four main secrets of Christmas happiness are 1) Lots of wonderful food, 2) Plenty of love and attention for everyone, whether they're family or not, 3) Some home-made presents under the tree – remember, not everything has to be perfect to be beautiful, and 4) A few good slugs of mulled wine to tide you over the chaos.

'Mulled wine,' Magda exclaims, as Fliss comes back into the room. 'We forgot we usually have a huge vat of that on the go at the bake sale. We can make it tonight if we've got all the ingredients and then warm it up on that camping hob of Jared's.'

'Great idea. That'll fill a corner of the table. Let's get going.' But before they can start to collect their ingredients, they hear the distant sound of the doorbell.

'Now what?' says Magda, stomping to the hall to see who's disturbing them at this inconvenient moment. Her heart skips a beat when she opens the door and finds Den on the step, a bulging shopping bag in each hand. Hoping that the children will stay upstairs for a few more minutes, Magda lets him in without a word. He looks down at her, as if trying to gauge the mood.

'I don't know if I'm welcome here, after being so out of the loop when you must have needed a hand, but I decided to come anyway,' he says. 'Time's ticking away and the mince pies are all done, so I've brought everything I need to make dinner for us all. The kids can help me if you and Fliss want to get on with the important stuff?'

'Well . . . I guess that'd be okay,' Magda says, then, realizing how ungrateful this sounds, adds, 'But I thought you'd be busy clearing up at school and then rushing back home to be with Virginia?' Let him think she's not heard the gossip about his wife leaving again, she thinks grumpily, still stinging from Fliss's comments.

'We all had a very quick tidy-up but I could see everyone was desperate to get away and get the wine chilling, so we'll be meeting for a bigger sort-out before we go back in January.'

'I've had a few issues of my own to sort out this week,' Magda says. 'It's good of you to come round and we really need the help tonight, but—'

'Mr Archer, you came back!' shouts Will, hurtling into the hallway.

'Were we good today?' Desi asks, joining her brother and coming to a halt in front of her head teacher and looking up hopefully.

'You were both fabulous. Great acting, amazing singing, and a fantastic line in ad-libbing,' he says. Magda's glad he refrained from commenting on the fact that Desi's speaking again. She's terrified of jinxing this lovely new development.

'What's ad-libbing?' Will says, skipping along after the others as Magda leads the way to the kitchen.

Den begins to explain, but Will is fizzing like a sherbet fountain. 'Let's make the presents first,' he says. 'Did you get everything, Granny?'

Magda shows them the row of equipment laid out on the table. 'I thought that might be the first job. It won't take long,' she says. 'I got my collection of shells down from the loft, and Laurence brought us some plaster of Paris. Here are a couple of terracotta plant pots too.'

'Hey, can I take charge of this before I make the dinner?' asks Den, rubbing his hands together. 'It's years since I made plaster of Paris presents. We used to do them at school but it got too expensive.'

Magda leaves him to it, relieved not to be going through the sorting of the shells. The memories of hunting for them with Hope are too poignant. They always discarded more than they brought home, but there are still hundreds there.

As she assembles her baking ingredients, she watches Den and the twins get to work, overwhelmed with a tenderness that's not just for her beloved grandchildren, so absorbed in making something beautiful for their parents. Her heart goes out to the man whose dark head is so close to the fair, curly ones. She realizes with a jolt that Den is the sort of partner she's thought only existed in romantic stories. Remaining single has always seemed the best option if the alternative is sharing her life with someone who isn't remotely right for her, but now it's no good trying to deny it any more. Den is a person of integrity, with a quirky sense of humour, twinkling eyes that often seem to be laughing, and the kind of body she longs to curl up next to on cold winter evenings. That said, he isn't hers and he doesn't seem keen to explain what's going on with his marriage. She wonders if Virginia can really have gone for good and if so, what if could mean for the two of them. He's studiously avoiding mentioning Virginia's name and Magda isn't about to ask questions. Any next steps have to come from *him*.

34

Saturday, 23 December

Two Days Until Christmas

The morning of the bake sale starts rather earlier than Magda would have liked when Desi wakes her at five o'clock, sobbing.

'What's the matter, my love?' Magda says, lifting her into bed and snuggling her up in the duvet. 'Have you got a tummy ache again?' As she cuddles her granddaughter and kisses the top of her head, Magda realizes that this all feels completely normal now. She's feeling a little bleary but not in the least irritated at being woken up at such an uncivilized hour.

'Desi, what's the matter?' she repeats hopefully. 'Come on darling, try and tell me. I know you can if you want to.'

The little girl shakes her head, tears flowing down her cheeks. She burrows into Magda's shoulder as Will enters the room.

'She had a bad dream. She thinks Mummy and Daddy aren't ever going to come home,' Will says, yawning. 'She still says it's your fault that they're not here.'

'But I thought I'd explained all that. Mum and Dad need to be in America for their work.' So much for completely normal.

Magda had congratulated herself too soon. Now she feels the familiar tendrils of frustration creep into her head again.

'Of course they're coming home,' she says, holding them both close. 'I'll ring them in a bit and tell them about the play and how great you were. They'll be desperate to see you!'

'Or they might have got lost in that big city,' Will says.

Magda cuddles the twins until they're quiet, calming them down and managing to persuade them back into bed for an extra hour, but when she gets back into her own bed, her mind is still whirling. She'd really thought she was winning the battle of making grandparenting fun, but they seem to be going backwards. It seems as though this won't be over until Jared and Annika have returned.

Her eyes fall on the heap of colourful holiday brochures that live on her bedside table. They're well thumbed, because the bright photographs of sunny beaches and azure-blue seas have been her constant study since she retired. Her dream is to cruise through those tranquil waters, relaxing on deck before wandering down the gangplank to explore yet another tiny Caribbean village or swim in the warm ocean. The money in her savings account has been gradually mounting up, waiting for the perfect moment. There's nearly enough now.

But maybe there's a better way for her to spend the nest egg. Magda reaches for her laptop before she can change her mind and puts through a Skype call to Jared and Annika. They'll probably be just going to bed, but with luck she'll catch them.

The ringing tone seems to go on forever. Just as Magda's about to give up, Jared appears on the screen, rubbing his eyes.

'What's up, Mum? Is everyone okay?' he says. 'I'd just nodded off, we got away from the theatre quickly tonight. I was going to FaceTime you tomorrow to talk about . . . well, you know.'

'We're not exactly okay,' Magda says. 'But this is nothing at all to do with the other issue.' She fills her son in on Desi starting to speak again at last and then this morning's emotional backslide. Annika's in the frame now, leaning over Jared's shoulder to see what's going on. 'Will's really sad without you both too. I need to do something to cheer them both up. It's too long for them to wait to see you.'

'But we can't do anything about that,' says Jared. 'We've got a contract. They're relying on us.'

'I know you have. That's why I've got a suggestion. Why don't I bring them to see *you*? No, let me finish,' she says as Annika tries to interrupt. 'We could come over just after Christmas. I can book us into a hotel near yours and they can maybe see you in a matinee. We can do the sights and celebrate the New Year together.'

'That's insane, Mum,' says Jared bluntly. 'It'd cost a fortune. Have you got any idea how much flights and a hotel room would be over the Christmas holidays? And then there's food for you all on top of that. It'd be amazing, but you can't afford it.'

'I can if I use my cruise fund,' says Magda defiantly. 'What's more important? Making the kids happy, or me having a fat cat holiday and eating and drinking way too much?'

'But you've been saving up for your cruise for ages,' says Annika. 'It's a lovely thought but we can't let you do it.'

'I'm going to have to dash now because there are sounds of mayhem coming from the twins' room, but let's talk about it as soon as Christmas Day's over, shall we? I'm sure I can get some last-minute flights. Honestly, it's something I really want to do.'

Magda blows kisses to them both and rings off before they

can say more. Another hour in bed for herself and a big hot bath is what she really wants, but for now, a quick shower and into her jeans and a big fluffy jumper is the reality. It's going to be a long day.

When Magda and Fliss reach the Town Hall in their taxi, ready for the bake sale, the place is already bustling. All the usual stallholders are there, busy loading up their allocated areas, and the din of old friends greeting each other and sparring good-naturedly about who has the best spaces is almost deafening. Will and Desi have been dropped off with their best friends for the morning, and Magda sends Fliss in to find their space while she unloads. In seconds, Den is emerging from the hall to help with a couple of his cronies in tow. Wordlessly, he takes the heaviest box out of Magda's arms and makes a beeline for the best spot in the corner, near the tea stall, where two long tables have been set out at right angles to each other. Fliss is busy spreading Hope's best embroidered cloths over them but her expression is serious.

'I'd forgotten how much room they always give us,' she says. 'We've done our best with the baking, but even with Den's mince pies and the mulled wine it's going to look really thin compared to our usual loaded tables.'

When all the boxes are in, Den helps to set up the mulled wine station, while Magda and Fliss lay out their produce. The cakes with their layers of marzipan and fondant icing have been decorated by Fliss with tiny Christmas trees and houses from the craft shop. Magda spreads them out as much as she can, taking care not to crumple the little gingham frills around the tops of the jars of apple jam and lemon curd. Their colourful labels add the finishing touch.

Magda has to admit that the crowning glory of the stall is the mince pie area right at the centre. She's displayed Den's creations on a set of pretty cardboard cake stands, three layers on each, and added tiny sprigs of artificial holly leaves and berries. The red and green of the decorations glows against the snowy white of their dusting of icing sugar. Magda's stomach rumbles. They smell wonderful – rich, spicy and appetizing. She's just trying to make the plates of iced short-bread and gingerbread men look like twice as many when someone taps her on the shoulder.

'Hello,' says the woman by her side. She's wearing a long camel coat with a fur collar, and her make-up is flawless. Magda has a momentary pang that she hasn't spent longer on her own appearance before facing the public, but there was only time to throw on jeans and her warmest polo-neck sweater before they all dashed out of the house this morning.

'We haven't met before but I'm Jenny,' says the smart lady, smiling at Magda. 'I'm from Midcaster. My hairdresser, Sophie, told me you might be a bit short of baked goods this year? I've made you a batch of lemon curd tarts. The lemon curd's from your mother's recipe book. She taught our ladies' group how to make it when she did a cookery class for us a few years back. We all loved Hope. She had a way of making you feel you could do anything if you tried. Sorry there's not more, but my teens love these and they pinched one or two.'

Magda has only just overcome her surprise and started to thank Jenny profusely when a second woman appears with an older man in tow. His grey beard is neatly trimmed and his thick fleece almost matches his twinkling blue eyes. He beams at Magda as if he knows her well.

'Hiya. Sophie said you needed a bit of back-up with the

cakes,' says the woman. 'This is my dad. He's made you six date loaves.'

The man hands over a box covered with a checked tea towel and waves away her thanks. 'You look a lot like your lovely mum,' he says. 'It's good to see that you're not letting the side down. She'd be proud of you for doing all this. I've used your mother's method for these,' he says, gesturing to the box. 'We were at school together, Hope and me, so we were old mates, but even so I had to bribe her with a big box of her favourite chocolates to get the date loaf recipe out of her when I took up baking a few years back. It was worth it. She was a fine woman, was Hope. Glad to help.'

Magda and Fliss are almost overwhelmed with emotion as more and more local people whose lives Hope has touched turn up with offerings throughout the next hour or so. Some are well known to them, others only vaguely familiar, but all of them explain that they have taken tips from Hope over the years, and these are their own specialities, developed from Hope's basic recipes. One woman tells Magda that her mother's economical recipe for chocolate crunch pudding saved her from homesickness when she was an impoverished student. She looks as if she's trying to relive those days, Magda thinks with a smile, dressed in a biker jacket, torn jeans and heavily scented with patchouli oil. Another, wrapped up warmly in a beautiful home-knitted cardigan in russet shades, raves about Hope's contributions to the Women's Institute teas over the years, and the way she was everyone's friend, but especially the ones lacking confidence with their baking.

Two men with attractively weathered faces come along next, and introduce themselves as brothers, members of the Gardeners' Guild in the next village. 'We've made some of

Hope's trademark chocolate brownies,' the older one says. They both carry large cake tins which they hand over with pride.

'Your lovely ma used to win our baked goods competition every year with this recipe,' the younger man says. 'She always challenged us to beat her but we never could. Rob here thinks this batch of his are about as good as Hope's, but I reckon mine are better. You can be the judge.'

Magda thanks the two men profusely but hopes fervently that the brownies are all sold before she's asked again to make such a tricky decision.

Laurence appears two minutes later, carrying ten little boxes of his home-made chocolate and brandy truffles and two large baskets full of decorated cookies. There are Christmas trees, bauble shapes, holly leaves and stars, all beautifully decorated and packed in layers of sparkly tissue paper.

'You're a star yourself,' breathes Fliss as she carefully unpacks the treasures. Her eyes are shining, and Magda wonders if this huge effort is merely Laurence wanting to help a good cause, or whether it's actually in aid of something more ambitious for his future happiness. Either way, the gesture is lovely.

As opening time draws nearer and Fliss rearranges the table over and over again to make room for the new arrivals, one of Fliss and Laurence's oldest customers at the craft shop brings strings of red and gold bunting that he's made specially to go around the edge of the stall.

One by one, the various stalls are filled with a tempting array of goods. There are three plant stalls, two tables covered with beautiful greetings cards and several laden with knitted toys and baby clothes, plus a whole range of bric-a-brac and some rather lumpy hand-thrown pottery. There are no other cake stalls. The people of Periwinkle Bay have always acknowledged that Hope reigned supreme in that area. By the time the chief organizer rings the bell to let them all know he's opening the door, the bake sale stall is so packed with home-cooked goodies that there isn't an inch of tablecloth visible. The delicious smell of the sale items is enough to draw people to the stall, and they look even better than they smell.

'Well, you've outdone yourselves again, girls,' says Den's next-door neighbour, Freda, as she elbows her way through the throng already queuing up to have first choice of cakes. 'I've bought you a batch of my Eggless Nutties to sell. They're like little baby flapjacks, only better. It was your mum's recipe originally, but I've added a few extras. I was very fond of Hope. I saw a lot of her after your dad's accident; it was a very tough time for her. We've been firm friends ever since. Were, I mean,' she adds sadly.

'She did tell me how good you were, and that you looked after me afterwards lots of times,' Magda says, giving the woman a hug.

'Well, she repaid me many times over through the years, teaching me her recipes and propping me up when I lost my own husband. We used to call ourselves The Merry Widows, even though we often didn't feel that merry, if I'm honest. We always cheered each other up, though. The cakes are to say an extra thank you.'

'That's so kind,' Magda says, still unable to take in how many people have come forward to help them fill the stall.

'It's no trouble. Your mum meant a lot to me, love. We shared some difficult times but she never lost that sunny smile of hers . . . By the way, have you decided what to do about your Christmas lunch, Denis?' she adds in a whisper, just loudly enough for Magda to hear. 'You know you're welcome to come round to mine. My gang are coming over but I can easily squeeze another one in.'

Den looks across at Magda. 'I haven't had the chance to tell people about my wife leaving again yet,' he says. 'But Freda knows all about it as she unfortunately had to witness some of it. Sorry again, Freda,' he adds. 'Anyway, Virginia's gone. And she isn't coming back this time. We had a long talk and she's going to make her home in Wales for good now. I think we both knew it was time things were over.'

'And she took the dog,' Freda says, with a hearty sniff. 'The cheek of it.'

'Not really, Freda. I think she actually came back to see Blondie and to sound me out about taking her away with her. Virginia missed the dog much more than she missed me. But that's okay. All good things come to an end. And I'm just glad we had a chance to clear the air.'

'So, Christmas dinner?' Freda asks again.

Magda can see Den struggling to answer and she decides to help him out. 'He's going to have the day with us, thanks Freda,' she says. 'I bagged him first.'

Freda nods and bustles off with her loaded shopping basket.

The final contribution is from Belinda, who arrives with a tray of Christmas puddings in pottery basins, covered with circles of red and white checked cloth and tied up with string.

'I guess you probably decided it was too late for you to make these for the stall,' she says. 'It isn't, though. Hope told me last year that she'd discovered years ago that microwaving her Christmas puddings meant she could make them much later. You can always boil them on the day if you want to make it feel more authentic and fill the kitchen with steam. I've made a big one for your family, in case you hadn't bought one already.'

Magda doesn't let on that they've already discovered this tip, thinking to herself that they could never have too many, anyway. She can't think of the words to say how much this means to her but she hugs Belinda tightly instead. The puddings are the perfect finishing touch. She shuffles everything around with difficulty to make space for Freda and Belinda's contributions. All will be well now.

As Belinda bustles away, Magda turns to face Den properly for the first time that morning. He smiles down at her as warmly as ever but seems hesitant when he speaks.

'Are you sure you want me to come to yours for Christmas dinner?' he says. 'You don't have to bail me out, you know, but I'd love to be with you . . . all.'

'So long as you didn't feel press-ganged into it?'

'I think you know I don't. There's nowhere I'd rather be. Also, we do need to talk.'

'I'm not sure if there's anything more to say, is there? Anyway, it'll have to be after New Year now,' she tells him. 'I'm planning to take Will and Desi to see their mum and dad. It's the only way I'm going to cheer them both up.'

'But . . . how . . . when . . .?' Den falters, clearly disappointed, and Magda can't help but enjoy his reaction. 'That's crazy. It'll be a nightmare trying to get flights at this time of year, and hotels and everything. And Mags, it'll cost an arm and a leg. They'll be home in a fortnight anyway. Can't you just wait a bit longer?'

Magda shakes her head. She knows what she has to do. 'Two more weeks must seem like forever to a five-year-old. They need to see their parents. I'm going to book flights as soon as I wake up on Boxing Day, in the sales. We'll manage it somehow.'

A fresh wave of customers distracts Den from arguing any more, but Magda can tell by his expression that he's not going to let the subject drop easily.

Much later, when she's back home at last with the twins tucked up in bed and a substantial log fire blazing, Magda lies back on the sofa and flexes her tired shoulders. She can hear Fliss coming downstairs after a long, hot bath and knows she should really stir herself to make a pot of tea or pour some wine for them both, but exhaustion is making the prospect of either seem impossible.

Fliss, clad in her huge fleecy dressing gown, pads into the room. 'You look how I feel,' she says. 'Was it worth all that back-breaking effort, do you think? I'd forgotten what hard work the sale is. Your mum never seemed to mind. She took it all in her stride even up to last year.'

Magda's just about to answer when her mobile rings. She glances at the caller display and sees Den's name lit up. Fliss, looking over her shoulder, raises her eyebrows.

'Hi, Den,' Magda says, sitting up straight and trying to sound as if just the sight of his name hasn't made her heart skip several beats. 'I thought you'd be in the pub by now, celebrating the yearly session of hard graft being over.'

She listens and then lets out a cheer, quickly silencing herself when she remembers Desi and Will are only just asleep. 'No kidding? But that's amazing. I'll tell Fliss right away. Okay . . . well . . . thanks for letting me know.'

Magda ends the call and turns to face Fliss, who is grinning in a most irritating way.

'Oh, stop it,' Magda says, pulling a face at her. 'He was only ringing to let us know about the proceeds from the sale.'

'Of course he was. And . . .?'

'Only the best result we've ever had! The cake stall doubled what we made last year because of all the extra contributions, and the whole event has made enough money to begin the setting up of Den's idea for a "Feed a Family" scheme. Did I tell you about that?'

Fliss shakes her head, coming over to sink into the sofa next to Magda. 'Go on,' she says.

'He ran it past the fund-raising committee last month but they didn't think we'd make enough money. Our contribution has tipped the balance. Den wants to start a drop-in centre in the town to provide hot meals. The food bank's doing a great job already but the problem is that some families are struggling to pay their fuel bills so cooking's an issue now.'

'So . . . he'll want volunteers to make soup and so on? Cheese and potato pie? Lovely stodgy puddings?'

They look at each other and laugh. 'I reckon we need to sleep on this before we start offering our services. You've got to take care of yourself at the moment and my track record isn't great in that area,' Magda says.

Fliss smiles. 'But getting better all the time. And I'm okay most of the time, so long as I don't rush at things. You know what, Magda? I think we can probably tackle anything we put our minds to these days.'

Christmas Eve, Three Years Ago

'Honestly, Mum, you *could* help more with the food prep, you know. I'm trying to learn my lines. The new play starts in January and Annika's still busy making costumes. Gran can't do it all herself.'

Jared's words cut into Magda's thoughts as she frantically scribbles down a list of everything the family want her to do before she can at last get into a hot bath and go to bed. She stares at her son in amazement.

'You really have no idea, do you? I'm meant to be looking after the twins for you both all day long, which means taking the double buggy round the town so I can get all this last-minute stuff you all suddenly desperately need, and I think Will and Desi are both getting colds and, and, I'm tired, Jared. I'm really, really exhausted.'

Jared folds his arms and frowns, his dark brows almost meeting in the middle. He's normally ridiculously handsome but Magda can't help thinking this isn't one of his better days. He hasn't showered or shaved yet today and his hair is standing on end. Sweat pants and a baggy jumper instead of his usual black jeans and smart shirt also add to the overall effect of a student after a night on the tiles. She can't really criticize, though, because in an attempt to throw herself into the festive spirit Magda is wearing possibly the most hideous Christmas jumper ever, bought at a charity shop in the town. The garish depiction of Rudolph with a flashing red nose and furry antlers isn't doing a lot for her mood but at least it's made the twins giggle.

'I'm just thinking of Gran, that's all. I'll help her later, so will Annie, but we need to get our act together this morning. I don't think you realize how much she does in the kitchen at Christmas. She's no spring chicken, you know.'

'Yes, I *had* worked that out for myself as she *is* my mother, but thank you so much for your kind reminder.' Magda's trying to keep a lid on her temper, but it's tricky. It's never been easy with her and Jared. 'Fliss is with her, and they're quite happy, I checked. Now do you want me to do my own bit today or would you rather look after your own kids? *For a change.*'

She whispers the last three words, but her son has the hearing of a bat.

'What did you say?' His voice is ominously quiet now.

'Nothing. I'm going to get the twins ready.'

'Now hang on a minute. Is this the woman speaking who palmed her own child off as often as possible so she could work? If it wasn't for Fliss and a few neighbours all those years, you'd have been really stuck.'

'When are you going to let go of all this resentment? I was a single parent, Jared. I had to do it.'

'Yeah, yeah . . .'

At this, Magda is on her feet and has him by the shoulders. 'How dare you? I did my best for you, I really did. You just love to stick the knife in, don't you? Over and over again.'

Slamming out of the room, Magda feels more like the teenage version of Jared than her much more mature self. She wants to scream and rage, but the children are upstairs with their mum, waiting for Magda to take over. Exhaustion almost swamps her. Her son never seems to remember what her life was really like back then and how hard she's still working. It had been eleven o'clock last night when the last baby had finally appeared and she still had to write up her notes when she got home.

'Granny?' shouts Desi, as she climbs the stairs. 'We're here. Where are you?'

'Coming,' Magda calls back wearily. It's a good job she loves them all so much. At some point she's going to have to make a huge effort and get to the bottom of Jared's bitterness. They both need to do some straight talking and get all these old resentments out of the way. If only she had more free time. A recent memory pops into her head unbidden. Her immediate boss has been ordered to streamline the workforce and has been sounding out everyone in the team about possible voluntary redundancies. Magda bites her lip. No, she can't . . . not yet anyway. She loves her career too much to give it up so that she can run around after the family even more. But maybe before too long she'll succumb to the lure of early retirement. Just maybe . . .

35

Sunday, 24 December

One Day Until Christmas

After the frantic bustle of the bake sale and an afternoon taking turns with Fliss to wrap presents upstairs, Magda is relieved beyond measure when she wakes to a peaceful house the next morning. In fact, it's not just quiet inside the cottage. An eerie glow from the window and a lack of noise outside tell Magda that something else has happened.

Sliding out of bed so as not to wake the twins, she crosses to the window, already with the fluttery anticipation in her stomach that makes her feel like a child again. Sure enough, more snow has fallen in the night. Proper, thick snow this time. It lies in drifts around the garden, and fat flakes are still floating soundlessly down. Magda gasps at the tranquil beauty of the scene, gradually becoming aware of faint noises coming from Will and Desi's room.

When she tiptoes in to investigate, half-hoping she's imagined the sounds, she finds all their bedding on the floor and the two ancient wooden clothes-horses from the spare bedroom being used as the base of a large construction.

'Erm . . . what are you doing?' she whispers, half-hoping she's still dreaming.

'We're making a boat and then we're going to sail across the big sea to fetch Mum and Dad home,' says Will, equally quietly. 'It's a secret. Sshh.'

Magda creeps back to bed, snuggling down and luxuriating in this bonus time. When she finally decides she should get out of bed and make it downstairs, the twins are still busily boat-making and Fliss is already in the kitchen, fetching in the vegetable delivery that came from the market stall yesterday and has been left outside the back door until now. She unpacks a cauliflower, a stick of sprouts, and bunches of carrots with their froth of green fronds, laying them out along the worktop and lining up the saucepans ready.

'We'll do the veg prep today and make the stuffing and the bread sauce,' she says. 'The turkey's already in the pantry on the coldest shelf . . .' Magda can feel relief flooding through her whole body as she listens to Fliss rattling on about the Christmas food prep. This, to Magda, is the proper meaning of a family Christmas. She and Fliss might not be blood relatives, but this is what Christmas has been for her, for as long as she can remember.

'Mags?' Fliss is asking now. 'I was wondering about Laurence . . .'

'Oh my life, I didn't give him a thought,' says Magda. 'Should we invite him now or will he feel like an afterthought? Oh wait, who cares? Say no more. Ring him as soon as it's past silly o'clock. One more won't make any difference and if he comes round early enough he can play with Will and Desi.'

Magda watches Fliss tapping away on her phone straight away and marvels at how relaxed she looks. It seems that

Fliss is finally coping well, despite everything, and Magda can't help but think the charms of Mistletoe Cottage have helped her get there. The anxious look has gone from her eyes and a couple of times she's even inquired about their plans for the potential makeover of the outhouses. She's pretending to just be intrigued, but Magda can tell she's on the cusp of being convinced and is looking forward to the prospect of downsizing.

'There's another thing,' says Fliss. 'Did you realize it's Den's birthday on Boxing Day, and it's his fiftieth?'

'No! He's never mentioned it before to us, has he?'

'I don't think so. I found out quite by chance when I was talking to Freda yesterday after the sale. What can we do to make it special for him? He's helped us out so much. It's way too late to get a present ordered.'

Magda sighs. Just when she thought they were on top of the Christmas organization, a curve ball appears out of nowhere. 'He'll be here for Christmas dinner but we can't let him celebrate the day after all on his own. I'll have a think. Leave it with me.'

The morning passes quickly and Magda and Fliss sit down with the twins for a steaming bowl of soup at lunchtime. There's no church service because everyone's saving themselves for Carols by Candlelight tonight. Will and Desi are still mad with excitement. They've been playing in the snow until their fingers turned blue with cold and their noses were bright red, but they don't seem in the least bit tired.

'Have you put out the carrot for Rudolph and the mince pie for Father Christmas?' Magda asks the twins as they all clear the table, remembering the rituals that Hope had introduced to her as a child and that Jared had loved so much in his turn.

'Yes, but there should be some of that yucky brown stuff,' says Will, capering around the kitchen.

'He means Hope's cream sherry, I think,' says Fliss, digging in the kitchen dresser for a dusty bottle. 'I don't think anyone's touched this since last Christmas.'

'Hooray,' cheers Will, spinning Desi around until they both fall over.

Fliss takes them each by the hand and guides them over to the table. 'Look, sit here again and calm down, both of you,' she says gently. 'If you want to stay up late and still have enough energy to hang up your stockings before you go to bed, you're going to have to give your granny a hand or we won't have finished our jobs in time to sing carols.'

'Good idea. What's still to do?' Magda asks.

'Can you three have a go at GG's apricot and chestnut stuffing next?' says Fliss. 'It's dead easy. You can't go wrong.'

A couple of weeks ago, those last four words would have made Magda roll her eyes in disbelief and make every excuse under the sun to pass the job on to someone else, but now, she fetches Hope's book from the shelf and gets to work, with a twin either side of her. Her hands are soon too sticky to turn the pages but even with the recipe book propped in front of her, Magda can feel the positive vibes flowing from it.

She talks to Fliss again about how much she regrets not learning her way round the kitchen from her mother while she still had the chance as she mixes the breadcrumbs with the eggs that Will has beaten ready, and supervises Desi, who's snipping apricots into small pieces with very blunt scissors.

Fliss has an unusual twinkle in her eye. 'So what were you

doing while all this kitchen activity was going on?' she asks. 'Lying on the sofa, eating grapes?'

'No, of course I wasn't,' Magda retorts quickly.

'I didn't think so. Well then, what *were* you up to?'

Magda considers the question. 'Actually, I was dashing about doing all the jobs that the rest of them hadn't had time for. Last-minute shopping, tidying up, cleaning the bathroom, wrapping presents . . .' she stops, seeing Fliss's grin.

'I'm trying to get you to see that everyone's got their part to play. They were all blissfully happy in the kitchen cooking up a storm even if they might have huffed and puffed a bit about being busy, but you were doing other useful stuff. And now it's your turn to enjoy the cooking part.'

'Enjoy?'

'Yes. You're loving it all now, aren't you? Working with the kids, showing them how it's done, the fantastic smells of Christmas food cooking all around. And I never thought I'd say this, but *I'm* liking having more of a back seat for a change. It's no fun getting a diagnosis like the one I've just had, but we're all dealing with it, aren't we? This is just a new kind of Christmas.'

Magda thinks back to that first meeting she and Den had in his office, when she was panicking about how to look after the children and still make Christmas feel like *Christmas*. He had mentioned something very similar back then. *Christmas can still be just as good, but in a different way*, he'd said. She had doubted him at the time, struggled with how she was going to make that happen, but now, with Fliss repeating his sentiment, she realizes: *I'm already doing it.*

Much later, wrapped up warmly against the chilly night air, Magda walks down to the church hand in hand with Will and

Desi. Fliss is getting a lift with Laurence and he's picking a couple of the older choir members up too, so there's no room for Magda and the children. Luckily, their frosty walk feels wonderfully festive. They peer in at all the brightly lit windows, commenting on the various trees and sparkly decorations. When they reach the church, the door is open wide, and a stream of people are hurrying towards the light from all directions.

Magda waves to Jean, who this time has the box of matches firmly clutched in her hand, and hands the twins over to Fiona, who shepherds them towards the other children at the front. The choir are already assembling, dressed in their favourite Christmas jumpers, with a fair sprinkling of Santa hats amongst them. Den waves from the organ bench. He's wearing an enormous red pullover with the sleeves pushed back, and smart black chinos. Magda has a sudden urge to rush up to him and wrap her arms around his waist, burying her face in the soft wool. She gives herself a mental slap and goes to sit with the altos, wishing she'd found something more glamorous to wear than the huge sweater with the picture of Rudolph on the front that she's pulled from the back of her wardrobe. His flashing red nose is already getting on her nerves and his furry antlers look distinctly moth-eaten.

Den's playing a medley of the quieter carols when they first arrive, but when the time approaches for the start of the service, he ups the volume and the swelling, heart-lifting chords of 'God Rest Ye Merry Gentlemen' ring out. The congregation all stand and join the choir to sing with as much gusto as anyone could wish for. As the last chorus of O *tidings of comfort and joy* dies away and everyone sits down, the main lights go out in the church and there's a collective gasp as hundreds of tiny tea-lights glow in the darkness.

The altar is traditionally lit by the Advent wreath and a magnificent array of thick red church candles, interspersed with holly and ivy. As Jean stands to introduce the choir and their first carol, Magda feels as if she's being transported back in time to her childhood. Nothing much has changed over the years in the way the church is decorated for this event, and that's the way she likes it. The stable at the front has its carved wooden animals and a manger filled with straw, and the Christmas tree glows and twinkles in one corner, a heap of brightly wrapped gifts for the junior members underneath it. Even the horse/donkey has its ears on straight, for once. But just as she's thinking this, she suddenly notices something that *is* different.

Looking round the church from her place in the choir, Magda has already spotted several unfamiliar faces. There's always a good turnout for this event and not all the congregation are regulars, but on the back row sit a line of teenagers. They're all wearing T-shirts sporting the words *Lantern Lighters*.

'Who are the back seat gang?' she whispers to Fliss out of the corner of her mouth, nodding over towards the newcomers.

'They're from Midcaster High School,' Fliss murmurs back, under cover of the carol's introduction. 'Good, eh? They're in charge of getting the lantern parade organized.'

Magda thinks about this development as she starts to sing. It's been a long time since they've had an influx of new blood and it makes the future of the chapel seem a whole lot brighter. It's early days, but it's a start. Den and Fliss's words about change sometimes being a positive thing at Christmas come back to her. She will make a point this year of treasuring the old ways but also celebrating the new traditions, she tells herself firmly. No looking back.

The highlight of the service, as always, is the part where the children, hurriedly helped into a jumble of costumes by Belinda, Natasha and Fiona at the side of the church, process round the church and up the central aisle. Den plays the organ quietly in the background and then the congregation sing 'Away in a Manger' as the children assemble around the stable, at least ten angels and shepherds mingling with wise men.

Mary and Joseph come forward to the manger and Mary places the baby in the straw. Magda's relieved to see that Desi has relinquished her starring role tonight and is wearing an angel outfit complete with wonky tinsel halo, so Jesus can safely have his original name. Will is a wise man this time and has bagged the gold-wrapped parcel. He's carrying it under his arm to make sure nobody snatches it.

As the service draws to a close, people begin to shuffle their feet and discreetly put on scarves and hats. The teenagers have already gone outside ready to dish out their assorted lamps because it's time for the lantern procession through the town, to the marketplace, where the Anglican vicar will meet them and take over from Jean for the final carol and prayer. The lanterns are waiting on the path outside, their tea-lights already lit, and as each person leaves the church, they're offered one to carry. This is a much better system than usual, Magda reflects. It's normally more like a rugby scrum. She congratulates the boy who gives her a lamp and he's obviously delighted with the compliment. She hears him passing it on to his friends as she moves away.

Magda is near the back of the line as they move slowly towards the town centre and the giant tree. She can see Will and Desi safely in the band of children, but when they reach the meeting point, the two turn anxiously to look for her and nudge Fiona to tell her they're going to join their granny. They run over to her excitedly, and as they come nearer, eyes shining, Magda experiences an overwhelming sense of their love for her. At long last, she's getting it right. Jared had never given her this whole-hearted sense of appreciation as a child. There was always an edge . . . or maybe she's only imagined it, lost in the depths of her own guilty feelings of failure.

Putting an arm around each of the twins, Magda joins in the final carol, 'O Come All Ye Faithful'. Den is now leading them from a portable keyboard set up near the tree, and the sound of the mingled voices is so joyful that Magda wants to save this perfect moment, to somehow preserve it forever. A time when everything, for a little while, is absolutely right, the childish voices and soprano tones blending seamlessly with deeper bass notes from the older men. Magda can even hear Den joining in with the chorus. He doesn't usually sing when he's playing the organ, but tonight, he's giving it his all. As if he senses Magda watching him, Den turns and smiles straight at her. Magda finds her throat has closed up for the moment and she can't sing. If only Jared and Annika were here to see how well their children have behaved tonight and how they are trying their best to join in the singing.

'*Hocum let ussa door i . . . im,*' Will bellows, and Desi is clapping along too, although not making a sound. As the music dies away, the vicar says his prayer for peace in the world.

'And this Christmas, my friends, let us not forget those who are outside our traditional circle. This town welcomes everyone, whether from far or near,' he says.

Desi yawns widely and Magda's just wondering how soon she and Fliss can escape to get the children to bed when the sound of a car engine breaks the silence that follows the vicar's words. Everyone turns, as a taxi rumbles to a standstill at the edge of the crowd and both back doors open at once.

'Somebody's left it a bit late to turn up,' grumbles Laurence, who's standing with a protective arm around Fliss, Magda notices.

'I don't think so, actually. It's more like they're just in time,' breathes Fliss, as Jared and Annika emerge, blinking in the light of the massed lanterns and the tree.

36

Magda thinks Will and Desi are in danger of self-combusting when they finally realize who is getting out of the car. Their excitement is contagious, and soon everyone around is cheering and slapping each other on the back. When the mad joy of seeing their parents has died down and the twins are finally home and tucked up with their mother reading them a bedtime story, Magda and Jared sit side by side on the kitchen sofa nursing large brandies. The hour since Jared and Annika have arrived has passed by in a blur for Magda. She's longed so much for the children to have their parents safely home in Mistletoe Cottage for Christmas, but now the new arrivals are actually here, she's able to admit to herself that she's wanted them back for herself too, for her family to be all together in one place.

'I can't believe you didn't warn us you were coming,' she says, definitely not for the first time. 'This is all just so amazing. How long did you say you can stay?'

'We've only got three days. Our main man, Joshua, has recovered from the bug he had, and he was determined he was going to do at least two of the Christmas performances. Anyway, if ever there was a moment that we could take a day or two off, especially with the break for Christmas Day, this felt like the time, so we seized it. We can't be away long, though. I suppose I should also confess that I had something of a eureka moment and realized I was doing to Desi and Will what I'd always resented you for: putting myself and my job ahead of my children. And I decided that I can't keep berating you for having done it if I'm not going to fix it myself, can I?'

'But you came all that way for such a short time. You knew how much the children needed to see you, even if it's just for a little while. And I did too,' Magda adds. 'I've been doing a lot of pondering on the past lately.'

'So have I. All the way over I've been thinking about all the things I want to say to you and wishing I'd said them before. There was a lot of turbulence at one point and I started to panic that we'd crash and I'd never have the chance.'

They sit in silence for a while, sipping their brandy. Magda isn't in the least bit tired now that her three large cups of coffee have kicked in, and Jared's body clock is all over the place. For the first time in a long while, it feels as though there's no rush between them. Eventually she turns to face him properly.

'Right, I'm going to make a start,' she says, taking control of the conversation. She is the mother, after all. 'I've thought a lot about how it was when you were little – me working so much and no dad around. I've felt guilty for such a long time that I don't quite know how to stop, but I feel like I've learnt a lot over the past few weeks with the twins. I've been using Mum's old recipe book and it feels like she's been speaking to me through it . . . anyway, I really think there's been enough resentment and regret now.'

There's silence for a moment and then Jared reaches for her hand. 'I know you did your best, Mum,' he says. 'It was cruel of me to criticize you so much and so often. When you said you were willing to sacrifice your cruise ship fund to make the kids and us two happy it got me thinking how many other times you've put me first. I'm really sorry.'

Magda's throat aches with unshed tears.

'I think I just really wanted to get out there and deliver babies,' she said. 'I've always loved my job. And maybe, yes, I could have been away from you less if I'd tried harder to get a better work-life balance, but I always found it very hard to say no if I was asked to do extra shifts. I just always wanted to be out there helping people.'

'Well, it doesn't matter now, anyway,' Jared says, squeezing her hand. 'You took me away from the city and brought me back here just in time.'

'How do you mean?'

He sighs. 'Well, it's nothing specific, but I was just in with the wrong people, and about to make the wrong decisions for my future. The guys I was at school with didn't think it was cool that I liked acting, for example. I wanted to quit and give everything up, before I'd even had a chance to get started. But coming back to a small village, where everyone supported each other? It was life-changing for me, I just couldn't see that at first.'

Magda sits in silence, letting him get the words out. 'Looking back now, I reckon we escaped just in time. I know I gave you a hard time because of it. I didn't want to leave Leicester, but now I can see it really was the best thing you could have done.'

'Really?'

'Yes. Being with you and Gran and Fliss in this peaceful place saved me, although I thought I'd go off my head with boredom for a little while. But being brought up by three strong women? Even with no dad? There are definitely worse scenarios.' He's grinning now, but Magda isn't prepared to let him get off too lightly.

Celia Anderson

'Well, you nearly drove *all* those three strong women crazy to begin with,' she says, shuddering at the memory of the wild-eyed boy who could hardly bear to be in the house for more than fifteen minutes at a time before taking off to run down the long lanes to the beach and pound along the shore until it got dark. He'd only been able to cope by exhausting himself physically or spending long hours at Fliss and Laurence's craft shop, helping them to redecorate the place.

'It all worked out in the end,' Jared laughs. 'As you know, Laurence introduced me to his drama group, and the rest is history.' Here, he takes a swig of his brandy and pauses for a moment. 'But anyway, I really want to talk to you about my dad. Well, he doesn't really deserve to have me call him that, but "my father" sounds so formal and I don't know what else I would say.'

Magda waits as Jared, lost in thought, stares unblinkingly at the twinkling lights around the dresser.

'Giovanni?' she prompts, when he seems to have drifted too far away.

'Ah, yes. At first I was really excited to meet him. I jumped at the opportunity to email him back and meet him as soon as possible – I felt like I'd been waiting for this moment for so long. That's when I emailed you. I guess I didn't think of the impact that email would have on you, either. But anyway, my excitement didn't last long, to be honest. I started feeling resentful that he thought he could just stroll into my life, and even try to see you again, with barely an apology.'

'And now?' Magda prompts, when he finishes speaking.

'Well, now I've had a bit of time to think. Just before we came back to Mistletoe Cottage his eldest daughter, Tanya, emailed me. Giovanni had finally opened up to her about you

320

and me and his life in Leicester. We batted a few messages back and forth, but we eventually gave up on the online conversation and had a really long talk on the phone. She sounds . . . kind of nice, Mum. She was shocked to find out about us, but she wants to meet me and Annika when we go back, and one day we might even take Desi and Will over for a holiday. How do you feel about that?'

Magda shivers. The past is catching up with her at a gallop. She reaches for the recipe book instinctively, searching for the kind of comfort she knows lies within its pages. It's sitting on the kitchen table already, waiting patiently to give her the final instructions for the Christmas feast. As soon as she's holding the book, Magda feels a delicious surge of happiness flooding her body, even stronger than usual, and so powerful that she gasps out loud.

'Are you okay, Mum?' Jared's looking at her anxiously.

'Oh. Oh yes, I'm fine. I was just . . . just thinking about your gran.' This is the time to be calm and magnanimous, but oh, it's so hard. Magda grits her teeth. 'As for Giovanni and his daughters, it's a decision you have to make without me. They're *your* half-sisters, Jared, they're not really anything to do with me. I think you need to go with your gut feeling, love.'

'Thanks, Mum. It's just that . . . I've now got this whole other family over there. Tanya says they're a great bunch and that as soon as they find out about me, they'll all want to meet us – that's Annika and the kids, too. She says as far as she knows, her dad was never unfaithful to her mum. He adored her and he's been an emotional wreck since she died. Maybe he's changed.'

'Well, maybe . . .' Sudden fear that her son, daughter-in-law and the twins are about to be taken away from her for good leaves Magda breathless, but she rallies as quickly as she can.

'Anyway, of *course* you want to meet them all. It's natural. Whatever Giovanni was or is like, he'll always be the start of the best thing that ever happened to me. You.'

Their arms go around each other, and the unaccustomed warm hug brings tears to her eyes. She holds her son tightly and, feeling his own hot tears on her cheek as they cling together, Magda tells herself sternly that she must make much more of an effort to drop the thought that she isn't enough family for him. As far as she's concerned, there's room for as many other people in his life as he chooses to get to know, and it's time to move forward.

'Right, let's start looking to the future now, Mum. We've done enough soul-searching about the past to last us a long time,' says Jared, giving her a final squeeze before he releases her.

'Ah, Well, it's funny you should say that.' Magda heaves a sigh of relief that they seem to have got past several very sticky moments. 'I've done something I hope you'll agree with too.' She outlines the idea of Fliss moving in when they manage to convert the outbuildings and back room of the sprawling cottage. Jared is, predictably, just as positive about it as she'd hoped he would be. He always did love his Aunty Fliss.

'Thank goodness,' Magda says, breathing a huge sigh of relief that turns into a yawn halfway through. 'Now all we need to do is sort out the money.'

The grandfather clock gives its usual creaky warning that it's about to strike eleven. Christmas Day is nearly here.

'Happy Almost Christmas, son,' says Magda, leaning in to kiss his bristly cheek.

'Happy Almost Christmas, Mum. It's going to be a different sort of Christmas Day this year, isn't it? And actually, I can't wait for it. It's nice to break traditions, sometimes, isn't it?'

Magda smiles knowingly. It seems as though she's heard that line a *lot* in the past two weeks. And on this occasion, finally, she couldn't agree more. Suddenly, there is a loud banging. Jared's head whips around and he sounds puzzled when he speaks.

'Hang on, was that a knock at the back door? It couldn't have been, surely? Nobody would turn up at this time on Christmas Eve.'

Magda gets up and goes to check, only to find Den standing on the doorstep, clutching a bottle of wine.

'I'm sorry, Mags, I know this is silly but I just had to talk to you alone, before the craziness of Christmas Day starts and we won't get a moment to ourselves,' he says, his words rushed. 'Can I come in? Just for ten minutes? I saw the light was on or I wouldn't have bothered you, but I didn't want to wake the whole household by ringing the doorbell.'

Jared clearly hears most of this from his seat at the table. He exchanges wry glances with Magda and excuses himself, saying he'll see both of them in the morning. After he's closed the kitchen door behind him, Magda looks up at Den, the intensity of the green eyes staring back at her making her blink. She beckons him in properly, intrigued. She clears her throat and goes over to the radio on the dresser, hoping for some soothing Christmas music to break the unfamiliar silence between them.

'So what do you want to talk to me about?' she prompts him.

'Can I sit down?' he replies, avoiding her question. Magda

nods and he slips off his long overcoat and drops it over a chair, sinking on to the old sofa with a sigh of relief. 'What a day. I bet you're shattered, too?' It feels to Magda as though he's trying to dodge the real reason he came here.

She nods silently, waiting for him to say more. He links his fingers together as she comes over to sit beside him and, after a few moments, Magda realizes that she's still watching his hands rather too closely for comfort. He has long, strong fingers, perfect for playing the piano or organ, but equally at home just being peaceful and still. It's warm in the kitchen and the soft background music is soothing. The sound of Bing Crosby crooning about a 'White Christmas' conjures up the image of a whole different life, one she's never had. Den still seems to be considering what he wants to say.

Magda's mind wanders to what it would feel like to snuggle down in front of a roaring fire, watching the glow of the lights on the tree and drinking mulled wine . . . to have Den's hands touching her, maybe massaging her aching shoulders, or stroking her cheeks. Horrified at the sudden heat that's rising to her face, she pulls herself up sharply and goes over to the table where Den has put the wine, killing a little time finding a corkscrew and fetching them both glasses.

'Let's have a drink,' she says brightly. 'Although we'd better not have more than a glass of this because tomorrow's going to be a busy day.' She can sense that she's rambling but can't seem to stop.

Den gets up again and joins her before she can babble any more, filling both glasses with the deep red claret. He raises his wine in a silent toast and they both take rather a large gulp. Magda puts her glass down and tries to get her racing thoughts in order, without much success.

Get a grip, she tells herself sternly. *Den's a whole lot younger than you, he's only just out of a long marriage and he's your grandchildren's head teacher, for goodness' sake. Imagine the talk in the town if you dragged him into your bed.*

Den gives her a warm smile that sends shivers right the way down her spine and makes her swallow hard. 'I've just got so much to say to you, I don't know where to start,' he finally says.

'Go on.' Her voice is croaky and she sips her wine, trying hard to make it last rather than drink it all at once. This conversation definitely needs a clear head.

'Okay, here goes. When Virginia left the first time, I thought everything was coming together for me at last. We'd run our course, but neither of us wanted to admit it until she made the move. Then I started to get to know you more and we just . . . kind of connected, didn't we? Being here with you seemed so natural and right. I couldn't help wondering what it would be like to spend a lot more time with you . . . and I thought that now I was free, and that if I could be patient and find ways for us to gradually get to know each other better, we might have something really good going for us. What do you think?'

Magda tries to take all this in. She takes another gulp of wine and splutters slightly. Den pats her on the back and waits. 'I . . . well, it's a lovely idea,' she says when she's recovered.

'I'm sensing a *but*, though?'

'No, not exactly a *but*. You must be able to tell that I want us to . . . I mean, I'd really like us to see if we've got something more going for us than mince pies.' They grin at each other. 'It's just that I'm not used to all this. It's been so long . . . I'm finding it hard to accept that you're ready to move on from

325

Virginia, I guess. There's no way I'm going to leave myself wide open to getting dropped at a moment's notice if she comes back again.'

There, she's said it. Magda holds her breath.

'She won't,' says Den firmly. 'I told you, we're well and truly done, and the best thing about it is there don't seem to be any hard feelings. We're still friends, parents to the boys but . . . she isn't you, Mags, that's what it comes down to. I wanted so much to say all this before, but I kept losing my nerve when I saw you at choir practice and school. You seemed to like me, but nothing was happening. Then everything changed all of a sudden. We did the cooking together, we made each other laugh and it was great. I was like a teenager again. Smitten, besotted, all those things. I played my old CDs, all the songs with cheesy lyrics, and fantasized about you and me, about what might happen next.'

'You did?' But already, the look in Den's eyes convinces Magda he's serious. The track on the radio changes, and she hears the opening bars of 'The Greatest Gift of All' begin to play.

'Oh! One of my mum's favourites,' says Magda, remembering with a pang the warm smile on her mum's face whenever she heard this particular song. 'She had a soft spot for Dolly Parton and Kenny Rodgers. This one's really cheesy, but I love it too.'

'Magda,' Den says huskily, standing up and reaching out for her. 'Come here and dance with me.'

As Magda gets rather shakily to her feet, Den's arms go round her and she leans into the incredible strength and sensuality of his body against hers. She wraps herself around him, lost in the fading scent of a subtle aftershave on warm skin. They fit together perfectly, and as they start to sway to the music, and he leans down to kiss her, Magda feels as if, at last, she's got it right. The kiss seems to go on forever, and when they break apart, Den can't stop looking at her.

'You're amazing, Mags,' he says softly. He kisses her again and time stands still, until the old clock creaks into life to tell them that it's now officially 25 December.

'Happy Christmas, beautiful Magda,' Den whispers. 'I'm going home now, because if I don't, there's a danger we're going to do something very unsuitable for family viewing on this sofa, and I'd hate for us to be disturbed. It might ruin the family day you've got planned.'

He kisses her one more time and grabs his coat, letting himself out of the back door with a wave and a blissed-out grin. Magda sits down at the table and reaches for her wine. She can hardly believe all that just happened.

Christmas Day, Last Year

The grandfather clock in the corner of the kitchen clears its throat, creaking with the effort. It strikes midnight in the usual lazy way, telling Magda that Christmas Day is here at last. On top of the Aga, a large saucepan of red wine laced with cloves, orange peel and cinnamon sticks is simmering gently, its fragrant steam making her mouth water.

'That smells amazing, Mum,' Magda says, rubbing her tired eyes. It's been a very long day. Christmas Eve at Mistletoe Cottage, as usual, has been the time when everyone gives her a list of last-minute jobs that they haven't had the inclination to do before now. Her mother has been cooking since the early morning, and now only the two of them are still awake. The twins have finally gone to sleep, and Jared and Annika have finished the frantic stuffing of stockings for Will and Desi, who will no doubt be bouncing out of bed at dawn. Magda doesn't usually feel old enough to be a granny. She's full of bounce herself as a rule and she likes to think she doesn't look anywhere near her age, but tonight, her sixty years are weighing heavily.

'You look shattered, love,' says Hope. 'They take advantage of you sometimes, they really do.'

Magda pulls a face, debating whether or not to mention that it was Hope's own request to source a very exotic moisturizer for her granddaughter-in-law Annika's stocking that had taken a good chunk of her afternoon. She decides against it. They've already had one spat about Magda's lack of help in the kitchen.

'Maybe we should test the mulled wine?' Magda says. She watches her mother straighten up and massage the small of her back. 'A small glass won't hurt. It might ease your aches and pains and help you to sleep.'

'You make me sound like an old crock,' says Hope, frowning over her reading glasses at her daughter. 'I'm not in my dotage yet, you know. They say eighty is the new sixty. I heard it on the radio. Mind you, we should really see if this stuff is up to scratch, I guess.' She winks. 'It's a tough job, but someone has to do it.'

Ladling out a measure for each of them and sipping her own slowly, Hope takes a final look at the book open on the dresser. Her recipe for mulled wine is legendary in Periwinkle Bay, but this batch is just for the family. She scribbles a brief note in the margin to remind herself to add another twist of lemon and a dash more freshly grated nutmeg just before serving.

Time seems to slow down as Magda and her mum sit down opposite each other at the table.

'What's your favourite thing about Christmas, Mum?' says Magda idly, still mentally running through the list of jobs she's ticked off today.

There's a long silence, and Magda begins to wonder if Hope missed the question. Just as she's about to repeat it, Hope stirs herself.

'Is that one of your deep questions or are you just asking me what festive food I like to eat?' she says. 'I could never tell when you were growing up whether you were being philo-sophical or just nosy when you interrogated me.'

Magda frowns. 'What do you mean?'

'Oh, nothing.' There's a pause and when Magda doesn't reply, Hope continues. 'Well, if you must know, you sometimes made me edgy when you were younger. Always wanting me to tell you things, as if you were trying to trip me up somehow. Fliss never did that.'

'But Fliss isn't your daughter, Mum.' There's another long silence, this one more awkward. Hope drains her glass and puts it on the table. Before her mum can make her escape to bed, Magda reaches out to touch her hand.

'I suppose I just wanted to know more about you,' she says. 'I used to worry about you a lot when I was growing up.'

'Did you?'

'Yes. There was just us two. I was . . . afraid what would happen if you weren't here any more.' Magda stands up suddenly. 'And on that subject, did you put that letter from the hospital somewhere safe?' she asks, leafing through a pile of discarded post on the dresser. 'No, you didn't, it's here.'

'Waste of time,' mutters Hope. 'I hate doctors. I don't know what they're fussing about. It's just a routine check-up, and I'm not ill. Let somebody else have the appointment, someone who needs it.'

Magda puts the letter in a prominent place on the dresser amongst the Christmas cards. She drinks the rest of her mulled wine and switches off the twinkling fairy lights.

'We should get to bed,' she says. 'Will and Desi are bound to be up at dawn. Happy Christmas, Mum.'

'And a very Merry Christmas to you too, my pet,' says Hope.

There's a moment when they almost hug, but as usual, something stops them. It's not what they do. Hugs are for the twins when they tumble over in the garden, or for the odd occasions when emotions run high. Magda sighs. Perhaps she should make a New Year's resolution to put her arms around her mother and Jared and Annika just because she wants to, and to cuddle the twins much more often. It'll take some time to get the hang of it and they'll probably all be too surprised to appreciate it for a while, but you have to start somewhere.

37

Monday, 25 December

Christmas Day, This Year

Magda's morning begins even before the twins wake up, when her laptop pings with an incoming email. She curses herself for forgetting to switch it off when she finally fell into bed, but she'd been so absorbed in daydreaming about Den that she'd not given it a thought.

Lying staring at the ceiling, Magda resolves not to get up to see who's messaging her at this ridiculous hour on Christmas Day. After ten minutes of this, however, her curiosity gets the better of her and she eases herself out of bed as quietly as possible, reaches for her dressing gown and pads across the polished boards to the table by the window.

As she draws the heavy curtains back and sits down in front of her computer, Magda's eyes are drawn to the view in front of her. It's still dark, but her room, which is tucked away at the back of the house, overlooks the wide sweep of the salt marshes and the distant bay. Through the gap in the trees at the end of the garden, Magda can just see the faint outline of the row of fishermen's cottages along the coast road. Bright stars hang in the sky, like the random sprinkles of glitter on the Christmas cards the twins made for her at school.

Distracted by the beauty of the scene, it's a moment or two before Magda remembers why she's shivering in the chilly bedroom instead of snuggled under her duvet. She clicks on the email, her stomach lurching when she sees who it's from. She closes her eyes. The thought of just wiping the offending message is very tempting. No, best to know the score in the long run, she supposes. She squares her shoulders and starts to read. It's mercifully brief.

Magda
Message received and understood. I won't be in touch again. Unless you ask me too, of course. Merry Christmas, Giovanni

Magda deletes the email and waits for a few moments for her heart to stop pounding. It's time to draw a line under what happened so long ago and start to build on her talk last night with Jared. The future is the thing now. Giovanni can't hurt her any more.

She glances at the clock on the wall. The twins are bound to be awake soon. Magda lies down again on her bed and concentrates on getting ready for the day. She needs to be calm. The most important thing is to make sure everyone has a wonderful Christmas, but also not to put too much pressure on her own shoulders to deliver that. Some arrogant blast from the past isn't going to spoil it for them. If Jared wants to be in touch with his biological father, that's up to him, and in the pre-dawn calm of her bedroom Magda makes a pact with herself never to stand in his way.

As anticipated, squeaks of excitement are now coming from Will and Desi's room, and Magda hears their door crash open and the sound of two sets of footsteps pounding across the landing towards their parents. She feels a momentary pang that they're not heading for her own room, and then gives herself a mental ticking off. Two weeks ago she would have killed for an hour more in bed, without the sounds of their little feet pattering towards her. But she's been displaced again now, and rightly so. Jared and Annika get the joy of the stocking opening. Her turn will come later when the twins see all the presents piled under the tree in the hallway. Yawning, she makes her way downstairs to make the first of many pots of tea, and a stack of hot buttered toast for the early risers.

Magda and Fliss have agreed to restrict themselves to giving each other just one present, having predicted how many parcels there will be under the tree for the twins and how long these will take to open. After some discussion, they've decided to have a luxurious spa day in a few weeks, and have given Jared and Annie the same thing between them. This simplifies matters, but the present opening is still intense, and by mid-morning, Will and Desi are so overexcited that they can't sit still. It's a huge relief when Den and Laurence make an appearance.

'Hooray,' shouts Will. 'They can help us to build our trampoline.'

'But I thought I was going to do dinner prep?' says Den, and Laurence nods hopefully, clearly both of them wishing for the warmth of the kitchen, rather than trampoline-building in the chilly back room.

'No, no,' says Annika firmly. 'There are plenty of us in the kitchen already. And we've already got the tool kit out ready for you two. The trampoline's still in its box. Here are some scissors. Off you go!'

She shoos the two newcomers out to the large, high-ceilinged storeroom at the back of the kitchen, where a space has been cleared for the new piece of kit. Will and Desi dance around their legs as they go, cheering wildly.

Jared turns to Fliss. 'Mum's been telling me that you might think about moving into this madhouse if we can go ahead with the work on the outbuildings. It could be a great little apartment for you.'

Fliss smiles at him. 'It's great that you don't mind the idea, but nothing's settled yet.'

'Isn't it?' Magda had thought Fliss was close to being committed to the plan, or had hoped she was, anyway.

'I'm still mulling it over. It's a lovely idea though,' Fliss adds hastily. 'And you're all very generous to offer me the chance.'

'There's plenty of time yet to decide,' Annika says, pouring all the adults a large glass of chilled, very dry sherry, the kind they only drink on Christmas morning for some unknown reason. Magda flops into her mother's rocking chair, recipe book in hand, to make sure she hasn't forgotten anything vital. Turning to the Christmas section, she's struck afresh by the familiar rush of confidence and love flowing from the pages, along with the pungent fragrance of cloves. It seems as if every time she reaches for the book, the feeling is stronger.

Fliss comes over to sit near Magda on the sofa and smiles at her. 'Hope's still with us in so many ways, isn't she? Keeping us on track and making sure we do all the most important things in order. Can I have a look?'

For the first time since she rediscovered her mum's book,

Magda feels able to pass it over to Fliss without any resentment. She watches her friend leafing through the pages.

'I love this poem she's written in the Christmas section, don't you?' Fliss says. 'I hadn't noticed it before.'

'What poem?'

Fliss passes the book back, open at the page after the stuffing recipe. 'I know she often used to write funny little verses in our birthday cards, but I can't remember ever seeing a full-length version.'

'That's odd,' Magda says, frowning. 'I've been through my mum's recipes and notes so many times lately that I practically know them off by heart, but I've never seen this.'

'Maybe a couple of pages stuck together and I've just loosened them? Anyway, read it out loud. She must have written it not long before she died.'

Magda clears her throat and starts to recite the poem. Jared and Annika have gone through to see what's happening with the trampoline and the kitchen is very quiet, as if it too is listening to her voice.

> *My Christmases*
> *By Hope Conway, aged 80*
>
> *Throughout my life, I've spent my time*
> *in Periwinkle Bay*
> *And often in my memories*
> *I'm here on Christmas Day.*
>
> *The springtime brings the leaves and flowers*
> *A garden full of birds*

A season full of growth and joy,
With beauty beyond words.

In summer I have walked the beach
My footprints in the sand
Watching waves and swimming far
Content in this fair land.

Autumn's mellow in the woods,
The leaves begin to fall
But now I'm on the countdown to
The happiest time of all.

So never let your Christmases
Go speeding by too fast,
Enjoy each precious moment
And make the good times last.

'Oh Mags, that's so lovely,' says Fliss. 'She was such a joyful person, wasn't she?' She pauses for a second or two, as if unsure whether to go on, but then continues. 'And so are you now-adays.'

'Am I?' Magda glances at her friend to see if she's teasing as she normally is, but Fliss's face is serious.

'Yes, you've changed a lot in the last few weeks. You're much more optimistic, and it seems as if you're . . . oh, I don't know . . . more comfortable in your own skin?'

Magda thinks about this. It's true, she's learning to be more flexible when it comes to the ups and downs of being with young children. She's listened to and tried to assimilate all that

Fliss has said to her regarding her own part in the family and about not being so hard on herself too. But most of all, and she can't quite believe this, she thinks it's the baking. Something about the routine of it has soothed her, the time spent with her grandchildren, and, most of all, opening this recipe book every day, which has made her feel closer to Hope than she's been for years, even when she was still alive.

'Well, it's a work in progress, but I think I might be getting there, wherever *there* is,' Magda says. 'Thanks to you.'

'Not just to me. You needed to step outside yourself for a little while, that's all.'

A short while later, the others pile back into the kitchen from the trampoline construction, cheering.

'We've done it!' shouts Jared. 'We've created a masterpiece. Who's going to be the first to try it out? It's definitely a moment for celebration, Mum. That job was a lot harder than we expected.'

Will and Desi take their slippers off, ready to demonstrate whose turn it must be first, while Laurence goes over to the fridge and retrieves the two bottles of champagne he put in there earlier. As the corks pop and Fliss helps him to fill the glasses, Magda looks around the room at all the happy faces, and for once, feels completely and utterly at one with herself. Maybe Fliss is right, and she really *is* learning to be as joyous as her mum always was.

Feeling this new contentment has made her realize she no longer needs to compete, with anyone, and Magda finds herself wondering whether Fliss is right and it's time to start thinking about making her mum's recipes available to everyone. There are definitely enough recipes in there, and her mother's random additions in the margins would only add to the charm. The quirky notes would certainly add an extra touch of readability.

Magda tries to imagine what such a collection would look like on the shelves, or displayed on a table in the middle of their local bookshop. It would need to tempt the reader in, to show that this isn't a run-of-the-mill cooking by numbers book. There could be a whole new generation of bakers inspired, just as she has been, by Hope's encouraging comments and easy way of explaining her methods. Perhaps she could use water-colour paintings instead of photographs for some of the illustrations, especially for the cover.

Magda realizes now that she still has the recipe book open at the page with the poem, and as everyone jostles for a glass of the champagne, she bends her head and very gently kisses the words, then closes the book and places it back on the shelf. Everything is in hand. She's followed her mum's instructions for a Christmas Day that's turning out to be as near perfect as possible and that's plenty good enough, as Hope had always said herself.

The enormous Christmas feast finally makes it to the table at two o'clock, and even self-critical Magda can't find anything they could have improved on.

'That was the best turkey I've ever tasted,' Laurence declares, leaning back in his chair and watching Fliss set fire to the magnificent pudding. 'And that stuffing – incredible. What's the secret, Magdalena?'

'Apricots, walnuts, chestnuts, and all sorts of other things,' says Magda vaguely, trying to remember the details. 'Also, Desi and Will made it with me.'

'It was the best *everything*,' says Jared. 'I may never eat again though. After we've had pudding, of course,' he adds hastily.

Magda is lost in happiness as she watches her family and friends eat, finally experiencing, as her mother must have done for so many years, the pure delight of cooking *with*, and cooking *for* those dearest to her. She recalls her mum's words, and now they mean even more than they did when she first read them. It's as if her mum is there too, cheering her on and helping her to create a team of chefs and helpers who have pulled together to make this such an amazing day. She remembers in particular one of Hope's extra notes in the book. *Christmas is for sharing. My family love food, and food is on a par with love in this house.*

'Den, I've been meaning to ask you this but I kept forgetting while we were cooking,' Fliss says now, leaning across the table. 'What are you doing to celebrate your birthday tomorrow? We didn't realize the significance of Boxing Day for you in time to get a present, but we all want to do something to make it fun.'

Den considers the question for a moment, his eyes on Magda. Then he smiles rather nervously. 'That's a lovely thought, Fliss,' he says. 'Actually, there is something I could ask for, and like all the best things in life, it's completely free.'

'Go on,' Fliss says, sounding intrigued.

'I'd like to borrow Magda for the whole day,' he says. 'You don't have to do anything else, just hand her over as soon as she's ready and I'll return her later.'

'I'm not a package,' says Magda defensively. 'You sound as if I should be gift-wrapping myself.' She's not sure whether to be flattered or annoyed, but Den's eyes are on her now and she can feel her cheeks burning and her heart beginning to beat faster.

'It's funny you should say that,' says Laurence. 'I was going to ask a similar thing, only it's not my birthday.'

'You want to borrow me too?' Magda asks, completely bewildered.

'Ah, no. That's not to say you wouldn't make a great gift, Magdalena, but it's Fliss I'd like to kidnap for the day. Both of you have been working so hard for weeks. It's time we did something good for you for a change.'

Jared and Annika are grinning now. 'You don't mean you're leaving us alone with these two reprobates for the day?' Jared asks, pointing at the twins, who were just about to slide under the table to make their escape.

'What's a reppo . . . bait?' Desi says.

'I don't think it's a good thing,' Will answers.

'It's a very good thing when it's referring to you guys,' says Annika. 'That sounds like a fabulous plan. We'll take care of everything here and have a slap-up dinner waiting for you all when you get back. Half past six? Is that long enough for these gallant knights to scoop you up and take you both away on their white chargers?'

Den and Laurence nod, both beaming from ear to ear. As they all get up to clear the table and make coffee, Magda has a momentary qualm, mixed with the mounting excitement of the thought of a whole day with Den. Her mind flits from one possibility to the next, each one more enticing. Whatever escapade he has in store for the two of them, the bonus is that they will be on their own together all day long. Magda's stomach is full of butterflies. She just can't wait to find out what Den has planned.

38

Tuesday, 26 December

Boxing Day

When she wakes the next morning after a fitful night's sleep, Magda lies quite still for a few moments, thinking about the day ahead. Her whole body is tingling with anticipation and she wonders how she's going to be able to pass the time until Den comes to call for her. She springs out of bed and goes to the window, suddenly filled with horror at the thought that it might be raining. It isn't. Perhaps a long, leisurely bath will calm her nerves.

She can hear Will and Desi chatting away in their parents' room as she climbs into the old-fashioned tub. Hope's original bathroom suite is back in fashion, she thinks with a smile. This pedestal bath is deep and has plenty of room to stretch out. Magda tops up the hot water, luxuriating in the feeling of not being in charge. Looking after the twins has been much more fun than she'd expected, of course, but it's very good to know that today, Jared and Annika are doing everything, including the cooking. Letting the water out and wrapping herself in the largest, fluffiest towel she can find, Magda vows to enjoy every moment of this treat. She's not going to worry about anything today.

Magda chooses her clothes with more care than usual and lays them out on the bed. All she's been told is to dress warmly, so she selects her thickest jeans and layers up with a vest top, long-sleeved T-shirt and a fleecy cherry-red hoodie. Woolly red socks complete the look. Her walking boots are already by the door.

This is the time to break out the large bottle of expensive moisturizer Annika brought back for her from America and gave her for Christmas, Magda decides. The fragrance is like summer mornings and she applies it all over, rubbing it into her skin and releasing even more of the delicious scent as it warms up. Her face gets the same treatment, only with an even more exotic cream that smells of freesias and makes her feel completely pampered. Annika has really gone to town on her gifts this Christmas.

Fully dressed, Magda looks at herself critically in the long mirror on the wardrobe door. Make-up wise, she's stuck to a couple of layers of waterproof mascara and a slick of glossy lipstick, not wanting to look as if she's tried too hard. Her hair has fallen into shape, thank goodness. The pink cheeks and eyes sparkling with excitement are nothing to do with any cosmetic you could buy.

When Den rings the doorbell at nine o'clock, Magda's been ready for half an hour. Fliss is in a similar state of nerves and they look at each other for a moment.

'We're acting like teenagers,' says Fliss. 'This is just two friends, taking us out for the day. We need to get a grip.'

Magda giggles and goes to let Den in. He's in faded jeans too, with his old donkey jacket and a thick forest-green scarf finishing off what Magda thinks of as his let-out-of-school look. He's got a large rucksack on his back and is wearing very muddy boots.

'Happy birthday from your gift of the day,' Magda says, wishing she'd got something a lot more impressive than her own company to give him. 'Will and Desi are making a giant card for you later from all of us, but it may take till next year to dry. They don't believe in *less is more* when it comes to glue and glitter.'

'That sounds great. All the best things are worth waiting for.' Den smiles at Magda and she shivers in anticipation. The adolescent fizz is back again. 'Are you ready? Grab a scarf, it's still a bit nippy out there,' he says. 'I'm not coming in because I forgot to knock the mud off my boots after the last time I went through the woods. And by the way, you look stunning, Mags. All glowing and . . . sort of . . . younger?'

Magda winces. This is too near her secret fears to be funny, but she can tell it's well meant. 'I'll accept that as a compliment, the younger part, and hope it's not that you think I usually look much older.'

'Definitely. But maybe I'm just not that brilliant at compliments.'

Den's eyes are shining even more brightly than Magda's as he shouts goodbye to Fliss, and holds his arm out for her to take.

'Where are we going?' she asks, glad of someone to hang on to as they slither down the hill over the frosty cobbles.

'You'll see. You don't need to think about anything today. Just relax.'

At these words, Magda feels the last of her sense of grown-up responsibility fly away and abandons herself totally to the delight of someone else taking charge of decision-making. It's not something she's used to doing but, oh, it feels so good.

Soon, they're leaving the almost deserted town behind them and making their way between the twisty old trees into the woods that lead to the sea marshes and the beach. Den looks down at Magda and takes her hand. She twines her fingers in his, loving the warmth and the feeling of security mixed with sensuality.

'Did you have breakfast?' he asks.

'Erm . . . not much. Why?' She doesn't want to say that she was too excited to eat but Den seems to understand.

'Me neither. That's excellent news though.'

They walk on in silence, and Magda wracks her brains trying to think if there's somewhere nearby where he might be taking her to eat. The little beach café only opens between Easter and October. The only other places are in the town, but even they won't be open on Boxing Day.

Finally, they cross the wide expanse of marshland on the tarmacked paths and end up at the edge of the beach. The tide's out, but instead of heading for the shoreline, Den steers Magda into the dunes that line the west side of the bay. They climb to the top and walk along the slippery ridge until he pauses.

'Here we are,' Den says. He drops his rucksack on the sand with a grunt. 'This was heavier than I thought, but it won't be so bad going back. Have a seat.'

Magda sits down on the tartan blanket that he's spread on the sand for her, and watches as Den unpacks a disposable barbecue, a frying pan and a small cool bag. He gets out a gas lighter and fires up the barbecue, before delving into the bag again and producing a flask. Magda accepts a tin mug of coffee and sips appreciatively as they wait for the flames to be steady enough.

'Bacon, sausages, or both?' Den asks. 'I didn't bring eggs because I didn't trust myself to get them here in one piece.'

'Both please,' says Magda, delightedly, suddenly realizing

how hungry she is. The crisp sea air and the electricity between them is exhilarating.

After a while, Den settles the pan in the centre of the barbecue's grid and sloshes in some oil from a tiny bottle he produces from the rucksack. Laying sausages and bacon side by side, he's soon created a sizzling sound and tantalizing smell that makes Magda's stomach rumble loudly.

'That's not very romantic,' Den says, grinning at her.

'Is this meant to be romantic then?' she asks. 'Not just two old friends having a fabulous breakfast picnic on the beach?'

'It's whatever it turns out to be. I'm fifty years old today, Mags. This is how I want to celebrate it, and better still, you're the only person I want to be with to mark this momentous occasion. Half a century! Can you believe it? *I* can't."

'Oh Den, I'd forgotten it was a special birthday. I should have made a cake . . .'

He laughs. 'If you'd said that a few weeks ago I'd have run for the hills, but you actually could do that now, couldn't you? Hang on, let me turn the bacon and sausages over and then there's one other thing in the bag.'

'Is it tomato ketchup?' she asks hopefully.

'Well, okay, there are three things, if you count the sauce and the bread.'

He tends to the food then rummages in the bag and fetches out a half-full bottle of ketchup, two small baguettes and lastly, a tissue-paper-wrapped bundle. Opening it, he reveals a sprig of mistletoe.

'Hey, have you been scrumping from my oak tree?' Magda says, cursing herself for the blush that's flooding her cheeks with colour. Her hands are shaking and her heart is thumping so hard he must be able to hear it.

'I have, but it was in a good cause,' Den says. 'It seemed a shame not to bring some for luck when it's just sitting there asking to be picked and used wisely.'

'But is this wise?'

Den's standing up now, and holding out both hands to Magda. She lets him pull her to her feet, and it seems natural to come forward and snuggle into his arms.

'I'm only doing this to keep you warm until your breakfast's ready,' Den says, unwinding Magda's scarf and nuzzling her neck. 'It's for your own good. And it *is* my birthday after all,' he adds, just before he kisses her.

It's some time before they can tear themselves apart, and if the smell of burning food hadn't alerted them, Magda thinks they might still be there, locked together, as if they've discovered the joys of kissing for the very first time. In the event, Den just manages to rescue the bacon and sausages before they're blackened beyond help, and eventually they sit down on the blanket to eat the doorstop sandwiches.

'I think this is the best fiftieth birthday Boxing Day picnic I've ever been to,' says Magda, throwing her last bit of crust to the seagulls who have been getting closer by the minute.

'That's high praise. Me too. It's not so bad being fifty, is it?'

'I can hardly remember,' says Magda, laughing.

Den, however, is serious. 'You know I don't care if you're sixty, seventy or eighty, right?'

'That's lovely, but I'm not sure if you've really thought it through. Aren't you worried that everyone in Periwinkle Bay will gossip about us . . . and say I'm . . . oh, I don't know . . . just way too old for you?'

He turns to face her. 'I've never bothered that much about what random people think of me, Mags, and you shouldn't either. So long as the ones we care most about are onside and we don't hurt anybody, it's up to us what we do with our lives. Anyway, whatever's said or not said in the town, nothing's going to change the way I feel about you.'

She takes the words in, her heart singing, but Den hasn't finished yet.

'And now for the next part of my present. We'll leave the rucksack here, have a good long walk along the beach, maybe find a few shells, and then I get to take you back to my house.'

'Do you?' This is something Magda hadn't considered. She's glad they're sitting down, because her legs seem to have suddenly turned to jelly. She's always thought that was just a well-worn cliché but it turns out to be a thing after all.

'Yep. And . . . we're going to watch a film.'

'Oh,' Magda feels her shoulders sag slightly and she sits up straighter.

He opens his eyes wide. 'Magda Conway, I do believe you sounded disappointed then. What were you thinking I was suggesting?' There's a glint in his eye as he says this, and Magda realizes, mortified, that she's really given the game away now. He's seen the desire in her eyes, felt the power of it in her kisses, and has – accurately – guessed exactly how she's imagining spending the afternoon.

'Let's just see how things pan out,' Den says. 'It's only half past ten. We've got eight whole hours before we report back for dinner. Who knows what might happen in that time?'

39

Magda and Den make it back to Mistletoe Cottage with only ten minutes to spare, and see Fliss and Laurence hurrying towards them.

'Where have you been?' Fliss and Magda say in unison.

Laurence laughs. 'They sound like clones of each other, don't they, Den? Both so nosy.'

'We were only showing an interest,' says Magda, laughing. 'And if we seem similar, it's because we're best friends. That's just the way it is.'

She unlocks the door to let them in and they all pile into the hall, Magda and Den stamping their feet to get rid of any mud and sand still clinging to their boots.

'Perfect timing,' shouts Annika from the kitchen. 'Jared's just uncorking the wine.'

Will and Desi come bounding down the stairs and hug everyone in turn, saving their biggest squeezes for Magda. 'We missed you, Granny,' says Desi.

'It's not so nice without you here,' agrees Will. 'Don't go out again. Not for so long, anyway, okay?'

Magda leads the way through to the kitchen, a twin hanging on to each hand. Her face is still glowing from the friction of Den's kisses. *I'm not used to stubble-rash these days,* she thinks with a smile. Her head is still full of the day's glory. The picnic, the exhilarating windswept walk along the beach, the long,

349

lazy afternoon in front of the fire cuddled up on Den's enormous sofa, watching a cheesy rom-com and eating chocolates. It's all left her with a surreal, floaty feeling.

'Was it a good day?' Fliss asks quietly, as she and Magda go upstairs together to tidy themselves up and get changed.

'This reminds me of when you used to come round here after the school discos so we could debrief. I felt like a teenager again today, and I still do.'

Fliss grins. 'Me too, but you haven't answered my question about your day.'

'It was fantastic. You?'

She nods. 'The same. Oh, I've been meaning to ask you, what did you wish for when we made the puddings?'

'Ha! That's a secret.'

'But you're allowed to tell if it's already come true, aren't you?'

Magda smiles. 'Well, I suppose so.' She pauses. 'If you must know, I wished to be able to make a fun Christmas happen for Desi and Will.'

'Two out of two then, because mine gets a *yes* as from today too. I got a belated Christmas present, actually,' Fliss says, holding out her left hand. On the ring finger gleams the most beautiful antique gold ring Magda has ever seen. It has a cluster of amethysts and a single diamond at its centre.

'Wow,' she breathes. 'Go, Laurence. That man's got taste, I've always said it.'

'Mags, he's bought a little bungalow here in Periwinkle Bay. He wants to put it in joint names and give us a fresh start. And I think I want that too.'

'Really? I always thought you two were brilliant together and it was such a shame when you parted, but I never thought this would happen. Your eyes are sparkling like that diamond on your finger, so it's got to be the right thing to do.'

'So . . . what about you?'

Magda sighs. 'Well . . . we kissed so much my lips are sore and my face feels like it's been sandpapered.'

'And?'

Magda's about to say more but the sound of Jared's voice telling them that the food's going cold and the wine's getting warm makes her stop and head for the door. 'Come on, it smells wonderful. Turkey curry, my favourite,' she says.

Later that evening, when Laurence has gone home, and everyone else has wearily gone upstairs to bed, Den and Magda move to sit together on the sofa.

'I wrote you a letter before I came round here today, Mags,' he says, looking at the floor. 'I was going to throw it away because I wasn't sure if you'd think I was a bit of an idiot writing all this when I was going to see you later, but I'm going to ask you to read it anyway.' He reaches into his pocket and pulls out a rather crumpled envelope. 'Look, I can't watch you, it's too embarrassing. I'm going into the kitchen to wait. I'll unload the dishwasher or something.'

'Okay,' Magda says, taking the letter. She looks down at it, already unbearably touched that whatever's in it, he's made the effort to write to her. When she's sure he's safely out of the way, she tears open the envelope and pulls out two pages of Den's large scrawl.

Dear Mags,

I can't remember the last time I sat down to write a proper letter rather than an email or a text so let's hope this makes sense. To say all these things to your face is too difficult because the more time passes, the more it seems that when you look at me I go to pieces and just lose the thread.

When we talked at school in my office, it wasn't the right place or time, but I was desperate to let you know how I felt about you. With Virginia gone for good it's time to go one step further and think about whether we could have a future together. I believe we could and should. You're an amazing person, and I probably don't deserve you, but it's definitely worth our very best shot.

I'm guessing you'll be worried about what people think for a while, about the age gap, about committing yourself to one man after being so independent and probably a hundred and one other things I haven't even thought of, but we can deal with all that together. I don't believe there's anything you couldn't do if you put your mind to it.

Mags, I've watched you change over the last few weeks. Ever since we first met, I've known you were a strong, generous, caring person, but as you tackled all those challenges with the twins and the baking, you've become calmer and happier and more confident, and with every day that's gone by I've loved you more and more. I know we're right for each other.

This letter is to say that I can wait as long as you need me to if there's a chance, even though I would much rather sweep you off your feet right now. There will never be anyone else but you for me, Mags. The more I see you, the more I adore you. I'll be patient unless you tell me to leave you alone. If you do that, I'll keep out of

*your way as much as possible, although in a small town
like this, it could be tricky.*

Either way, I'll never, ever stop loving you.
Yours, either with or without the mistletoe,
Den xxxx

Magda feels tears trickling down her cheeks. She wipes them away before they can drop on the page and blur the lovely words. She's never had a romantic gesture like this made for her. Reading it through again, her heart sings. He really does care. And what's more, he really does *know* her. It feels wonderful to feel this understood. Now all she needs to do is to decide if she can overcome her misgivings about the age difference and the prospect of tittle-tattle in the town and just go for it.

After a few more minutes she stands up stiffly, stretching her shoulders as if she's been asleep for a hundred years, like Sleeping Beauty. And in a way, she has, because no man has really got through her guard ever since Giovanni caused so much damage. She tiptoes along the corridor, aware of all the sleeping people on the next floor. Meanwhile, Den is sitting at the kitchen table scratching his head, with sundry utensils in front of him.

'I put away everything I could find a home for,' he says, getting to his feet. 'But some of these things got the better of me,' he adds sheepishly. He points to the letter in Magda's hand. 'How did I do?'

Magda goes over to stand in front of him. 'Promise me that every now and again, even if we're living in the same place, you'll write me more letters? I love this one so much. Nothing as romantic as this has ever happened to me in my life.'

'I've never been called romantic before,' Den says. 'But then

I've never wanted to write my feelings down before. Seeing them in black and white on paper was quite a big moment for me. So . . . what happens next?'

Magda looks up at him. 'For us? Or for me?'

'Let's start with you.'

'Okay . . . well . . . talking of getting important things down on paper . . .'

'You're going to reply to my letter?'

'No, or not today, at least. I'm going to write a book. Not a novel,' she adds hastily. 'I don't think I'm ready for that yet. But Mum's recipes are wasted with only us to use them. It was Fliss's idea and I hated it to start with, but I feel like I've grown a lot since then. I'm going to get them set out properly, including all her notes in the margins, my own memories and stories about her from her friends. Then I'll see about getting the whole lot published.'

Den puts his arms around Magda and pulls her close. 'That sounds like a terrific idea but you're still looking worried about something. Come on, let's have it all.'

Magda closes her eyes for a moment, loving the feeling of coming home that she gets when Den is so near. 'It's the magic,' she says eventually. 'I'm so afraid of losing it.'

'Not quite sure what you're getting at here, but carry on.' Den looks puzzled now.

'Okay, I'll try. I really want lots more people to benefit from her wonderful recipes, and I'm determined to publish this book, but I'm scared if I make them public, I'll lose my personal link with her. There, does that sound mad?'

Magda holds her breath, hoping against hope that Den hasn't now got her marked down as batty. But after only a second or two, he nods.

'I can see why you're anxious, but from what I remember about Hope Conway, she wasn't a person to begrudge anybody anything. I think if she knew she was helping a whole new generation of prospective bakers to be more confident in the kitchen, and better still, that it was her own beloved daughter who'd made it happen, she'd be bursting with pride. There's no way you'll lose sight of the magic. Have faith, Mags. I've got faith in you, so you need to trust your mum's ability to carry on making a difference.'

These words mean so much to Magda that she can't speak. She leans her head on Den's shoulder and lets herself believe that her dream of a published cookbook really could become a reality. She can see the book already in her mind's eye. It will be a classy hardback, with a view over the marshes to the sea on the front cover and the title in gold, or something else just as shiny. Maybe there'll be a plate of mince pies or a fruit cake in one corner. She thinks she'll call it *The Magic Art of Baking*, and then underneath those words it could say *With love from Mistletoe Cottage*.

The grandfather clock in the corner creaks and begins its ponderous striking. Den looks up. 'It's getting very late and you're going to have a lot to do tomorrow, with Jared and Annika getting ready to jet off again. I'm going home now, but you still haven't told me what I've been waiting to hear.'

'I don't know what you mean.'

'Mags, I poured my heart out to you in that letter but maybe the main message got lost in all the words. I love you.'

Magda gets the message at last. She stands back from Den so she can look him in the eyes.

'I love you, Denis Archer,' she says. 'I love you so much I don't know how to explain it. I might even explode with the excitement of it all. Actually, I think you're the one I've been waiting for all my life. There, will that do?'

He pulls her into his arms and kisses her for an answer. The grandfather clock ticks away to itself in the corner. Time's passing, but there's no rush. A kiss as mind-blowing as this shouldn't be hurried. It's a close-run thing but Magda doesn't explode, which is lucky because she's got a book to write, a final magical link with the woman who gave her life and helped to make her the person she is today. Hope Conway's legacy will live on. Magda will make sure of that.

Hope's recipe book never gets to sit on the shelf by the kitchen window these days. It still has a view of the garden, but usually it's open and propped up on the desk, very close to Magda's laptop, recklessly giving away its secrets.

One day, a whole host of new people will share in the life-enhancing joy of making Hope's recipes. They'll smile at her quirky notes, bake her marvellous creations, share them with the people they love and be very proud of themselves. Maybe the sparkle will be there for them. Perhaps their fingers will tingle too, and new confidence will flow through them like the river that winds its way down through Periwinkle Bay to the sea. After all, the magic of Hope Conway's recipes is irresistible.

A Selection of Hope's Favourite
Recipes for You to Try

Quantities are given in pounds and ounces as these were from the original versions (1oz is the equivalent of approximately 25g). Hope used cups, tablespoons and guesswork for a lot of her measurements, but always weighed the ingredients for pastry. Her cooking times were also often instinctive and rather random.

And a note to the reader, in the hope you're already donning your favourite apron: these recipes are all completely authentic. There really was an Aunty Ruby, an Aunty Vera, a Freda (my dad's cousin) and many more relatives who have contributed to the family recipe books over the years, including my mum, Joyce, who made the best soup and date loaves ever and my mother-in-law, Margaret, who taught me the magical art of Yorkshire puddings, Victoria Sandwich and the Very Easy Fruitcake, amongst many other things.

I've been lucky with my family. Food has always been a priority, and still is – my daughters are carrying on the tradition and my grandchildren are already baking with them. Now it's over to you!

Celia x

Aunty Vera's Apple Jam

(Use instead of apple sauce with roast pork, chicken, turkey, etc., or in apple turnovers/pies)

Ingredients
1lb peeled and chopped cooking apples
1lb 6oz granulated sugar
1 tablespoon lemon juice

Method
- Place the chopped apple in a large microwavable bowl and cover with the sugar.
- <u>Do not stir.</u>
- Microwave on full power for 10 minutes.
- Beat well.
- Return to microwave for 9–10 minutes.
- Stir in lemon juice.
- Leave to cool and then put in sterile jars.
- Seal and label.

Aunty Ruby's Lemon Curd

Ingredients
4 lemons – juice and grated rind
3 large free-range eggs
8oz granulated sugar
4oz butter

Method
- Strain the lemon juice and eggs into a heatproof bowl.
- Add the rind, sugar and chopped butter and mix.
- Place over a saucepan of boiling water but don't let the bowl touch the water.
- Cook until mixture thickens, stirring often.
- Cool slightly and pour into heatproof jars.
- When cold, label and store in the fridge.

Hope's Very Easy Fruitcake

Ingredients

12oz mixed dried fruit

8oz glacé cherries

6oz soft dark brown sugar

4oz margarine or butter

A small tin of crushed pineapple (or blended chunks)

1 teaspoon nutmeg, freshly grated if available

1 teaspoon ground ginger

1 teaspoon cinnamon (or any spices to taste)

8oz self-raising flour

2 eggs, beaten

Grated rind of an orange or lemon (optional)

1 tablespoon demerara sugar (optional)

Slug of brandy or rum (optional)

Method

- Mix everything except the flour and eggs in a large saucepan and bring to the boil. Stir thoroughly.
- Add flour and beaten eggs. Mix well.
- Pour into a greased and lined tin – large loaf tin or 8-inch round. Sprinkle with demerara sugar if desired.
- Bake for 45–60 minutes in a medium oven, gas 3, electric 160 degrees, fan oven 150 degrees. Test with skewer after

45 minutes. If skewer comes out clean, cool on baking tray. If not, test every further 5 minutes until cooked.

This cake does not need any maturing time so is ideal for a last-minute Christmas cake, but will keep well if wrapped in greaseproof paper and foil.

Magda's Grandmother's Christmas Puddings

Ingredients

2lb mixed dried fruit
A handful of candied peel (optional)
4oz glacé cherries (Hope always added double this amount)
½ a nutmeg, grated (or ready-ground, 1 teaspoon)
1 large potato, a large carrot and an apple, all grated
½ cup golden syrup
A heaped tablespoon of chopped stem or crystallized ginger
Juice of an orange or a lemon (Hope added the grated rind too)
½ lb suet
½ lb ground rice
½ a small white loaf, made into breadcrumbs
4oz sugar, any kind but dark brown is good.
2 eggs, beaten with a cup of milk

Method

- Mix all the ingredients together, and don't forget to make a wish.
- If the mixture feels too stiff, add more milk.
- Put into basins, as many as you like depending on how big you want the puddings to be.
- Cover with greaseproof paper and then a double layer of foil. (Hope's mother used muslin cloths and string over the greaseproof paper.)

- Steam the puddings for 6 hours in large saucepans in a couple of inches of boiling water. Top the water up regularly.
- Alternatively, microwave – without the foil! Cook on defrost for 25 minutes for a pudding in a 2-pint basin or 12–13 mins for a pint version. They are cooked when dry on top. When serving, reheat on defrost for 8–10 mins (2 pint) or 4–5 mins (1 pint).
- On the day of serving, either boil again for a couple of hours or microwave.
- Serve with custard or white sauce, brandy butter, double cream, ice cream, or all of these. It's Christmas!

Freda's (and Hope's) Eggless Nutties

Ingredients
½ cup self-raising flour
½ teaspoon salt
2 cups porridge oats
½ cup soft brown sugar (or any other sugar)
½ cup chopped nuts
½ cup sultanas/raisins/glacé cherries/chopped dates
3oz margarine or lard
1 tablespoon golden syrup
½ teaspoon bicarbonate of soda

Method
- Mix flour, salt, oats, sugar, nuts and fruit in a bowl.
- Melt margarine/lard and golden syrup together and stir into dried ingredients.
- Add bicarbonate of soda stirred into 2 tablespoons boiling water.
- Make into small balls and space them out on a greased baking tray. Makes about 18.
- Bake for half an hour in a cool oven, gas 1–2, electric 150 degrees, fan oven. Check after 15 minutes as it may not take this long. Depends on the size/how many you decide to make.

Acknowledgements

Writing my first ever Christmas book has been great fun, but also a difficult journey in parts. The first challenge came when the ever-inspiring editors at HarperFiction, Lucy Stewart and Martha Ashby, suggested a proper structured plan for this one. Oh dear. Planning anything in great detail has never been my strong suit, even as a teacher, but I trust the excellent judgement of these brilliant ladies so took a deep breath, found some real-life future diary dates as a framework, broke out the chocolate digestives and prepared to have a go.

We were in the run-up to Christmas 2021 at this point, most of us looking forward to family get-togethers after the cancellation of the previous one under lockdown, so the excitement level was high and the story bowled along at a great pace. Even in January, with the decorations mostly packed away (although I kept out a few fairy lights to preserve the mood), the festive feeling was still around. I almost delayed a routine mammogram to bring forward a trip to see my grandchildren on the south coast, but was persuaded to get it done. That detail out of the way, I packed up my laptop ready for the visit and put all hospital thoughts out of my head.

You can probably tell where this is going by now. When we got back, a referral letter was waiting and the following speedy run of tests and appointments finally delivered the shocker that I had breast cancer. I'll skip over the waiting time for a mastectomy, which was mercifully brief thanks to the efficiency of the fabulous NHS in a crisis, but during that period, finishing the first draft of this book was a welcome distraction.

Later, when the edits came through, I simultaneously recovered and wrote at a gentle pace, fully supported by Lucy and Martha plus, as always, my wonderful agent Laura Macdougall and her lovely assistant Olivia Davies. Mistletoe Cottage and its cast of characters will always be very close to my heart for this reason. We went through big changes together. Hopefully, I've been lucky. My problem was spotted early and the prognosis is good, thanks to the mammogram system and swift action and excellent after-care of the staff at Queens Hospital, Burton-on-Trent.

The super-efficiency and kindness of Lucy, Martha, Laura and Olivia has been massively appreciated, and grateful thanks go to everyone else who has had a hand in this story, not forgetting ace copyeditor Sarah Bance, proofreader Anne O'Brien, cover designer Caroline Young and publicist Susanna Peden. The very long list includes the fabulous Yamak and Laycock gangs in the south, Laura, Hakan and Ida, Hannah, Mark and Levi, and of course my beloved Ray here at home, who provided his own brand of jigsaw, wine and hugs therapy, plus all the other much-loved family members and friends both local and further afield. They constantly held my hand via FaceTime, email and WhatsApp when we had to isolate before and after the op, sending flowers, stunning gifts, cake, more cake, hot dinners, more flowers, superb Romaniac care packages and yes, more cake.

Special thanks go to Della for her inside information on nursing training in the Midlands when Magda would have been starting out, and midwifery advice for her later career.

The mobile hairdresser in this story, Sophie, is based on my own dear friend Angie, whose visits always brighten up my day and leave me looking a lot tidier! Angie has been going through tough times herself this year. Sending her all the love.

Also a big thank you to the fabulous Crafty Ladies (Anne, Heather, Kay, Lynda and Rose, and Lynda's dog, Lady, who unknowingly modelled for Blondie). Week on week, this sterling bunch have listened patiently to my ramblings about Christmas food and knotty character issues. Extra shout out to Kay for the chilly but very enjoyable plot walks. Who knew park benches could be so useful as planning tools?

They say it takes a village to raise a child, but it takes a whole lot of love to give birth to a book in a crisis. I'm a few pounds heavier and with an extra chin or two but am very, very relieved to be here. I hope you enjoy the result. Mince pies not included.

A Q&A with
Celia Anderson

***Coming Home to Mistletoe Cottage* is your first festive novel. What inspired you to write a Christmassy book, and create this particular story?**

Christmas is my absolute favourite time of the year, and the festive food that goes with it is literally the icing on the cake! I wanted to write a story that included the atmosphere and the food preparation in the build-up to Christmas, with everything gearing towards that short time, but not forgetting the tensions that can arise when people have mixed emotions about the season's pressures. I remember once when my children were small and I was child-minding too, trying to juggle childcare, Christmas shopping and present wrapping, and my dad (who also adored Christmas) saying to me 'So, I bet you're all ready now, aren't you, love?' I had to bite back a very loud scream. Nowadays, Christmas is much less stressful for me, but Magda has been plunged right back into the middle of all the chaos. Her frustration was my inspiration.

In particular, Magda is a strong, independent woman who has faced some hardships, but is determined to make the best of it. Is it particularly important to you to write characters like this?

Although I've been married for almost all of my adult life, it's very important to me to also focus on characters who are perfectly happy and strong being single, especially where child-care is involved. Although there is romance in this book, it isn't the vital part of it. Magda has dealt with some very tough times on her own and emerged unscathed apart from a sense of guilt. I think so many of us, whether parents or not, carry unnecessary guilty feelings for one thing and another. I'm always fascinated with what makes a person stronger as opposed to damaging them. Magda is an example of someone who has worked her way through her insecurities and discovered what's really crucial in her life.

This book is set in another picturesque but small coastal town, with a great sense of community. What is it about this setting that particularly draws you?

I love the idea of a community pulling together and keeping an eye on each other. Having grown up in a very down-to-earth mining, and now ex-mining, area in the Midlands, I have experienced the friendliness (and sometimes over-whelming curiosity) of neighbours, and have always felt very much at home there. Sometimes, as in the case of this Christmas story, a sense of place is there even before the characters fully emerge. Over the years, I've spent some very happy times in the little town of Rye in East Sussex, and also read E.F. Benson's wonderful books about Mapp and Lucia. The author lived in Rye in the beautiful Lamb House and wrote in the midst of the salt marshes and cobbled streets. When working on *Coming Home to Mistletoe Cottage*, I imagined a similar place to this and the characters appeared quite naturally after that.

What's your general process for writing a book – could you tell us a bit about what your writing day looks like?

My mornings typically start very early, sometimes before the birds are awake, but before I get up on a writing day, I spend an hour or so thinking about the work-in-progress and making plans for my characters. This is where the real magic happens for me. My thoughts gallop along very quickly and soon I'm ready to get up, make a pot of tea and start writing. I usually manage a couple of thousand words before breakfast and then come back to it later on and revise/write more. This isn't every day, I hasten to add, I'm definitely not a writing dynamo, but it often occurs when I'm getting the first draft down. Sometimes I plot when I'm out walking with my husband, and quite likely bore him silly with ideas about who does what. He never fails to come up with useful advice. A second opinion is very handy when it's from someone who really knows what makes you tick. I also have a lovely group of friends who listen and chip in with their own ideas and my plot walks with my friend Kay are always super-productive, in fact we're hoping to start writing a children's book together very soon.

What would you most like readers to take away from *Coming Home to Mistletoe Cottage*?

In practical terms, it would be wonderful if readers tried some of the recipes included in the back of the book. Sharing home-cooked food with my family and friends has always been very important to me, and the legacy of my mum, Nanna, Mum-in-law and various other lovely relations is very strong, now carrying on down the line through my daughters, who already bake with their toddlers.

On a more emotional level, I would like to pass on the message (something I'm only just really getting the hang of myself) that the things we've done in the past all go towards forming and strengthening our characters, but it's unnecessary and self-destructive to carry on beating ourselves up for past mistakes. We're not that person anymore. To grow and develop is the important part, but to still be able to hold on to the useful lessons we've learned along the way. That answer actually got deeper than I meant it to!

Do you have any book recommendations for any readers who love your books, but can't wait until the next?

I have lots of current favourites, particularly anything by Susanne Fortin, Catherine Miller, Vanessa Savage, Sally Page and Libby Page, to name but a few. One of the most unexpected joys of getting published for me, as an avid reader, has been the amount of fabulous proofs of new books that regularly drop through my letterbox or arrive by email. I'm currently reading *When I First Held You* by Anstey Harris and *Small Miracles* by Anne Booth, two very different stories but both gripping and very moving. I've just finished reading *The Dazzle of Light* by Georgina Clarke and *The Weekend Before the Wedding* by Tracy Bloom; an absolute delight in both cases. Happy reading, everyone – I hope you find something here to dive into.

If you enjoyed
Coming Home to Mistletoe Cottage,
don't miss Celia's other novels,
all available now in paperback,
ebook and audiobook . . .

'A brilliantly original and enchanting tale'
The Sun

May Rosevere has reached the grand old age
of one-hundred-and-ten. But there's so much more
to May than her remarkable age. She has a secret.
One that no one has ever discovered . . .

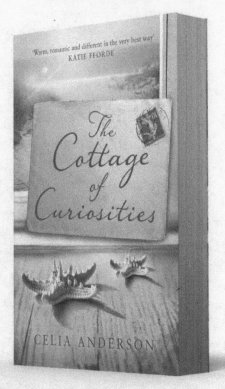

Fifty-four-year-old Grace Clarke arrives in Pengelly
determined to uncover the secrets of her past.
Standing outside the little cottage, she feels sure that
the answers she craves lie inside. The truth about
her mysterious long-lost mother and the even more
mysterious gifts she was born with . . .

'Uplifting with a magical quality'
Woman

After fifty-eight years of playing it safe, Lucia Lemon
wants something more from life.

Until she receives a compass from an old friend that
will change her life forever. For the first time ever,
life feels full of possibility and the open road is
calling. If only she's brave enough to answer it . . .